# A Bargain Struck

ALSO BY LIZ HARRIS
FROM CLIPPER LARGE PRINT

The Road Back

# A Bargain Struck

## Liz Harris

**W F HOWES LTD**

This large print edition published in 2014 by
W F Howes Ltd
Unit 4, Rearsby Business Park, Gaddesby Lane,
Rearsby, Leicester LE7 4YH

1  3  5  7  9  10  8  6  4  2

First published in the United Kingdom in 2013
by Choc Lit Limited

A CIP catalogue record for this book is available
from the British Library

ISBN 978 1 47125 427 7

Typeset by Palimpsest Book Production Limited,
Falkirk, Stirlingshire
Printed and bound by
CPI Group (UK) Ltd, Croydon, CR0 4YY

*For my very good friend, Stella*
*She knows why*

# CHAPTER 1

*Baggs, Wyoming Territory; July 1887*

The stage came to a halt in a cloud of dirt and grit.

Ellen O'Sullivan lifted the oiled leather flap that covered the glassless window and looked out. Dust kicked up by the horses' hooves swirled up around the sides of the coach, and she coughed. With one hand holding her poke bonnet firmly in place and the other covering her mouth, she leaned slightly out and glanced around.

They'd stopped in front of a tall, wood-framed building. As far as she could see, it was the first in a line of buildings that straggled a wide, dusty track. Hitch racks had been dug into the ground along the front of the building, and a number of saddle horses were tied to them. Several men clad in worn, dirt-covered jeans hovered among the horses; a few others stood talking in groups in front of the entrance.

One of those men would be Connor Maguire, she thought, and she dropped the flap.

She sat back against her seat and breathed

1

heavily. Beads of cold sweat gathered on her forehead – she could be about to make a dreadful mistake, a mistake that she might have to live with for the rest of her life.

She took her handkerchief from the small bag that hung from her waist and wiped her forehead, pushing back her fear.

She couldn't let herself think like that, not after enduring four uncomfortable days on an overcrowded train, and one seemingly never-ending day on a jolting stagecoach; not after choking day after day on whisky fumes and tobacco smoke, unable to escape either the rancid odour or the open stares of her fellow passengers. She'd put up with it all just to meet this man, and now that she'd reached her destination, it was much too late to question what she'd done.

Or rather, what she'd not done.

But she'd had no choice. To have stayed in Omaha would have been a mistake. She'd been right to come to Wyoming in search of a new life, and if Connor Maguire could understand why she'd not been completely honest with him, and if he could forgive her, then that new life could be a good life.

The door of the stage was flung open. Dust and the stench of manure and sweating horses filled the coach, and she coughed again.

'This is it, ma'am. This is Baggs. It's just you to get off,' the driver told her, and he stood aside to let her get down.

Her hands shaking, she pulled her hat more closely around her face and climbed slowly down

2

the steps, her limbs stiff and unwilling to move, her petticoats sticking damply to her legs. She reached the ground, straightened her skirt and looked about her.

Some of the men had stopped what they were doing and were staring at her, openly curious, but no one appeared to be making a move to come over to her. She glanced to her right, saw that her travelling bag had been unstrapped from the back of the stagecoach and thrown to the ground, and went over to it. Grit crunched noisily beneath her high button boots at every step.

Her heart beating fast, she took up a position next to her bag, tied her bonnet ribbons into a tighter bow and stood waiting, her eyes firmly on the ground.

'Be you Mrs O'Sullivan?'

She gave a slight jump. Shaking inwardly, she drew in a deep breath, and looked up. A tall man in a suit was standing in front of her, twisting a broad-rimmed felt hat in his hand.

'I am. Yes,' she said. Piercing blue eyes scrutinised her face. She attempted a smile. 'And you must be Mr Maguire.'

He nodded, his eyes never leaving her face.

Self-conscious, she put her hand to her cheek, then slid it to the ribbon beneath her chin. Her heart pounding, she untied her bonnet, took it off and smoothed down her hair. 'My hair is thick with dust. I fear I'm very travel-stained.' She could hear the nervous edge in her voice. Fixing her gaze on the broad shoulders in front of her, she stood very still.

Silent, he stared at her. Then he cleared his throat. 'The Justice of the Peace is waiting in the roadhouse. With two witnesses.'

She forced herself to raise her chin and look directly into his face. 'And you still wish this?'

It was a moment before he spoke. 'I believe in honourable behaviour, ma'am, and I always honour the agreements I make,' he said quietly. He bent down and picked up her bag.

A lump came to her throat. 'Thank you, Mr Maguire. I promise, you will have no cause for regret.'

'That is to be hoped,' he said flatly. 'For afterwards, I've ordered you a room for the night, and a tub of hot water. You will feel stale after so much travel, I'm sure, and you will wish to bathe. And there will be a meal for you. For my part, I'll go straight to a friend – we have business to talk over. I'll come by for you tomorrow morning, when you've had breakfast. We must start early if we're to reach the house before sundown.' He paused. 'I hope that this suits.'

'It does suit. Thank you, Mr Maguire.' She put her hat back on and tied the ribbon tightly.

He nodded again. 'Then we can go.' And he started to walk.

Guilt swelled up inside her. Swallowing hard, she followed a few paces behind him.

\* \* \*

His face impassive and his eyes fixed on the infinite horizon, Connor headed the wagon out of Baggs and across a vast expanse of blue-green sagebrush spiked with clumps of golden rabbitbush and spears of purple asters.

Sitting next to him, clutching the side of the wagon with one of her hands and gripping the wooden seat with the other, Ellen clung on tightly as the wagon raced across the uneven ground at full speed, jolting her sharply whenever it hit a rock or a deep rut. From time to time, she turned to stare from one side to the other, watching mile after mile of emptiness fly by, an endless wilderness of sage-green shrubland, broken only by patches of yellowing grass and the occasional glimpse of an isolated claim shack.

More than once she glanced across at Connor and wondered about trying to strike up a conversation with him. But while he looked more relaxed than he'd done the day before, having changed into denim jeans and a light-blue flannel shirt, the grim set of his mouth daunted her. Instinct told her that any attempts at conversation would prove unwelcome, and each time she'd turned away from him and continued to stare in silence around her.

As the morning drew to a close, the desolate beauty of the brush desert gradually gave way to gently undulating hills and lush green meadows. A line of trees in the distance suggested that they were following the course of a river, and soon she saw Connor pull on the reins to angle the wagon so that it was heading in that direction.

As they drew closer to the trees, she caught fractured glimpses of a verdant meadow beyond the foliage and blue-green water. Reaching the first of the trees, Connor slowed the wagon and began to guide the two horses skilfully between the slender trunks of the tall aspens and aromatic pines. A heady scent enveloping them, they made their way beneath a canopy of branches until they came out of the shade and on to an open expanse of grass that led to the water.

She gazed in front of her. On the other side of the river which was meandering across the meadow, sparkling in the bright light of day, a wide, tree-studded patch of green stretched far into the distance where it met a line of dark-blue mountain ridges that were framed by an azure sky. Her face broke into a smile and she turned to Connor.

He continued to stare fixedly ahead, clicked on the reins and increased the speed of the horses. She turned away and held on to the side of the wagon more tightly.

'We've gotta cross the river,' he shouted above the creaking of the wagon and the pounding on the ground of the horses' hooves as they gathered pace, his voice breaking up at every jolt of the wagon. 'The crossing will be easy. There's been scant rain this summer and the water's low. Hold tight.'

With a loud clatter as their hooves hammered

across the white pebbles that lined the water's edge, the horses dragged the wagon into the shallow depths, its wheels grating stridently. Water splashed up its sides, spraying Ellen's dusty boots and dampening her skirt. She gripped the wagon more tightly as the horses pulled them deeper into the water, their necks straining.

They reached the other side and the wagon gave a mighty shudder as the horses pulled it clear of the river.

'Are you all right, ma'am?' Connor asked, glancing across at her as he pulled on the reins and brought the wagon to a halt.

'Ma'am?' she repeated in surprise, turning to him. She glanced down at her left hand, at the thin gold band that glittered in the light, and she looked back up at him. 'Not Ellen?'

'No, not Ellen, ma'am. I don't know you.'

'Then in answer to your question,' she said, her voice shaking, 'I am all right, thank you. The dress is calico and it will soon dry. Thank you for asking.'

He nodded, dropped the reins and jumped down to the ground. 'We'll break now – the horses have need of water and we must eat.' He unhitched the horses, took the bits from their mouths, pulled off their bridles and gave them a slight push in the direction of the water. With a toss of their heads, they made straight for the river, their flanks steaming.

Ellen climbed to the ground. Aching all over, she stretched herself, put her hands on her hips

7

and arched her back. Then moving her shoulders in circles to rid them of their stiffness, she walked down to the water's edge and stood a little way downstream from the horses, watching them drink their fill from the water that lapped against the pebbles.

The late morning sun beat down upon her, and without the cooling effect of the wind that the moving wagon had thrown back at her, she began to feel hot and uncomfortable in her tight bodice. Kneeling down, she gathered her skirts and petticoats and bunched them between her knees, then she cupped her hands, scooped up some of the clear water and lowered her face into it. Then she ran her wet hands across the back of her neck. Feeling slightly fresher, she dried her face on her underskirt, stood up again and smoothed down her damp garments.

'If we don't have rain before long, we'll see the rivers dry up like the springs have done. The land's startin' to crack up.'

She turned sharply and saw that Connor was only a few steps away from her. He was standing in the water, which was trickling over the toes of his brown leather boots, his hand shielding his eyes from the glare of the sun as he scanned the river in both directions. He'd rolled his sleeves up to his elbows and the tanned skin on his forearms gleamed gold.

She swallowed hard.

'It certainly is hot,' she ventured, her mouth dry.

'Now that we've stopped, I can feel the intensity of the sun.'

'It sure is intense, as you put it,' he said, his eyes still on the river. 'It's been an unusually hot summer with little rain, same as last year. I've known years when we've woken on a morning in August and found a light frost, but I doubt it'll be that way this year.' He turned to her. Deep-blue eyes stared at her from a sun-browned face, eyes without warmth. 'Reckon we'd better eat now and be on our way again.' He started to walk back to the wagon.

She watched as he took a large canvas bag from the back of the wagon, carried it over to the cottonwood tree and sat down in the shade of the wide, silvery branches. As she stood there staring at him, at his face which was dappled from the sunlight that slipped between the leaves, she ran her hand slowly down her cheek. Then she tightened the ribbons of her bonnet so that its sides were flat against her face, and she went and sat under the tree a little way back from him.

He opened the bag and pulled out two packets of food and two canteens of water. Leaning across to her, he passed her one of each, then he sat back upright, opened the other packet, took out a slab of cornbread and started to eat. At the sight of the food, she realised how hungry she was, and she hurriedly unwrapped her parcel and began to eat the cold chicken and cornbread that she found inside it.

Neither spoke as they ate.

His meal finished, Connor stood up. 'You might want to freshen up – put water on your face, make yourself more comfortable. We won't see a river again until we reach the house. The creeks between here and there are dry. I'll see to the horses, and I'll fill the canteens again. If you'll pass me yours.' He held out his hand.

She finished the last of her water and handed the canteen to him. He went down to the river, refilled the canteens, then stood nuzzling the mouths of the horses, his back to her.

Understanding that he was giving her privacy, she ran quickly to a nearby clump of bushes. When she'd finished, she went down to the river, rinsed her face and hands, and wiped her face dry.

Returning to the tree, she saw that Connor had already cleared away the remains of their lunch and had hitched up the horses again. He was standing on her side of the wagon, waiting to help her up to her seat. She hurried over to him. As she reached him, he offered his hand to her.

She took a step towards him, went to take his hand and stopped. 'Are we not to talk at all?' she asked, trying to keep the tone of her voice light.

'Not if we want to get to the house before sundown. Of course, you may prefer to go slow enough to talk, and then bed out beneath the stars tonight. It can be mighty cold when the sun goes down, but if you want to do that . . .' He shrugged his shoulders.

'No, I've no wish to do that,' she said quietly, and she gave him her hand and allowed him to help her up.

The moment she'd cleared the steps, his hand released hers and he went around to the other side of the wagon, climbed up to his seat and picked up the reins. One of the horses threw back its head, whinnied and struck the hard ground with its hoof in impatience. He clicked the reins and moved the horses forward.

She glanced across at his profile. His face was cold, distant. Not once, from the moment that she'd come to an agreement with him after their exchange of letters, had she allowed herself to look forward, to think about how he might react when he saw her, saw what the bonnet wouldn't be able to hide completely, but if she had done so, she wouldn't have expected that. Angry, maybe, or bitter and accusing, but not coldly polite, and silent.

She felt a chill inside her. She should never have come to him like she had.

Anxiety building up within her, she faced the way ahead and stared with unseeing eyes at the mountain ridges veiled in a haze of deepening blue.

# CHAPTER 2

The sun was sinking behind the mountains, smothering the grassland with lengthening shadow that slowly spread out from the deep grey hills, when Connor steered the wagon sharply to the left, on to a broad, heavily rutted track that stretched out ahead of them into the gathering gloom. Their heads down, the horses gained speed, and the wagon swayed wildly from side to side as its wheels ground against the deep-sided walls of the ruts. Ellen clutched her seat with both of her hands, and fixed her gaze on the blurred shapes that were taking form at the end of the track.

This must be Connor's land, she thought, and that must be his homestead. They'd soon be there. Her stomach gave a sudden lurch.

The shapes took on features and became buildings. She guessed which one was the main house from a faint amber glow that came from within one of the structures. She couldn't see the house clearly, though, half hidden as it was by a large barn which stood a little way back from it between the track and the house, but she could see enough to know that it was made of sawn wood, not logs, and that beyond the house there was another large barn, and a few smaller buildings behind that.

They reached the low fence that encircled the yard and the buildings, and Connor pulled back on the reins and brought the wagon to a halt in front of a wide, cross-beamed gate.

'We're here,' he said. He turned slightly and nodded towards the grey-hazed fields to their right. 'You can't see it now as the light's almost gone, but Liberty Creek flows across our land. Even when the water level is low, as it is now, we still have water, and that makes us better off than a lot of our neighbours.'

She heard his love for his land in his voice.

'You have a good position,' she said, and she ventured a smile in his direction.

'I've got my folks to thank for that.' He jumped down, went up to the gate, pulled up the iron bar and swung the gate open. Returning to the wagon, he climbed back up and urged the horses forward. 'Yup,' he said. 'Back in '65, two years after the law had said they could, my folks staked their claim here. Five years later, it became theirs in the eyes of the law, one of the first of the homesteads in the Territory of Wyoming, and we Maguires have been here ever since. They're gone now, my ma and pa, but the land that they claimed has served the family well, and will continue to do so long after we've gone.'

They pulled up in front of the house. Through

the window, Ellen could see that the light was coming from a lamp. Her heart missed a beat. She put her hand to her bonnet. 'Will I meet your daughter tonight?'

'Nope,' he said, getting down and going around to her side. 'She's with my neighbour, Peggy Thomas. She and her husband, William, live further up the creek. Bridget will not be back till after sunup tomorrow. And Aaron and the men will be in the bunkhouse by now. Aaron's my foreman. He'll have done the animals and lit the lamp for us before finishing for the day. So you'll not meet anyone tonight.'

He offered her his hand. She took it and started to climb down, her joints stiff in the cooling air. When she reached the ground, he let her hand go and moved to the back of the wagon.

'Will I cook us dinner?' she asked as he lifted out their travel bags.

'There's no need. Peggy will have left a meal when she collected Bridget. She's a mighty fine neighbour. So, no, you've no chores to do tonight. I'll fill you a tub of water as I expect you'll want to wash, and then we'll eat. When I've filled the tub, I'll come out here, rub down the horses and feed them. And I'll check on the rest of the animals. Aaron's a good foreman, but . . .' He shrugged his shoulders.

'Thank you,' she said quietly.

He nodded. 'You're welcome, ma'am.' He picked up the bags and led the way into the house.

★　　★　　★

The kerosene lamps that stood on the shelf and on the wood table in the centre of the room threw out a warm glow as they ate the meat loaf that Peggy had left them. Neither spoke to the other. Ellen finished first, and she sat quietly, waiting for Connor to come to the end of his meal. The moment he did so, she pushed her plate away from her, moved the lamp to one side and stared at him across the table.

'We've had our food and you've still not spoken to me. You didn't speak on the journey. I can understand that it would have been difficult to have been heard above the noise of the wagon, but you didn't speak to me at lunch, and that would not have been difficult, and now not at dinner. Are we never to talk?'

He sat back in his chair and looked at her. 'Why didn't you tell me?'

'Tell you?' she echoed.

'You know exactly what I mean.'

She paused a moment. 'You're right, I do,' she said. 'And I'll answer that – of course I will, you're entitled to an answer. But first of all, I'd like to ask you something.'

He shrugged his shoulders. 'Sure, if it helps.'

'Why did you advertise for a wife?'

'Because my daughter needs a woman in the house, someone who can tell her a woman's things. And I need someone to do a woman's work around the place. Bridget is eight now and she'll be going to school. She's helped me a deal since her ma

15

died last year, but now that she's gonna to be gone for much of the time, I need someone to do what she's been doing. I've got men to help with the men's work, but the men wouldn't do a woman's work. A man wouldn't.'

'And Peggy Thomas? Couldn't she help?'

'I rely on her too much already. She's a good woman, and a true neighbour, but she lives half an hour away. When the snow melts and the rains come, the track's all but impassable because of the mud. And no one can leave their home in the winter. We get snow several feet deep and blizzards that last for days. Besides, Peggy has her own house to look after. I can't expect her to look after mine, too.'

'You could have got a housekeeper; you didn't need to take a wife. A housekeeper would have lived here and looked after the house. And she'd have helped with your daughter.'

He glanced across to the window. 'A man has needs,' he said bluntly. 'And going to the rooms at the back of the roadhouse in town is not for me.' He turned back to her. 'Having a woman in the house, doing all the things a wife would do – exceptin' one – it wouldn't be easy. I wouldn't want to be in that position and I wouldn't want to put any woman in that position either. And there's Bridget to think of . . . Taking the woman who was gonna live in my house for a wife seemed the right thing to do.'

'I can understand that.'

'And I want a son,' he added. 'I want a boy. I love my daughter, but she'll never be able to run the place. A boy would. A son would take over from me, just like I took over from my pa.' He leaned forward, his forearms on the table. 'I've answered your question, so now will you answer mine? Why didn't you tell me?'

'I will in a minute, I promise. But first, did you get many replies to your advertisement?'

'A fair number. Why?'

'And why did you choose me out of all of them?'

'I guess I wanted a woman who knew about farming, but she also had to be a woman with some education. Bridget's education is important. It was for my wife, Alice, rest her soul, and it is for me. You had education so you'd be able to help her with her lessons, and you knew farming. And you've been married before, so you'll know what a woman needs to know – about the house and everything.' His face broke out in a sudden smile. 'And I picked you for your name.'

'My name!' she exclaimed, sitting back and staring at him, puzzled. 'You mean Ellen?'

'No, I mean O'Sullivan. I come from Irish stock, and I want Bridget and my son, if God gives me one, to know their heritage. I thought they might learn it through you. I figured your husband was Irish, and Irish men marry Irish girls so I thought you would be, too. And I was right – you told me your family originally came from Ulster, just

17

like mine.' His smile faded. 'Well, do I get my answer now?'

'You wanted someone educated, who knew about farming. And as you said, I *am* educated and I *do* know a bit about farming. I'm a widow so I know what to expect from a man and how to keep house. I'm of childbearing age and might give you a son, and I have an Irish background. So in me you got what you wanted, and that's all that really matters.' Her voice shook on her last few words, and she bit her lip.

'But it's not, is it, ma'am? I saw the way that folks in Baggs looked at you. You can pull your bonnet across your face as much as you like, but it's not enough. I saw their faces when you got off the stagecoach and I saw them when I collected you this morning. And my daughter will see those looks of distaste, too. She'll see them every time she goes into town with you, every time that her friends come to the house, if her friends still want to visit. I have to think of Bridget as well as me. You should have told me before you came and let me decide.'

'If I had, you'd never have given me the job.' He opened his mouth to speak. 'No, don't try to deny it; you know it's true. You've as good as said so yourself. If I'd written to you that I had the mark of a horse's hoof on the side of my face, that it covered the whole of my cheek, you'd never have picked me – you'd have taken one of the other educated women with an Irish heritage, who can

18

farm and look after a house. That's why I didn't tell you. Just because I'm marked by an accident, it doesn't stop me from being everything you wanted in your wife.'

He looked her squarely in the face. 'And you really believe that? Truthfully?'

She held his gaze, then dropped her eyes and slowly shook her head. 'Of course I don't. I know that the way that I look matters, but I wanted a home and a family very much, and I knew that this was my only chance.' She raised her eyes to his. 'I know I should have told you, and I'm truly sorry that I didn't for your sake, but not for mine.'

'So you—'

'Please, Mr Maguire,' she went on quickly, trying to keep from her voice the desperation that she felt growing within her. 'Please, let me show you that I can be a good wife to you. After all, you married me after you'd seen my face. You went ahead with the wedding, and you brought me all the way here to your home. You could have said no. You could have walked away the moment you saw me, but you didn't. So please, give me a chance.' She stopped abruptly. Her forehead creased in a frown. She put her hand to her cheek and stared at him in puzzlement. 'If my appearance was so important, why *did* you marry me?'

He held up his hands. 'I don't know; I really don't know. I spent last night asking myself the same question and I couldn't come up with an answer. Maybe it's like I said in Baggs, it's being true to my word. We made an agreement and you left Omaha to come here because of that agreement. Maybe it's because I'm running out of time – Bridget starts school in about four weeks. Maybe it's just that I didn't want to write any more letters to women. Maybe it's that I'm not looking to have again what I had with Alice – no one could ever find that a second time – and you'd do the chores as good as anyone else. I guess it's one of those, or a bit of them all.' He paused and stared at her. 'Well, I reckon that means that you get the chance you want.'

She looked him steadily in the eyes. 'You won't be sorry that you married me, Mr Maguire. I promise you.'

'That's as may be.' There was an awkward pause. 'You must be tired.'

'Yes, I am,' she said, and she stood up.

He got up, picked up the lamp from the table and handed it to her. 'I'll be in shortly. You go ahead.' She took the lamp from his hands, and he turned away. As she went through to the bedroom, she heard the front door close behind him.

Connor stood with his back to his house and stared ahead of him at Liberty Creek. Moonlight stroked the flowing water, which gleamed with ebony lustre in the black of night.

Behind him, he could hear the sound of someone moving around inside the bedroom, the someone he'd taken to be his wife.

20

He thrust his hands into the pockets of his jeans and strolled forward.

Why *hadn't* he walked away the moment he'd seen her face, seen the red rawness of her cheek, the garish, mottled folds of skin which starkly ridged the side of her face where her wound had ill healed? He could have turned and left her there, and no man alive would have blamed him. But he hadn't. *Why* hadn't he? He'd been asking himself that question since the moment that the Justice of the Peace had said the words that made them man and wife.

He'd certainly been furious enough to walk away.

It had been all he could do to keep his voice steady as he'd talked about honourable behaviour and then to lead the way to the roadhouse and the Justice of the Peace.

He'd wanted to shout at her, to show her how let down he felt, and how angry he was that his daughter would have to suffer the cruel taunts made by those around them. He'd wanted her to feel the weight of his frustration at knowing that he didn't have time to start his search all over again, not with the distances involved, not with Bridget being about to go to school – yet he'd kept silent.

Why?

He stared ahead into the darkness. Was it that, if he was being truly honest with himself, he had felt another emotion, too, an emotion that he didn't want to admit to himself, didn't like himself

21

for feeling? Was it that he'd felt an overwhelming sense of relief when he'd seen her face?

Was that was the real reason why he hadn't turned away from her?

If the woman he took for his wife had been a beautiful woman, there was a risk – only a slight risk, but a risk nonetheless – that he might have begun to feel about her in a way that he didn't want to feel.

He would never love another woman the way he'd loved Alice. His heart would belong to Alice until the day he died, and that was only right. In truth, the moment that he'd looked on Ellen O'Sullivan's face, an anxiety that he hadn't even realised he'd felt had lifted. It would be so much easier to remain true to Alice's memory if he were living with someone who looked like Ellen. And he'd felt a tremendous relief.

He had loved Alice since he was nine years old and she'd walked into the schoolhouse on her first morning there, an eight-year-old carrying in one hand a small tin pail with a cloth over the top, and a slab of grey slate in the other.

As she'd turned to push the door shut behind her, she'd knocked over the water pail that stood on the bench next to the door. The other children had burst out laughing, and she'd gone red. But he hadn't laughed. He had jumped up as fast as he could, run over to her and picked up the water pail. As he'd straightened up, the pail in his hand, he'd looked into glistening green eyes that were shining at him with gratitude, and he'd fallen in love at that moment.

Long before their school years had ended, they'd known that they would stay together forever. Only it hadn't been forever – he'd been nineteen when they'd wed and they'd been married for less than nine years – and his grief at losing her a year ago was still every bit as intense, every bit as painful, as it had been on the day when she'd slipped away from him.

He'd waited as long as he could before bringing another woman into the house, but now that the time had come that he must do so, he was glad – yes, glad – that it was someone who looked like Ellen, someone who could never touch his heart, someone who'd never threaten his daughter's memory of her mother.

He felt guilty for finding a benefit to himself in another person's great misfortune, but that was the way he felt, and there was nothing he could do about it.

He turned to look back at the house. It was silent. She'd stopped moving around; she'd be in the bedroom, waiting.

He took a deep breath and went towards the house.

Ellen sat on the edge of the bed in her flannel nightdress, just beyond the reach of the pale glow which spread out from the lamp that she'd set down next to a large china bowl on the table in the far corner of the room. Her long brown hair fell over her scarred left cheek; her right cheek faced the door.

The door opened. She felt herself stiffen, and she made a conscious effort to relax.

Connor came into the room, closed the door behind him, hesitated and then walked over to her. Standing square in front of her, he looked down at her. 'This be all right with you?' he asked, his voice tinged with awkwardness.

She pulled her hair further across her cheek, glanced up at him, her hand against her hair, and tried to smile. 'Of course. It's part of our bargain, isn't it? You've kept to your word, and I'll keep to mine.'

He nodded, and went across to the table, pulling his braces down over his shoulders as he walked and tugging his shirt free from his jeans. She glanced at him just as he started to undo his shirt, and she caught sight of a lean, sun-browned chest. A lump came to her throat, and to her dismay, her eyes filled with tears. She put her hands to her eyes and tried to push them back.

He slipped off his shirt, dropped it on to the table and started to unbutton his denims. Then he looked across at her, and stopped. His hands fell to his sides and he took a step towards her.

'What is it?' he asked. 'You've been married before so you know what to expect. I won't hurt you. Is that why you're afeared?'

She pulled her hair further across her cheek and turned away from him.

'I'm being stupid,' she said, her voice shaking. 'Please, don't pay any attention to me.'

He didn't move, and she felt his eyes on the side of her head.

'Is this too soon for you?' he asked. 'We've had a long day, and I can sleep in Bridget's room tonight, if you wish.'

She shook her head. 'No, I don't wish. I want to begin our life as man and wife tonight. I'd like you to lie beside me. Please, Mr Maguire.'

He gestured helplessly. 'Then why are you crying?'

'I'm not really.' She paused. 'It's just that I wish . . . I wish . . .' She stopped.

He waited a moment, then sat on the bed next to her, leaving a small space between them. She turned her face further away from him.

'What is it you wish? Tell me, will you?'

She took a deep breath, turned around and looked into his face, her hand holding her hair in place. 'I wish I didn't look as I do now. I know you wouldn't have chosen me if you'd had the chance to see me before I got here, and I wish that my face was as before the accident. If it was, I think you would not feel such distaste for me. For this.'

He met her eyes.

'No, I would not have chosen you, ma'am . . . Ellen . . . That's true. But as you said yourself earlier

25

this evening, I agreed to marry you after I'd seen you. I needn't have. And I told you that I would like to have a son.' He gave her a wry smile. 'As far as I know, there's only one way to bring this about. So my distaste, as you put it, cannot have been so very great. Wouldn't you agree?'

She gave him a watery smile.

'But before we go further, I think we must free your hands,' he said. 'If you are to live here as my wife, you must get used to me seeing your face.' He leaned across, gently took her hand and moved it aside. Then he gathered up the hair that hung in front of her left cheek, held it to one side and stared at her scar.

She edged back from him.

He released the hair, and smiled at her. 'There, now I've seen it so you've no need to hide yourself from me any more. One day I'll ask you about the accident, and you'll tell me about it if you want to, but not tonight. Tonight's about sealing our bargain.'

He stood up, went across the room to the lamp and lowered the wick. The flame extinguished, when he turned back she was lying beneath the quilt, waiting for him.

His hand went to the buttons on his denims and he walked forward.

# CHAPTER 3

Tying her blue and white checked apron behind her back, Ellen hurried out of the house into the white intensity of the morning sun. Momentarily blinded, she stopped abruptly and blinked a few times, then she pulled her white cotton day bonnet further forward and made her way across the worn-down grass to the fence that enclosed the house and yard. Leaning against the wooden post at the side of a small gate that opened out on to the meadow, she stared at the view.

An expanse of grass sloped gently down to the edge of the creek which cut across the verdant landscape, a deep-blue ribbon of water bordered with scattered rocks and pebbles that shone white in the sunlight. On the far side of the river, clusters of spreading cottonwoods, tall pine trees and sage-green aspens with silvery trunks dotted the low undulating hills that stretched back to meet the distant blue mountains.

Coming from somewhere behind the house, she heard the lowing of cows and the occasional whinny of a horse. The watery call of a meadowlark rippled the air above her, and she looked up in time to see the solitary bird outlined against the endless wide sky. Catching the clean, spicy scent of the pines in the air, she closed her eyes and inhaled deeply.

The thud of an axe hitting wood made her jump. Her eyes flew open and she turned sharply in the direction of the noise. Connor was further along from her, naked to the waist, just inside the fence. He had his back to her and was lifting a section of log on to the sawn-off stump of a tree.

She stood still for a moment and watched him lift his broad axe high above his head and swing it down hard, splitting the log in two.

He must have started working long before she got up, she thought with a twinge of guilt as she saw the pile of chopped wood beside him and the glistening rivulets of sweat that were running down his bare skin. She remembered how considerate he'd been with her the night before, and her guilt deepened. Tightening the ribbon of her bonnet, she went over to talk to him.

'I'm sorry to be so late in rising,' she said, walking around the back of the stump to stand facing him. 'It won't happen again, I promise you.'

He stopped in the act of bending down to pick up another log from the pile and straightened up. Resting his booted foot on his axe head, he leaned against the handle and wiped the perspiration from his forehead with the back of his arm.

'You had a long journey,' he said, 'and not an easy one. I didn't think to see you before now.'

'As you say, it *was* a long journey, but I'm revived now and you can be sure that I'll be up early tomorrow.'

'If you need to sleep late tomorrow, you sleep late. I reckon it'll take a few days to get over your journey.' He glanced at her day dress and bonnet. 'I'm guessing you found the jug of water I stood in the bowl, you being dressed.'

'Yes, I did. Thank you.' She glanced towards the house. 'Either Bridget isn't back yet or she's extremely quiet.'

'You got it right with your first shot.' He grinned at her. 'As you'll find out soon enough, your second couldn't be more wrong.'

'When do you expect her back?'

'Any time now.' He glanced at the pile of logs waiting to be chopped and frowned slightly. 'I guess I should show you around the place before she gets here.'

She followed his gaze. 'You've a lot to do, and I ought to get to know the inside of the house before I see the outside. To begin with, I must see what there is to eat in the kitchen. You'll be wanting food soon, and your daughter and Mrs Thomas will have an appetite when they arrive. You can show me around another time, when you're not so busy.'

'That's mighty understanding of you. Winter can come unexpectedly upon us, so at this time of year, we're racing against the weather. It could turn cold very soon and we'll want this wood when it does. I need to finish what I'm doing and get it into the woodshed.'

She nodded.

'And we've gotta get the rest of the grass cut and baled before the autumn rains,' he added. 'Aaron's taken on extra men to help with that. Because of the drought, much of the grass has dried out and we can't risk losing what's left – we'll need it for the animals in winter. Winter can last a long time in these parts. I've known it to snow as late as June.'

She straightened her bonnet. 'Will I meet Aaron today?'

'Maybe later. He and the men have taken their food to the fields. Most working days you'll fix them lunch here, but not today. They're staying out there so's not to break off getting the hay in, which means it'll be just us. I mean Bridget and Peggy, too, of course.'

'I'll go and see what I can find in the kitchen. And I want to look at the wood-burning stove. I've never cooked on one before – we fed coal to the black iron stove we had in Omaha.'

'There are folks around here who've got those, too. But since we've got our own trees, why buy coal? There were trees on the homestead when my folks started out, but they planted more and now we've got a better supply of wood than most of our neighbours. I'll be giving Peggy a pile of cut logs to take back with her.'

'That's kind of you.'

'Not really. It's me being neighbourly to someone who's been more than neighbourly to me.' He took his foot off the axe. 'You'll have seen the pump by the kitchen sink. It connects to a narrow well right next to the kitchen wall so you can pump water into a bowl in the sink. But you might also want to use the well in the backyard. It's the other way from the outhouse, going towards the bunkhouse – it's the one the men use. Filling pails is quicker at that well. If there's anything else you wanna know, just holler.'

'And the vegetable garden will be back there, too, I suppose?'

'Yup, it's behind the house before you get to East Barn. That's the barn that's just past the woodshed. The corrals are on the other side of the vegetable patch, and beyond them you've got West Barn. The wheat and hay fields, and the corn fields, they're all behind the barns. Everything's ripening well, though of course the corn's still yellow-green. But as for the garden, you'll not find much there now. Bridget's been looking after it since her ma died, and she's done the best she can, but there's a limit to what a child of her age can do on her own.'

'I can see that. It must have been difficult for her. For you both.'

'It was.' He grasped the haft of his axe with both hands and started to raise it. She turned away, went a few steps towards the house, stopped and turned back to him.

'There's just one thing I'd like to ask before you start chopping wood again,' she said.

He stopped mid-action, lowered the axe and looked at her. 'What is it?'

'I was just wondering.' A trace of awkwardness crept into her voice. 'Should I call you Mr Maguire? I remember what you said yesterday about us not yet knowing each other, and when you called me Ellen last night, I think you were just being kind. Before your daughter returns, I'd like to know what to call you.'

He gave her a dry smile. 'I guess that having lain together, we've gotten to know each other a whole lot better since yesterday morning, and that's good enough for you to be Ellen, and me to be Connor. Or Conn, as folks around here often call me. If that suits.'

She smiled up at him. 'It does. It suits very well. Thank you. I'll get off to the kitchen now before . . .'

'And since we're kinda getting to know each other's ways,' he cut in. 'If I may say one thing, ma'am . . . Ellen. Maybe folks in Omaha, Nebraska, put on a bonnet every time they step out of the house, but folks in Liberty, Wyoming, don't. It can be hot work, running a homestead, and it's hard work, hot or cold. If you want, you leave off your bonnet and your corset – if you'll forgive me mentioning a lady's undergarment – and all those petticoats and you be comfortable when doing your chores.' He glanced down at his bare chest. 'Like I am.'

32

She followed his eyes to the taut muscle that rippled beneath the golden skin, and she flushed.

'I'm thinking that if I wear a bonnet, it will be easier for your daughter,' she said, swiftly looking back up at his face. 'Don't you think that is so?'

'Alice never wore a bonnet like that, exceptin' when we went into town for something special. Bridget will find it a mite strange, you being in a hat all the time.'

'But my scar.' Her hand went to her cheek.

He shrugged. 'She's gonna see that, bonnet or no bonnet. Might be better to let her say her piece when she meets you. Get it over with.'

'If you think that's best.'

'I do.' He lifted the axe, brought it down with a powerful swing, and clove the wood in two. 'Yes, ma'am, I do.'

By the time Connor had finished piling the wood for Peggy in front of the house and stacking the rest of the chopped logs in the woodshed, the sun was at its height. He closed the door, bolted it, and stood staring towards the house as he wiped the back of his neck with the grey flannel shirt he was holding.

He saw the kitchen door open and Ellen come out, a pail in each hand. He ought to go across and offer to give her a hand, he thought, this being her first day, and he hurriedly put on his shirt, pulled his braces up over his shoulders, and took a step forward.

Then he paused. No, he wouldn't; he'd let her be. She was obviously busy, and it'd surely be easier for her to get on with what she was doing if he wasn't around. And it wasn't as if she'd had any problems that morning. She hadn't needed to bother him at all about anything. Thinking about it, she'd probably be glad to have as much time as possible by herself while she was finding her way around the place. Instead of interrupting her, he'd do better to go and see if there was any sign of Peggy and Bridget.

He thrust his hands into his pockets, turned to the right and made his way along the narrow path at the foot of the fields of ripening grain in the direction of the track they'd be coming down. It felt good to be out in the open. Having been working in the same place since the break of day, he'd needed to stretch his legs more than he'd realised.

The clank of the pump arm being lowered and raised reached him from behind, and he began to walk more quickly.

Yes, he was definitely doing the right thing by giving her more time to herself. And it suited him, too, if he was perfectly honest. After chopping logs all morning, the last thing he'd felt like doing was making polite conversation with a lady. There'd be plenty of time for that later. First there'd be lunch, and then he'd sit down with her that evening and run through the daily routine. The quicker she settled into Alice's way of doing things, the quicker they'd all adjust to the new situation. Above all, the less disruption there'd be for Bridget.

Bridget. He felt a sudden surge of anxiety about her, and about whether she'd still be as angry with him as she'd been when he'd set off for Baggs. Never before had she drawn away from him when he'd tried to hug her.

And it had been entirely his fault.

He should have listened to Peggy when she'd told him to tell Bridget as soon as possible what was going on. Learning that he'd found a woman and was gonna marry her was certain to be a mighty shock for her, Peggy had repeatedly told him, and he should give Bridget sufficient time to get used to the idea before he brought the woman into the house.

But he hadn't listened to her. He'd been pig-headed and ignored her advice, persuading himself that he had to wait for the right moment to bring up the subject. But there hadn't been a right moment, and he'd ended up telling her just before he left for Baggs. That had been a big mistake on his part. His mishandling of the situation meant that it would now take Bridget a mite longer to get used to Ellen O'Sullivan being around the house.

In his own defence, however, he could never have imagined that she'd be quite as stunned as she was. It was the moment he'd seen the anger and hurt on her face that he'd realised how badly he'd got it wrong. And unfortunately, he'd had no choice but to leave her in that state of mind. He'd had to get to Baggs before the evening so that he'd be there the following day when the stage-coach arrived.

Of course, there was always a chance that in the two days since he'd left for Baggs, Peggy might have been able to help Bridget to understand the situation a little more clearly, and might have been able to soften her towards him. He certainly hoped that she'd been able to do so, for both his and for Ellen O'Sullivan's sake.

But even if Bridget were still hostile, that was sure to pass as soon as she saw how much easier her day had become. When that happened, she'd completely forgive him and be glad that he'd got someone in to do the chores, and to teach her sewing and things, and to answer the questions she would have asked her mother.

And there was that one unforeseen thing that had helped him, and it might just help Bridget, too.

If a part of her anger at him was fear that his new wife might try to take the place of her mother in his affections, the moment she saw Ellen's face she'd know that that would never happen. The scar would be the first thing that she'd see, that anyone would see – it was even bigger and redder in the bright light of day, and looked more raw. And when she saw the ugliness of his new wife's face, she'd know that this was a business deal and nothing else, and that it would never be anything more than that.

He felt a sudden impatience to get the introductions over with so that their life could start running smoothly again in the way that it hadn't since Alice's death, despite the efforts they'd all made to get it back on track. He shaded his eyes with his hands and stared across the fields to the track to see if there was any sign of Peggy's wagon, but the hayracks blocked his view, so he walked on.

They'd be back very soon, he was sure. Peggy had already kept Bridget longer than he'd expected, but that was her being considerate, knowing that he had a new wife and thinking that he'd want time to get used to her without his daughter being around.

But *had* he started to get used to his new wife? He reached the fence that ran alongside the track, climbed up on to it, settled himself on the top beam and stared in the direction that they'd be coming from. It was hard to say if he had. It was early days, and most of the time that they'd been together, they'd been travelling, and that had made it impossible to talk.

Not that he'd wanted to talk to her.

After his first sight of her, he'd been in too much of a turmoil to want to make any attempt to get to know her. But conversing with her after they'd eaten their meal the night before had helped him to clear his head, and although he was still angry with her, he understood why she hadn't told him and he'd lost some of his fury.

And that had helped him to lie down in the bed beside her.

Being close like that with anyone other than Alice was something that he'd held back from thinking about when advertising for a wife, but if he *had* thought about it, what had happened last night was just what he would have sought – a straight-forward sealing of their bargain, but no more than that. Nothing that was in any way a betrayal of Alice. He'd wanted a woman in his bed who could give him a son, but he would never want any more from her than that.

Maybe it meant that he *was* getting used to her. It was hard to know.

Not that it really mattered much. She had her work to do, and he had his. Apart from in bed, they'd probably only meet at meals, and in the evening Bridget would be with them. And when Bridget was asleep, he'd have the sorts of things to do that he wouldn't do in the day, such as repairing any worn out bridles or mending the cinches, and she'd probably have some sewing or reading to do. He'd noticed that she'd brought some books with her. So no, he couldn't see their lack of familiarity with each other causing any problems.

And he didn't anticipate any real difficulty with his daughter. Or not for long, anyway.

Bridget had a good heart. She loved Peggy, and she loved Oonagh Quinn. Oonagh having been in her life since she was born, a friend of both his and Alice's, it was natural that Bridget would care for her. Of course, whether that warmth would survive Oonagh becoming her schoolteacher, it was too soon to know, but he was pretty sure that it would.

Whatever he might think of her, Oonagh had been good to both him and Bridget since Alice had passed on. She'd supported them throughout that terrible year, she and Peggy. He didn't know how they'd have got through it without their help.

The sound of horses' hooves reached him, and vibrations rattled the fence. He glanced along the track and saw the wagon, a distant speck half hidden by a cloud of dust. A sudden wave of anxiety shot through him. Bridget would be home very soon. If he was still out in the fields, the first person she'd see would be Ellen O'Sullivan.

He had to get back to the house before the wagon reached it. He jumped off the wooden bar, spun around and started to run back along the path. He had to stop Bridget from speaking too plain when she saw the woman's face. Whatever she'd done or not done, the woman he'd wed didn't deserve the hurt that would cause.

# CHAPTER 4

Ellen heard the clumping of horses' hooves and the creak of a wagon as it drew to a halt in the yard, followed by the sound of a high-pitched voice. A child's voice. She knew that she should go outside at once, a smile on her face, but she couldn't move. Standing in the centre of the living room, her back to the front door, anxiety gripped her limbs and paralysed her.

She thought that at last she'd got used to people staring openly and to the cruel remarks they made within her hearing, that they no longer bothered her and she no longer feared them, that going outside to meet Connor's daughter and his neighbour would hold no terror for her, but it did. And she stood there motionless, chill dread creeping through her.

She heard the door behind her open. Two narrow columns of light fell to the floor in front of her and she whirled around, her heart beating fast. But it was only Connor standing in the doorway, his broad shoulders cutting off the light.

'The wagon's here,' he said, drawing his breath in ragged gasps. 'I've been running. I wanted to get here before Bridget. I see you've put your travel bonnet on. It's my wish that you take it off and come outside and meet her.' He stood back from the doorway to let her through, and the stream of light flooded into the room, trapping her in its harsh glare.

She stepped aside, into the shadow.

'Take off your bonnet and come now,' he repeated, a trace of impatience in his voice.

She didn't move.

He walked across the room to her.

She put her hand quickly to the crown of the bonnet. 'I think it would be better if I kept my hat on,' she said. She could hear her voice shaking. 'To make it slightly less noticeable. Not every day, of course, but today. Until she is more used to me. To the way I look. I've been thinking about this and I believe it would be wiser.'

She looked at the floor, and bit her lower lip.

He was silent for a moment. She sensed him staring down at her.

'And I think differently,' he said at last, quietly but firmly. Positioning himself squarely in front of her, he removed her hand from the bonnet, untied the bow beneath her chin and let the yellow ribbons hang loose.

She caught hold of the ribbons and inched back from him.

'I should have told you when we exchanged letters,' she said, her voice rising. 'I'm sorry I didn't. It was unfair on you. Unfair on your daughter.'

'Yup, you should have told me, Ellen. But you didn't, and you're here now. And you're my wife. Bridget must see your scars some time, and that time should be now. That's what I think.'

She glanced past him to the doorway, and she felt the blood drain from her face.

'We'll go out together,' he said, and he took the bonnet from her head. 'It's only right that your husband is at your side when you're introduced to his daughter, and I will stand with you.' She watched him as he leaned across to the table, put the bonnet down and turned back to her. 'If you're ready, we'll go.'

'Yes, I am,' she said, hastily gathering together some stray strands of light-brown hair and tucking them into her French knot. 'Yes, I think I am.'

He started walking towards the door, and she followed close behind him. As they went through the doorway, she brushed against his arm and she felt tension coiled inside his hard muscle. A wave of guilt ran through her.

They came out into the sun as a plump woman was just beginning to climb down from the wagon, her back to them. Instinctively Ellen raised her hand to her face, but Connor caught it and placed it gently at her side. He gave her a slight smile.

She tried to smile back, and then looked again at the wagon. The back of a girl's head could be seen in the rear, just above the side, but she seemed to be making no attempt to get out.

42

Leaving Ellen standing in front of the doorway, Connor went across to Peggy Thomas and helped her down the last step.

'Thank you, my dear,' Peggy said, smiling broadly at Connor as she raised her hands and made an attempt at pushing wisps of greying brown hair into the loose bun that hung low on the back of her head.

'You sure kept Bridget a good amount of time, Peggy,' he said as he led the horses to the short rail in front of the house and looped the reins over the rail. 'We appreciate that.'

'It was a pleasure. It always is,' she said cheerfully, turning towards him as she brushed the dust from her worn blue cotton skirt and shook stubs of dry grass out of the folds.

Connor glanced back at her and laughed. 'I'm not sure how true that is.' He pulled a couple of pails of water in front of the horses. 'She's awfully full of energy,' he said, returning to Ellen's side. He took her by the arm and turned her to face Peggy. 'I only hope she didn't wear you out.'

'Don't you worry, Conn. Your daughter's good company. When she's around, that is,' she added, looking towards the back of the wagon. 'Come on, gal,' she called. 'We're here now. I think your pa's got someone he wants you to meet.'

She turned to Ellen with a broad smile. A look of surprise crossed her face, and her smile wavered. She glanced up at Connor, her eyes questioning. He stared back at her, his face expressionless.

She looked again at Ellen, then she went forward,

her hand outstretched, her smile welcoming. 'Mis' Maguire,' she said warmly, shaking Ellen's hand up and down. 'I'm mighty glad to make your acquaintance. I hope you'll be real happy with us here in Liberty.'

A bolt of relief shot through Ellen, weakening her with its force.

Her knees trembled and she leaned against Connor. He put his hand under her elbow to steady her.

'I'm real pleased to meet you, Mrs Thomas,' she said, feeling her strength return. 'Connor's told me what a good neighbour you are.'

'I've been glad to give a hand now and then. But there's more here that needs doing than I can do, and I've been telling Conn for a while that he must get in proper help. Someone to be here all the time. That makes you a very welcome sight, my dear.' Peggy stopped abruptly, and stared at Ellen in horrified embarrassment. Ellen went red. 'There aren't so many of us hereabouts that a new neighbour isn't always good to have,' Peggy added quickly. 'So you're real welcome.'

'Thank you, Mrs Thomas.' Ellen's voice shook with gratitude.

Peggy leaned forward and patted Ellen on the arm. 'You'll be fine, my dear. There's nothing for you to worry about. For the most part, the folks in Liberty are easy-going. And something else they are, is much less formal than the folks back East. Round here, everyone calls me Peggy.'

'And I'm Ellen.'

Peggy turned to Connor. 'If you don't get that gal of yours out of the wagon, she'll take root along with the potatoes she's sittin' on. Reckon she's feeling a mite shy in front of your new wife.'

'I guess you're right at that,' he said, and he went over to the back of the wagon.

'Ellen here is waiting to meet you,' he said. 'D'you want a hand getting out?'

'I can get out by myself.' Bridget's voice was sharp. 'I don't need anyone to help me.' She clambered over the back of the wagon, put her foot on the large metal wheel, jumped down and landed on the ground with a light thud. She had vivid red hair, Ellen noticed.

Connor turned around to walk back to Ellen. As he did so, he held out his hand to Bridget, but she ignored her father's outstretched hand, folded her arms in front of her, waited for him to walk ahead and then trailed along behind him, her eyes on the ground.

'This is my daughter, Bridget,' he said, stopping in front of Ellen. He looked back down at Bridget. 'This is the woman who's become my wife.'

Bridget raised her eyes to Ellen, her expression hostile.

Her forehead creased in sudden amazement and she took a step back. She looked up at her father, bewilderment clouding her face, then she looked again at Ellen. Her mouth fell open and her arms dropped to her side. The hostility in her eyes gave

45

way to revulsion, and she took another step back. 'What's wrong with your face?' She wrinkled her nose in disgust. 'It's red and ugly.'

Connor moved closer to Ellen's side. 'That's no way to speak to anyone, Bridget. I'd like you to apologise.'

'Why did you marry someone ugly like her?' she asked, her tone accusing, her eyes still on Ellen's face. 'I don't want her anywhere near me.' She rounded on him. 'You should have married Miss Quinn if you had to get married at all. Miss Quinn's real pretty, not like *her*. Miss Quinn would have married you. You know she would.'

'You're old enough to know better than to talk like that, Bridget,' he said quietly. 'What must Peggy be thinking of you? And Ellen. You say that you're sorry to Ellen at once.'

Bridget's mouth set in a hard line and she stared up at him, her face cold. 'What for? For telling the truth? Well, I'm not sorry for what I said and I'm not going to pretend that I am. She's ugly and I don't want anything to do with her.'

'Go to your room.' His voice was steely. 'I'll bring your things in from the wagon.'

She tossed her hair, pushed past him and went into the house.

Ellen stared at the ground, feeling heat rise to her face.

'I'm sorry, Ellen,' Connor said. 'I figured she'd have something to say, but not that she'd say it

46

quite as rudely. I guess me having a wife is gonna take her some getting used to.'

She looked up at him and shook her head. 'You've nothing to apologise for. It's my fault. I should never have come here. Not without telling you first. I'm sorry, Connor. I really am.'

'Her feelings are all mixed up, my dear,' Peggy said, patting Ellen on the arm. 'That's all it is. She'd have found it difficult, whoever Connor married. She'll come round soon enough. She's a good girl. You mustn't think badly of her – she's still hurtin' after her ma. All this'll take her some getting used to.'

'I don't think badly of her at all. I know this is a difficult situation for her, and the fact that I look like this makes it even harder. I blame myself, not Bridget. I didn't tell Connor what I looked like before I met him and I should have.'

'Blamin' people's no good, my dear, whether you're blamin' yourself or others. It don't alter anything so it's a waste of your time. It'll work out fine; you'll see.' Peggy gave Ellen a reassuring smile, then glanced up at the sky. 'I reckon I'll be on my way now.'

'Surely you'll eat first!' Connor exclaimed. 'I was about to grain the horses, and Ellen's done some food for us. You'll have lunch with us before you set off, won't you?'

'Yes, you must join us,' Ellen said. 'It's not much – I've made a thick bean porridge and flavoured it with a bit of salt pork that I found – but we'd like

47

you to share it with us. Wouldn't we?' she appealed to Connor.

He nodded. 'We sure would.'

'That's sure neighbourly of you,' Peggy said. She smiled at Connor. 'If your wife can do that on her first morning here, I reckon you've got yourself a woman who can cook.' She turned back to Ellen. 'Most times I'd stay and eat with you, my dear, but this isn't most times. And I thought it wouldn't be, so I brought me some bread and ham, and I'll have that on the way home. The three of you need time by yourselves. Bridget will settle down soon, so don't you worry. I'll let you help me back on to the wagon, Conn, and then I'll be off.'

A heavy silence hovered above the table.

Ellen spooned the porridge into three dishes, dreading the meal ahead. She passed the first to Connor, picked up the next and held it out to Bridget. Bridget's hands remained beneath the table and her eyes stayed resolutely on the table-cover. Rising slightly from her chair, Ellen leaned across and put the plate in front of Bridget. Then she took the last dish for herself.

'I hope you like it,' she said, picking up her spoon. 'I don't know where everything's kept yet, but if one of you shows me where you store the rest of your provisions later on, I can be more adventurous tonight.' Her nervous smile encompassed them both.

'Maybe Bridget will show you after we eat,' Connor said, glancing at Bridget.

'And maybe she won't.' Bridget stuck out her lower lip.

He frowned at her, and turned back to Ellen. 'Peggy was right. You've done well to make us something for lunch. It can't have been easy in a strange place, and with a stove you're not used to. I really shoulda shown you around this morning.'

'It's of no matter. Having time to find my way around the kitchen on my own really helped, and the stove was easy to use. And I'm guessing that the trap door in the pantry floor will lead to a cellar where I'll find a lot of the things that I'll need,' she added with a slight smile.

'You guess right.'

She fell silent.

'This is good,' he said after a few minutes. 'In fact, it's real good.' He paused. 'Isn't that right, Bridget?'

Her eyes on her plate, Bridget continued to eat, a sullen expression on her face.

'It's nice of you to say so, Connor,' Ellen said. 'It's not much.'

'We'll go into town at the end of the week,' Connor said after a few minutes, breaking the silence that had fallen again on the table. 'There'll be things you need to buy. We'll all go,' he added.

Bridget looked up, alarm in her eyes. 'I'll stay here. There's nothing I want in town.'

'You've forgotten that you need things for school.

49

You need a lunch pail, and you need books and a slate for a start, and the only place to get them is Massie's. And you'll need a new dress. That's woman's stuff. We'll go to Massie's together, and then you and Ellen can go to O'Shaughnessy's while I go to the livery stables. So like I said, we're all going into town together.'

Bridget's lips tightened, and she glared at her father.

'I'm thinking that it might be better if you and Bridget went alone, Connor. I could give you a list of what I need. Yes, I think that would be better.'

'So do I,' Bridget said sharply.

'And I don't agree. We'll go into Liberty as a family.'

Bridget threw him an angry glance, opened her mouth to say something, caught his eye and closed her mouth.

They continued eating in silence.

'How far is Liberty from here?' Ellen asked, breaking the silence.

'About as far away as Peggy's, but in a different direction. You go north for Liberty and east for Peggy's. Our neighbours, the Careys, live to the west of us. It takes about half an hour to get into town by horse, a bit longer by wagon,' Connor told her. 'The schoolhouse is on the edge of the town. I reckon it'll take Bridget an hour and a half to walk there. Isn't that right, Bridget?'

Silence.

'But she's a strong girl and she'll do it,' he continued. 'And when the winter blizzards come and she can't get there, she's got someone in the house who can help her with her letters. Ellen's got education, Bridget.'

'If you'd wanted a teacher in the house, you should have married Miss Quinn,' Bridget said bluntly. 'She's got a licence. She'd have been able to help me with anything I couldn't do.'

Ellen glanced swiftly at Connor, then at Bridget, then looked quickly back at her plate.

Connor nodded. 'That's true. She's been a good friend to you – to both of us, in fact – and I'm sure she'll continue to be so. But now you've got Ellen and she can also help you.' He took two pieces of cornbread from the bowl in the centre of the table and put one of the pieces next to Bridget.

Throwing Ellen a look of dislike, Bridget dug her fingers into the cornbread, crumbled it into pieces and pushed the crumbs away from her.

Ignoring Bridget's action, Connor took a bite of his cornbread. 'So what did you do at Peggy's?' he asked.

'Fishin'. I went fishin' with William.'

'What bait did you use?'

'Worms. Just after we started, I thought it was gonna rain and I wanted to go back to the house, but William said that fish bite well in the rain so we stayed put. And then it didn't rain.'

'I sure wish it had! We're well overdue for some rain. And did you catch anything?'

'Yup, several.'

'And?'

'And nothing. We took 'em back to Peggy and she cut their heads off. Then she covered them in cornmeal and fried them in the pan. We had them for supper and they tasted real good. Peggy sure is a fine cook. And so is Miss Quinn.'

'And luckily for us, so is Ellen. If you ask—' The sound of a buggy pulling up a short distance from the house stopped him mid sentence.

'I'll see who it is.' Bridget jumped up and ran across to the window. She pressed her nose against the glass and stared in the direction of the gate. 'It's Miss Quinn! I'll do the gate,' she cried, and she dashed to the front door, flung it open and disappeared outside. 'Miss Quinn,' they heard her scream in unmistakable delight.

Connor rose from his chair.

Ellen's heart sank. She hastily pulled her hair further across her face. Keeping it in position with her hand, she turned in her chair towards the door, inwardly steeling herself to meet the person that Bridget would clearly rather have had as her father's wife.

A moment later, Bridget appeared in the doorway.

'It's Miss Quinn, Pa,' she said, her eyes shining. 'She came to see if we wanted anything. She didn't know that you'd got some woman here. She said she's gonna go home now. Tell her she's gotta come in, will you?'

Connor moved towards the door.

'I'm sorry to disturb you, Conn.' A voice full of apology came from behind Bridget. 'I was wondering if you needed anything and I stopped by to ask. But I'll go now.'

'You must come in now you're here, Oonagh,' Connor said. He sounded uncomfortable, Ellen thought.

Beaming, Bridget came further into the room, closely followed by a tall, slim woman.

'I didn't realise you'd have a visitor, Conn,' the woman said. 'I'm sorry for interrupting, but Bridget insisted that I come in.' She smiled warmly at Bridget, and then at Connor.

'It was a mighty kind thought to see if we were needing anything,' he said, going around the table to stand beside Ellen, 'but we're fine. We'll be going into town on Saturday.' He hesitated imperceptibly. 'Ellen's more than just a visitor, Oonagh. She's my wife.'

With a sharp intake of breath, Oonagh turned from Connor to look at Ellen.

'This is Miss Oonagh Quinn, Ellen,' Connor went on. 'Her pa is Liberty's bank manager. I've known her for just about all my life – we were at school together. She's been a real good friend to the family. Oonagh teaches school and is gonna be Bridget's teacher.'

Ellen's hand fell from her hair. She rose from her chair and stared at Oonagh.

Oonagh's jet black hair had been skilfully swept to the top of her head, its dark lustrous sheen a

53

sharp contrast with the creamy white skin of her face and neck. The fashionably tight-fitted bodice of her pale-blue calico dress emphasised her tiny waist, as did the lightly gathered skirt that fell naturally over her slender hips. She raised her eyes to Oonagh's face and stared at the classic features, at the perfect curve of her lips.

Oonagh Quinn was beautiful.

Envy washed through her. And fear.

# CHAPTER 5

Oonagh took a step forward. Striking violet eyes stared back at Ellen, eyes that were filled with amazement. And with anger, too, Ellen saw in surprise.

'Your wife?' Oonagh's voice rose in disbelief. She turned to Connor, shaking her head slightly.

'Yup, my wife,' he repeated. 'Ellen and I got back from Baggs last night. Peggy brought Bridget home this morning. But she wouldn't stay and eat, and I believe that there's food left over if you were minded to join us.'

'No, I won't stay. As I said, I only came over to see if you wanted anything.' She turned back to Ellen and went forward, her lips in a wide smile, all trace of surprise and anger gone from her face.

'As Conn told you, I'm Oonagh Quinn,' she said, shaking hands with Ellen. 'I'm real pleased to meet you, Mrs Maguire. Real pleased. I hope I didn't seem rude just now. It's just that learning that Conn had wed again took me by surprise.' She gave a little laugh. 'But it was a good surprise. He and Bridget needed help in the house. I wish you well in your marriage. Both of you.' She turned her head a fraction to include Connor in her smile.

He acknowledged her with a slight nod.

'I'm delighted to meet you, Miss Quinn,' Ellen said. 'I haven't been here long, but in the short time since Bridget returned, she's talked much about you.'

Oonagh glanced down at Bridget, her expression affectionate. 'So Bridget's been talking about me, has she? How dull for you.' She laughed and looked back at Ellen. 'Perhaps one day, I'll do some talking, too. I could tell you some things about Conn that he probably won't be telling you himself. I've known him all my life, and Alice, too. She was my best friend. Yes, I think I might just do that.' She laughed again, glancing mischievously at Connor from under her long eyelashes.

Ellen looked up at Connor, but his thoughts were impossible to read. She turned back to Oonagh. 'I'd like to think that we can be friends, too, Miss Quinn.'

'Of course we will.' Oonagh's voice was full of warmth. 'But getting to know each other better will have to wait till another time. I must go now. This was only ever going to be a quick visit. With school starting in a few weeks, I've a number of things to do. It's been a real pleasure to meet you, Ellen – I hope I may call you Ellen – and I look forward to seeing you again before long. I live in Liberty itself, and Conn must bring you to visit me when you come into town. My ma and pa will want to meet you, too.'

'Thank you. You're very kind. And yes, please do call me Ellen.'

'I'll see you out,' Connor said, moving forward. Bridget ran quickly to Oonagh's side. 'No, Bridget,' he said firmly. 'You sit down again. You've not yet finished your meal.' He went across to the door, pulled it open for Oonagh to pass through, and went out after her.

Bridget returned to her seat and sat down with a flounce. Scowling at her plate, she stirred her porridge with ferocity.

Ellen sank to her seat and picked up her spoon. She looked at her plate, but all she could see was the beautiful face of Oonagh. And the way that Oonagh had looked at Connor.

So why hadn't Connor married Oonagh?

She sat motionless, her eyes directed towards her plate, her spoon in her hand. Connor had needed a wife. Bridget was clearly very fond of Oonagh and would have welcomed her into their home. So why, with a woman such as Oonagh Quinn so close to him, who was so clearly willing to share his life – or so it had seemed just now – had Connor written to a Nebraskan newspaper in search of a wife?

The sound of the buggy driving off broke into her thoughts, followed by the grinding of metal hinges as Connor swung the gate shut behind it.

She took a spoonful of porridge and was putting

the spoon to her lips as she heard the click of the front door as it closed behind her. Connor walked past her, went to his end of the table, took his seat again and picked up his spoon.

'Miss Quinn looked real pretty today, didn't she, Pa?' Bridget said, pushing her plate away from her.

'She's a good looking woman,' he said bluntly.

Bridget turned to Ellen. 'Like Pa said, Miss Quinn's real good lookin'. How come you look so ugly?'

'Bridget!' Connor banged his spoon on the table, his eyes blazing with anger.

'It's all right, Connor. It's a fair enough question.' She turned to Bridget. 'I didn't always look like this, Bridget. I was in an accident.'

'What kind of accident?'

'You don't have to answer that, Ellen,' he cut in quickly, glaring at his daughter. 'Bridget shouldn't have asked you. It's up to you when you tell us, and it may be that you never want to tell us, and that would be fine by us. We're not gonna force you to remember something you'd rather forget. Bridget should never have asked that.'

'You've got a right to know what happened, so I'll tell you. After all, you're both going to have to look at my face.' She attempted a smile. 'Robert and I were out in the buggy one afternoon – Robert was my husband. There was a four-in-hand wagon coming towards us. It was being driven too fast for the narrow track, so Robert tightened our reins. All of a sudden, something spooked one of the wagon's horses, and the horses bolted towards us. To this day I don't know what spooked them, and it doesn't matter anyway. Our two horses hadn't long been broken, and they took fright and reared. Robert just couldn't hold them. Our buggy overturned and we were thrown to the ground in front of the wagon horses. They trampled all over Robert, and I got a hoof in my face.' She touched her left cheek. 'As you can see.'

'I guess the fact that you're here now tells us what happened to Robert,' Connor said quietly, his voice full of sympathy.

Ellen felt a lump come to her throat. She swallowed hard. 'You guess right: he was killed instantly.' She forced a smile. 'But that was almost two years ago, and as you say, I'm here now.'

'Bridget and I are real sorry about the accident. Aren't we, Bridget?'

She stared at her father. 'Yeah, of course we are. But it doesn't make me want her here, lookin' like that. Everyone at school will laugh at me. And they'll think you've gone mad, takin' such a woman to be your wife. You shouldn't have married her.'

'Well, I did,' he said shortly. He sat back in his chair and looked at Ellen, anxiety sweeping across his face. 'You having such an accident puts a thought in my mind. I've gotten you a saddle horse to ride as that's the easiest way of getting around. Pa staked the full hundred and sixty acres they were allowed, and that's a whole lot of land. But you may have become afeared . . .'

59

'I haven't. As soon as I was healed, I made myself ride again. But it's considerate of you to think that way. Thank you.'

'Your horse is in the shed with the other horses, and the equipment you'll need. It's the shed just behind East Barn. You won't find a whip there as we don't use them here, and you'll find that your spurs be so blunt they wouldn't hurt so much as a man's skin. In Wyoming Territory we rule our horses with our voices and with a slight pressure on the snaffle bridle. That's our way. I hope that suits.'

She nodded. 'It does. It's a good way to be with horses.'

'And one other thing. Alice used to find the distances hard to cover sittin' side-saddle on the horse, so she'd ride like a man when she was on the ranch, pulling her skirts up as far as she must. I've given you a youth saddle, which is what all the ladies around here use, but you can ride your horse in whatever way you want.'

'Thank you. I've never ridden a horse sitting it like a man. I've never even thought of doing so, but if I had, Robert's parents would have considered it unseemly. But as you've said before, things are different in Liberty from in Omaha. And what you say makes sense, given the size of the homestead and the nature of the ground.'

'I've gotta go out in the fields with the men tomorrow, so I suggest that I take you to see your horse before sundown this evening, and I'll show you where your harness and the rest of the equipment is kept. Then you can practise when you want on your own. We'll go before we eat. At the same time, I'll show you quickly the other barns and the woodshed. You need to get an idea of where everything's stored.'

She smiled and nodded.

'And tomorrow Bridget will take you through your day's routine.'

'I can't. I've got things to do for school.'

'You've a few more weeks before school. There's nothing that can't wait a day or two. You'll help Ellen tomorrow.'

She scowled at her father, and then at Ellen.

'Don't worry, Connor. I can probably work out most of the things for myself. I guess that I sweep out the stove, re-lay it and set it alight as soon as I get up, and then collect the eggs for breakfast. When I've done the breakfast, I feed the chickens and hogs. And I milk the cows after that. Is that right? It's the order I used to do the tasks when Robert and I lived on his parents' farm.'

'Yup, that's the way we do it here, too. You'll have seen that we've got a good flock of Plymouth Rocks. They give us a mighty fine number of eggs, and Bridget will show you where to look for them. Not an egg can escape her eyes; not even the ones that are hidden beneath the clumps of sage-brush that we've got around the place. Isn't that right, Bridget?'

Bridget kept her eyes on the table.

61

'We get sage hens here, too. There's a shotgun for them just inside the kitchen door,' he went on. 'You don't need to be much of a shot to hit them. At times you can't see the sky for the birds. And Alice once got four of them with nothing but a stick, they were so thick on the ground. They're a danged nuisance, and I'd rather have them on my plate than in my fields, eating the clover and grass. If they're young and tender, that is. The adult hens are as tough as a bale of swamp grass.'

'And the cows will need milking in the evening, too, I expect.'

'You're expecting wrong about everything,' Bridget said sharply. '*I* collect the eggs, and *I* do the milking. I've been collecting the eggs for Ma since I was real little. And doin' the milking, too. They're *my* chores. They *are*, aren't they, Pa?'

He leaned forward to her. 'I appreciate all the hard work you did when we had your ma, honey, and everything you've done to help since her passing,' he said, his voice gentle but firm. 'But things must change now. You'll be starting school soon, and that means you'll be leaving home early in the morning, and you'll be back late in the day. You won't be able to do all the chores you've been doing, and it wouldn't be fair on you to expect it. That's why Ellen is here. She's gonna take some of them off you.'

'But we've got on all right by ourselves, just you and me. And I like doin' the things I've been doing and I want to carry on helping you. You

62

always said how well I did everything and that you wouldn't be able to manage without me. I can do the chores before I go to school and when I get back.'

'Your ma would have been real proud of you, and how well you looked after the house and me. But at the same time, I reckon she'd be mighty angry at me if I let anything come in the way of you getting an education, and you know that.'

'I wouldn't have minded sharing the chores with Miss Quinn.'

'She teaches school. With both of you out of the house all day, who'd look after the vegetable patch, do the preserving, do the cooking, and not just for us, but for the men we hire? They need three meals a day, like we do. Who would wash the clothes, clean the house and do all the things a woman does when she runs a home?'

'She could stop teaching school.'

'Maybe she doesn't want to. She's very comfortable, living with her folks and teaching school. I've heard she's been offered for on many occasions, but she's always said no. What's more, I reckon that if she ever changes her mind about living alone, it'll be to the town that she looks for a husband, not to any homestead. The life of a homesteader is not the sort of life that Oonagh's ever wanted.'

'You don't know for sure. You could have asked her. I know she likes me, and I can tell she likes you. Anyone can see that.'

He straightened up. 'I think we'll let the subject be, Bridget. Enough has been said, don't you think?'

An ache of misery deep within her, Ellen rose from her chair. 'I'll take the empty plates.' She went around the side of the table and leaned across in front of Bridget to pick up her dish. Her hand brushed against Bridget's arm.

The girl drew back sharply. 'Don't you touch me!'

'Enough!' Connor stood up and pushed his chair noisily back. 'I reckon I've had just about enough of your rudeness, girl. Apologise at once, and then go to your room.'

Stony-faced, Bridget looked up at Ellen. 'I'm sorry for speaking my mind.'

Connor pounded on the table with his fist. 'I don't call that an apology. Make a better one than that.'

Bridget clamped her lips together.

'I accept her apology, Connor,' Ellen said quickly. 'I'm sure Bridget's tired, and all this – meeting me, seeing my face – it must have been a shock for her.'

Bridget turned and looked Ellen in the eye. 'I'm sorry you had that accident, and I'm sorry about your husband. But I don't want you here, and you won't get around me by trying to be nice, if that's what you think.' She stood up. 'I'm glad I'm going to my room now, Pa. It's better than sitting here, looking at *her*. Anything's better than that.'

She turned around, ran to her bedroom and closed the door firmly behind her.

Connor gestured helplessly. 'You won't see Bridget again this afternoon. We don't need meat tonight – just do what you can with whatever you find. I'm gonna go and see how Aaron's getting on.'

A moment later, the kitchen door slammed shut behind him and Ellen was left at the table, alone in the room.

Ellen pulled her shawl around her shoulders and stepped through the open doorway into the pine-scented night. Pausing a moment, she stared ahead at the distant horizon.

The sun was dropping behind the hills, and the streaks of crimson and orange that arched the heavens were slowly being consumed by widening bands of deep grey that were reaching out across the sky. Stark against the darkening horizon, the branches of isolated trees formed an intricate network of black lines. But as she stood and watched, they gradually blurred into a formless mass, overcome by the inexorable advance of night.

She inhaled deeply and began to stroll across the yard in the triangle of yellow light thrown out by the lamps within the house. Reaching the pinpoint of the tapering beam, she moved into the shadows, sat down on the chopping-block tree trunk and leaned forward, her elbows on her knees. The scent of newly cut wood filling her senses, she gazed in the direction of the river, a ribbon of gunmetal glinting beneath the light of the moon, and she felt herself begin to unwind. It had been a long day, and a difficult one.

For someone who'd shied away from people for the past two years, to meet as many as she had in the one day, and so soon after reaching the homestead, had been hard to cope with.

In the back of her mind, she'd known that she'd meet Bridget soon after her arrival, but she hadn't given any thought to the actual meeting, nor to how Bridget might react when she saw her. Prior to leaving Omaha, all of her thoughts had been focused on the effect of her appearance on Connor and whether he'd turn away from her.

The degree of Bridget's relentless hostility had thrown her, and her discomfort had further deepened upon meeting Oonagh, who was beautiful, and who was so clearly admired by Bridget. She'd done her best to hide the increasing strain she was feeling, but she was pretty sure that Connor had sensed it and made sure that Aaron and the hired men didn't go near the house that day. Certainly there'd been no sign of anyone when he'd shown her the horses late in the afternoon and had given her a quick tour of the barns.

But she wasn't the only person to have been put out by Oonagh's unexpected arrival: Connor, too, had seemed unsettled, and it wasn't hard to work out why.

Bridget must be wrong in thinking that he hadn't

proposed to Oonagh. His explanations to Bridget seemed too quick to hand. More likely, he'd been one of the men who'd offered for her and been turned down. Seeing the woman he'd wished to be Mrs Maguire next to the damaged woman he'd married in her stead must have brutally reminded him of what might have been.

While it was hard to believe that any young woman would turn down an offer of marriage while living in a small town where there were unlikely to be many unmarried men, and few of them as ruggedly handsome as Connor, that must be what had happened. There was no other possible explanation.

Connor must have been so devastated by her refusal that he hadn't cared whom he married. And that was why he'd gone through with the wedding after he'd met her.

The fleeting anger she'd glimpsed in Oonagh's eyes when they'd first been introduced must have been on Bridget's behalf. Oonagh would know better than anyone else the cruelty of children, and she would have realised at once that Bridget would suffer because her father had wed a woman with a damaged appearance; that Bridget, too, would become the object of jeers and stares every time they went out together. She may not have wanted to share Connor's life, but she still cared about him and Bridget. That much was obvious.

And what, she wondered, were Connor's feelings for Oonagh.

Did he blame Oonagh for the position he now found himself in? If he did, had his resentment killed his desire for her? Or did he still feel as strongly about her as he had when he'd proposed to her? If that was so, she hoped very much that his feelings would lessen with the passage of time and would allow some room for her.

She didn't expect to be loved by him. She'd known from the start that that would never be possible. And for her part, she would never be able to love another man in the way she'd loved Robert. Only once in a lifetime could a woman feel a love like that. But although Connor would never replace Robert in her heart, any more than she would Alice in his, she would like to feel that they could be some company for each other.

A high-pitched yelp pierced the night air.

Startled, she sat upright. Coyotes, she thought, and she shivered. She stood up and pulled the shawl more tightly around her as she walked quickly back to the house. They'd need to keep an eye on the chickens, just like they'd had to do in Omaha.

Once inside the house, she leaned back against the bolted door, shut her eyes and let Robert's face fill her mind.

They hadn't had long enough together. They'd married when she was twenty, a few months after they'd met at the church she'd just started attending in Omaha, and they'd had little more than a year together before the accident. In that time, though,

68

she'd known a degree of happiness that she wouldn't have believed possible, and in the dreadful two years since he'd died, she'd found herself drawing repeatedly upon the strength that his love had given her.

Opening her eyes, she looked around the cold, empty room, and she knew she was going to have to rely on that strength a whole lot longer if she was going to cope with the situation she'd got herself into.

She went over to the lamp on the wall, turned down the wick and extinguished the flame. Then she picked up the lighted lamp from the centre of the table and went across to the bedroom where Connor would be waiting for her. As she put her hand on the door handle, she wondered fleetingly if he'd summon the image of Oonagh's face to his mind as he raised himself above her and prepared to enter her.

Shaking the thought from her head, she opened the bedroom door. She mustn't let herself think like that. To allow such thoughts to enter her mind could destroy any chance of happiness she might have, and that would be folly indeed. She closed the door firmly behind her.

# CHAPTER 6

Connor glanced across at the lean, weather-lined man who was working on the fence alongside him.

'Take a break, Aaron,' he said. 'I'll just finish fixing this beam and then I'll stop a moment, too.' And he turned back to the fence.

'Sure thing, Conn.' Aaron threw the hammer to the ground, went over to his horse and pulled a canteen from the leather bag that hung from the saddle. He walked across to a nearby cluster of rocks, sat down, unscrewed the top of the canteen and took a swig of water. 'It sure is hot,' he said, wiping his forehead with the red bandanna he wore around his neck. 'Mind you, it may still be hot in the day, but it's beginnin' to get colder mornings and nights. It's my guess we'll soon be seein' yellow leaves on the trees.'

Connor nodded. 'Yup, I reckon you could be right.' He paused and glanced over his shoulder at Aaron. 'You and the men didn't need to start eating in the bunkhouse, you know. You've always eaten in the main house or in the fields. You did with Ma and Pa, and you did with Alice. No need

70

to change now just because I've gotten me a new wife.'

'I know we don't have to, but we want to. You and Bridget have gotta get used to bein' with her, and that'll be easier without us there. Besides'—he gave a sudden grin—'the men like to be able to speak their minds when relaxin', maybe cuss a bit, too. They don't want to have to think about what they're sayin', like you have to do when you're with a lady. And I guess I feel the same.'

'It wasn't a problem with Alice.'

'You and Alice were already together when your ma and pa took me in. I've always known Alice. You could say anything in front of her and she wouldn't take amiss. We don't know your new woman.' He took another drink of water. 'You know, that's about the first thing you've said all morning. You bin mighty quiet since we set off. In fact, you bin mighty quiet all week. If I'm not out of place to ask, are you and the new wife gettin' on all right?'

Connor turned away from him and stared across the stretch of yellowing grassland to the line of hills on the far horizon. 'I guess.'

'Only, we don't normally ride the fences till nearer the fall, not when there's things to do in the fields.'

Connor pulled himself up on to the fence and sat on the top beam, facing Aaron. 'Well, if I'm honest, things aren't right peaceful at the house. I knew it'd take some getting used to, having

71

another woman around the place, but I guess I hadn't realised quite how difficult it'd be. Bridget's taken it real hard.'

'She would. She still remembers her dear departed ma.'

'It's not just that. It's Ellen being like she is. You know, her face.'

Aaron nodded.

'I've never known Bridget like this, and I've gotta say, it's trying my patience. I feel real bad about that, with her being so young, but the girl snaps at the woman every time she speaks. And at me, too,' Connor went on.

'Bridget sure don't look too happy of late.'

'You should've seen her this morning when Ellen was getting ready to go out to do the morning milking. That's one of the chores that Bridget likes best. I took one look at Bridget's face – it was the image of Alice's face when she was mad. She opened her mouth, and it hit me real hard that we oughta be making a start on fixing any broken fences. As a matter of urgency,' he added with a grin.

Aaron nodded. 'Good thinkin'. I ain't complainin'. We've almost gotten the hay in so they don't need us in the fields today. And the fences have gotta be checked before the end of fall anyway, so we might as well make a start on them now.'

'I figured we both needed a change from lookin' at cut grass,' Connor said, and he jumped down, collected his canteen and went and sat down near

Aaron. He took a drink, then leaned back against a rock, linked his hands behind his head and stared across at the hills, which were taking on a rose-pink blush in the late morning light.

How much longer before things eased up at home? His red-haired Alice had shown at times that she could be mighty stubborn, and Bridget had got the same red hair and stubbornness as her ma. Alice had always known when to stop, though; but not Bridget. And that didn't make for an easy life.

He felt a momentary anger with himself. He shouldn't really be blaming Bridget – she was only eight. He was partly to blame for not better preparing her before he took a wife. And some of the fault, too, lay with the woman he'd married. A lot of the fault, in fact, and maybe he'd been too easy on her.

He'd always seen himself as a man of his word, and when he'd first met her, he'd instinctively done what he'd felt to be right, which was to honour their agreement to wed. But now that he could see the effect of his decision on Bridget, he'd been wondering if maybe his instinct had let him down for once, and as he'd lain in bed the last few nights, he'd started to ask himself if he'd done the right thing in going through with the wedding after he'd seen her face.

It was no wonder that he couldn't sleep at night. And it clearly wasn't much easier for Ellen.

She'd taken to going out to the front of the house

73

and sitting in the dark while he was walking around the homestead, checking that all the gates and barn doors had been bolted for the night, but even after she must have heard him return to the house, she'd remain out there in the shadows.

On the first couple of occasions that he'd seen her out there, he'd wondered whether he ought to join her. But each time he'd decided against it, figuring that they'd both had a long day and that she probably needed some peace and quiet as much as he did, and he'd gone to bed.

Later on, when she'd get into bed beside him, he'd turn to her as her husband and she'd never shy from him. She would raise her nightdress to her hips to make it easier for him, and then when he'd finished, she'd turn on to her side and lie there, her back to him. Increasingly, he'd found himself watching her as she lay there, caught in the white moonlight that seeped in around the curtains, and he'd wondered what she thought about the situation.

She certainly thought something, that was for sure.

Once or twice in the past few days, he'd seen a flash of anger come into her eyes when Bridget had been rude to her, and he'd half expected her to talk real sharp to Bridget. But she hadn't. She'd just sat there, very still, accepting everything, and the spark within her eyes had died away. It was as if she was waiting for Bridget to wear herself out. But that wasn't happening, and it wouldn't. He knew his Bridget. It was pretty clear that she wanted Ellen out of their lives, and she wasn't going to stop till she had her way.

What did Ellen think about him? Not as a man, of course – theirs wasn't a marriage like that – but the way in which he ran the homestead and the way he was raising Bridget. Maybe she blamed him for Bridget's rudeness. He felt a momentary irritation. If she did, she shouldn't do. He was doing all he could to make things easier for Ellen.

That first day – the day that Peggy brought Bridget back – he'd gone out to Aaron and asked him to keep the men well away from the house, and to finish early in the barns and corrals so that he could show Ellen around that evening without her having to face anyone else that day.

And he'd told Aaron about Ellen's face.

He was sure she'd be dreading what the men would say when they saw her, and the look on their faces, so he'd asked Aaron to tell the hands about her injury, hoping they wouldn't make anything of it when they finally met at lunchtime the next day. He figured she'd heard enough on the subject from Bridget without the hired hands starting on her, too.

He sat up, had another drink of water, settled back against the rock again and stared up at the wide, cloudless blue sky.

With luck, it wouldn't be too many weeks before Ellen had news for him about a baby. That would give everyone something else to think about and discuss, and that would be no bad thing. A fleeting image ran through his mind of Ellen's back turned towards him as they lay alongside each other at night, and he felt sure that she was hoping the same.

'I saw the churning's been done,' Connor said as Ellen put a plate in front of him and Bridget, then went across to the stove, came back with a plate for herself and sat down. 'Was that you or Bridget?'

'It was her,' Bridget said. 'That's why she's here, isn't it?'

Ellen wanted to sigh, but didn't. 'Bridget's right. I did it. Your cows give a lot of milk. I'll need to do the churning twice a week.'

He nodded. 'That's what Alice did.' They ate in silence for a few minutes. 'You obviously know farm work,' he said suddenly, 'but you don't sound like a woman who was brought up on a farm. Were you?'

'No, I was born and brought up in Omaha itself. But when I got married, I went to live on the farm owned by Robert's parents. It was just outside the town. We were going to take it over from them when they couldn't run it any longer. I didn't know the first thing about farming, and they all had to teach me what to do, but it was one of the best years of my life, if not the best. And then there was the accident.'

'You weren't tempted to stay on with them afterwards?'

76

'I didn't have the chance. Robert's parents didn't want me around. They said I reminded them too much of what had happened, and I understood that. So I went back to Omaha and moved in with my brother and his family. My father was already living there. He'd gone to live with my brother after my mother died of influenza.'

'You should have stayed there,' Bridget said bluntly.

'That's enough, Bridget,' Connor said tersely. 'We're gonna eat this meal in peace. But if you want to do something helpful, you can get me the catchup,' he added.

'I don't.' Bridget scowled at her plate and picked up her knife and fork.

Ellen stood up.

'Sit down,' he said, getting up. 'I'll get it myself. I like it with meat.' He went across to the pantry, returned to the table with a jar in his hand and sat down. 'Peggy gave us this. She brings us a few jars whenever she makes it.'

'I can make you some. Robert liked it, too.'

He nodded. 'Don't forget to take a look at what's in the pantry and kitchen, and also the vegetable garden, such as it is, and make a note of anything you need from town. We'll be going there tomorrow. And put down anything you need for yourself. You, too, Bridget.'

Bridget leaned across the table, picked up the jar of catchup, put a large spoon of it on to her corn and stirred it in. Scooping up as much of the red mixture as she could, she raised the spoon to her mouth. Just before it reached her mouth, the spoon twisted in her fingers and the mixture of corn and catchup fell on to the front of her pale-green cotton dress.

'Shucks!' she exclaimed. 'I've spilt it, and I reckon it'll take a mighty lot of washing to get it clean. Catchup's like that.' Clear green eyes turned towards Ellen, a challenge in their depths. The green eyes returned to the dress and to the red mass sliding slowly down to her waist.

Ellen ran for a cloth, dampened it, and with a clean knife, scraped off the mixture as best she could. Then she gave the cloth to Bridget and asked her to wipe the dress down.

'If you take it off when you've finished eating, I'll put it into the tub to soak,' she said, sitting back down.

'Good job there's someone here to do the chores, isn't it, Pa?' Lightly flicking the cloth across the widening red and orange stain, Bridget turned to Ellen and smiled, her eyes ice-cold.

Ellen's eyes met Connor's across the table. Then she glanced at Bridget, at the slight smile of satisfaction on Bridget's face, and she opened her mouth to speak. She closed it again. Both she and Connor looked down at their plates and continued eating.

Connor hovered by the dinner table. He stared across the room at the empty chair at the end of the small table by the window. Sitting at the other end of the table, Ellen was bent over one of Bridget's muslin petticoats which had a tiny hole in it.

He hesitated a moment, then came forward. 'May I?' he asked, indicating the empty chair.

She threw him a quick glance. 'Of course,' she said, and looked back at the petticoat.

He sat down, leaned back against the chair and looked around the room.

'It's a while since I've sat at this table in the evenings,' he remarked after a short silence.

'Indeed,' Ellen said. She pulled the kerosene lamp closer to her, held her needle up to the flickering halo of orange light and slotted a piece of thread through the eye.

'Have you put Bridget's dress in to soak?' he asked.

'Yes. I did it as soon as we'd finished. I fear the catchup will have stained it, though.'

'It sure is hard to know what to do about her. It's getting to be a relief when she's gone to bed, and I feel real bad about that.'

'It *is* a difficult situation. Very difficult,' she repeated, and she started to darn the hole.

'I don't want you to think I don't criticise Bridget for her behaviour,' he went on, 'because I do. But if I punish her every time she's rude or drops food down her dress, I'll harden her against you, and I'll be blaming her for something that's partly my doing.'

79

'*Your* doing?' Ellen stopped sewing and stared at him in surprise.

'Yup. I should've given her time to get used to the idea of me marrying again before I brought you home, but I didn't. I'm at fault for that, and I recognise it.' He paused for a moment. 'But I reckon you deserve some of the blame for what Bridget's feeling, too,' he added.

'So do I,' she said. 'I don't blame Bridget for any of this. I understand how unwelcome this all must be for her, and I can see that I've made the situation worse than it needed to be. I'm sorry for that.'

'At least we agree on that.'

'And I'm sure we can also agree that this would have been hard for her, no matter how much time you'd told her in advance, and no matter what your new wife looked like. She's had you to herself for a year and she won't want to share you with anyone. It's natural for her to feel the way she does.'

'I don't know that I do agree. You're forgetting, she wouldn't have had a problem with Oonagh. You heard her.'

'Oonagh has one big advantage over me, and I don't mean her face.' She gave him a quick smile. 'It's that Oonagh isn't married to you. Bridget won't see her as a threat in any way. But if you'd actually married Oonagh, Bridget might well have found that hard to accept. She might even have found it harder to accept Oonagh than she finds it to accept me.'

He shook his head. 'I can't agree with you there. There's no reason for you to think that.'

'With such a good-looking woman for your wife, Bridget might have feared that one day Oonagh would replace her mother in your heart. If so, that would completely change her attitude towards her. But every time she looks at me, she can see that I'll never be any sort of threat to her mother's memory.'

He nodded slowly. 'OK. I take your point.'

'But I admit that she might have accepted me more quickly if I had just been plain, and not scarred as I am. And that's my fault. I didn't think how it would be for her, me looking like this. I thought only of how much I wanted a home and a family.'

He leaned forward, his elbows on the table, and stared at her in curiosity. 'But you were in your brother's house. And your father was there. Was that not home and family enough for you?'

'I'm afraid not. My brother's in comfortable circumstances. He's an ambitious man, and his wife is ambitious for him. So, too, is my father. My brother's always wanted to be a senator and is hoping to get elected to the Nebraskan legislature. When I moved into his home after the accident, I was told by him, his wife, and by my father that I must do nothing to ruin his chances. I was there to look after my brother's three children, and I must never be seen. I had to remain in the kitchen or in my room whenever they had visitors.'

'But was there nothing else you could do? It takes a strong woman to do what you did – travel a distance to marry a man you'd never met – and strong women have no need to rely on a man to provide a home. You have education. Could you not have found work in Omaha and set up home by yourself?'

'It's an overcrowded city, and everyone's looking for work. It wouldn't have been easy for a woman as scarred as I am to find a job. I would have had to take anything I was offered, no matter how unpleasant, no matter how badly paid. Omaha's full of tired, overworked women, who have insufficient to eat in the winter, and who fear daily that they'll lose their jobs. I would have become one of them, except that I'd have had the extra burden of a damaged face, which means that I'd have lived with an even greater fear of losing my place of work than most.'

'I can see how that wouldn't have been a good life.'

'And I wouldn't have felt safe, living alone in a place where there's such a fearful amount of gambling, drinking and worse. So many of its leaders are corrupt that there's little being done to clean up the town, and there's unrest everywhere, which has led to riots. I felt that I had no real choice but to go to my brother's house. But with my life there being so unpleasant . . . living in his home in the way I was . . . and then I saw your advertisement . . . But I should have been honest with you from the start.'

'You're right about that. But I can understand why you did it, and I reckon we can put that in the past now, don't you?'

'Thank you.' She hesitated. 'While we're talking about Omaha, something you said earlier started me thinking. Why didn't you try to find a wife in Wyoming or in some other place closer than Omaha?'

'I didn't really want the people of Liberty to know what my thoughts were. There was a chance that they'd find out if I advertised in the area. Denver and Cheyenne felt too close to risk it, so I thought I'd try Omaha. It's on the railroad so anyone living there could get to me.'

'I'm glad that you did.' She paused. 'You know that I don't ask for anything from you, Connor, except kindness, and maybe a little warmth,' she said awkwardly. 'I ask for no more than that. You should realise that.' She moved the petticoat closer to the lamp and resumed her sewing.

'I do,' he said. His eyes were drawn to her bent head, to the sheen on her light-brown hair which she'd tucked behind her ears. He lowered his gaze to her cheek.

As Ellen pushed the needle through the material, she felt his eyes on the side of her face. Resisting the impulse to pull her hair back across her cheek, she glanced up at him.

'Is there anything I can get you?' she asked, putting the petticoat down and starting to stand up.

'No, not a thing. To be honest, I was thinking that

I'd fair forgotten what it was like to sit and talk with someone at the end of a day's work.'

A sense of pleasure rose within her. Sitting back down, she picked up her needle again.

'I'm sorry for you, Ellen,' he went on quietly. 'You've not had an easy time since your husband's death. You'll not find me making many demands of you.'

She looked up at him, words of gratitude hovering on her lips, and she saw his clear-blue eyes on her face, eyes that were warm with sympathy, and her words wouldn't come.

Unable to tear her gaze away from him, she traced the planes of his face, hewn out of gold in the light of the lamp, the firm line of his jaw, the sun-browned chest, visible through the open neck of his flannel shirt, and she felt an overwhelming urge to reach out and touch his skin.

She looked back into his eyes.

A sudden sharp ache stabbed her in the pit of her stomach, and her mouth felt dry. Her eyes threatening to fill with tears, she looked quickly down at her sewing.

# CHAPTER 7

Liberty lay ahead of them, a sprawling patch of brown set on a wide expanse of open grassland. Beyond the town, a line of trees marked the passage of the river that flowed down from the purple-hazed hills and meandered across the plain. From the town itself, plumes of white smoke rose from the stovepipes that broke through the roofs of the wooden houses, and drifted upwards to the endless blue sky, dissolving into nothingness in the cloudless heights above.

By the time that they'd reached the first of the town buildings, steam was rising from the flanks of the horses that were pulling their wagon. As they turned on to the wide dirt track that cut through the centre of the town, Connor tugged on the reins to slow the horses, guiding them with skilful ease between the wagons and horses that moved through the town at varying speeds and in different directions. Clouds of dust, thrown up by feet and hooves, climbed the sides of the wagon, and Ellen tasted grit.

She wiped her mouth with her hand, glancing

from one side to the other at the people walking along the sidewalks.

'I reckon Liberty must seem mighty small to you after Omaha,' he said, 'but it seems pretty big to us. When Ma and Pa settled here, there were buildings on only one side of the street. All they had was one store, a meeting house, and a few small cabins with only two or three rooms. But look at it now.' He indicated on either side of them. 'We've got a general merchandise store, which is where we're heading first of all, a bank, a telegraph office, a blacksmith's and a livery stable that'll take a fair number of horses. And there's O'Shaughnessy's for ladies' clothes and sewing things. And we've even got a sheriff. We've also got a saloon with a billiard parlour, and a roadhouse. And a school and a church, of course. And a doc.'

'It's larger than I thought it'd be,' she said, and she pulled on the ribbons of her bonnet, hugging it closer into her face.

'And it's still growing,' he went on. 'Those two blocks haven't been up long enough to have gone grey.' He pointed to the left-hand side of the street, to a row of pine buildings fronted by a board sidewalk lined with hitching posts and occasional troughs of water. 'They've also recently built a town hall with jails in it just back from the road. That's where the sheriff has his office.' He looked back to the track ahead. 'Nope,' he said in satisfaction. 'There's not much you can't get in Liberty now.'

86

'It has the air of a fine town,' she said. 'And there's no smell of slurry or stock pens, not like the towns the train stopped at. Most of those towns were crowded and noisy, and they reeked of animals, sweat and stale grease. But Liberty seems very pleasant.'

He smiled at her and opened his mouth as if about to say something.

'Martha!' they heard Bridget scream from behind them. 'Wait for me!' A loud scrambling came from the back of the wagon, and Bridget's face appeared in the gap between their arms. 'Stop, Pa, I wanna get down. I've just seen Martha. She's gonna be startin' school, too, and we've gotta talk.' Her head disappeared and they heard her call again to Martha.

'Martha's one of Abigail and Elijah Carey's two children. They're our neighbours who live in the opposite direction from Peggy,' he said, pulling on the reins and bringing the horses to a stop just before they reached a large, high-fronted building made of wide, grey boards, which stood by itself a little way back from the track. He indicated the building. 'That's Massie's. It's where we're headed first of all. And then you'll be wanting O'Shaughnessy's. You'll find that almost opposite.' He climbed down, looped the reins around the nearest hitching post, and moved to the rear of the wagon.

'OK, Bridget, out you get,' Ellen heard him say. She moved on her seat to watch him as he unhooked the thin metal bar that ran across the rear of the wagon. Bridget stepped over the back, put her foot on the large wheel to her right and jumped down. 'You can go and say hello to Martha now,' Conn said, 'but leave the rest of your talking till later on. We've got chores to do first.'

Turning back to face the front of the wagon, Ellen tied the ribbons of her bonnet more tightly.

Her back on her father, Bridget ran, beaming, to where her friend was waiting for her on the sidewalk.

'What are you getting today?' Martha asked. 'Pa's getting me material for a new dress, and a slate and other things for school.'

'Me, too. What colour dress are you gonna have?'

'Red, I guess. Or maybe blue. Ma's already made me a grey smock. What about you? I saw Annie earlier. Her ma's made her a green dress and a green smock.'

'You're lucky, and so's Annie. Pa said I had to get a brown dress. I've got to get it from O'Shaughnessy's. I'd rather have any colour other than brown. Brown's boring.' Bridget pulled a face.

Martha giggled.

'But brown it's gonna be, Bridget,' she heard her father call.

'Please, Pa, can't I have a coloured dress?' she begged, turning towards him.

'Brown,' he repeated, his voice firm, and he finished helping Ellen down from the wagon and started walking towards the line of pails at the foot of the steps leading up to Massie's.

Martha jumped from the sidewalk on to the track, took a couple of steps forward and stared open-mouthed at Ellen.

Looking around her, Ellen stopped abruptly when she saw Martha. She put her hand to her bonnet.

'Who's that ugly woman with your pa?' Martha asked loudly, a look of disgust on her face.

'Pa's gotten her in to run the house,' Bridget said, narrowing her eyes as she looked past Martha to Ellen. 'She's gonna do the chores. Now that I'm startin' school, I'll be out all day, and he's gotta have someone in the house to do all the things I've been doing.'

'Is that just till he marries Miss Quinn?' Martha asked.

'Who said he's gonna marry Miss Quinn?'

'My folks. The whole town knows he is. You're so lucky. She's real pretty, and she'll be able to dress your hair and make you look pretty, too.'

Bridget pulled at her red curls. 'I wish I had dark hair like yours. No one could make my hair look pretty.'

'I bet Miss Quinn could.'

Bridget shrugged her shoulders. 'Anyway, Miss Quinn teaches school so she wouldn't be able to do the milking.'

'Come on, Bridget.' She glanced up and saw her father standing by the wagon, a pail of water in each hand. He put the water in front of the horses and stroked their manes. 'Time to be moving,' he said. 'Since you're over there, maybe you'd get the empty kerosene can from the back of the wagon.' He gave a nod to Martha. 'Give my regards to your ma and pa, won't you?'

'Sure thing, Mr Maguire. See you later, Bridget. I can't wait to tell Ma and Pa what a funny-lookin' woman your pa's taken on.' And she ran off.

Feeling red with embarrassment at being in any way associated with Ellen, Bridget reached into the back of the wagon and pulled out the empty kerosene can. She stood still, glaring at her father, waiting for him and the woman to walk off towards Massie's, then she followed slowly, keeping a distance behind them.

They reached the steps that led up to the entrance to the general merchandise store and climbed up to the porch. Connor sensed Ellen slow down and he stopped. He saw her glance at the open door, and take a step back. 'You and Bridget go on in,' she said. 'I'll wait here. It's better that way,' she said, her back against the wooden railing.

'I don't think so. I'd rather you came in and chose for yourself the things you put on the list,' he said quietly. 'You're gonna have to go in some time. Better to get it over with now when we're all together. You'll not be alone. I'll be with you, and so will Bridget.' He looked behind him and saw that Bridget was still at the foot of the steps. She was tapping the bottom stair with the toe of her boot. 'I'll go and talk to her,' he said with a sigh, and he went back down the steps, two at a time.

'What are you waiting for, Bridget? If carrying an empty can was too much to ask you to do, you can give it to me and I'll get it filled, but there are things you need from the store, and that means you've gotta come in with us. When you've done that, you and Ellen can go to O'Shaughnessy's and see about a dress for school while I go to the livery stables. So can we go in now?'

Bridget kicked the step hard. 'I reckon I can look for a dress by myself. I don't need help.'

'Well, I think you do, and I want you to go with Ellen. If your ma had been here, she'd have gone with you. She wouldn't have let you choose by yourself.'

'But she's not here, is she? I haven't got a ma.' She looked up at him, her eyes filling with tears. 'Please don't make me go with her, Pa. Please.'

He glanced helplessly up at Ellen. She gave him a slight nod, and he turned back to his daughter. 'All right, then. You can go to the store by yourself. I reckon Ellen and I can get the things you need from here. When you've found a dress, you come back and tell me, and we'll go and look at it together. And don't forget, I said a brown dress. They don't get so dirty-looking.'

'Thanks, Pa.' She wiped her eyes with the back of her hand, turned and ran across the street to the opposite sidewalk. Connor watched her until

91

she'd disappeared into one of the stores, then he went slowly back up to the porch.

'Well, I guess that was to be expected,' he said. 'Come on. Let's make a start on the list.' He held out his hand to Ellen. A look of surprise crossed her face, and she hesitantly took it.

'Thank you,' she said, her voice little more than a whisper.

He glanced down at her. 'It'll be all right. They'll soon get used to the way you look. The first time is the worst, and there's only one first time. After today, you'll not be afeared.' He gave her a wry smile. 'And nor will I. I've gotta face it just like you have. You think they won't be talking about me? Well, they sure will. So come, Ellen, let's go in.'

He turned to face the dark interior of Massie's, drew in a deep breath, and led her through the doorway. He saw that her eyes were firmly on the thin veil of sawdust covering the floorboards as she walked beside him into the shop. Then his hand felt empty as she pulled hers away and moved instantly to the side wall.

He made straight for the board counter, which ran for the length of the building. Nodding at the man in dusty blue denim overalls next to him who was looking at a seed catalogue, Connor stood the empty can on the counter and glanced along the shelves that lined the wall behind the counter, scanning the tin pans, pots, lanterns and bolts of different coloured cloth.

A thin young man came forward to serve him. Connor pushed the can across to him. 'Fill this, would you, Ezra?' he asked. 'And I need some more salt to put in the glass bowl of the lamp. It's low and I don't want to risk the kerosene exploding.' He took his list from his pocket and ran his eyes down the items again.

'You fill the can, Ezra, and I'll serve Conn,' a voice boomed out. Connor looked up and smiled at the large red-whiskered man who was walking down from the far end of the store, wiping the dirt from his hands with his dark-grey apron.

Connor nodded at him. 'Thanks, Jack. I'll begin with the slate. Bridget's startin' school soon.'

'That sure don't seem possible,' Jack Massie said, reaching behind him to a pile of slates and flat wooden frames. He turned back to Connor and put one of each in front of him. 'Only minutes ago, she was nowt but a wee bairn.'

'Isn't that the truth?' Connor ran his fingers across the smooth, soft-grey surface of the slate, then fitted it into the frame that Jack had put next to it.

'And you'll need a slate pencil. That'll be a penny. Now what else is on that list you're fingering?'

'We need some sugar and things for the kitchen.' He turned to look for Ellen, and saw her in the shadows on the opposite side of the room, walking slowly along, hugging the wall, her face turned towards the ploughs, kegs of nails and rolls of wire

93

that were stacked up in piles beneath the saws, hammers, hatchets and knives that were hanging from higher up on the wall.

'Ellen!' he called to her. 'Come and choose the sugar and coffee you want, and the rest of the things on your list.' He turned back to Jack Massie.

'You said *we*,' Jack remarked with a grin. He raised a bushy eyebrow. 'From what folks have been sayin', you'll not have been referring to Bridget alone. We sure are wantin' to meet your new wife, Conn.' He saw Jack Massie gaze past him towards the other side of the store.

'Folks should have better things to talk about,' he said bluntly. He turned around again. Ellen was still on the other side of the room, her back to him. 'Come here, Ellen,' he repeated, a note of impatience in his voice.

Her heart beating fast, Ellen gave a final tug on her bonnet to bring it as close as possible to her face, turned slowly and took a few steps towards him.

'Ah, Ellen! I thought I'd find you in here.' Oonagh's voice came from the open doorway.

Ellen stopped short and turned in dismay towards the door. Out of the corner of her eye, she saw Connor turn at exactly the same moment to look at Oonagh, and that he kept on looking. Then he glanced at Ellen, caught her eye and looked back down at his list.

'How did you know we were here?' she asked as Oonagh came up her.

'This is the first place Connor always comes,' Oonagh said, glancing across at him and laughing. 'Isn't that so, Conn?' She turned back to Ellen. 'And seeing Martha also helped. She told me you'd come to Massie's. So, what do you think of Liberty?'

'I like it. It seems to have all the shops you could wish for.'

'I'm not sure about all of them, but there are a good number. And it has more than just shops,' Oonagh said. 'It has entertainments, too. For example, we ladies meet at intervals for a sewing bee, usually at my house. Alice used to come to the bees, and you must come, too.'

'I don't much like to sew. I can mend clothes, of course, and if I had to I could make them, but I don't do that so well.'

Oonagh gave a dismissive wave of her hand. 'Oh, the sewing is just an excuse for us to gather together and talk. You must come along the next time we have one. You may bring your darning, if you wish,' she added with a laugh. 'Or you can come to one of our dime sociables. There's no sewing there. All we do is talk and maybe have some cake.'

'I don't know. I . . .'

'I hope you'll join us for something, Ellen,' she cut in. 'It's the neighbourly thing to do. I think most people know already that Conn has taken a wife, and after today, they will all know. Everyone will want to meet their new neighbour. We town dwellers are your neighbours just as much as the Thomases and the Careys, you know.' The warmth of her smile embraced Ellen. 'And apart from that, I am not so much older than you that we can't be close friends. I'd like that.'

'I'd like that, too,' Ellen said, and she did her best to return a smile. 'Thank you, Oonagh. I promise I'll come to one of your activities just as soon as I've settled into my routine.'

'I'll tell Conn to make sure that you do.' Oonagh laughed again, and she smoothed down the bodice of her dress.

Ellen's eyes went to Oonagh's high-necked violet and white striped calico dress, to the low-waisted bodice that emphasised her slim waist, to the sleeves which hugged her arms from her wrists to her elbows and then filled out to her shoulders, to the skirt which was fuller at the back than the front. Raising her eyes to the rough-straw bonnet with its lining of violet silk, she saw that the shade of violet matched exactly both her eyes and the violet stripes on the dress

'Your dress is very fashionable,' she said, trying to push back a rising sense of envy. 'Did you make it yourself?'

'Yes, I did. I didn't really have a choice. I generally wear a blouse and skirt when I'm teaching school, but I wouldn't want to wear such clothes at other times, and I would never wear the only sort of clothes I could buy in a small town like this.'

'Pa said I've got to get a brown dress for school, Miss Quinn.' Bridget's voice came from behind Oonagh. 'Brown's horrible, isn't it? Martha will have a red dress.'

Oonagh turned sharply. Ellen saw Bridget standing there, staring up at Oonagh.

'I didn't see you there, Bridget,' Oonagh said, a hint of discomfort in her voice. 'So you're getting a new dress for school, are you?' she asked brightly.

'Yes, and Pa said I have to get a brown one, but I don't want to. Like you said, they don't have nice clothes here. They only had one brown dress and it was ugly.'

Oonagh bent towards Bridget. 'I'll tell you a secret,' she said in a loud whisper. 'We dress to please men. So if the most important man in your life wants you to wear a brown dress, then brown is what you must wear.'

'Hello, Oonagh,' Connor said, coming over to them with a sack in each hand. 'I gave up waiting for you, Ellen, and gotten what I thought would do.' He glanced down at Bridget. 'You're not still complaining about having to wear brown for school, are you? If you are, you should know that I'm getting a mite tired of it.'

Bridget glared at him. Her look embraced Ellen, too.

'A brown dress can be very smart,' Oonagh said quickly. 'A few little touches can make even a brown dress special. When I was your age, my mother made me a dress of brown wool, lined with brown cambric. I cried all night because I thought it looked plain and unattractive. But you should have seen it when she'd finished with it.'

'What did she do to it?' Bridget asked, pulling a curl into her mouth and sucking on the end of it.

'Well, first of all, she sewed small brown buttons down the front, and then she put a plaid trimming on either side of the buttons and around the bottom. It had red and golden threads running through it, and they shone in the light. Then she made a high collar out of the plaid material, and fitted a little white lace inside the collar so that it fell over the top. I couldn't wait to wear the dress when she showed it to me.'

'There's a brown dress at Mrs O'Shaughnessy's. Will you make it pretty for me, Miss Quinn? Please?' Bridget pleaded, her eyes shining.

Oonagh laughed. 'I think your pa would prefer it if Ellen did it.'

Connor turned to Ellen. 'Can you do the things that Oonagh was talking about to the dress that Bridget's seen?'

Ellen's heart sank. 'I'm sorry, Bridget,' she said apologetically. 'I really wish I could do that, but I think it's beyond my ability. I could probably sew piping around the wrists and collar, though.'

'But that's not what I want. You don't want me to look pretty. That's why you won't do it.'

'Bridget!' Connor exclaimed. 'That's enough. If Ellen says that's all she can do, then that's what you'll have.'

Oonagh glanced at Connor. 'It's up to you, of course, Conn, but if you'd like me to put some buttons and plaid, or something similar, on the dress that Bridget's chosen, I'd be happy to do that. We could go and get the dress now, and buy the trimmings at the same time.'

'Oh, Pa, please,' Bridget begged. She jumped up and down, beaming up at Oonagh.

Connor gestured in despair. 'Well, if you're sure you don't mind, Oonagh. It's mighty kind of you to offer.'

'You know me, Conn. When have I not enjoyed looking for clothes, or making them, or improving the ones I've got? We've known each other for most of our lives, so you know that there's nothing I like better. Come on then, Bridget. Let's see what we can find.' She held out her hand to Bridget, who eagerly took it, and they made their way towards the doorway, with Connor following close behind.

Ellen stood for a moment and watched them go, then she began to walk slowly after them, a chill of foreboding creeping through her.

# CHAPTER 8

Ellen turned the handle of the large barrel churn that stood on wooden legs in the small shed behind the house, rocking it gently as she did so, her eyes on the cream in the churn, her mind on Connor.

If he'd wanted to push any lingering thoughts of Oonagh to the back of his mind, he hadn't had much of a chance to do so in the past month or so, she thought bitterly. Trimming Bridget's dress had brought Oonagh into the homestead several times in the run-up to the start of school – almost certainly more often than had really been necessary, she couldn't help thinking. And although Bridget was now at school all day and returning home tired every evening, she wasn't too tired to praise Oonagh nightly on her return.

Oonagh may have chosen not to marry Connor, but even when she wasn't physically there, thanks to Bridget she'd become an invisible presence at their table.

Her arm suddenly tired, she stopped turning the handle and shook her hand a few times as she leaned over the churn and peered inside. To her relief, the pale-yellow cream had finally broken up into grains of butter swimming in buttermilk. She pulled a round wooden butter bowl towards her, skimmed the grainy butter into it, pressed the remaining drops of buttermilk out of the butter, salted it and packed it into tubs which she covered with stretched muslin.

She took a jug from the shelf and poured the buttermilk into it. There was more than enough buttermilk to make both doughnuts and soda bread the next day, she thought as she put the jug on the table. The doughnuts would make a change from flapjacks. Bridget would like them, she was sure, and she was equally sure that Bridget wouldn't admit it. All of her appreciation was reserved for Oonagh.

She sat down on a stool and poured herself a mug of buttermilk. Sipping the milk, she wondered if Oonagh was now regretting her the decision to turn Connor down. It was certainly beginning to look like it. She seemed to be searching for reasons to come to the house, and she couldn't do enough for Bridget and Connor. Striking up a friendship with Connor's wife, which she clearly wanted to do, could be just another way of staying close to him.

If Oonagh, seeing someone else in the position that she might have held, felt a sense of regret, or even jealousy – no, not jealousy; no one could ever feel jealous of her with her ugliness – it could explain why Oonagh didn't like her.

Of course, she didn't know for sure that Oonagh disliked her, but her every instinct told her that this was the case. Although Oonagh had always been very pleasant to her, she was certain that her importance to Oonagh was merely as an access to Connor, not for herself.

She finished her milk, stood up and started to pile the butter tubs on to a tray.

But what if she were wrong about Oonagh? She had become so used to the cruelty of people in Omaha, who'd been unable to see beyond her scars, that she could be in danger of imagining something that wasn't there.

Peggy had shown her that not everyone thought of her as little better than an animal, and Connor, too. Also Aaron and the hired men. Their eyes had been curious at first, but they'd never looked away, nor had they been anything other than polite and respectful. It could be that Oonagh did truly want her as a friend and that she was misreading the situation. She'd like to think so. And she'd also like to think that she wasn't pushing people away from her and losing the chance of being happy. No, it was time that she started to make a real effort not to be so suspicious of people, nor to expect the worst of them, she decided, putting the last of the tubs on to the tray.

She picked up her bonnet, raised it to her head, then stopped midway and lowered it again. Clutching it in her hands, she stared at it.

After that first morning six weeks ago, Connor

had never again said anything about her not wearing a hat. He'd left the decision up to her. She'd chosen to wear her bonnet lest she meet any of the men while she went about her chores, but in truth the men had done nothing to make her feel it was necessary. It was habit more than anything else.

She had to start trusting people more, and this could be a beginning.

Her heart jumping nervously, she tied the end of the ribbons together, slipped her arm through the loop she'd made and tucked her hair more neatly into her French knot. Then she put the jug of buttermilk on the tray and picked up the tray with both hands. Using the heel of her boot, she pulled the door shut behind her and made her way across the flattened grass to the house, her bonnet hanging from her arm and swinging at her side.

She went into the kitchen, rested the tray momentarily on the nearest ledge and closed the kitchen door behind her.

'I'm afeared I bin stoppin' your man from workin',' Peggy called to her from the living room.

'I expect he was glad of a break,' she shouted back. She went into the pantry, put the tray on the side and smoothed her hair down again. Then she took a deep breath and went out into the living room. Peggy and Connor were sitting at the table in the centre of the room. Seeing them there, her steps faltered. 'He'll have enjoyed talking to you,' she told Peggy, and she forced a nervous smile. 'I would have joined you sooner but there was a great deal of milk, and the butter took me longer than I'd expected.'

She went across to the small table by the window, pulled the ribbon loop off her arm and put the bonnet on the table. Pausing a moment, she stared down at her hat and slowly ran her fingers along the rim, then she turned and went over to Connor and Peggy.

She saw them glance at her hat at the same moment, then exchange a quick look with each other.

Connor picked up his mug of coffee. 'Our cows are good milkers. Always have been.'

Peggy smiled up at Ellen. 'They must like you. Cows don't milk well for people they don't like.'

'Then for the sake of our butter supply, I hope their affection for me lasts. And talking of butter, would you like to take a tub or two back with you?'

'Thank you for the offer, my dear, but we've plenty. The lack of rain doesn't seem to be troubling the cows. But now that you've finished churning, why don't you come and sit with us? I'm sure you could do with a break, too.'

'All right, I will. But first of all, you must let me get you something else to drink.' She moved towards the kitchen. 'More coffee, or some peppermint tea maybe?'

'Coffee would be fine,' Peggy said.

A few minutes later, Ellen returned from the kitchen, a pot of coffee in one hand and a plate of small seeded cakes in the other. She put both on the table, poured coffee into the mug that Peggy had pushed towards her, took a mug from the shelf for herself and filled it, then she sat down.

'About the butter, Connor. I was wondering if I should try to sell some to the store in town,' she said. She leaned across to fill Connor's mug, but he put his hand across the top.

'Not for me, thanks. I reckon I've had enough to drink.' He stood up. 'The butter's a good idea. It's what Alice used to do. And now it's time that I watered the animals and fed them, so I'll leave you ladies to talk.' As he went past Ellen's chair, he stopped. Looking down at her, he put his hand lightly on her shoulder. 'It's real good to see you like that, Ellen,' he said. 'It makes me think you now feel at home.'

A lump came to her throat, and she looked up at him. 'I do, Connor. Thank you.'

He nodded at them both and went across the living room. A moment later, they heard the kitchen door close.

Peggy sat back in her chair and looked at Ellen. 'It must be five or six weeks now since you got here, my dear. You and Conn have obviously settled well. And what about Bridget? How are you getting on with her these days?'

'It's hard to say. She still resents me being here, and I can understand why. I'm doing the things

105

in the house that she used to do, and it looks to her as if I've taken over her place, which I have to some extent. She feels that she's no longer as important to Connor. Of course that isn't true, but she doesn't want to hear that, and she can be mighty difficult when we're all together. She's deliberately awkward whenever she can be, but maybe she isn't quite as openly rude as she was when I first arrived.'

Peggy nodded. 'And she's gone all day while you're at home with her pa, is how she'll see it. She'll be feelin' that she's not as close to Connor any more, and she'll be blamin' you for that.'

'That's right. And me being scarred like this has made things worse. I'll never forget how embarrassed she was the first time we all went into Liberty together and we met Martha. And something Connor said at the time made me realise that he, too, was feeling awkward about the way I look. I hadn't thought of that before, that people would stare at him, wondering why he married someone like me. But they do. I've seen their faces, and I've seen his. Him being such an attractive man, they will have expected a lot of his wife, and me looking like this must make it very difficult for him.'

'I'm sure you're wrong about that, my dear. It's not like Connor to worry about what other people think.'

She shrugged her shoulders. 'He's only human. As for Bridget, if she could have felt proud of me, it might have helped her to accept me. But she can't; she's ashamed of me.'

'I know Conn's a mighty busy man, but is he trying to help with Bridget?'

'I guess he's doing what he can, but we can both see that if he keeps punishing her, she'll turn against me even more. But as I said, she's not as rude as she was, and I expect she'll get even better as more time passes.'

'At least you seem to be getting on with Conn.'

She nodded. 'I think we're doing well together. He's always very polite, very considerate; maybe too much so. It's hard to know what's going on inside his head. I just hope he isn't still hurting too much over Oonagh.'

'Over Oonagh? Oonagh Quinn?' There was a note of surprise in Peggy's voice. 'What d'you mean?'

'Oonagh was a frequent visitor to the house before Bridget started school, and now that Bridget's at school, she's always telling us over dinner what Oonagh's done to help her that day. I can't believe that Oonagh makes the same effort to impress all of her pupils as she does Bridget. With never a day going by without her name coming up at some point, it can't be easy for Connor to put her behind him.'

'Oonagh and Conn have been friends since they were real little. But what makes you think he's hurtin' over her?'

'It's just that I've noticed that he always behaves

107

differently when she's here. He's quieter, more distant, maybe. With her being so beautiful, he must have been very keen to marry her, and very hurt when she refused him.'

Peggy sat up straight. 'Well I never! You sure do surprise me. I never knew he'd even offered for her. All the town thought he would, and they thought she'd say yes, her folks included. But then when you arrived . . .' She shrugged her shoulders. 'Well, I sure am knocked flat that she turned him down. There were those in town who used to think she'd been sweet on him from far back when they were young'uns, even though everyone always knew that he'd marry Alice.'

'Did he never show an interest in Oonagh?'

'Nope, never as we could see. We thought Oonagh would marry Niall, and if not Niall, Jeb Barnes. Not that she loved Jeb – she didn't – but Jeb's pa had several thousand head of cattle, and Oonagh Quinn has liked fine clothes since she was knee-high to a grasshopper. She'd want a husband who could provide for her as well as her pa has done, or even better. Jeb's money; her looks. It would have been a fair bargain on both sides.'

'Why didn't she marry one or the other of them?'

'I don't rightly know. There was some talk that Jeb asked her to marry him and she turned him down, but whether that's what happened, I couldn't say. In the end, he went and married a woman whose father also had a lot of cattle. I reckon it was the fathers did the deal. Mind you, things

108

aren't so good for either family after the last winter, or so I hear. Anyway, Oonagh didn't seem to mind that Jeb was no longer hangin' around her – she'd always been closer to Niall, anyway. But nothing came of that, either, as Niall left Liberty not long before Connor married Alice.'

'Did Niall live in the town?'

Peggy glanced swiftly at her, then looked down at her coffee. 'I reckon you could say he did,' she said, and she leaned across to the plate and took a seed cake. 'He and Jeb used to spend a lot of time together. They had hideaways all over the place, usin' them as bases for their huntin' and fishin'. Or they'd be off drivin' cattle for one or other of the stockmen in the area, and hangin' around the cowboys, playin' cards with them. But not Connor. Niall was a very different boy from Connor. Conn never had any time for Jeb.'

'To go back to Oonagh, having heard what Connor said to Bridget, I'm wondering if the reason she turned Connor down was because she didn't want to be a homesteader's wife. She obviously likes living in the town, and with a bank manager for a pa, she must live in greater comfort and ease than she would on a homestead. Or maybe she realised that Connor was still in love with Alice and always would be, and being a beautiful woman she'd feel she could do better than take second place to a dead wife.'

'And what do *you* feel about being in second place?' Peggy asked.

'If I still looked as I did before the accident, I think that I, too, might have found it difficult to accept. But after the accident . . . well, I'm grateful for what I have.'

'I reckon what you say about Oonagh does make sense. I can't see her churning the butter or rolling up her sleeves and getting down to the weekly wash, and Conn still has strong feelings for Alice – that's natural as she's only been gone for little more than a year. But Oonagh's not the sort of woman who would find that easy to live with. She'll know that he'll not forget Alice. And he couldn't if he wanted to: Bridget looks just like her.'

Ellen nodded. 'He's told me that. It must make it even harder for him.'

Peggy shook her head. 'They'd have made a good-lookin' couple, Connor and Oonagh, but I think he'll have a better life with you, my dear.'

Ellen smiled warmly at Peggy. 'Thank you. I hope you're right.' She leaned forward a little. 'Would you mind me asking you how Alice died, Peggy? In all the weeks I've been here, Connor's not told me what happened, and I've not liked to ask.'

'She died in childbirth. She'd lost two babies since Bridget was born. They hadn't even lived long enough to come into the world. And then she found herself with child again. This time she went real careful. Connor wouldn't let her do a thing in the house, he so wanted this child. She

110

went to the end of her time, bless her, but the baby was born dead. It was a boy. Alice caught the fever and died a few days later.'

'How awful for him to lose them both at once. And for Bridget, too. No wonder they're still suffering.'

'But that's something you have in common with them, isn't it? You probably still hurt when you think of your Omaha husband, just like Connor does when he thinks of Alice and his son.'

'Yes, I do. I understand Connor because I know that I, too, could never feel about anyone else as I did about Robert. But I also know that if Connor *was* ever able to love someone else again, it wouldn't be someone who looked like me. I don't hope for anything more than kindness from him, and I've told him that. And for my part, I intend to do my best to make him happy. I know the kind of life I'd have had if he'd rejected me, and I'll always be grateful to him for letting me have a home here.'

'You're right about him bein' a kind man. I've a lot of time for Connor. He's one of the best.' She stood up. 'If I'm gonna be home before sundown, I oughta be goin' now.'

Ellen rose from her chair. 'It was real nice talking to you, Peggy. Thank you for visiting.'

'You're welcome, my dear. You must come over to us soon. Come with Connor and Bridget once the harvest's in. We can take a picnic with us and go berrying. There's a spot near the mountains where more wild huckleberries and blueberries grow than we'd ever be able to pick. William knows where to find it. We'll fill every pail and basket we've got, and then you'll be able to make huckleberry pie and blueberry pudding, as well as jams and jellies. Bridget's real keen on huckleberry pie.'

'I'd like that,' Ellen said, following Peggy out of the house.

Peggy unlooped the reins from the rail and went around the side of the wagon. She made a move to climb up to her seat, but she paused and turned to Ellen. 'You don't need to apologise for the way you look, ya know. You're doin' fine. And Connor, he looks to me to be doin' pretty good, too.'

Pleasure welled up in her. 'Don't be a stranger, Peggy,' she said, and she gathered up her skirts and ran to open the gate.

# CHAPTER 9

'We'll start on the corn on Monday,' Connor told Aaron as they walked through the rows of ripening corn, pushing aside the long, yellow-green leaves as they went.

'You agree that it's ready, then?'

'Sure do. It's going to be a fine crop this year – nearly every stalk's got two ears, and some have got three. But I told you it'd be good. It always is when it's knee high by the Fourth of July.' He stopped walking, ran his fingers down the thick green silky tuft of hair that hung from the tip of the green cornstalk next to him, and parted the husk. 'Yup, we'll definitely make a start tomorrow,' Conn said, studying the kernels. 'The ears are full and the tufts are about to turn brown. We'll do the wheat immediately afterwards.'

'Right you are. I've let a couple of men go now that we've done the baling, but I've kept on enough for the corn and the wheat. You think your wife will be able to help with husking the cobs and cutting the kernels? We'll need as much help as we can get for that.'

'I reckon so. I'll sharpen the knives tonight, ready for the cutting, and then I'll have a word with her.'

Aaron nodded. They walked along in silence for a few minutes. 'Your wife knows about farming, I can tell,' he said.

'She lived on a farm with her husband before the accident.'

'Thought it might be something like that. Shame about the accident – she'd have been a good-lookin' woman before it. But a scar don't stop her from bein' mighty pleasant,' he added quickly. 'She's a fine woman.'

'I guess she is. I don't ever think about her. She's got her work to do, I've got mine, and that's the way it is.'

The last light of day was fading away, losing itself in the mellow dusk of twilight that was silently falling around them.

'Bridget!' Ellen called, walking towards East Barn. 'Bridget, where are you?'

'She's over here,' she heard Aaron call out from some distance away to her left.

Glancing around, she saw him standing on the far side of the corrals, just in front of West Barn, a pitchfork in his hand.

She waved an acknowledgement at him, and he went back inside the barn as she started to retrace her steps. Making her way along the back of the house, she went past the corrals to West Barn, and through the open barn door.

A pungent smell of rotting hay and damp manure hit her as soon as she entered the cool, dark interior, and she saw a heap of steaming, dirt-filled hay behind the barn door. Putting her hand in front of her nose and mouth, she went across to Aaron, who'd just started to drag the hay from inside a stall towards a pile of sodden hay outside the neighbouring stall. He caught sight of her and straightened up.

'I guess it does stink when you're not used to it,' he said with a grin. 'She's down there.' He nodded towards the far end of the barn, and Ellen saw the back of Bridget's head sticking out from above the wooden side of the stall. 'She's been helpin' me. Soon as I've changed the hay and put in fresh, she waters the cows and fills their buckets.'

She removed her hand from her mouth. 'I hope you don't mind if I take her, but I need her back at the house now.'

He nodded. 'We done the worst of it, anyway.' He looked towards the end of the barn. 'Bridget!' he called. 'You're wanted.'

Bridget turned, put her face above the side of the stall, saw Ellen, and ducked down out of sight.

Ellen gave Aaron a rueful smile, then walked along to the end of the barn and stood in the opening to the stall. 'I want you to come back to the house now, Bridget. I know your pa's already told you that we're going to church tomorrow, and that means that you'll need to have a bath before you go to bed. I've filled the tub with hot water and you can have the first bath. I've put the screen up ready.'

Bridget shrugged her shoulders. 'I'm busy. I'm helping Aaron. If the water gets cold, you can add some hot.'

'If the water gets cold, you'll have a cold bath. But that'll be your choice. I'll not be heating up any more drums of water for you.' She turned and started to walk towards the barn door.

'You're here to look after Pa and me,' Bridget called after her.

Ellen paused and looked back at her. 'You need not be afeared on your pa's behalf. I'll heat up the water for him, just like I've done for you. Hot or cold bath, Bridget? It's up to you.' She continued to walk away, nodded at Aaron as she passed him, and went out of the barn.

A moment or two later, she heard footsteps behind her, and she smiled to herself.

By the time she'd reached the kitchen door, Bridget had let herself catch up. Ellen went into the kitchen and turned back to Bridget. 'I'll be in the bedroom, sweeping. If you want me to scrub your back, give me a call.'

'I won't.'

'As you wish. I've left soap and a towel next to the tub, and your nightdress is on the chair. Let me know when you're done.'

★    ★    ★

She finished sweeping the bedroom floor, rested the willow-twig broom against the wall and sat down heavily on the bed.

The sounds coming from the kitchen told her that Bridget was still in the bath tub, splashing. At regular intervals, she heard water washing over the side of the tub on to the kitchen floor. Despite it being a small tub, with little space inside it in which to move, Bridget was clearly doing her best to make as much mess as she possibly could.

She was filled with a sudden lassitude.

For a time she'd thought that she and Bridget were drawing closer to each other, with Bridget not being quite as rude to her as she'd originally been, but she had been mistaken. The girl still resented her every bit as much as when she'd first arrived. She could sense the well of loneliness deep within Bridget and she desperately wanted to help her, but Bridget wouldn't let her near enough to do so, and her antagonism went on.

It wasn't that Bridget commented about her face any longer – she rarely did. It was more that she took every opportunity she could to backtalk or to make things difficult. Just as Oonagh could do nothing wrong, she could do nothing right. And it was wearing her out to be continually on the receiving end of Bridget's hostile attitude.

On several occasions she had come close to speaking her mind and telling Bridget what she thought of her attitude. But then she'd remembered Bridget's age, and how she was obviously still grieving for the loss of her mother and for what she saw as the loss of her father, and she'd remembered that if she'd been honest with Conn from the start, none of them would have been in the position in which they now found themselves, and she'd bitten back her words.

Did she regret not being more honest with Connor when she'd answered his advertisement? In the early days, when she'd seen the expression on the faces of everyone who met her, and the anguish her appearance had caused Bridget, and the discomfort felt by Connor, too, she'd thought that she did. But now?

She glanced down at the place on the bed where she lay with Connor, night after night. Leaning across to his pillow, she ran her hand slowly over the place where he rested his head. A wave of intense longing shot through her and pooled in the pit of her stomach.

Her heart racing, she lay back on the bed and stared up at the ceiling.

That night, they'd lie there again, side by side, and as with every other night, she'd hide her hunger for the moment when he raised himself above her, for the moment when she felt his body hard against hers, for the moment when he slid deep inside her. And that night, as with every other night, she'd allow herself to imagine what it would be like to be kissed by Connor, and she'd hold back her burning desire for more . . . so much more . . .

A shiver ran through her.

The light hairs on her forearms stood up, and she knew that if she were truly honest with herself, she no longer felt any sense of regret. None at all.

Connor placed the sharpened knives on the shelf next to a heap of husking pegs, went out of East Barn, swung the door shut behind him and bolted it. He glanced up at the sky. The pale moon was milky white against the black sky. Just as well we're beginning the harvest soon, he thought; we'll be seeing frost before long.

He started to walk slowly back to the house.

Bridget would be in bed, and Ellen would have cleared away their meal by now and would be sitting at the window table, mending something or reading one of the books she'd brought with her. He'd go and join her, he decided, and they could talk some more. In fact, when he thought about it, he'd rather become accustomed to sitting with her in the evenings now. He'd found that she was quite pleasant to talk to, and joining her after he'd finished his evening tasks, or bringing his work into the living room and sitting with it opposite her, seemed to have become a part of his routine without him realising it.

She was still a little formal with him, a little too polite, and much too apologetic. But once or twice recently, he'd seen a spark of fire within her, and a liveliness in her eyes, and for a moment he'd thought that he was about to see the woman she'd been before she'd been made to feel that she had to make herself as invisible as possible. But the spark had died away, leaving him feeling strangely disappointed, and increasingly he'd found himself looking forward to seeing that burst of fire again.

So why had he been so dismissive about her when he'd spoken to Aaron as they'd been walking through the ripe corn that morning?

His steps slowed and he came to a halt, frowning.

It was true that he never thought about her as a woman; that he never paused in the day as he used to do when he thought about Alice, and with a burning ache in his groin, find himself longing for the night ahead, for the touch of her soft skin against his body.

However, he did enjoy his conversations with Ellen in the evening. And he knew that later, when they went into their bedroom and extinguished the light, he didn't recoil from doing what he had to do in order to get a son. Although he'd never be able to love her as a woman, he was finding her a pleasant companion for when he'd done his day's work, and he shouldn't have been ashamed to tell Aaron that.

Ashamed?

Yes, if he was truly honest with himself, he felt ashamed that he enjoyed being with her, but he didn't quite know why he should.

Had he felt obliged to distance himself from Ellen because Aaron, like the whole of the town, had expected him to marry Oonagh, and had been shocked when instead of Oonagh, he'd wed a woman with a badly damaged face? Was it that he was embarrassed deep down to admit that he was able to find enjoyment in the company of a woman who looked like that? Or did he feel that in some way he'd be betraying Alice's memory if he let himself admit that he was looking forward to spending any sort of time with another woman?

He resumed walking.

He didn't know the answer. Maybe he'd said what he had for one of those reasons, or maybe it was for something entirely different. It didn't really matter. All he knew was that he felt as if he'd let himself down by not being totally honest with Aaron, and that by saying what he had, he'd been unfair to Ellen.

# CHAPTER 10

Aware of the curious stares of the people who hadn't seen her before, Ellen walked out of the wooden cabin into the shadow thrown by a white wooden cross that was fixed to the sloping roof of the church. She glanced at the people clustering in front of the church, their eyes on her face, and she left Connor's side and went quickly to a place on the edge of the crowd. Standing there, her eyes firmly fixed on the ground, her face shaded by her bonnet, she waited for Connor and Bridget to finish exchanging words with their friends and neighbours and to be ready to return to the homestead.

'Be you all right?'

She looked up and saw Connor standing in front of her, concern on his face. She nodded. 'I'm fine, thank you.'

'We'll say hello to the Reverend, and then we'll go home,' he said. 'By we, I mean you and me.'

She looked again at the ground, and bit her lower lip. 'If you wish.'

'Pa!' Bridget ran over to him and put herself between him and Ellen, her back to Ellen. 'I want to go and visit with Martha. Her ma and pa said I can. Her pa said he'll bring me back before supper. Can I, please?'

He shook his head. ''Fraid not. Another time, you can, but you've got things to do for school this afternoon and I want your help with cutting the corn from the cobs.'

She stamped her foot. 'It's not fair. All my friends were allowed to sit with Miss Quinn in church, but you made me sit with you and *her*. It was horrible. Everyone from outside Liberty stared at us when they saw her face.' She turned and scowled at Ellen. 'And I don't blame them.' She turned defiantly back to Connor. 'I did what you asked me, and now I'm askin' if I can go to Martha's.'

'We came as a family and we're leaving as a family,' he said firmly. 'Now go and say goodbye to Martha while I introduce Ellen to the Reverend. And then we're leaving.'

Bridget glared at her father. 'She's *your* family, not mine.' She threw another black look at Ellen and ran off in the direction of Martha and her family.

'I could speak to the Reverend another time,' Ellen said. 'He . . .'

'We're gonna speak to him now,' Connor said firmly. He slid his hand under her elbow and urged her towards the tall man in a black suit, who was shaking hands with the members of his congregation who had lined up to speak to him.

123

'Good morning, Reverend. That sure was one fine sermon,' Connor said when they reached the front of the line. 'I'd like you to meet my wife, Ellen.'

Ellen looked up at the Reverend. She saw his eyes run across the part of her scar that was visible beneath her bonnet, then he held out his hand, his smile steady.

'I'm mighty pleased to meet you, Mis' Maguire,' he said, and he turned to Connor. 'I was happy to hear you'd taken a new wife, Connor, and I've been praying you'd find your way back to the church.' He smiled again at Ellen. 'I can see that my prayers have been answered, praise the Lord.'

'We're trying to get back to normal,' Connor said.

The Reverend nodded. 'I hope that Sunday School is part of that normal. Bridget should be learning her verses along with the other children. I'm sure you and Mis' Maguire can teach her many things,' he said, 'but Miss Quinn has a certificate for teaching Bible, and you'd do a fine thing for your daughter if you let her be instructed by Miss Quinn on the Sundays between my monthly services.'

'We'll see,' Connor said.

'As I said, it's been a long time since you joined us on Sundays, Connor – too long – and I'm real glad to see you here today. And to meet you, ma'am.' He inclined his head towards Ellen.

'Thank you,' she said, and she turned to move away.

'You've done a fine thing by takin' in a woman that looks like that,' she heard the Reverend tell Connor. 'You've been a true Good Samaritan. There's many here that wouldn't have done what you've done.'

'Good day, Reverend,' Connor said. Ellen heard a trace of anger in his voice. She glanced quickly at his face as he came to her side and she saw fury burning in the depths of his eyes. She looked at him anxiously. He met her gaze, and his expression softened. Giving her a rueful smile, he took off his jacket and slung it over his shoulder. 'Don't mind him, or people like him. I'll get Bridget and we'll leave. You can wait by the wagon, if you wish.'

'I'll do that,' she said, and she turned away and began to walk quickly towards the group of horses and wagons tethered to the nearby hitching posts.

When she reached Connor's wagon, she climbed up into her seat, sat back and sighed with relief at being away from the townsfolk. At least that first visit to the church was over. The worst must now be in the past as there couldn't be many people left in the area who hadn't yet seen her face. As Connor had once said, the first time for a thing was always the worst, but there was only ever one first time.

She closed her eyes and let the conversations that were taking place in front of the church recede into a low buzz behind her, a distant hum broken every so often by the chirrup of a bird or the warning cry of a hawk overhead.

After a few minutes, she moved her head to one side to look at the fields on the right of the wagon. The rays of the sun had found the patches of yellow rabbitbush dotted throughout the green expanse and had painted them gold. She stared at the view for several moments, a smile on her lips, then she tilted her face towards the sun, pulled the rim of the bonnet so that it shielded her scarred cheek, and let the sun's warmth creep through her body. For the first time that day, she felt herself truly begin to unwind.

After a few minutes, she sat upright and looked back at the church to see what Connor and Bridget were doing. She saw they were still talking to folks from Liberty, so to pass the time while she was waiting for them to return, she took off her bonnet and began to roll up the first of the ribbons that hung from each side, trying to rid it of the creases that had come from being tied to the other ribbon. When she'd finished rolling the first ribbon, she started on the second. Then she stopped abruptly and looked up.

She was being watched.

At the height of the midday heat, she felt a cold chill wrap itself around her. Her skin prickled and goosebumps ran along her arms.

Frowning, she stared in front of her towards Main Street, but there was no one to be seen in the street ahead. It was empty of everything except for the tethered horses and wagons. And the small part of the sidewalk in Main Street that she could

126

see from where she was sitting, that, too, was deserted. And in the fields on either side of her, there was no one to be seen. She turned around and looked back at the yard in front of the church. Everyone there seemed engrossed in conversation: no one appeared to be paying her any mind.

Turning back, she bit her lower lip. There really was no one to be seen. She must have imagined it. But the sensation that had come over her . . . For a moment it had felt very real to her that someone had been watching her. Not staring at her – she was used to that – but actually watching her.

She shivered, wiped her clammy hands on her skirt, then shook loose the coil of ribbon, put her bonnet back on, tied the ribbons firmly beneath her chin and sat upright. Connor would soon return, and when he was sitting next to her, she'd be able to laugh at her silliness.

'Are you going to sit in the back or up in front, Bridget?' Connor voice came from just behind the wagon. Bridget's reply was to scramble noisily up into the back.

She felt herself relax a little.

He came around the side of the wagon, pulled the reins over the top of the post and climbed up into his seat. Glancing in the back, he told Bridget to sit down and to stay sitting, then he shook the reins and started the horses along the narrow track that led to Main Street.

'I'm glad you're back,' she said as he turned into Main Street.

He looked across at her in slight surprise. 'I wasn't exactly far from you, nor gone for long.'

'For a moment or two, I thought someone was watching me,' she said, keeping her voice low. She looked quickly behind her and was relieved to see Bridget didn't appear to have heard what she said. She was too busy staring over the side of the wagon, waving at the people they passed.

'People often look at you, Ellen,' he said quietly. 'I know this cannot be pleasant for you, but . . .'

'No, I mean really watching me, Conn. Not staring at my face. It was more than that.'

'Who was it?'

'I don't know. And I don't know that there *was* anyone there – I certainly couldn't see anyone – but it felt as if someone was watching me. Just for a moment or two.' She shrugged her shoulders dismissively. 'Ignore me. I think I must have imagined it. I doubt if there was anyone there.'

She turned away from him and stared at the sidewalks on either side of the track as they drove slowly through the centre of town and out on to the open range.

'Is this the first time you've felt eyes on you?' he asked after a while, pulling back on the reins to keep the horses at a gentle gait.

'Yes, it is. But I feel easier in my mind now that I've told you, and now that I think I was mistaken.'

'Maybe so. But I reckon I'll tell Aaron and the hands to be extra vigilant.'

128

'Thank you. I would like to think I was wrong and it was my imagination.' She gave him a half-smile. 'I normally don't like being proved wrong, but in this case I would be happy if it were so.'

He grinned at her. 'Then I reckon you're no different from any woman I've met. No woman of my acquaintance has ever wanted to be proved wrong, no matter how wrong they are.'

She laughed. 'I'll have to let that pass. Men are well known for their stubbornness and determination to get their own way, and if I argue that women are more willing to accept being at fault than men, you'll use it as proof that no woman ever wants to accept that she's wrong.'

'So we're stubborn, are we?' he asked, amusement in his voice. 'Then the least I can do is try to live up to your opinion of men. If I do that, you'll have the pleasure of knowing that you're right, and I'll enjoy stubbornly asserting myself. We'll both benefit. Yup, I like this way of thinking.'

'I'm not so sure that *I* do,' she said, laughing again. 'I rather think I've unintentionally given you permission to adopt a characteristic that would be hard to live with. I think I'd do well to change the subject.'

'As you wish,' he said, turning to her. His face broke out into a lazy smile. The blue eyes that ran across her face were flecked with gold in the late morning sun, she noticed.

She met his gaze, and smiled back. For a long moment, their eyes lingered on each other, then

129

each turned at the same moment to look at the path ahead.

'How did you feel, going back to church for the first time since Alice died?' she asked after several minutes.

'That we did the right thing for Bridget. When Alice was first gone, I didn't feel much like church, and nor did Bridget. And later on there was always something to do on the farm and we never even got as far as hitchin' up the wagon. But we must start going again for Bridget's sake, if for nothing else. It's what Alice would have wanted. And what about you? I know you've not mentioned going to church since you got here, but back in Omaha, were you a churchgoer?'

'Not since Robert died. In a town as large as Omaha, there were services every week. My brother went with his wife and children every Sunday, but I wasn't allowed to go with them, and I sure was glad about that. Some of those worthy God-fearing folks could stare the hardest and be the meanest. I hated going anywhere where I'd be seen.'

'I think you're finding that folks in Liberty don't stare as hard as folks in Omaha. Leastways, most of them don't.' He glanced across at her. 'Don't let the horses that took your husband and destroyed your face, destroy your life, Ellen. My house isn't your brother's house.'

'Thank you,' she said quietly. 'I'm very grateful to you.'

He burst out laughing. She looked him in surprise.

'I reckon I'm getting to know you,' he said cheer-fully. 'And I guess we've reached the point where you can stop being a mouse about the place all the time, always being grateful, never saying what you think. You've shown me that you can give back as good as you get, so that's the way it's gonna be from now on. Liberty Homestead is *your* home now as well as mine, and it's time you started to relax and act normal.'

'So thanking someone who's been kind, and feeling grateful for that kindness, isn't normal, is it?' she asked, smiling at him. 'If it isn't, I shudder to think what your normal is.'

He grinned at her. 'Well, it sure isn't creeping around and whispering thank you all the time. Nor is it letting a rude miss get away with it,' he added, his face suddenly serious. 'OK, I'm as much to blame as you for the last one – more so, in fact, as she's my daughter. But you're to start saying what you're thinking. When she's rude, you can tell her so, and I will, too. I reckon we've given her long enough to settle.'

'I'll do that.'

'What I'm trying to say is, I want you to be like you used to be when you lived with your husband . . . with Robert, I mean.'

'How do you know I was any different when I was married to Robert?' she retorted lightly. 'Maybe I thanked him daily for taking me to live on his parents' ranch. I've already said that that was one of my best years.'

'Instinct,' he said with a grin. 'It's not only you women who've got instinct. We men have it, too. And my instinct tells me you can be quite spirited, when you're not thinking you mustn't be seen or heard, that is. I've seen a look in your eye that I used to see in Alice's. You're both Irish, and Irish women have a liveliness that makes them good company. It was one of the things in my mind when I got myself another Irish wife.'

'Maybe my family has been in America for so long that we've lost all of our Irish characteristics,' she said with a sideways smile.

'Maybe that's true. You certainly don't sound Irish. On the contrary, you sound like a town-bred American. When did your family leave Ireland?'

'My great-grandparents came over in the late 1700s. They settled near the port where they'd landed as they couldn't afford to move inland. When they'd made something of themselves, they went to live in Chicago. After they died, my grandparents moved south to Omaha. They wanted to be seen as full Americans, and they thought that that would be easier in a town which didn't have such a large Irish community as Chicago has. So I was brought up as an American first and foremost.'

'Do you feel at all Irish?'

'Strangely, I do. I know I don't know much about my Irish heritage, which is another reason why I probably shouldn't have answered your advertisement. But whether that means that I have the lively Irish spirit you were looking for, I wouldn't know.'

'I'm inclined to think you have, and I wanna see more of the Ellen from before the accident, and less of the Ellen from after it. And that's an order.'

'Aha! You're now proving that I was right when I said men were stubborn and determined to get their own way. Am I allowed to thank you for the smug self-satisfaction that I now feel?'

They turned to each other, a smile on their lips. Again their eyes met and held. Slowly their smiles faded away, and her heart missed a beat.

'What's the matter with you, Pa? We're never gonna get home today if you don't go faster,' they heard Bridget call out from behind them. 'What are you talkin' about?'

They swiftly turned to look at the path ahead, and Ellen straightened her bonnet. Bridget's face appeared next to Connor's elbow. 'Like you said, I've gotta get things ready for school and do my chores, Pa. And I'm hungry.' The face disappeared and there was a thud as she slid back down to the floor of the wagon.

'OK, Bridget. Hold tight!' Connor shouted back to her. 'You, too, Ellen.' And he urged the horses into a gallop along the rutted track.

Her heart beating fast, Ellen gripped the side of the wagon with one hand, and held her bonnet to her head with the other. If only Bridget hadn't chosen that moment to bring their conversation to an end, she thought in despair. She'd been enjoying it, and she thought Connor had, too. And they'd seemed to connect. It was just for a moment, but it was a connection all the same. Maybe . . .

No, she thought, angry at herself. There *was* no maybe. Once again, she was in danger of letting herself see something that wasn't there. There wasn't a maybe, and there never would be.

# CHAPTER 11

Ellen stopped checking the rows of cobs that she'd put out earlier in the day to dry in the sun, straightened up and looked anxiously around her. Not for the first time that day, she felt as if she were being watched. It had been no more than a vague suspicion at lunch time, and she'd decided that she was probably imagining it and hadn't said anything to Conn or Aaron, but the feeling was stronger now. There was definitely someone out there, someone she couldn't see, but who could see her, and that was frightening her.

Until that afternoon, she'd been inclined to think that her fear after church two days ago had been the result of imagination combined with the midday heat and the discomfort caused by the stares of people who'd never seen her before. But to feel the same sensation again . . .

She took a few steps forward and stared hard in every direction.

Once again, there was no one to be seen. But this time, the feeling was so strong that she had no doubt there was someone there.

Wiping her hands on her apron, she made her

way quickly across the yard to East Barn, where she knew she'd find Connor along with Aaron and three hired hands. They'd been there since lunch, sitting on milking stools, working their way through the huge pile of corn cobs that they'd pulled from the stalks both the day before and that morning.

Earlier on in the afternoon, as soon as she'd finished clearing away the lunch, she'd gone out and joined them, helping to remove the stalks and long dry leaves which would be used as fodder for the young stock, adding her share to the large heap on the ground behind them. She'd then started stripping the husks from the ears of corn, using the husking peg strapped to her mittens, but she'd taken a break to check on the cobs that were in the sun, drying.

She went back into the barn. Almost all of the bushel baskets had been filled with the bare ears of corn, she noticed, and there was only a small pile of cobs left to do.

Connor had his back to her, but Aaron saw her approach. 'It's your wife, Conn,' he said, indicating with his head that Connor should look behind him.

Connor turned and smiled. 'We won't be much longer – we're about ready to stop for the day. We thought we'd leave cutting the kernels from the cobs that we aren't gonna sell till tomorrow. You could help with that tomorrow morning, if you were so minded. And if you think we need to dry more cobs, you can take them before we begin and put them out tomorrow. We don't wanna run out of food in the middle of winter. Certainly not if next winter's anything like the last. Some of the blizzards lasted for days on end.'

'I'm not here to do the corn,' she said quickly. 'It's about something else. You know that I thought someone was watching me on Sunday. Well just now, out in the vegetable garden, I had exactly the same feeling, and not for the first time today. I'm certain there's someone there, even though I can't see them.'

Connor glanced at Aaron and the hands. 'Have any of you seen anything out of the ordinary today or in the last couple of days?'

'Not me,' Aaron said. 'And I bin watchin' out ever since you mentioned it on Sunday.' The hired hands shook their heads.

Connor turned back to Ellen. 'I reckon it's your imagination. You had that feeling on Sunday, so being watched was probably still in your mind today.'

'I don't know . . . It felt very real to me. Both times.'

He glanced down at the pile of cobs. 'We'll easily finish by noon tomorrow so I reckon we can stop for today.' He stood up. 'I suggest we all get a gun and take a look around the place, just to be sure. You three men ride out to the far fields and see if there's anything happening there. There's not been any rustling for a while, but maybe someone's planning on starting up again, though that wouldn't explain why Ellen would be of interest to anyone watching. Aaron, you come with me. We'll go through the barns and outbuildings. And when we've done that, maybe, you'd ride the fences and start checking for damage.'

Aaron and the hands stood up.

'We're on our way,' one of the men said.

'While you're making a start on the fences, Aaron, I'll take the wagon and go for Bridget. If there's the slightest chance of trouble around, I don't want her walking home by herself. When I get back, I'll ride out and join you. As for you, Ellen, you go back to the house and bolt the door till I return. Be sure to bolt the front door and the back. I doubt there's anyone here who shouldn't be, but we'll make real sure of that.'

'That's the barns and all the outbuildings clear,' Aaron said as he and Connor started to make their way towards the horses' shed. 'And all the animals are safely penned in the corrals. There's no sign of any visitors. You think she was right?'

'Maybe, maybe not. So far we've not found any damage to the property or the animals, and there's no sign of any strangers havin' been here, but that doesn't mean to say that there's no one interested in what we're doing.'

'That's so. But it sure ain't Injuns. We ain't had Injun trouble in these parts for ten years or more. Nope, I reckon it was her imaginin' things.'

Connor shrugged his shoulders. 'You're probably

right. But my mind keeps going over the same thought. It's that Ellen said someone was watching her on Sunday. She wasn't at the farm at the time – she was in town. And she thought they were watching her again today. Checking the buildings and land was the obvious place to start, but this might just be to do with Ellen. Or with me.'

'With you? How d'you figure that?'

'I went to the church with her and Bridget, and I'm always around the farm. Anyone watching could have been looking for me, not Ellen. She doesn't strike me as a fanciful woman, and I'm more inclined to think that someone has been watching us than not. And that's why I'm going for Bridget now. When I've got her safely back, I'll come out and join you.'

'You do that,' Aaron said with a grin. 'But I still think we ain't gonna find so much as a dead rattler.'

'You've been very quiet since you got back today,' Connor said, sitting down on the edge of Bridget's bed and looking thoughtfully at her. 'Is it because there seems to have been a lot going on around the ranch since I dropped you back here?'

'Nope.'

'Well, is it that you're not feeling well, then?'

'I'm fine.'

'Only you hardly spoke on the way back from school, and you weren't much more talkative at dinner. And you weren't rude to Ellen – not even once. And you weren't rude to me. That's got us real worried about you,' he said with a grin.

'Very funny. There's nothing wrong with me.' She wriggled further under her quilt.

'I know you, honey, and I know that something's bothering you. What is it?'

'It's nothing.'

'Yes, it is. Tell me what's wrong.'

'It's Miss Quinn, if you really want to know. She wasn't like she usually is. She was different today.'

'In what way different?'

'She was very quiet.'

He grinned at her. 'Maybe you caught that from her. If so, I hope she'll be very quiet again tomorrow. It makes for a peaceful evening for us.'

She pulled herself back up in the bed and stared at him, a worried expression on her face. 'Be serious, Pa. It was like she was thinking about something else and not about us. We all thought that. We were especially good, and we sat learning our spellings all afternoon and didn't move from our desks. We didn't even have a recess. And then she didn't test us before we came home, and she always tests us.'

'I guess that does sound unusual, but the answer could be a simple one – she may have been feeling unwell. There are times when a woman doesn't feel so good, and today could have been one of those times.'

'Maybe. I didn't like it, though, and I was mighty pleased to see you when I came out of school. So was Martha as it meant she didn't have to walk so far.' She giggled.

'I sure wish I could collect you more often. I like hearing about the things you've done at school. Usually, by the time we sit down in the evening these days, you're too tired to tell me much about what you've been doing. It was lucky that I urgently needed more molasses from town today as it meant that I got to have time with my daughter, you didn't have to walk home and Martha didn't have to walk as far as usual.'

Bridget turned her head and stared at the door. 'You'd have more time to talk to me if you didn't have to talk to *her*, and if she didn't feel she had to talk to us,' she said sharply.

'I see that the old Bridget is returning,' he said, and he stood up. 'I'm now convinced that there's nothing wrong with you so I'll be off and you can get some sleep.' He leaned over, kissed her on the forehead and left the bedroom.

'Is she all right?' Ellen shouted from the kitchen as he went back into the living room and sat down at the window table, opposite Ellen's chair.

'She's fine. It was about Oonagh,' he called back to her. 'She's been acting strangely today. But nothing to worry about.'

'At least she's not feeling poorly.' She came into the room, holding a pail. 'I'm going to get some water from the outside pump. It'll be quicker to use that one, and there's nothing to worry about since none of you found anything amiss today.'

Ellen opened the kitchen door, went out into the backyard and walked across to the pump, glancing up at the sky as she did so. The riot of orange and red that had earlier blazed a path across the sky was slowly purpling into the muted shades of night. She paused for a moment and watched the colours meld and deepen into a canopy of black that reached as far as the eye could see. As she watched, the first of the stars appeared.

And she heard a sound.

Not the sort of sound she was used to hearing break into the silence of the night. It wasn't the loud report of a fallen branch as it snapped beneath the weight of an animal scurrying across it, nor the call of a bird, nor the hoot of an owl, nor the yelp of a coyote. It wasn't the subdued murmur of the water in the distant creek, nor the quaking of the aspen leaves as the wind played between the branches. No, it was a different sound.

Puzzled, she took a few steps forward and stared across the fields in the direction of Liberty.

She heard the sound again. It was too faint to make out what it was, but it definitely wasn't in her imagination.

The ground beneath her trembled and she heard it again, this time more distinctly. It was coming closer, getting louder. In a flash, she realised that she was hearing the clip-clop of metal-shod hooves as they pounded the hard, dry earth.

She spun around and ran back into the house.

'Connor! Someone's coming!' she cried as she ran into the living room.

He jumped up, went swiftly past her to the kitchen, flung open the kitchen door and went out to the yard. He stood still and listened. She followed him outside and hovered close behind him.

'They're heading for the front,' he told her. 'Run and tell Aaron. Then come back and bolt the door behind you.' He quickly stepped back into the house, and she saw him reach up above the door, lift down a thick wooden plank and lean it against the side of the door. 'When you've bolted the door, slot the plank into the iron holders. That'll keep you safe.'

He picked up his shotgun.

Her heart seemed to stop. 'Why do you need a gun? Who do you think it is?'

'No idea, but I'm thinking it's kinda late for neighbours, but not too late for rustlers. We may only have twenty head of cattle, but it's still worth their taking.'

'It could be the person who was watching me. There could be more than one.'

'Maybe. Only one way to find out. Now be gone. I'm gonna go out front to meet our visitors. When you get back, bolt the door and stay in the house.'

She went a couple of steps up the path towards the bunkhouse, then turned back to look at him. 'You'll be careful, won't you?' she called to him.

'Sure will,' she heard him say as he pushed the kitchen door shut behind him, his rifle in his hand.

As she slid the wooden plank into the metal holders on either side of the door, she heard the thwack of boots hitting the ground at speed as Aaron ran across the backyard towards West Barn. She went quickly to the front door, bolted it, then ran to Bridget's bedroom and stood with her back to the closed door, staring across the living room to the front door. Cupping her hands together, she breathed deeply into them, trying to push back her fear.

She heard the muffled sound of a horse drawing to a halt on the other side of the gate. Only one horse, she thought, and she relaxed slightly. Connor would be a match for whoever it was.

'Hello, the house!' a strange voice called, and the cry was followed by laughter.

Connor said something in reply, but she couldn't make out what he'd said. There weren't any gunshots, though, just Connor speaking to another man.

The talking stopped and the gate creaked open on its hinges. The clip-clip of a horse being ridden up to the front of the house was followed by the clang of the gate closing and the grating of the iron bolt as it was slotted into place. Footsteps approached the house. That would be Connor, she thought. A horse whinnied outside the front door, and she heard the dull thud of leather boots landing on the hard ground. And that would be the other man. She drew her breath in sharply.

'Hello, the House, indeed,' she heard Connor remark from just outside the door. 'No warning was necessary. We don't shoot strangers on sight in these parts.'

His voice sounded cold, but he seemed to know the man. More of her tension drained away. He called to her to unbolt the door and she quickly did so.

Connor was the first person to come into the room, his face tense and strained. She took a step forward. A slim, dark-haired man in a wide-brimmed brown felt hat followed closely behind him. The man was carrying a large leather bag which he'd slung over his shoulder. The smell of woodsmoke, horses and leather came into the room with him.

'This is Niall,' Connor said. 'My brother.'

# CHAPTER 12

'Your brother?' Ellen echoed. 'The Niall that Peggy mentioned a while ago, the friend of Jeb? I didn't realise he was your brother. In fact, I didn't know you had a brother.' She stared at him in surprise.

'I kinda forgot I had one,' he said bluntly, 'he's been gone so long. He walked out on us around ten years ago and no one hereabouts has heard from him since.'

Niall took off his hat and threw it to the table. Brushing past Connor, he went up to Ellen. 'Aren't you gonna introduce me, Conn?' he asked. She saw his eyes run across her face and settle on her left cheek. He glanced over his shoulder at Connor and raised an eyebrow, then he turned back to her, and smiled broadly. It was Connor's smile, she saw with a start, but coming from a leaner face. 'Not that I need an introduction. From what I hear in town, I've gotten me a new sister.' He held out his hand.

She glanced at Connor, but his eyes were fixed on the back of Niall's head.

She took Niall's hand. 'Hello, Niall,' she said. 'I'm pleased to make your acquaintance.'

'Likewise, I'm sure.' He released her hand and looked around the room. 'Well, what do you know, Conn? You've made this mighty pretty.' Amused eyes settled on her once again. 'Or is that your doing, ma'am?'

'Call me Ellen, won't you?'

He gave her a slight bow. 'I'll be glad to do so. And the young 'un, Conn? A girl, I believe.'

'In bed.'

'I guess I'll have to wait till tomorrow to see her.'

'Since she's eight year's old and you've never yet set eyes on her, not so much as even once, I reckon one day more won't hurt too much.'

'Eight is she?' Niall said, shaking his head. 'How time flies!' He crossed to the living room table with a leisurely gait, sat down and stretched out his legs. 'I was real sorry to hear about Alice. She was a fine woman.'

Connor took the seat opposite Niall. Ellen went into the kitchen and pulled the coffee pot across to the stove. 'You seem well informed about me and my family,' she heard Connor say, his voice chill. 'How come you know so much?'

'Why, from Oonagh, of course. First person I looked for when I rode into town. She's turned into a real beautiful gal, I must say. I sure was amazed to learn that she wasn't already taken.' He turned around as Ellen came back into the room with a plate of doughnuts. 'Beggin' your pardon, ma'am, but I'm gonna speak my mind to my brother here.' He turned back to Connor. 'I sure was surprised that you and our Miss Oonagh didn't wed each other, what with Alice gone and Oonagh still not wed. She always was sweet on you.'

Ellen's heart missed a beat. She put the plate in the centre of the table and moved back towards the kitchen. Hovering just inside the living room, she waited for the water to heat up, hanging on to every word that Niall and Conn spoke.

'It was you and Jeb she hung out with, not me,' Connor said tersely.

'You can't tell me that you didn't know she'd have had you for the asking.'

'I guess I was too busy looking at Alice to be interested in figuring out what was going on in Oonagh's mind. But it's what's in your mind that I want to hear. Why've you come back, Niall? What do you want?'

'Why, you're sounding a mite unfriendly, brother,' he drawled. 'That wouldn't be much of a welcome for a stranger, and it's even less of a welcome for a brother. And you a churchgoer, too.' He shook his head and clicked his tongue in disapproval.

Ellen stepped forward to put two mugs on their table. 'The water's almost ready. I'll bring you some coffee in a minute.'

'And then I think Niall will be on his way,' Connor said. He met his brother's eyes.

Ellen stared from one to the other.

'And then I think Niall will be given a bed for the night,' Niall said quietly, his gaze not leaving his brother's face. 'And for as many nights as he wants. This is Niall's home, too. As the older son, it's his birthright, if you like.' He sat back, gestured with upturned palms and smiled across the table. 'Look at us both, Ellen, sitting at the same table after all these years. This is just what our ma and pa would have wanted – their two boys under the same roof, running the homestead together.' He laughed. 'And I'm thinking that we should do just that. Yessir; I am.' He laughed again.

Ellen went out and soon after returned with a pot of coffee. She filled their mugs and turned to leave.

'Pour a coffee for yourself, Ellen,' Connor said, 'and sit with us. Whatever Niall has in mind – and I'm sure he has something in mind – it'll affect you as much as me.'

'That's right, sister.' Clear-blue eyes looked up at her, amusement dancing in their depths. 'Do come and join us.'

She got a mug for herself, poured a coffee, put the pot in the centre of the table and sat down between Connor and Niall.

'Now,' Connor went on. 'Maybe you'd tell us the real reason why you've come back to Liberty.'

Niall picked up his coffee. 'Like I just said, you and me, running the homestead together. I'm thinkin' that sounds a real good idea.'

'And I'm thinking something different,' Connor said quietly. 'You never took to farm work, and that's why you left. It's always been cattle you wanted.

And not just a small ranch at that – you wanted to go into cattle in a big way. You and Jeb, you went on every drive that you could, and you were forever up at his ranch, working with his pa's cattle when you should've been working here with us. And what I'm thinking is, you're not gonna suddenly take to homesteading now.'

'This farm's as much mine as yours, brother. More so, in fact – I came along a year ahead of you, in case you've forgotten,' Niall said, his voice steady.

'I haven't forgotten anything. I haven't forgotten how you walked out the day after Pa was laid to rest in the cemetery aside of Ma, and how you left me to run the place by myself, still a lad and not yet married. Didn't want to be trapped, you said. You walked out without one thought about me and what it would do to my life. There wouldn't be any farm today if I'd gone after my freedom like you did. So as far I'm concerned, you lost your rights to this farm on that day. This is my home now, not yours. I've earned it.' He stood up. 'You can bed down here for a few days, but then I'll expect you to move on.'

Niall sat back in his chair and smiled at Ellen. 'Your husband sure is a hard man,' he said, shaking his head. He looked up at Connor. 'I'll grant you that, Conn. The homestead would be long gone if it weren't for you. But it *is* still here, and as it is, I do still see myself as having rights.' He finished the last of his coffee, got up and stretched. 'We'll talk some more tomorrow. I'm ready to bunk down now. Am I gonna be in our old room?'

'Bridget's got our room,' Connor said, 'and Ellen and I are in Ma and Pa's room. Ellen will make you a bed in here. I'll put your horse in the barn for the night and we can talk in the morning, since you seem to want to do so. But whatever you're planning on saying, Niall, you'll not be staying here for long.'

The sun was sliding above the horizon, driving the chill from the early morning air, as Conn stepped out of the house. He paused and looked around him for a moment or two. Niall was over by the fence, leaning against it, staring towards the creek. Connor strolled over to the fence and leaned beside him.

Twisting a piece of straw in his fingers, Niall continued to stare ahead. Conn's eyes followed the direction of Niall's gaze. A light translucent vapour hung low over the water that wound across the milky-white meadow and veiled with silvery gauze the cottonwood trees and trembling aspens that grew on the other side of the river.

'I thought I'd find you here,' Connor said. 'The river sure is beautiful at this time of day. At any time of day. And when the aspens are changing from yellow to the deep red of fall – and you'll see that they're doing that now, when the mist rises – the view is something you'd have to go a long way to beat. I never tire of looking at it.' He turned to Niall. 'You must've missed it, being so far from home for so long. Leastways, I'm thinking you must've been miles away since we've seen neither hide nor hair of you since you left.'

'Yup, the river is a mighty pretty sight,' Niall said, nodding. 'Almost as good as the sight of sunup on the open range when you're on the back of your horse, breathing in the earthy scent of wet ground and of sagebrush that's too new even to be used for building a fire. And you're sittin' up there, watchin' a thousand head of cattle – your cattle – grazin' out on the grass as far as the eye can see.' He turned to Connor. 'Now that sure is a sight that takes some beating.'

Connor grinned at him. 'Why, you almost make that sound like a challenge, and you know how much I like a challenge. Let me think . . .' He eyed Niall with amusement. 'Since I can't rustle up a thousand head of cattle to gladden your eye, I've come up with something else that might be a pleasing sight for you to behold until you go back to your ranch and get the view you hanker after. I'm seeing in my head eighty acres of ripe golden wheat, stretching out to the horizon, just waiting to be harvested. Now what do you say to that vision?'

Niall put his head on one side and screwed up his forehead in thought. 'Nope,' he said at last. 'The cattle still comes first, and for my second choice, I'm of a mind to choose the town with all its dust and dirt, and with people coming and

152

going all the time, and playing hands of cards and the like. I guess the river's no higher than third place. And as for the wheat, I'm sorry, brother, it's so far down the list I can't even place it. Nope, I reckon I'll stay put and admire the third-best view.'

'OK, Niall. Let's quit funning now.' Connor took a step back from the fence. 'We could use your help, and as you're staying here a day or two . . . The temperatures are beginning to drop off and we could be looking at a freeze before too long. We've done the hay, chopped the winter wood and gotten the corn in. And now we've gotta harvest the wheat real quick if we're gonna get the ploughing done before the frost comes. If you can remember anything at all about farming, you'll know that it's essential to break the sod before the ground hardens, or it won't be ready for seeding come spring.'

'I ain't forgotten how to farm.'

'But I don't know that, do I? How would I? You've become a stranger to me.'

Niall glanced sideways at Connor. 'Talkin' of strangers, where'd you get that wife of yours? Or maybe I should say, *why* did you take a woman who looks like that for a wife?'

'We're not talking about my wife. We're talking about the wheat. We got ourselves a reaper-binder a few years ago, and that cuts a fair patch on a good day so we don't need to take on as many men as we used to. But we still need men to shock the bundles, throw them on to the wagon and haul them to the thresher. We've obviously hired some men, but we can always use another hand. The more we have, the faster we get it done. The men'll soon be going out to the wheat fields, and I'm about to hitch up a team of horses to take out to them. What about coming out with us?'

Niall shook his head. 'I dunno, brother. I just arrived. Seems like I haven't had time to settle in yet. And think of your gal. Bridget, didn't you say her name was? She'll be real anxious to meet her uncle. Nope, I reckon I oughta stay near the house.'

'She's finishing getting ready for school,' Connor said sharply. 'She'll be leaving any minute now by the back of the house, so you'll not be seeing her till tonight. It's better that way. So, are you gonna help us or not?'

'I think not. Not today, anyways.' He gave an exaggerated sigh. 'If I can't get to know your daughter this morning, I guess I'll have to make do with your wife. Now, she looks a mighty interesting woman.' He threw a sly glance at Connor. 'I guess you knew what you were doing. A woman like that must be real grateful to have a man.'

Connor looked at him, his eyes two shards of ice. 'Well, she needn't be. She can farm as good as any other woman. I take it that's what you meant?'

'What else?' Niall raised his hands in helplessness. 'Yup, that's what I'll do; I'll go and get to know her.'

'She's busy. When Bridget's gone and she's done her morning chores, she's gonna be working in the vegetable garden. With winter on the way, she'll be pulling up any beets, turnips and parsnips she can find. And then she's gonna dig up the carrots and potatoes. And while she's doin' that, she'll also be making lunch. And not just for us – she's gotta make lunch for the bundle-haulers, too. She's a farmer's wife, Niall, and she's busy. Let her be so she can work in peace.'

'Why, what a hive of activity,' Niall drawled in tones of exaggerated admiration. 'Then I'm thinkin' the best thing I could do is leave you both to get on with everything. After all, you'd have had to do it without me if I hadn't returned. Isn't that right?' He pulled out his watch and glanced at it.

'I see you've still got that old Pitkin watch that Pa gave you,' Conn said. 'Thought you would've lost it in a poker game or such by now.'

'Not this ole watch,' he said, sliding it back into the pocket of his jeans. 'It's about all I got from Pa. You got the rest, down to every last cob of corn. This watch is all I got and I'd never so much as wager it. I trust it, and when it tells me that it's time for me to go for a stroll around the farm and then take myself off into town, I listen to it. And I'm listening to it now.'

'So you'll not be helping us today. But that's not exactly a surprise.'

'It's fair worn me out, hearin' the chores for the day, and I reckon I'd be helpin' you all if I took

155

myself off to Liberty later this morning and tried to find me a conversation that didn't involve talking about turnips. That way, I'd be one less mouth for that woman of yours to feed. Yup, that's what I'll do.'

'You haven't changed, have you, Niall? Not one little bit. You always thought only of yourself, and you still do.' Connor's voice was full of disgust.

'Aw, shucks. That's hardly the way to talk about your brother. No, sir, it isn't.'

'Just tell me one thing before you set off. Ellen felt sure on a couple of occasions that she was being watched. Was that you watching her?'

'I can't deny that it was. I wanted to see how you'd gotten on over the years, and to have a look at your wife, before coming into your life again.'

'What you mean is, you wanted to see if it was worth your while returning. If the farm hadn't looked thriving, I'm guessing we wouldn't have been seeing you.'

'You could be right, brother. But that's me. You always were the good son. I'm the prodigal son, and the prodigal son is back. I don't reckon the good son in the Bible was any keener to see his brother than you are to see me. But I kinda hope that when the shock wears off, you'll feel some degree of pleasure at seeing me again. A more brotherly welcome when I get back from town would be mighty pleasing.'

'I'll work on it,' Conn said dryly.

'As I may not be back today, you've got time to

get it right. Keen as I am to meet your daughter and get to know your wife, I may be held up by a different sort of woman. Leastways, I sure hope I will be.' With a lazy smile, he eased himself away from the fence, put the piece of straw he'd been twisting into his mouth, touched his hat to Connor and strolled off in the direction of the horses' shed.

Conn stared after him. 'He's up to no good, I'm sure,' he said aloud. 'But what sort of no good could that be?'

# CHAPTER 13

Ellen stood up and rubbed her back. Every bone in her body ached.

She should have done as Connor suggested and left the vegetable garden until the end of the week when Bridget was home from school and could have helped her with the work. If she'd dug up the potatoes, and Bridget had followed her, picking them up, she'd have gotten through the work much more quickly than she was doing. She probably also would have been able to pull and top the carrots, beets and onions in the time it was taking her to deal with the potatoes alone.

But no, she'd insisted on making a start at once, and now she'd have to break into another day to do what she and Bridget could have done together in less than one.

And there was another reason why it would have been a good idea to have had Bridget working alongside her, she realised as she carried the potatoes over to the wooden chair that she'd brought out from the house.

She dropped the potatoes into a large basket on the ground next to the chair, dragged two empty bins over to the chair, and sat down. Leaning forward, she started to sort out the potatoes, dropping the seed potatoes that she'd later cut up and plant in the furrows into one bin, and the potatoes to be stored for eating throughout the winter into the other.

Yes, she'd missed what could have been an excellent opportunity to spend time alone with Bridget, she scolded herself. It was proving almost impossible to find more than a few moments in which to talk to Bridget in the short evenings after she'd returned from school, and the same was true of the busy weekends. If she was going to break through the lack of closeness between them, and the lack of any warmth and friendliness on Bridget's part, she needed to take advantage of every genuine reason to spend time with her.

As for Niall, how his return would affect things with Bridget, she had no way of yet knowing.

She sat up and wiped her forehead with her apron. In fact, why *was* Niall back? And how long was he planning to stay? Not for long, she hoped. In the short amount of time since his return the previous night, the atmosphere in the house had changed.

Connor was on edge in a way that she hadn't seen before, not even in the early days when he'd been coming to terms with her failure to warn him of her injury. When he'd come to bed the last night, he'd turned straight on to his side, his back to her, and had lain there, motionless. She'd sensed his anxiety and she'd raised herself slightly to look at him, wondering if he wanted to talk, but she'd seen that his eyes were shut and she'd sunk back down again. As they'd lain there in silence, side by side, neither touching the other, his breathing had given him away, and she'd known that he was as wide awake as she was.

And this morning, from the snatches of conversation she'd picked up between Connor and Aaron as she'd been on her way back from the milking, Niall had gone out of his way to provoke Connor before he'd left for town.

Connor was visibly worried about Niall being there, so she was worried, too.

'Somebody talk to me,' Bridget said, her voice a whine. 'Neither of you said a word during dinner, except about food. Usually you never stop. Miss Quinn was acting real funny in school today, and now you are, too.'

Ellen looked to Connor, wondering what he'd say.

'You must be tired, Bridget,' Connor said. 'Now that you've eaten, you'll be wanting to go to bed. It's school tomorrow.'

'It's too early to go to bed. I want to stay up longer.'

'And I want you to go to bed,' Connor said firmly.

'That's because you want to talk behind my back. You want to talk about Uncle Niall, don't you?' She flung the words at him accusingly.

Connor and Ellen exchanged glances. 'Who told you about your uncle?' he asked.

'Miss Quinn. She thought I already knew about him, and that I knew he was stayin' with us. She thought my pa would've told me. And now you wanna talk to *her* about him'—she glared at Ellen—'and not to me, and you don't want me to hear what you're saying. But he's *my* uncle, not hers, so you should be telling me, not her. It's only right.' She turned back to her father. 'Why didn't you didn't tell me I had an Uncle Niall?'

'Because he'd gone long before you were born, and I thought he'd never be a part of our lives again. When he walked out ten years ago, he said he was goin' for good, and we've not had word from him since the day he left. Your ma and I didn't decide not to tell you – it just never seemed to come up. Or to be important.'

'Not important! He's your brother. He's my uncle. Is he younger than you?'

'He's older by a year. I'm afeared that kinship doesn't mean much to your uncle. He left the homestead the day after your grandpa was laid to rest beside your grandma. I was just a strip of a lad, but he left me to run the hundred and sixty acres on my own, with just Aaron to help.'

'What about Ma?'

'I wed your ma soon after Niall left – we'd been sweethearts for years. She was a good woman, your ma. They were difficult years, working from sunup to sundown, but she never once complained. I reckon it was her working so hard that killed each of the babies that followed you. If Niall had worked the farm with us, maybe we wouldn't have had to work so long each day. Maybe you'd have had a brother by now.'

'I wish Ma was still alive and sitting with us now. Not *her*.' Bridget turned and scowled at Ellen, and she saw that Bridget's green eyes were brimful of tears. 'I look like Ma, don't I?' Bridget said, turning back to Connor.

Connor looked at her face, and nodded slowly. 'Yup, you do. You're just like her. And in your ways, too.' He reached across the table to Bridget and took her hand. 'You get more and more like her each day, honey,' he said softly, 'and that makes me real happy. She was a mighty fine woman.' Ellen saw Bridget relax. The eyes that looked up at her father were full of love. Then he released her hand and straightened up. 'Anyway, to go back to Niall, we didn't expect to hear from him, and we didn't hear from him. We were busy getting from one day to the next, and we had our sorrows over the years, and he went plumb out of our minds. And that's why no one told you about him.'

'I seen him, you know,' she said.

Connor stared at her in surprise. 'You couldn't have. You were asleep last night when he arrived, and he was outside the house when you were getting up and preparing to leave for school.'

'I saw him at recess. Miss Quinn came into the yard when we were playing Uncle John. She had a man with her, and we all wondered who he was. Then she called me over and told me that the man was my uncle. I thought she was funnin' at first and I started to laugh, but she wasn't. He said something about being pleased to meet me, and I shook hands with him. Then I went back and told Martha.'

'So Miss Quinn knew that you didn't know about your uncle,' Ellen said quietly.

Bridget shrugged her shoulders. 'I guess so. I don't know.'

Connor stood up. 'Niall is obviously staying on in town over night. He thought he might. I'll check outside now and then lock up. And you must get off to bed, Bridget.'

'Why's he come back to us now, Pa?'

'That's what I'm wondering,' he said, sitting back down again. 'Like he said, it was his home for years, and maybe he just felt like seeing the homestead again, and maybe me, too. I wouldn't know. Or it may be to do with money. He seems to have got a ranch, and he might wanna buy more heads of cattle than he can afford, and think that he's entitled to some of the money from the farm to help him out. Who knows with your uncle? I reckon he'll tell us in his own good time, and we'll just have to be patient till then. Come on now, Bridget. It's time you were in bed.'

She didn't move.

'Miss Quinn was wearing a real pretty dress today,' she said.

Connor looked at her in surprise. 'She always wears pretty clothes. She's careful about the way she looks.'

'She looked especially nice today. Usually she wears a white blouse and a dark-colour skirt for school. But she didn't today – she wore a dress. It was light blue. I've never seen her in school in a coloured dress before.'

'You haven't been going to school very long. She might often wear dresses, but just hasn't worn one till today. I can't see that it matters what she wears, unless, of course, the school board has told her what she should wear, and she's going against what they've said. But I wouldn't know about that. Now say goodnight and go to bed, please.'

Still Bridget didn't move. 'It's funny, Miss Quinn acting strange yesterday, and getting all dressed up today, don't you think, Pa?'

'All I'm thinking is that you should go to bed now.'

'Would you like me to help you get ready?' Ellen asked, starting to stand up. 'I'll read you a story, if you like.'

'I don't like,' Bridget said. She got up. 'Whatever you say, *I* think it's funny,' she said, and she turned to go to her bedroom.

Connor stood up. 'Stay where you are,' he said, his voice steely. 'You'll apologise to Ellen at once. We've just been talking about your ma, and this is not how she raised you. I've put up with your rudeness to Ellen for long enough, giving you time to settle into the situation, but it's almost a couple of months now and I reckon you've had sufficient time. I don't know about Ellen, but I sure have had enough of your backtalk. Now apologise.'

Bridget scowled at him, then at Ellen. 'I apologise,' she said stiffly, turned, walked over to her bedroom and slammed the door shut behind her.

'Thank you for getting her to say sorry,' Ellen said as Connor sat down again. 'I appreciate it.'

He nodded. 'It was time.' He stared down the table, his brow creased with worry.

'Talk to me, Connor?' she pleaded. 'Tell me what you're thinking.'

'I'm wondering if Bridget can be right about Oonagh,' he said at last. 'About what she's thinking, but couldn't bring herself to say.'

Her stomach turned over.

'Would this be difficult for you, seeing Oonagh with Niall?' she asked. She could hear the tremor in her voice. 'Would it?' she repeated, her heart pounding.

'It's what Niall's up to that I'm worried about.'

She felt herself relax a little.

'In what way? He has the same parentage as you, so can his character be so very different?'

'Truthfully, I don't know. I just know that I feel uneasy about him coming back. I'm real worried that his return means trouble for us, but I don't know why I think that, nor what trouble he could cause. It'd be a relief if this were just about money, and it might well be as it's not been easy for cattlemen since last winter. It would certainly explain him checking out the place before making his presence known. The thing is, I've never really known him. He was more like a brother to Jeb Barnes than to me. Both would play cards sooner than checkers, and they lived for hunting, shooting and fishing, and above all, for cattle.' He paused. 'I don't like to say it of my brother, but he and Jeb could be quite sly, and if they could get me into trouble with Pa, they did, and remembering that makes me feel uneasy. The sooner he returns to his ranch the better.'

He pushed his chair back, stood up, and looked down at her. 'I'm sorry, Ellen.'

'What for?' She put her hand to her throat.

'I was beginning to enjoy our evenings together.' He gave her a wry smile. 'Sure I had Aaron for company before you got here, but talking to a woman is a different thing. I hadn't realised how much I'd been missing it. Niall's return may spoil the evenings.'

A wave of pleasure spread through her. She rose to her feet and looked into his eyes. 'Niall can only spoil things if we let him. I, too, enjoy the time we spend together.' She felt herself going red. 'Me with my sewing,' she added quickly, 'and you repairing the harness or doing a chore like that.'

She felt the warmth in his eyes as they lingered on her face.

'To get back to the subject of chores,' she said,

putting her hand to her hair and pulling it further across her scarred cheek. 'I ought to clear the table.' She turned away from him, moved around the table and leaned over to pick up Bridget's plate.

He stood still, staring hard at her. 'Because of the way you're standing, I can see only the right side of your face. You must have been a very beautiful woman,' he said slowly.

She straightened up and faced him squarely. 'There is a left cheek as well as a right cheek, Connor. I never let myself forget that. Both are a part of me now. I'm not as I was before, and I never will be, so I prefer to forget that other time. That Ellen died when the hoof of the horse met her face.' She paused a moment. 'But you're very kind, and I'm grateful for it.' A sense of loss aching within her, she moved across the room towards the kitchen.

'She didn't die,' he called after her. She stopped and looked back at him, her brow wrinkling in surprise. 'She's still there, but she's scared to come out. One day she will, though, I'm sure. Every week I see a little more of her and I know that she's too strong to stay hidden forever.'

'I fear you may be wrong,' she said, and she continued to the kitchen.

With her every step, she was aware of him standing in the middle of the living room, staring after her.

# CHAPTER 14

Connor stepped out of his house, saw Niall and stopped sharply. He was sitting in the yard with his back to the chopping block, hat tipped down over his eyes, looking relaxed as ever.

'You're back, I see,' Connor called. 'Why, it must be the fourth or fifth time in the couple of weeks since you got back that we've seen you here so early in the evening, or at all, for that matter. Are there no poker games in town tonight?'

Niall pushed his hat off his nose and held it up with his finger. 'I thought I'd come back today. I stopped by the school, had a word with Oonagh and then with little Bridget, and then I hung around the town for a while, but there was nothin' doin', so I decided I'd come home. Thought I'd have dinner with my brother and his family. Yessir, I did.' He smiled at Connor and let his hat slip down again.

'This isn't your home any more,' Connor said sharply. 'But if you're hungry, I'll get you something now.'

'No need. I'm fine, thanks. I'll wait for dinner. I guess I could use a coffee though.'

168

'I'll get us both one and I'll join you.' He went into the house and reappeared a few minutes later, a couple of mugs in his hand. He walked across the yard to Niall, handed him a mug and sat down on a tree stump opposite him.

Niall glanced up at Connor, pulled himself up on to the chopping block and sat on it. 'That's better. Now we're seein' each other eye to eye, you might say.' He reached down, picked up his mug and took a swig of coffee.

Connor stared thoughtfully at him. 'What's this about, Niall? You've been restless since you got back. Don't you think it's time you went back to the place that *is* your home? I'm guessing that you put some men in charge of your cattle, and you trust them, but you need to be there to make sure you've prepared for winter as best you can. Two weeks is long enough to leave a ranch without a boss.'

'There ain't no ranch,' Niall said bluntly.

Connor leaned forward. 'What do you mean, there ain't no ranch? You talked about your cattle when you got here, didn't you?'

'You heard it like that because that was the way you wanted to hear it. But I was talkin' in a general sort of way. You might as well know, I lost everything in the last winter.'

Connor straightened up, feeling sympathy. 'I'm mighty sorry to hear that, Niall. I really am.'

Niall studied Connor's face. 'Yup, I reckon you really are. You know how much I always wanted my own place.'

'I sure do. But last winter . . .' Connor shook his head. 'That was a winter like we've never had before, and it went on for months. I heard tell that cattlemen across the Territory lost everything when the snow and ice finally melted and they saw that their cattle had died on the open range, trying to find food in the deep snow. But I never thought you might've been one of those cattlemen, not the way you were talking when you got here.'

'Well, I was. I had a nice little spread way north of here, and then too many people with fat wallets put an end to that. A few years ago, they came from all over to Wyoming, looked around them, saw free grass and the high price of stock in the markets, and they saw a chance to make easy money, so they flooded the open range with cattle.'

'I heard things had been getting tougher for small ranchers in the last couple of years.'

'Danged right they were! By the start of summer a year ago, you couldn't move for stockmen controllin' huge areas of grazin' land. They had herds that numbered in the tens of thousands. They were even drivin' herds up from Texas to graze on Wyoming grassland. There was big money behind them.'

'You need not tell me. I'm guessing they overgrazed the land.'

'Yup. The grass got too thin to feed the number of cattle on it. And then there was no rain all summer so what grass there was, dried up. By then the price of cows had dropped real low and I didn't want to sell.' He shook his head. 'I should've sold them last fall. If I had, I would've had something left for today. Instead, I figured I'd hang on till this year or even next, hoping the price might have gone up again by then, and I left my skinny animals out on the range for the winter. When the snow melted, there were bloated carcasses everywhere, lying where they'd fallen. I can smell them yet. I'd lost my cattle, and with them my money and my ranch.'

'That's real hard. I can imagine what losing your ranch will have meant to you. Ranching is all you ever wanted to do.'

'Ain't that the truth?'

They fell silent and sat for a few minutes, lost in their thoughts.

'Maybe between us we could try to get some money together for you to get started off with some cattle again?' Connor suggested, breaking the silence.

Niall shook his head. 'I think not, brother, but I thank you for the thought. I've done that, and it didn't work. I guess I've kinda burnt myself out of cattle. I know that I haven't the heart to start all over again. And certainly not in times like these, when it'd be real hard to get going. The days of the open range are over, and I don't see myself building barns and feeding the animals. Why, it'd be like bein' a farmer, and I don't want that.'

'Did you take a wife when you had your ranch?' Connor asked. 'You'd have needed someone to do

171

a woman's things while you were out tending the cattle.'

Niall glanced at him in mock horror. 'No, sir. I left the marrying to you. But you're right about me having a woman to work around the place, and what's more, the woman I had knew exactly how to pleasure a man.' He laughed. 'But I never married her. When I knew I'd lost everything, so did she. I came back home one day to tell her we'd have to leave the ranch, but she was already gone. Plumb cleared out.'

'I'm right sorry to hear that,' Connor said.

Niall shrugged his shoulders. 'It weren't nothing to me. I didn't have the feelings for her you need to have if you're gonna wed a woman.' He glanced at Connor. 'I guess you got my share of such feelings as well as getting my share of the farm.'

'We'll leave that comment be. So, have you been looking for work while you've been here? Is that why you came back? To find work in Liberty?'

'I came back because I couldn't think what else to do. The family homestead was here – mine and yours. I know you, Conn, and I knew you'd have made a success of it. I might have walked out ten years ago, but I've still got some rights in the place, and you know it. It's why you've wanted me gone from the moment you saw me.'

'I asked you if you'd been trying to find work in town.'

'There's nothin' to be had. Sure I could join a crew hauling lumber around the Territory and helping to make houses for newcomers, but I'm no carpenter and that's no work for me.'

'What about Jeb? Have you asked him to give you something? You'd be a good hand for them to have.'

'Sure I've asked. He was the other reason I came back. I knew that my best hope of finding cattle work was on the Barnes's ranch. But like everyone else, Jeb's pa lost a lot of stock last winter. He just about survived it and he's building sheds and barns now, and enclosing his land in barbed wire and wooden fences. He'll not chance what happened last year happening again, and in future he'll be bringing the cattle in before the freeze comes.'

'That means he's gonna restock then, so he'll need to take on men.'

'Sure, but it's never gonna be a big ranch again, leastways not for a long time. He hasn't got the money. And he's got men working for him that he's had for years, as well as Jeb and his two boys. There'd be some casual work there, but nothin' I could count on.'

'So what are planning on doing?'

'You telling me I gotta move on? You're gonna put me on the road that goes over the hills to the poor house?'

'Not till you've got somewhere to move on to. But you can't carry on like this, coming and going whenever you feel like it, sleeping in the living room, an extra mouth to feed when you're here, but one that didn't help produce the food. That's not right, and you know it. And suppose you got wed and had a family. The acres we farm wouldn't support a second family; not the way they're set out now.'

'Thanks, brother.'

'It sounds hard, I know, but I'm telling you the facts. I have to think about my family, about Bridget and my wife. And about the children I hope to have.'

'So you get everything left by Ma and Pa, and I get nothing? That's fair, is it?'

'You could've shared it with me, but you didn't want it. I wanted it, though, and I've worked hard for it, every minute of every year since you left. If you'd wanted to stick around and farm this land with me, we'd have built a second house years ago, or made this one bigger, and we'd have used the land differently, gone into areas we've not been able to go into.'

'Such as?'

'Sheep, maybe. I hear tell there's good money to be made in sheep. If we'd expanded, the farm would've been able to support your family and mine. But that didn't happen. You walked out because Ma and Pa had never wanted to invest in cattle in a big way, and you were certain I'd want to farm the place as they had. You didn't even stay long enough to try and change my mind. As you said, you're the older brother. I'd've had to listen to you. We'd have found a way of doing what we both wanted.'

'Maybe we could do that now, go into sheep. There's many a cowman turning to sheep.'

'Face it, Niall. It's life on the farm you didn't like. You told me many a time it was like being in jail. Sheep is farming, just as wheat and corn is farming, just as ranching cattle today will become like farming. When you walked out, I reckon you weren't just getting away from what we were farming, you were making a break for freedom from the life of a farmer. Life on the open range and a herd of cattle gave you that sense of freedom.'

Niall gave him a wry grin. 'I guess that's a no to sheep, then.'

'It'd be spending money on something new at a difficult time, and I wouldn't want to take that risk. Apart from anything else, I'd be gambling on you sticking to your word and not takin' off as soon as you got bored or heard of a job with cattle. And you *would* take off. You don't really want to spend your evenings with Ellen and me.'

'Ah, but you've forgotten Bridget.'

'I haven't; she'd be in bed. No, Niall. If you can't get work on a ranch, you'd be happier living in town.'

'Well, that sure is tellin' me.' He stood up, brushed the earth and twigs from the seat of his jeans and walked across to the fence. Leaning against the wooden bars, he stared ahead of him.

Connor got up and stood beside him, his eyes on the purplish-blue mountain ridges. 'What are you thinking?' he asked after a few minutes.

Niall turned his head and looked at him. 'I'm thinking that you owe me something even if I did walk out. You said you would have found a way to help me if I'd wanted to go into cattle again. I don't want money for that, but that don't mean I don't want any help from you, because I do.'

'What help are you expecting me to give you?'

'Money. Maybe you don't make enough to keep a second family, but you make more than you need. I'll wager you sell eggs, butter, potatoes, wheat, the hay you don't need for your animals. Why, you'll get at least two dollars for a bale of hay. I've been lookin' around and I reckon you'll have thirty bales or more to sell. And I saw you had a couple of four-year-old colts. You'll get at least two hundred dollars for each. I don't need to go on, do I?'

'Nope. As you said, I'd have tried to help you get into cattle again.'

'I'd find lodgings in town, and I can look around from there for any work that's going.' He gave a sudden grin. 'And with a stake in my hand, I might even be able to find me a game of poker or two.'

'OK,' Connor said. 'I'll give you something. It won't be a lot because there isn't a lot to give, but it'll help you to find somewhere to stay and it'll keep you going till you find work. I doubt it'll go far when it comes to cards since I'm guessing you'd only play for high stakes, but if you lose it, that'll be down to you. Let me know when you come across a place to stay and you'll have the money. I guess you deserve that much from the ranch.'

'I reckon I do.'

Connor nodded, turned away and walked back to the house.

# CHAPTER 15

Ellen stood staring down at the wooden tub on the ground outside the kitchen door. She ran the back of her arm across her brow, wiping the salty perspiration from above her eyes. It had been exhausting work, washing the first of the quilts and putting it out to dry, and she was going to have to figure out an easier way of doing the rest.

She'd forgotten how difficult it was to lift a wet quilt out of the tub, with water coursing from it to the ground, weighing it heavily in her arms, and then to wring it out and hang it over the line to dry. It had taken her almost all of the afternoon just to wash the quilt, and she hadn't yet replaced the straw in the tick from the bed she was cleaning.

She glanced towards the house. The afternoon light was already dying. She should have started earlier in the day. As it was, it was now too late to drag out the tick and empty it. She'd have to leave both emptying and washing it till the next day. Apart from the lack of sunshine, Bridget would soon be back from school, and she needed to get out the spare bedding they'd be using that night and then get on with the dinner. But if she made an early start the following morning, the tick would be dry before sundown and she could fill it with fresh straw and return it to the bed before night.

One good thing about having the quilts to wash was that it had kept her out of the way of Niall and Conn, who'd had a long talk in the front of the house after Niall's unexpected return from town that afternoon. Connor had been hoping to have a chance to talk to him, without it looking too contrived, and it had worked out well that he'd been near the house when Niall had got back, and she'd had chores to do in the yard behind the house. Conn had gone straight out to the fields when he and Niall had finished talking, but hopefully, he'd found out more about Niall's intentions and would tell her later.

She turned to go into the house.

'Uncle Niall,' she heard Bridget call from the direction of West Barn. 'You're home.' Bridget's voice was alive with pleasure.

She stopped halfway into the kitchen, took a step back and glanced to her right. Bridget was running between the empty corrals and the entrance to the barn, her lunch pail in one hand and her school bag in the other. Niall was just coming out of the barn, but he'd stopped at the sound of Bridget's voice. Even from a distance, with his hat shading his eyes, Ellen could see the broad smile on his face as he looked down at her.

She turned around and stood watching them.

'Hi there, Bridget!' she heard Niall say from afar. 'And how was that test?'

She went a few paces forward so that she could see them more clearly and hear them better. Niall's expression as he gazed down at Bridget was one of amusement. And of affection, Ellen noticed in surprise.

'The First Reader class had to answer questions this afternoon.' Bridget's voice jumped up and down as she hit out at a cloud of midges with her lunch pail. 'I got all my answers right,' she added. 'Martha got one wrong.' Ellen couldn't see her face, but she could hear the pride in her voice as she spoke.

'You're a clever gal,' he said. 'Just like your uncle.'

Bridget laughed.

'What're you goin' to do now?' he asked. 'I'm about to go over to the horses' shed to polish my harness. I sure could use some help with that. And while you were helpin' me, I could tell you about the time your pa disturbed a wasps' nest.'

'Oh, yes!' Bridget sounded so happy, Ellen thought. In the short amount of time that he'd been there, Niall had clearly gotten through to her, while Ellen still hadn't. A wave of envy shot through her. 'I'll have a glass of milk and then I'll come and find you,' Bridget said.

'You do that,' Niall said. 'I'll see you over in the shed.'

Bridget spun around, and saw Ellen.

She stopped. Her smile faded and her face hardened. 'I can't,' she said, and she turned back to Niall. 'I told Pa I'd milk the cows this evening. His wife's started on the fall clean today and Pa said she'd be too busy to get the cows done, too.' Ellen could hear the bitterness in her voice. 'And you have to do them the same time each day or they don't give you as much milk.'

Ellen saw Niall glance above Bridget's head in her direction. His face broke out into a grin when he saw her standing there, watching them. She took a step back. Inclining his head to her, he touched the brim of his hat, and then turned his attention back to Bridget.

'Like I said before, you're a real smart gal.'

'Will you tell me about Pa and the wasps when I've done the cows?' Bridget begged.

'I've got a better idea, honey. Why don't you and me do the milkin' together? I can tell you the story while we're doin' the cows. I can always polish the harness later.'

'Thanks, Uncle Niall!' Bridget jumped up and down in glee. 'I'll go and get my milk and be right back.'

'I'll wait for you outside West Barn.'

Clutching her bag and lunch pail in her arms, she spun around and half-ran towards the house, pushing past Ellen without acknowledging her as she sped into the kitchen.

Ellen looked across the corrals towards Niall. He shrugged his shoulders and walked away. She stared after him for a moment, then followed Bridget into the kitchen.

'Uncle Niall's gonna help me do the cows,' Bridget said, dumping her school bag and lunch pail next to the sink. 'But you were listening so you know that. I want a glass of buttermilk first.'

Ellen slid her hands into her apron pockets, stood still and stared at her.

'Please,' Bridget snapped.

'I'll get it,' Ellen said. She went into the pantry, lifted the trap door, went down the stairs into the cellar and came back up with a stoneware jug.

'I'll heat the milk for you, if you want. It won't take long.'

'I don't want.'

'As you wish.' She poured a glass of the milk for Bridget and handed it to her. Bridget reached out to take the glass. Her fingers closed around it, and she went to pull it towards her, but Ellen's grip held firm.

Their eyes met above the glass.

Bridget scowled at her. 'Thank you.'

Ellen released her hold on the glass. 'I need to start getting dinner ready,' she said, and she moved away from Bridget. Raising the pump arm at the side of the sink, she pulled it up and down, slowly filling the bowl in the sink with water.

Bridget finished the milk, put the glass in the bowl, pulled her school bag towards her and thrust her hand into it.

'Miss Quinn asked me to give you this,' she said,

her tone ungracious. She held a slip of paper out to Ellen. Ellen stopped pumping, lifted the glass out of the water, wiped her hands and took the paper from her. 'Though I don't know why she'd want you there, why anyone would,' Bridget threw over her shoulder as she crossed to the corner of the kitchen. She picked up an empty pail in each hand and left the house.

Ellen unfolded the piece of paper and read through the message. Oonagh was inviting her to a sewing bee, to be held at her home this Saturday. It would begin in the afternoon and last through the evening.

She'd obviously remembered Ellen's dislike of sewing as she'd written that those who liked sewing would be making themselves a dress for the forthcoming wedding of Hannah Carey, and those who didn't, would bring the dress they were going to wear, improve the fitting if necessary, and add any finishing touches they wanted. Also, they were all going to line their bonnets with material that matched their dresses. They'd help each other and have an enjoyable time doing so. And while they sewed, they could also work out who was going to bring what dishes to Hannah's wedding.

Just before she'd signed off, she'd added that she was sure that either Connor or Niall would bring her into town, and that Abigail Carey, Martha's mother, would bring her home. This was what used to happen when Alice joined them, she wrote. Abigail would bring Alice back home and stay overnight, and then Abigail would return to her own home the following morning. But if she would prefer, Oonagh had written, she would be very welcome to stay the night at Oonagh's house. Conn could collect her the following day.

It was kind of Oonagh, but she wouldn't go, Ellen decided. It was not the sort of thing she'd ever really liked doing, and she'd like it even less after the accident.

She tucked the paper into her apron pocket, went into the bedroom and started to pull one of the spare quilts out of a chest standing against the wall.

'I just saw Bridget,' Connor said, coming into the bedroom after her. 'She tells me that you've been invited by the ladies to their sewing bee. That's good. Alice used to enjoy them.'

'I'm not going,' she told him, straightening up.

He stared at her in surprise. 'Why not? This is not about your face, is it? They've all seen you in church or in town so they know what you look like. You should go, Ellen. You might enjoy it. When is it?'

'This Saturday. No, it's not about the way I look,' she said quickly. 'It's just that Abigail Carey would have to bring me back and stay over, and there isn't room for her; not with Niall here. Oonagh did invite me to stay at her house, but I would not like that.'

'Did someone say Niall?' Niall's voice came from behind Connor. 'I coulda sworn I heard my name.'

184

Connor glanced at him over his shoulder. 'Ellen's been asked to go to a bee in town on Saturday. She wants to go, but she's worrying where we'll sleep Abigail Carey. Abigail's gonna bring her home.' He turned back to Ellen. 'There's no problem. We'll do what folks do in these parts, make up a bed in the living room. I'm sure Niall can find himself another place for the night.'

'No need for any of that,' Niall drawled. 'I'll be in town myself on Saturday. I can easily take a wagon, and then I can collect you at the end of the evening and bring you back with me. No need to trouble Abigail Carey.'

'Thanks, Niall.' Connor turned back to Ellen with a smile. 'So, no reason not to go.'

She hesitated a moment, then glanced at Niall. 'Thank you, Niall. I'll go then, and I'd be grateful if you brought me back.'

'My pleasure,' he drawled. 'And now I oughta go and give Bridget a hand. I only came back for another pail, and also to tell you that I've decided to join the hands in town this evening when I've done the milking with Bridget. They're gonna be spending the money Aaron's paid them now that their job's done, and I'm of a mind to relieve them of some of it. There's talk of setting up a game of cards. So if you'll excuse me from dinner, ma'am.'

He grinned at them both, put a short piece of straw between his lips, touched his hat to Ellen and walked out.

185

Connor turned to her with a wry smile. 'I think that maybe you didn't really want to go, and Abigail Carey was just an excuse. But I'm pleased you're going. They don't have these bees very often, and it's a good chance to meet the ladies and get to know them better. Especially with Hannah Carey's wedding coming up so soon. It would be real good for you to have met a few more people before we go there. Look on it as another first for you.'

She glanced at Connor, gave him a resigned smile, then she carried the quilt across to the bed and threw it on to the straw tick. Leaning over, she started to straighten the quilt.

Connor moved swiftly to her side and together they spread the quilt across the bed. As she reached across the bed to flatten the corner, her hand brushed against his. She went to pull it back, but he caught hold of it, and held it.

She stared down at their linked hands.

'You've no reason to hide from people, Ellen,' she heard him say through the pounding in her ears.

He tightened his hold on her hand.

Her heart beating fast, she glanced up at him and saw warmth and understanding in the depths of his eyes. Then he released her hand.

'I'd better water the horses,' he said, his voice sounding awkward, 'or I'd have to hold off graining them till later. We wouldn't want them getting colic.'

She nodded.

He stood still for a moment, staring at her, and then went out.

She put her hand to her mouth, drew in a deep breath and stood there, motionless.

# CHAPTER 16

Bridget dropped her nightdress over her head and shrugged it into position. 'It's not fair that I had to have my bath tonight. Saturday night's bath night; not Friday,' she shouted from the kitchen to Ellen.

Ellen stopped folding the square of silk with which she was going to line her bonnet, and sighed. 'It's good to have a change every now and then,' she called back, trying to keep the irritation from her voice.

Bridget pushed the screen aside and came into the living room, her face sullen. 'I wanted to go and say goodnight to the calves, and now I can't.'

Ellen resumed folding the material. 'The calves will still be there tomorrow.'

'That's not the point.' Bridget went up at the dinner table and sat down heavily on her chair.

Ellen glanced at her. 'I think it is. There was no other way of doing things, as you well know. You must have a bath before Sunday School, and I'll be at the sewing bee tomorrow evening, which makes work for you and your father if you choose to have a bath tomorrow night.'

Bridget kicked Ellen's basket of sewing things away from the foot of the table.

'Of course,' Ellen went on, ignoring the upturned basket and the needles and thread scattered on the floor, 'you might have been hankering after pumping the water from the outside well into the large drum, and watching your father boil the water and then pour it into the bathtub, a bucket at a time. And you might have been looking forward to emptying and cleaning the tub when you'd finished your bath. If I'd known you wanted to do that, I could have left the tub out after I'd had my bath tonight and you could have had your bath tomorrow. Then you could have spent those extra few minutes with the calves this evening. If that's what you would have preferred to do, then I apologise.'

She bent down, pulled her basket back to the side of her chair, put the strewn contents back into the basket, and placed the folded piece of silk on top of them. Then she put the basket on the other side of the table, out of Bridget's reach.

She felt Bridget's eyes on her as she sat back up, and she smiled at her with exaggerated sweetness.

'I'll need these, too, I suspect,' she said, seeing her scissors on the floor by the leg of the table, and she bent down to pick them up.

'You don't talk to Pa like you talk to me,' Bridget said, her tone accusing.

Ellen stopped mid-action, sat upright and stared

at her in surprise. Puzzled green eyes stared back at her.

'Of course I don't. I wouldn't talk to you in the same way as I talk to him. Your pa's a grown man, and he's my husband. You're a child, Bridget. A clever child, but still a child.'

Bridget flushed. 'That's not what I mean.'

'What do you mean, then?'

Bridget bent down and picked up a reel of thread from by her foot. She put it on the table between them. 'If I say something I shouldn't, you tell me. You didn't at first, but you do now. Though not always when Pa's around.'

Ellen smiled at her. 'That's because underneath the backtalk, I suspect there's a very pleasant little girl, and I want to make sure that everyone sees her. But they might not if I let her continue to get away with being rude. When your pa's here, he can deal with you.'

Bridget sat back in her chair, wrapped her nightdress around her legs, pulled up her knees and hugged them to her chin. 'How d'you know that I'm a very pleasant little girl?'

'From everything I've heard about your ma, she was a fine woman. And I know your pa. Two fine people made you, so it stands to reason, you must be a fine person, too.'

Bridget shifted her position. 'Uncle Niall likes me, doesn't he? He already thinks I'm pleasant.'

'Yes, he does. But you don't backtalk him, do you? You discuss things with him, talk to him normally. You don't talk normally to me, do you? Be honest now.'

'I guess not. But you don't talk normally to Pa, do you?'

Ellen stared at her in surprise. 'Of course, I do.'

Bridget let her feet slide to the floor. 'No, you don't. You don't say what you're thinking to him. I always know what you're thinking 'cos you tell me plain, but Pa doesn't know what you're thinking 'cos you don't tell him. Why d'you tell me, but not him?'

Ellen felt herself going red. 'I'm not clear what you mean.'

'Yes, you are. Sometimes, when you're with Pa and you think I've been rude, I can see that you're angry with me and you want to say so, but you don't 'cos Pa doesn't say anything.'

'As I said, it's for your Pa to correct you when we're all together.'

'But it's you I'm rude to,' she said bluntly. 'And another thing. Even if you don't want to do something, but Pa wants you to do it, you do it. Like the sewing bee tomorrow. I heard Pa tell Aaron that he suspected that you didn't really want to go, but you hadn't liked to say so. You're jealous of Miss Quinn because she's beautiful, and you don't like all the women saying how ugly you are. They'll all talk about your face when you go out of the room, and you know they will. But you didn't tell Pa that.'

'I know that he wants me to go,' she said quietly.

'This is your Pa's house, and a wife likes to please her husband.'

'That's not why you're doing it. Martha's ma, she's real quiet now. She thinks everything Mr Carey thinks and if he wants her to do something, she really wants to do it just because he wants her to do it. But you're not like Martha's ma. I've seen your face. Even though you've got that red mark all over it, I know what you're thinking. If you don't want to go, why are you going? You should speak plain to Pa like you speak plain to me.'

'I'm not sure why you're saying this, Bridget,' she said, standing up, 'but I know that I don't want to continue this conversation. Anyway, it's time that I had my bath. It'll soon be dark and the men will want to be able to come in for their meal so I must be quick.'

Bridget put her feet on the floor and stood up. 'I'm going to my room and I'm gonna look at a book.'

'That's a good idea. You'll find some of the books I brought from Omaha on the shelf over there. Why don't you take a look at them and see if there's anything you'd like me to read to you. I could read to you after dinner.'

She shrugged her shoulders. 'If you like.' She started to walk past Ellen, and paused. She ran her finger along the edge of the table. 'Ma used to read to me. I miss her.'

'I know you do.' Ellen said quietly. She put her hand on Bridget's shoulder.

'Don't,' Bridget said. She shook Ellen's hand off, and ran into her bedroom.

Ellen lay back in the warm water and shut her eyes.

When she'd first gotten into the tub, she'd heard faint sounds of movement coming from Bridget's room, but the sounds had gradually died away, and she was guessing that Bridget had either fallen asleep after her week in school, and the long walk there and back each day, or she was engrossed in her book.

She'd wake her, she decided, when it was time for them to eat. But for the moment, she was glad to have a short time in which to relax. With Connor and Aaron outside, finishing off for the day, and Niall in town, there was no one around to disturb her solitude. To have a few quiet moments before a day that was going to be long and stressful was very welcome.

First thing the following morning, she'd be going into town in the wagon with Connor and Bridget, taking with her the dress she'd be wearing for the wedding and her best rough-straw bonnet. She'd also be taking her sewing things.

Once they'd bought the necessary supplies for the homestead, they'd have something to eat in the roadhouse, and then Connor and Bridget would leave her at Oonagh's house, and she'd remain there until Niall came at the end of the evening to collect her. So from the time she got up until the time she got back home, she'd be surrounded by people, and for the most part they'd be people she hardly knew.

She was dreading the day.

Maybe, she thought, she should do as Bridget had suggested earlier that evening, be more honest with Connor about her feelings.

She sank low into the tub and looked up at the ceiling as the warmth of the water crept around her. It was funny, Bridget speaking to her like that, she thought, and she stretched out her arm for the soap.

As she rubbed the soap into her washing rag, her mind raced back to the days when she was with Robert. She stopped what she was doing. The soap slipped through her fingers into the water.

Leaning back, she rested her head on the rim of the narrow tub, and she let herself remember how Robert used to slide the soap-filled cloth across her back; along her arms, first one, then the other; how she'd stand before him and he'd bring the cloth slowly, very slowly down the length of her body, and let it fall to the water. She could almost feel again the touch of his fingers against her damp skin, his caress. And her body ached for him.

She pulled herself upright in the tub, her knees close to her chin. She shouldn't be thinking like that. Robert and the things they used to do together belonged in the past. Her future lay with Connor. The kindness that she'd received from him was far more than she'd dared hope for when she'd left Omaha, and she should be grateful for what he was able to give her, and not waste her time yearning for something she'd never have again. Bridget had told her that she should be more honest with Connor, and thinking in such a way about Robert was hardly being honest with Connor in her thoughts.

She retrieved the soap, picked up the cloth, rubbed the soap into it and started to wash her leg. Then she started to soap the other leg, and suddenly paused, frowning. Thinking back again to what Bridget had said earlier on, it really was strange the way in which she'd spoken to her. Not so much what she'd said, but why she'd said it.

Being only eight, Bridget was too young to understand the requirements of a wife and she'd see things in the stark way that a child did, so it wasn't surprising that she was mistaken in her way of looking at things. But it was the first time that Bridget had spoken up in a way that wasn't rude. She had openly said what she thought, and in a conversational way, not in a confrontational way. She had seemed to be trying to tell her to do something that would help her to be happy. It was almost as if she was beginning to see her as a person in her own right, and wanted Connor to see her as such, too.

She rubbed the soap vigorously across the cloth again. She was probably reading too much into Bridget's words. She didn't know what had gotten into her that evening, first of all thinking about

Robert in the way that she had, and then imagining that Bridget was starting to accept her into the family. All it had been was a few short sentences from a tired girl.

She finished washing, returned the soap to the dish and slid as far under the water as she could to rinse herself clean. She shivered. The water was getting cold. Glancing up at the window, she saw that the afternoon light was starting to fail. She must quickly get dressed and set the table. She'd set the table herself and not disturb Bridget until she absolutely had to.

She stood up, water coursing down her body, and stepped over the rim of the tub on to the floor. Strands of hair stuck to the back of her neck, and she raised her arms to push the wet hair back into the loose coil pinned on top of her head.

The door swung open, and Connor came in.

He exclaimed in surprise, stopped short and took a step back.

'I'm sorry,' he said. 'I thought you'd be done. I'll go.'

She lowered her arms and stood facing him. Rivulets of water ran down her skin and pooled on the floor at her feet.

'I'll go,' he repeated, gripping the door handle, his knuckles white.

He stood still, staring at her. Then he lowered his eyes from her face.

Trembling beneath his gaze, she started to lift

her hands to hide herself, but she stopped, let them fall to her side and stood motionless.

She heard him draw in his breath.

A wave of deep longing swept through her body, an overwhelming yearning that made her weak at the knees. Unable to stop herself, she took a step towards him.

He raised his eyes to her face, and they stared at each other, their breathing loud in the silence of the room.

He released the door handle, pushed the door shut with his foot, and walked forward.

Her heart missed a beat. Raising her arms, she crossed them in front of her chest.

He stopped inches from her. His clear-blue eyes never leaving her face, he moved aside first her right hand, then her left. For a moment he held both of her hands in his, then he gently lowered her arms to her side.

Her every nerve tingled as his eyes touched her skin.

'I've never seen you like this before,' he said, his voice thick with emotion. 'You are beautiful, Ellen.' He looked back into her face. 'Really beautiful,' he repeated, his voice full of wonder.

She shook her left arm free and put her hand against her damaged cheek.

He caught her arm and lowered it again.

Lightly, he ran his fingers down the ridges of her scar. She tried to pull back, but his hold on her was firm.

'More and more in the past few weeks when I've looked at you,' he said quietly, 'I've seen a woman who's made my house into a place that I look forward to entering each night, and who looks after my daughter with kindness, and I've been thankful for both these things. But until this moment, I hadn't seen how beautiful that woman is.'

The weight of his gaze fell on her face, on the whole of her face, and she closed her eyes as he ran his fingers along first her upper lip, then her lower lip. Then he slid his hands slowly down the curve of her body to her stomach. They lingered there. She gave a sigh of deep pleasure, and opened her eyes.

'You know how much I wish to see this rounded,' he murmured, rhythmically circling her skin. 'I'm thinking that this is something we should work on right now.'

'I think so, too.'

He put his arms around her and pulled her close to him.

His jeans rough against her soft skin, she felt his body hard beneath the denim. A wave of anticipation shot through her, and she put her hand to the buckle on his belt.

'Is that you, Pa?' Bridget's voice came from the bedroom.

They gasped, and stepped quickly back from each other.

'Pa! Is that you?'

There was a thump as Bridget jumped from her bed to the wooden floor.

Ellen reached for her towel.

With a heavy sigh, Connor eased his jeans away from his crotch and started to walk past Ellen towards Bridget's room. As he went by her, his arm brushed hers, and he stopped. For a moment they looked deep into each other's eyes, then he continued walking out of the kitchen.

She wrapped the towel around her and went quickly towards their bedroom.

'We were about to wake you, Bridget,' she heard Connor call through Bridget's door.

As she pushed their own bedroom door open, she glanced towards Bridget's room.

Connor was standing outside at the closed door, staring at her. Their eyes locked. Then with a rueful grin, he turned away, knocked and went in to Bridget.

# CHAPTER 17

Ellen ran her fingers through the pieces of material in her basket, checking that she had everything she needed for the sewing bee, then she put her box of sewing equipment into the basket and placed the dress she was going to trim with lace that evening very carefully on top of it. It was the best of the dresses she'd brought from Omaha, and the only one that would really be suitable for the occasion.

She ran her hand slowly across the vivid green material of the dress. It had been Robert's favourite. The colour brought out the green-gold flecks in her eyes, he used to say. Every time that she'd looked at the dress since his accident, she'd heard his words and she'd been certain that she would never be able to bring herself to wear it again. And she'd felt sure that she'd never again want to wear a dress in a colour so striking that it would attract attention.

In fact, she'd been so confident that she'd never wear it again that she'd tried to throw it away on several occasions. Each time, though, she'd found herself unable to discard something that reminded her so much of Robert, with the result that she still had the dress in her possession, and as she'd nothing else to wear for the wedding, she'd decided that she would put it on again.

She obviously wouldn't feel in it the way she used to feel when she wore it with Robert, but if nothing else, it would send a strong message of defiance to anyone at the wedding who stared openly at her when she encountered them. If Connor could accept her appearance, so could they.

But more important to her than that, the fact that she was prepared to wear such a dress told her that for the first time in more than two years, she was beginning to feel like a woman again.

And that was due to the evening before, to the feelings that Connor had roused in her. To the emotion she'd seen in the depths of his eyes.

While she'd been waiting for him to join her in bed, she'd wondered if he'd follow his usual custom of leaving it a few minutes, then raising her nightdress and entering her, or if he'd seek to recapture the mood they'd been in at the moment when Bridget had interrupted them. She'd even half-wondered whether to leave off her nightdress. But when she'd thought back to the dinner they'd had after her bath, to the lack of any special glance from him, any word, or anything to suggest a change in their relationship, she'd decided against it. It might not be the right thing to do; not without him first suggesting it.

She'd certainly made the correct decision about the nightdress, she thought, picking up the empty coffee mugs from the table and carrying them into the kitchen. Despite her hopes, last night had been no different from all of their other nights together.

No, she was wrong – there *had* been a difference, she thought, suddenly stopping, the mugs in her hand. As he'd raised himself on top of her, she'd looked up into his eyes and seen a grim determination that hadn't been there on any night before.

He was holding himself back, she'd thought in surprise, and she'd wondered why that should be. Being married and in the privacy of their bedroom, they should be able to go where their feelings took them. His instinct earlier had clearly been to want more, and he must have seen that she felt the same way, but then why deliberately hold himself back?

Unable to answer her question, she'd lain awake in their bed, watching him while he slept, and she was still unable to answer the question in the light of the new day. But nevertheless, something had changed between them the evening before. She couldn't say how she knew it, but she did.

She'd never been more certain of anything than that.

She put the mugs down in the kitchen, went back to the living room, picked up her basket, carried it over to the door and put it next to the drum which contained the tubs of butter that she planned to sell in town. Stepping back, she looked at the group of items clustered by the front door. She'd be so glad when the sewing bee was over and she was back at home.

Going back to the kitchen, she opened the door. 'Bridget,' she called out, untying her apron as she stood in the doorway. 'Come and wash your hands. It's almost time to leave. If you want to see Martha in town, that is.'

'I'm coming.' Bridget's voice came from behind the henhouse. 'I've just found some eggs that I missed. Don't go without me.'

Leaving the door open for Bridget, she went back into the kitchen. Her steps slowed as she passed the place where she'd been standing the night before when Connor had come in. The floorboards were still wet. She stepped into the centre of the damp patch and stood there. Her mind went back to the look she'd seen in Connor's eyes as he'd gazed at her body, to the longing she'd felt in his touch, and a tingle ran down her spine. Her skin broke out in goosebumps.

Would he seek to come upon her again like that? she wondered. She put her hands to her stomach and drew her breath in deeply. How she hoped that he would.

Steam rising from their nostrils, the two horses whinnied as Connor led them out to the wooden rail in front of the shed. He stopped by the two leather harnesses he'd earlier slung over the rail, and began to rig the first of the horses. When he'd

203

finished, he dropped the reins to the ground and moved to the second horse.

'There you go,' he said finally, putting his arm around each horse's neck in turn and stroking its nose.

What had that all been about last night? He ran his hand across the chestnut coat of the second horse. Where had those feelings of his come from? He was furious with himself. Ellen was never meant to be a threat to his memory of Alice. How could she be, looking as she did? But since last night, all he'd been able to think about was Ellen – Ellen; not Alice.

And that was the last thing he wanted.

He wanted a child and he hoped that she'd soon have good news for him, but he had never wanted the feelings – feelings that he knew from night after night of loving Alice – that could go along with the act of getting that child. Those feelings belonged to Alice alone – Alice who'd lost her life in trying to give him a son. He'd be betraying her if he let himself think about anyone else in the same way.

Yet that was the way in which he'd thought about Ellen when he'd seen her standing there, ghostly in the failing light. And beautiful.

He hadn't even noticed her injury. He'd seen only her naked body, water trickling down her bare skin, tracing curves that he hadn't seen until that moment. A sudden, powerful urge had kicked him with force in his groin, and he'd wanted to reach out and touch her, every inch of her.

All thought of self-restraint gone from his mind, he'd pushed the door shut behind him and had stepped forward.

A soapy warmth had risen from her, and that special scent of a woman, and he hadn't been able to keep himself from running his hands across her skin, her soft, soft skin. Desire, a stranger to him for more than a year, had swept through him and all but knocked him off his feet.

That Bridget had called to him at that moment was something he'd ever be grateful for. If she hadn't . . . Well, he didn't like to think of what might have happened if she hadn't.

It wasn't just Alice's memory he would have been betraying; it would have been unfair on Ellen, too.

He was highly satisfied with the bargain he'd made with her. His side of the bargain had been to give her a home; hers had been to run the house, look after Bridget and be a good mother to any children they might have together. But that was where their arrangement ended. Both had honoured their agreement, and he would have been wrong to ask more of her than that.

When she'd allowed him to look upon her last night, and when she'd responded to him in the way that she had, reaching out for him as she'd done, she would have been acting out of wifely duty, but that wouldn't have been what she sought, or expected, from a relationship based on mutual advantage and convenience.

He and Alice had had years together in which to

develop deep feelings, but he and Ellen hardly knew each other. Most of the time since she'd been there, he'd been outside the house and she'd been in the kitchen. True, in the evenings they would sit and talk awhile, and both seemed to enjoy their conversations, but that didn't give him the right to go beyond the understood boundaries.

And what's more, she would feel about Robert in the same way as he felt about Alice. He should respect that.

Last night had been a momentary impulse, brought about by an unexpected situation. It had been no more than that, and it should be forgotten.

Fortunately, by the time that they'd finished their dinner and he'd said good night to Bridget and joined Ellen in bed, he'd managed to get himself under control and he'd been able to keep his desire in check. But it had been difficult, and he wouldn't let either of them get into that position again.

He put the saddle on to the horse, and tightened the girth.

No, he thought, threading the harness reins through the bridle guides, he would never again do anything that could look as if he were trying to take advantage of her situation. She'd already suffered at the hands of her brother, and he must show her that he respected the limits of their marital relationship. He must never again come near to doing anything that could be seen as violating her.

★   ★   ★

'Hurry up, Bridget,' Ellen called towards her bedroom. 'Your pa won't want to be kept waiting.'

'I'm coming,' Bridget shouted back. 'I can't decide which dress to wear.' She came into the living room in her unbleached muslin petticoat, holding up two dresses. 'Which one shall I wear?'

'The green's nice,' Ellen said. 'It was my husband's favourite colour, and the dress I'm wearing next week is green. That's what I'm taking to the bee tonight. I'm going to trim it with lace so that it looks nice for the wedding. Robert always said it suited me best of all my dresses. With your colouring, green must look real lovely on you.'

'OK, I'll wear that. Tell Pa I won't be long.' She disappeared back into her room.

Ellen opened the front door and went out into the fresh morning air. As she did so, the ground trembled beneath her and she heard the sound of a horse being ridden up the track at speed. She stepped back into the house and closed the door.

Stones clattered loudly as the horse drew to a halt on the other side of the gate. She heard Aaron call out to the visitor. His voice was friendly and relaxed so it must be someone he knew, she thought. There was a squeak as the gate was opened. She hurried across the room to her bonnet, slipped it on and tied the ribbons beneath her chin.

The sound of the horse's hooves came closer, and stopped. She thought the horse had stopped in front of the door, but she couldn't tell if the rider had got down. She certainly didn't hear anyone jump down. She heard Aaron call out something to the visitor, then she heard footsteps as he ran along the front of the house, shouting for Connor. There was an urgency in his voice. She bit her lip and pressed against the door, trying hard to hear what was going on.

'William!' she heard Connor exclaim a moment later, surprise in his voice. 'I thought to see you and Peggy in town this morning, but not here,' he said, his voice coming closer. She heard the crunch of feet on gravel just outside the house. 'We were shortly gonna head into town. But come on into the house and have a bite to eat while you tell us what brought you here. There's water in the trough for the horse.'

She heard the sound of William getting down, and she opened the door and stood in the doorway, ready to welcome him in.

'I won't come in, Conn,' William said, his back to her. 'I thought you might be settin' off for Liberty pretty soon, and that's why I came as fast as I could. We've got a problem.'

As she stepped out of the doorway, she caught sight of the rifle hanging down from William's saddle, and the heavy band of ammunition around his waist. She looked swiftly at Connor in alarm.

'There's a gang of hunters in the area and they're slaughterin' animals for their hides,' William told Connor and Aaron. 'It's mainly the elk and the deer. A territorial official warned Massie to watch

208

out for them. Said they could be doin' some rustling, too. Massie vouches for the man. Says his word is beyond question. And we know there've already been newspaper reports of slaughtered beasts in other areas. The hunters seem to have started in Liberty now.'

'Can't say I'm surprised,' Aaron cut in. 'The game's in real good condition this year and as thick as anything on the foothills. It's easy enough to find the animals for those so minded, and there must be some mighty good hides for the takin'.'

'And that's just what the vandals are doin'. It's a right shame to see game wiped out for the few paltry dollars their hides'll bring, but that's what's happening.'

'I've said it before, it's time they started enforcing the law that protects the game from the hunters,' Connor said angrily. 'They've let the law become a dead letter on the statute books. If they don't do something before long, there'll soon be nothing left in the Territory but the jackass and the gopher.'

'I agree, Conn. As you can imagine, we're gonna do our best to stop the hunters. Massie's gone to the ranches north of Liberty this mornin', and men will already be on their way north of the mountains. I've bin to the Careys, and Elijah Carey will have already ridden off to the west with his hired men. I'm gonna head for the foothills, and I thought you might wanna come with me.'

Ellen drew her breath in sharply.

'I sure do,' Conn said.

A wave of fear ran through her.

Connor turned to Aaron. 'Not you, though, Aaron. I want you here at the ranch, keepin' an eye on the animals. I don't know when I'll return.' He looked back at William. 'What do you think, William? D'you reckon we'll be back tonight?'

'Depends, doesn't it?'

'Good day, William,' Ellen said, moving closer to him, her voice shaking. 'I heard what you said. Would you like coffee before you go? I can bring it out to you here. It won't take long.'

A movement in the trees beyond William caught her eye, and she saw that Niall was hovering near the fence, unnoticed by any of them.

William turned to her, took off his hat and smiled. His eyes were strained, she saw, and despite his smile, his face was creased with worry. 'Thank you for your offer, my dear, but I won't have any coffee. When the horse has drunk its fill and Conn's ready, we'll be off.'

'If you're sure.'

'I am,' he said, putting his wide-brimmed hat back on. 'You know, I reckon this is the first time I seen you outside of Liberty. We never did get that berryin' done that we were always saying we would. But there ain't been no time, we bin so busy gettin' ready for winter.' He paused a moment, glanced towards Conn, and then looked back at her. 'You're not to fret now. Conn and I know what we're doing. Isn't that right, Conn?'

'It sure is,' he said, and he moved closer to Ellen. 'If you heard what William said, you'll know I must go with him. We've not had any killing of animals in these parts for quite a while, and we've gotta keep it that way. But I'm wondering how you and Bridget are gonna get into Liberty. And you've baskets to take, too.'

'No need to wonder what to do, brother.' Niall's voice came from behind them. They turned towards him. 'I reckon I can help,' he said, strolling up to them.

'When did you get back?' Connor exclaimed. 'You were out last night when I locked up.'

'I got into a poker game and it ended real late. I reckon I got back at some point between sundown and sunup. 'Fraid I can't tell you closer than that. But I had me some sleep in the barn. I heard what William said and I was about to saddle up and go with you all, but it struck me that you might prefer it if I took Ellen into town. I know how much you want her to get to know the womenfolk there. Then I could collect her from Oonagh's this evening, like I was planning to do.'

'And what about Bridget?' Connor said sharply. 'She can hardly spend the day in the saloon with you, doing whatever it is you do.'

'You'll find Peggy in town when you get there, Niall,' William said. 'She's a mighty long list of things to buy and she's taken the buggy. She can take Bridget back with her, and keep her overnight.'

'Isn't Peggy going to the sewing bee?' Ellen asked in dismay.

William smiled. 'Peggy ain't never once bin to a sewing bee since we got wed, and that's a mighty long time ago. Don't you worry, she'll be real pleased to have Bridget's company while I'm away.'

'What are you saying about me?' Bridget called, running out of the house.

'Is that all right with you, Ellen?' Connor asked.

'Yes. Thank you.'

Conn put his arm around Bridget. 'You and Ellen are going into town with Niall. You're going back with Peggy for the night and Niall will collect Ellen from the bee.'

Bridget beamed up at William. 'Can we go fishing?'

'Not this time, darlin'. I'll be with your pa.'

'It does sound a good arrangement,' Ellen said. 'But thinking some more, I'm beginning to wonder if it wouldn't be better for you to take as many men with you as possible. Maybe Niall should go with you. I can stay at home today with Bridget. Yes, I think that would be better. There'll be other sewing bees.'

Connor grinned at her. 'I think not. You're going into town as planned. No reason not to. What's more, we'll most likely bed out in the woods for the night, and I'd feel a mite easier knowing that Niall was back here keeping an eye on things with

Aaron. We've paid off the hired hands, and my mind wouldn't be at ease, knowing that Aaron was alone out here when there might be rustlers around.'

'And I want to go to Peggy's,' Bridget said. 'I haven't been to stay with her since you got here. Peggy will want me to stay, won't she, William?'

'That's the truth.'

Bridget beamed up at him. She turned to Ellen, a challenge in her eyes.

'All right, then,' Ellen said with a slight shrug. 'If Niall doesn't mind.'

He doffed his hat to her. 'It'll be my pleasure, sister,' he said in a lazy drawl. 'Something tells me that Conn has already harnessed the horses. I'll go get the wagon.'

'I'll quickly get my things together, and you must, too, Bridget,' Connor said, starting to go through the doorway. 'I won't be a minute, William,' he called over his shoulder.

'And I'll just see if I can help. Excuse me, won't you?' Ellen hurried into the house after Connor, saw his broad back disappearing into the bedroom, and ran across to him. 'Conn,' she called to him, halting in the open doorway.

He stopped in the middle of pulling his bedroll from the wooden chest, straightened up and turned to her.

She took a step into the room, her heart pounding in fear. 'You will be careful, won't you?'

He smiled reassuringly at her. 'I will, Ellen. I promise.'

'I'll get you some food to take with you.' She turned and went towards the kitchen, trying to swallow the fear that threatened to choke her.

# CHAPTER 18

The weak rays of the late afternoon sun fell on the branches that arched the narrow dirt track that wound between the slender aspen trees. One behind the other, William and Connor rode beneath the leaves which formed a red-gold canopy in the filtered sunlight, their sweat-damp shirts sticking to their backs, their throats parched.

'Carcasses ahead!' William suddenly shouted, and he spurred his horse forward into a clearing surrounded by tall, dark pine trees. He swiftly dismounted and stood staring around him at an array of bloodied carcasses that had been left to rot on a thick carpet of pine needles.

Connor rode over to him and jumped down from the saddle.

'Obviously an elk,' he said in angry despair as he looked down at the remains of a slaughtered animal in front of him. He knelt down and touched the carcass. 'I reckon what warmth there is has come from the sun.' He stood up again. 'The flesh is cold beneath the surface. It'll have been dead awhile.' He glanced around the clearing. 'I reckon there be about ten or eleven dead'uns here. All this killing to make a few lousy bucks. The sooner they're stopped, the better.'

'Kill enough animals, and even at only a few bucks a pelt, you've got money in your pocket. That's what they're obviously lookin' to do.' William kicked the pine needles away from the area in front of him, looked down at the dusty ground and shook his head. 'It ain't gonna be easy to find them. The chances of following them are slim – the ground's too hard for tracks. An Injun might find somethin', but by the time we'd got one up here, the hunters would be long gone, if they're not already.'

'They will be,' Connor undid his horse's reins, let the reins fall to the ground, and walked slowly around the clearing, pushing the pine needles aside with his feet as he went. William did the same on the opposite side of the clearing.

'Nope, not a thing to be seen here,' Connor said, coming to a standstill next to William. 'But I guess we knew deep down that we were never gonna catch them today. This is more about letting them know we're ready to act. They'll have somewhere in the area where they can put up at night. They'd never risk travelling too far in the area where they were working lest they be caught. I'll wager that someone from hereabouts is helping them, and the sight of the Liberty men packing their rifles and a load of ammunition as they saddle up will send a mighty powerful message to that person.'

'Then let's hope he passes it on real soon.' William took off his hat and wiped his forehead with his sleeve.

'Oh, I reckon he will. And there's always a chance he'll give himself away. We oughta watch out who's suddenly got more money than normal. Massie's well placed to know who's spending too much in the store. And folk in the saloon should listen to what's said around them. Drink loosens tongues and someone might just start bragging about what he could tell us, if he were so minded. And we'll ask the girls at the back of the roadhouse if anyone's visiting more than usual. If we're watchful, we might just get him, and through him, the animal killers.'

'I sure hope you're right.' William looked up at the sky. 'The light's going. We're not gonna see anything else tonight so there's not much point in goin' on further. We could bed down here for the night and look some more tomorrow, or we could go home now. If we left now, we'd be clear of the woods before the light's completely gone and we'd find the rest of the way by the light of the moon.'

'I guess we oughta go back. We've no reason to think the hunters will still be around here. And anyway, before we go further into the hills, it makes sense to find out if the others have had more luck than we've had. If they have, we'll have a better idea of where to look tomorrow. I reckon we should head home now and meet up at the town hall first thing in the morning.'

William nodded. 'We'll do that.'

★　★　★

'That's it, ladies,' Ooonagh said, smiling at the women sitting in a semicircle in front of her. 'Every button is on, every thread-end has been knotted and clipped, every bias facing has been basted and every buttonhole made firm. We shall all look beautiful at the wedding next week.'

There was a wave of laughter. Ellen was aware of several sly glances in her direction as the women gathered up their newspaper pattern-pieces and their thimbles, folded their dresses and put everything away into their baskets.

Ignoring the looks, she tidied her things and picked up her basket, stood up and went across to the line of women waiting to thank Oonagh for her hospitality. Joining the back of the queue, she stood quietly, watching the women further ahead of her say goodbye and then drift off towards their homes in groups of two or three.

'Thank you for helping me with my dress,' she said when she reached Oonagh. 'It was very kind of you.'

'No, it wasn't,' Oonagh said with a laugh. 'I was giving myself pleasure. You know how much I like to sew, and fitting your lace collar on to your bodice is the sort of challenge I like. It had to hang correctly over the top or it would have spoilt the look of the dress. And it's good that you tried on the dress or you wouldn't have known that it needed letting out a little. That was an easy thing to do, too. You'll look lovely at the wedding, Ellen. Conn will be so proud of you.'

'The dress will look lovely,' Ellen said with an embarrassed laugh, 'but there's a limit to what a dress can do.'

'You are too hard on yourself,' Oonagh said with a dismissive wave of her hand. 'It's about what's inside you as much as what's outside.' She glanced around the room. 'I'm in luck tonight. You're the last to go. Everyone's left real quickly, and no one's chosen to stay over till morning. Some of the women who live further away sometimes do, but not this time, and I sure am thankful for that. But I don't mean you,' she added with a hasty laugh. 'I would have liked you to stay. In fact, I'm surprised you didn't take up my offer.'

'I know, and it was kind of you to suggest it. But Niall said he'd collect me. I don't know when Conn will get home, or even if he'll get home tonight, but whatever time it is, I want to be there to get him something to eat. He'll be tired.'

'As I thought, you are the perfect wife,' Oonagh said with a smile. 'Well, at least sit down and wait for Niall.'

'You'll be wanting to get to bed. I can wait for him outside.'

'Absolutely not. I insist on you waiting in here.' She gestured to one of the chairs, and Ellen sat down. Oonagh sat next to her. 'We hardly ever have time to talk to each other, so we must take advantage of the few minutes before Niall arrives. I'm curious to know how you're getting on with Conn.'

219

Ellen shifted uneasily in her seat. 'Well, I think,' she said finally.

'Only "well"?' Oonagh raised an eyebrow. 'We're friends, aren't we? Surely you can do better than that,' she said lightly. Ellen edged slightly back. Oonagh leaned forward, her face suddenly serious, and took Ellen's hand. 'Forgive me, Ellen. If you wish to leave it at "well", I shall understand. A true friend doesn't push someone into saying more than she's comfortable saying. I can see that you're reluctant to talk to me about Conn. You don't see me as the sort of good friend in whom you can confide, and I respect that. It takes more than helping with a lace collar to make a true friend.'

'Oh, I do see you as a good friend, Oonagh,' Ellen said quickly. 'You've been helping me all evening, haven't you? That's friendship.'

Oonagh, released her hand, sat back and smiled at her. 'You needn't say so, Ellen. I can see that you don't think of me as that sort of friend, and I'm not offended by it. We haven't known each other for long. We'll talk about something else while we wait for Niall.'

'You must think me real ungrateful,' Ellen said apologetically. 'And to show you that I *do* think of you as a friend, I'm going to improve on that "well". I'll add that Conn's an easy going man and not given to complaining. There, is that better?'

'Yes, it is,' Oonagh said with a laugh.

'He seems satisfied with the way I'm keeping house,' Ellen went on, 'and he can see that I'm doing my best with Bridget. So yes, I think he's content with the way things are.'

'I'm very happy to hear it. But it's only what I expected.'

'I didn't tell him about my face before I came, you know,' Ellen added after a moment's pause. 'If he'd refused to wed me when he saw me, I wouldn't have blamed him.'

'Oh, no; that wouldn't be Conn's way. If he's said he'll do a thing, he'll do it, even though he might secretly hate it.'

A wave of anguish shot through Ellen. She took a deep breath and nodded. 'I'm sure he did what he thought was the right thing to do when he went ahead and wed me, and that it wasn't what his heart would have chosen for him to do,' she said quietly. 'I could see that. But I realised that even though we were man and wife in name, there was no need for him to treat me as anything other than a housekeeper. In fact, I expected that. But I was wrong.' She stopped abruptly and smoothed down her skirt.

'As no more than a housekeeper? I think not!' Oonagh's laugh was shrill. 'The whole of Liberty knows that Connor wants a son. Alice tried hard enough to give him one, and I'm sure he'll be trying equally hard to have one with you. That's why he took a wife, not just someone to keep house.'

Ellen felt herself colour. 'As you say, the agreement was for a wife, not a housekeeper.'

221

'It must be difficult to follow in Alice's footsteps,' Oonagh volunteered after a short pause. 'They were very close, you know. We thought that he'd never be able to feel the same way about another woman.'

Ellen coloured more deeply. 'And I'm sure he never will. I understand that. I lost my husband, Robert, and I know what I still feel for him. I don't expect anything more than kindness from Connor. And respect, too, I hope.'

Oonagh's lips curved into a smile. 'I do declare, Ellen. You're going quite red. You're saying all the right things – in fact, I'm beginning to wonder if *you* should be teaching Sunday School, not me – but the colour of your face is telling me something different. I think I'll ask you again how you and Connor are getting on.'

Ellen burst out laughing. She stretched out her legs and surveyed the tips of her black boots. 'All right, then. We're getting on very well, I think.' She glanced across at Oonagh. 'See,' she said lightly, 'I immediately said "very well", and not just "well". Are you satisfied now?'

'No, not yet. We've only just started,' Oonagh said, laughter dancing in her violet eyes. She drew her chair closer to Ellen. 'When you say very well, just how well do you mean?'

Ellen giggled. 'While I've no desire to take your place at Sunday School – coping with Bridget is more than enough for me – I'm going to hold back on the details all the same. No, Oonagh, you'll have to be satisfied with what I've already said.'

Oonagh grasped her hand again. 'I'm so glad that there are details you can't even tell a friend. Connor's a good man and he deserves to be happy. And I like you, too, Ellen. It makes me real pleased to see that two people I like have drawn close to each other.'

'Which is particularly fortunate when they're married,' Ellen said in amusement.

'Yes, it is. Having to endure a man's attentions nightly in the way that some wives have to do, would be most unpleasant if one didn't feel very close to that man.'

Ellen changed her position in her chair. 'Maybe it would be more accurate to say that we're closer than we were, rather than very close. But I really think Connor is starting to feel a little more for me than just gratitude for the meals I make him,' she added with a smile.

Oonagh squeezed her hand and released it. 'Well I hope that his feelings for you get stronger and stronger.'

'Me, too,' Ellen said fervently.

'So you really like him, then?' Oonagh arched her eyebrow at Ellen.

'I wouldn't let myself think like that. Look at me, Oonagh.' She gestured to herself with her hands. 'And look at him. A man as attractive as Connor could have had anyone. I've no right to expect more from him than I already have, and I don't.' She paused. 'But I'll admit, I do like him in the way that a wife should like a husband, and I hope that I can give him the son he wants. More than one, maybe.'

'So Bridget hasn't put you off the idea of more children? You must be made of strong stuff.'

'She couldn't. I'd love a child of my own! It's not just Connor who wants one. Robert and I wanted a child, but it didn't happen in the short time we were married, and I didn't think I'd ever have another chance. I figured, who'd want to lie nightly with someone who had a face like mine? But now I *have* got a chance, and I'm real grateful to Connor for it.'

'But he has done well, too, Ellen. You're a good wife to him. Anyone can see that, and the things that Bridget has let drop has make that clear. No one in these parts could have made him a better wife, and I'm sure he knows that.'

Ellen hesitated. 'Maybe I shouldn't say this, but as we're talking in the way that we are . . . we're not just talking politely to each other, as strangers do, but really talking . . . You're beautiful, Oonagh . . . You would be an equal in looks with Connor. You and Connor belong together, and he must know that . . . will have known that. I've always thought . . . what I mean is, I'm thinking you turned Connor down because life as a home-steader's wife was not a life you wanted; not even if Connor was that homesteader.'

Oonagh tensed. She sat back in her seat. 'Did Connor tell you this?'

Ellen shook her head. 'No. This is not something he's spoken to me about, and I've never asked him. It's not for me to do so. But I've heard him say how happy you are living in town. And then when he told me how you used to go to the farm and help so much after Alice's death, I wondered if, apart from being kind in the way that you are, you were seeing how you would like to live that life, and you found that you wouldn't like it.'

Oonagh's shoulders relaxed a little. She hesitated, then sighed aloud. 'All right then. I wouldn't have told you, but since, as you say, we're talking like this . . . You're right in what you thought. I realised that I would not like to live on a farm. It showed me that Connor and I could never be happy living together.' She threw a mischievous smile at Ellen. 'I'm not saying that the nightly attentions, as I described them, wouldn't have been fun – I'm sure they would have been – but there would have been a lot of time to fill in between them. Too much for me.'

Ellen nodded. 'But it's not just Connor who wanted you for his wife. Bridget wanted it, too. It's why she's been so difficult with me. She loves you, and having lost her mother, her choice would have been for you and Connor to have wed. I've been a real disappointment to her, both because I'm not you, and because I look as I do.'

'Bridget will come to accept you; you'll see.'

'I'm sure you're right. She's already easier than she was. She's not as openly rude, for a start. But that's not a lot of progress in more than two months.'

'If ever I can help with her, you must tell me. Apart from trimming her dresses, I mean,' she added. 'Although I'm always happy to do that.'

'I'll remember that. Thank you.' She looked around her. 'I can understand you preferring your life in the town to being out on the land. Here you have a very comfortable home with your parents, and you have people all around you. You've made a good life for yourself, and you're highly respected. I can see you not wanting to change this.'

Oonagh sat up sharply. 'Then you are seeing things incorrectly. I wouldn't want to change my present life for the life of a homesteader, that's true. Not even for someone like Connor. It would be escaping one sort of jail for another. But that's not saying that I wouldn't exchange my life for a different life, I would, if it was a life that gave me some freedom.'

Ellen stared at her in amazement. 'Jail? What do you mean? Surely the life you have here gives you freedom?'

'Look at my life, Ellen.' She put her hand against her chest. 'All week, I'm the upright school teacher. On Sundays, I'm the upright Sunday School teacher. I'm the woman townsfolk turn to when they want someone to organise something, someone to lead a committee, put on a sewing bee. Don't you think I get real tired of all that? Well, I do. At times, I'm so close to standing up, walking out of the door and leaving all this . . . this goodness . . . behind me. At night I fall asleep and I dream of being able to be me.' She paused, and sank back against the chair. 'You don't understand what I'm saying, do you?'

Ellen shook her head. 'No, not really,' she said slowly.

'That's because you're living the life you want to live. I chose to remain an unmarried woman in a frontier town, rather than take up a life I would not like, but the price I paid for my choice has turned out to be my freedom. Of course, I didn't realise that at the time.'

'I still don't understand.'

'Then consider my life. I started working for my teaching licence while still a pupil myself, so I went straight from obeying the rules for students to obeying the rules for teachers. I must obey these rules or the trustees of the school will remove me from my position. And I live with my parents, which a teacher should do wherever possible. My parents are good, hard-working people, who'd need reviving salts if either of them so much as glimpsed a man near my room. So you see, every day I play the part of being Miss Quinn, a woman without passion, and I pretend that that is all there is to me. I'm in a jail as much as I would be if I were living on a homestead.'

'What life would you prefer to have, if not your present life nor the life on a farm?'

Oonagh held her hands up, palms facing up. 'I have absolutely no idea,' she said, smiling at Ellen. 'There probably is no such life. I'll wake up tomorrow and ask myself what I was talking about.' She waved her hand dismissively. 'Ignore me. Let's talk about something else, something that we'll both understand. We'll return to the social niceties, and you may thank me again for helping you this evening.'

Ellen leaned across, touched her gently on the arm, then withdrew her hand. 'Thank you for helping me this evening, Oonagh.'

'No need to thank me – it was a pleasure. We're friends, after all,' she said with a wry smile. 'There. As you see, we play our different parts very well.'

'I *am* grateful. I'm not playing a part.'

'Of course you are. You're playing the part of a woman who has no spirit. You feel that your voice has no right to be heard because of what happened to your face.'

Ellen stared at her in surprise. She opened her mouth to ask what Oonagh meant, but Oonagh gestured for silence, raised her head and listened.

'I think Niall's coming now,' she said, and she turned to Ellen. 'Before he gets here, let me tell you how much I've enjoyed talking to you. When we first met, I thought we would be friends, and I'm glad to be proved right. I hope this is the first of many such evenings.'

'I hope so, too, Oonagh,' Ellen said quietly. 'I've not spoken to a woman of my age like this for so long. Not since before . . . Well, not for a long time. I, too, have enjoyed the evening.'

Oonagh lifted her head slightly again. 'Yes, that's definitely Niall. Ma's talking to him. She'll keep him for a minute or two. Quickly, tell me how you're getting on with him. He's very different from Conn, isn't he?'

'Not to look at. There's a definite likeness physically. Like Conn, he's a good-looking man, though Connor's handsome in a rugged sort of way and Niall is smooth. But in his manner, he's different. Whereas Connor's a homesteader, at home on the land, Niall is the sort of man you see in a town, often in a saloon, sharply dressed, amused by everything, never taking anything too seriously, always ready to play a hand of cards, a favourite with a certain kind of woman.' She shrugged her shoulders. 'I sense that he's an opportunist, rather than someone who plans ahead what he's doing. There were men like him in Omaha, too.'

'But you get on with him, don't you?'

'I think so. I don't see much of him as he spends most of his time in town. In fact, Connor thinks he'll be moving into Liberty real soon. He'll prefer that to being on the farm. It can't be easy for him, seeing Conn in the house that could have been his, too. He doesn't appear to be jealous – the only things he seems to like about the farm are the cows – but I'm sure there must be some resentment deep down. And he likes Bridget, of course. He seems genuinely fond of her, and she of him.'

229

The sound of a man and a woman's voices came from the hall just outside Oonagh's door, and she stood up. 'I'll go and rescue Niall from my mother while you check that you haven't left anything behind,' she said, and she hurried out of the room.

Ellen heard the pleasure in her voice as she greeted Niall, and she smiled to herself. Oonagh might not be living with her parents for much longer, she thought. She might be about to start enjoying the freedom she yearned for. She picked up her basket and went out to join them.

As she walked out of Oonagh's house alongside Niall, she felt the weight of eyes upon her back. She turned around and saw that Oonagh was staring after her. Oonagh's face immediately broke into a smile, and she gave a little wave. Ellen waved back, then she turned and let Niall help her into the wagon.

# CHAPTER 19

Ellen walked into the living room and looked around. 'Connor's obviously not yet back. It must have been Aaron who lit the lamps for us. I don't like the thought of Connor being out all night, especially as the hunters might still be in the area.'

'He won't be back tonight. They'll have bedded down somewhere.' Niall took off his hat, hung it on a hook at the side of the door and went to the small table by the window. 'I'm sure Connor won't mind me taking his seat,' he said, sitting down.

'I wouldn't have said that was his seat.'

'I would. It's where he sits at night. Whenever I come back late in the evening, it's just you and him, sittin' together, pretty as a picture.' He grinned at her.

She gave an awkward laugh. 'If you came back more often, you'd know it was not always, but sometimes. If he doesn't have anything that needs doing in one of the barns, he sometimes sits with me.'

'I envy him,' he said. He leaned back and stretched his legs out under the table. 'It must be

231

real nice to sit here at night and talk about what you've been doin' in the day. Real nice. My brother's sure got it all.'

'But you could have the same for yourself,' she ventured, hovering at the side of the table. 'When you move into town, you'll likely find a woman there that you'd enjoy talking to.'

'You may well be right.' He locked his hands behind the back of his head and stared up at her. Amusement flickered across his lips. 'I guess I've had other things on my mind and not done enough talking with the women I've met so far. But I'm thinking that it's time I changed my ways. While I try to think of someone in town I'd like to talk to, I'll have a coffee, if you're offerin'.'

She hesitated. 'It's getting late. Connor might still be back tonight so I'll read in bed for a while. There's no need for you to wait up, too. Connor will try not to disturb you – if he gets back tonight, that is.'

He unlocked his hands and sat up. 'There may not be any need for me to wait up with you, ma'am, but it'll be my pleasure to do so anyway. We can sit in here together. Then, by the time you're as sure as I am that he'll not be back, we'll know each other a mite better. After all, we're brother and sister now, yet I know you so little that I feel I must say ma'am to you, not Ellen.'

She felt a moment's annoyance at being forced into a conversation with Niall when she'd spent the whole evening in conversation with those at the bee and she was ready for some time alone, but she couldn't see any way around it. 'I'll get you a drink,' she said.

She went into the kitchen and returned soon after with a mug of coffee which she put down on the table in front of him. She took a step back.

'Only one mug, I see,' he said, glancing pointedly at his drink. 'Since we're gonna be waiting together, why don't you take off your hat and have a drink with me?' Picking up his mug, he glanced up at her. 'I already seen what you look like, you know.'

'I had a dish of custard and some cake at the bee,' she said. She undid the ribbons, removed her hat and hung it on a wall hook. 'But I'll get a coffee, as you wish it. Would you like a piece of pie?'

'Not for me, thanks. But it's real kind of you to offer. And then you must come and sit opposite me, just like you sit with my brother.'

She turned and went across to the kitchen.

A moment later, she came back in, a mug in her hand. He was standing by his chair, hanging his jacket on the back of it. She sat down opposite him and put her coffee on the table in front of her.

Having made sure that his narrow lapels lay flat, he moved the lamp from the centre of the table to the side of the table, and sat down again.

'Is it all right with you that I've made myself comfortable like this?' he asked, indicating his waistcoat and shirt sleeves.

'Of course,' she said. 'I'd like to think that you felt comfortable here.'

'Thank you, ma'am . . . Ellen.'

A silence fell between them.

'It was kind of Aaron to think of lighting the lamps for us so that we didn't have to come into a dark room,' she said after a moment or two. 'It'll have been done for Conn, too, of course.'

Niall raised an eyebrow. 'Am I meant to say something about that? Is that what you and my brother discuss in the evenings – how light it is in the room?'

She laughed. 'Not exactly. I might begin by making a remark about whether it's too light or too dark, but it wouldn't lead to a conversation about it.'

'I'm mighty pleased to hear that. I was beginning to feel quite sorry for Conn, and to be thinkin' that I'd rather carry on missing out the talkin' bit. I'm real glad to know that you have some other topics of conversation.'

She smiled across the table. 'We've even been known to discuss the price of a bushel of wheat.'

'Well, I never,' he said, his voice full of admiration. 'Now that is a topic indeed.'

They both burst out laughing.

'To be honest, Niall,' she said, when their laughter had died away. 'I've no idea how we begin our evening conversations. One of us says something, maybe about what we've been doing in the day, and we just carry on talking. Sometimes we just sit quietly, doing whatever it is we're doing.'

'I see,' he said, an expression of exaggerated thoughtfulness on his face.

'As I suspect you very well know,' she said, amused. 'You and Oonagh talk to each other, don't you? Maybe you can't talk late at night when she's at home with her folks, but talk is talk wherever and whenever it happens. If you were with her now, you'd both be finding things of interest to talk about.'

'I guess.' He grinned at her. 'So you and me, what can we talk about that would interest both of us?'

She smiled at him. 'As you said earlier, we don't know each other well so that would be hard to say. And of course, when you're trying too hard, as we are now, you can never think of what to say. It has to be something that comes naturally.'

'You could begin by telling me something about yourself, Ellen. Then I can tell you something about myself. We'd know each other a little better if we did that.'

She hesitated. 'All right. But one thing only. If Connor hasn't returned by then, I'll think that you're right about him not coming back till tomorrow, and I'll give up waiting.'

He nodded, leaned back in his chair and stared at her, the light from the lamp reflecting in the depths of his blue eyes. 'You begin,' he said.

'My one thing is, although you and Conn are not close as brothers, there is still more between you than there is between my brother and me, and

I envy that. I think that whatever you say about each other, if either of you was threatened, the other would step forward to his defence. It was not like this with my brother,' she paused, 'and I have no sisterly feelings for him. And now it's your turn.'

A slow smile spread across his face. 'I think you credit me too highly, sister, and my one thing about myself will prove the truth of this.' He leaned closer to her. 'My one thing is that I would like to spend the night, or what's left of it, in your bed. And that makes me a not very good brother.'

She gasped, stood up and faced him. 'Good night, Niall,' she said sharply. 'If that's what you're like, I don't wish to know you further.'

He rose and moved swiftly to her side.

She took a step to go around him, but he blocked her path. A momentary panic arose in her.

'No need to be afeared, Ellen,' he said, looking down into her face, his voice soft. 'I ain't gonna force you. I've never forced a woman, and I never would.' He ran his finger down her right cheek. 'But I'm thinking that you might like a change, a bit more excitement, and I can give you that.'

'You've got me wrong, then.' She felt her panic start to subside, and she pushed his hand away. 'Very wrong.'

'I don't think so,' he said, slowly shaking his head. 'If you'd told me a second thing about yourself, it would have been that you wanted to feel like a woman again, to be pleasured in the way that a man can pleasure a woman. I've known many women, and I know the way they feel. I can sense what you want, and I know I can make you feel a woman again. And it's not just me bein' charitable – I'd extinguish the light and then I reckon I'd enjoy it, too. But only if you so wish.'

'I don't so wish. And you've got me very wrong if you think I do. Conn's been kind to you, and I'm truly shocked that you'd want to do something to harm his marriage. I'm going to bed now, and I'm going alone. Goodnight, Niall.'

'But we wouldn't be tellin' him, would we? I wouldn't want him to know any more than you would. And what he don't know . . .' He shrugged his shoulders and looked around him. 'The house is empty. It's just you and me alone, and the night ahead is long. We could have us some fun, and Conn would never know. There's no harm in that. So what do you say?'

'I say goodnight again, Niall.'

She turned to go, and felt his hand on her topknot. As she spun around, he pulled out the pin that held up her hair. Her hair tumbled to her shoulders. Very slowly, he raised his hands and combed his fingers through her hair, lightly touching her scalp with the tips of his fingers.

A shiver ran through her body, and her toes curled.

She didn't want to feel like this – not with Niall. She must abandon politeness and walk away from him.

237

'Just what's going on?'

Niall dropped his hands and they turned to the door.

Connor was standing there, caught in the amber light that fell out through the open doorway.

Niall took a step back.

Chill air slid around Ellen, and she felt the blood drain from her face. What must this look like to Connor? How hurt he was going to be by Niall's behaviour.

Niall moved slightly towards his brother. 'Sorry about you comin' in on this, Conn. I . . .'

Connor looked past him. 'Get to the bedroom, Ellen,' he ordered, his voice ice-cold.

'But . . .'

'Get out. I wanna talk to my brother. I'll speak to you later.'

Biting back her misery and frustration, she ran to her room.

# CHAPTER 20

His face grim, Connor closed the front door behind him, walked over to the table in the centre of the room and sat down. Niall went and sat opposite him, and waited.

'So why did you do it, Niall?' Connor asked at last. 'Was it that you saw my scarred wife as easy prey, and you were bored with the women in town? Is that what it was? Or was it that you could see that my life had some sort of order now after a year more terrible than you could imagine, and you couldn't bear the thought of me having a degree of happiness when things had gone so wrong for you?' He paused. 'Well, which was it?'

Niall stared at him. 'Why would I want to destroy your happiness?' He gestured in wide-eyed amazement. 'I've already got what I came here for. I came for some money and you've promised me some. You're a man of your word, and I've no reason to think you'll go back on that. And I wanted time to think and to sort myself out, and I've had that time. So why would I wish you ill?'

'Because you're jealous, maybe.'

'Jealous of what?' Niall exclaimed. He gave a

loud laugh of disbelief. 'We both know I don't want to farm. What you've got isn't my idea of happiness, so why would I be jealous of you? If I'd stuck around, I'd have had this, too. I didn't 'cos I didn't want it. I didn't want it then and I don't want it now.'

'You'd like the livin' it gives.'

'But I'm gettin' a share of it, aren't I, and all without doin' any work for it. And next year, too, and the year after. I'm back now, Conn, and I'll be takin' a share of the farm's profits each year. You owe me that.'

'If it's not about money, maybe it's about me being settled when you're not.'

'Believe it or not, I coulda got me a wife by now if I'd wanted one, and I could be having the same degree of happiness, as you put it, that you've got.'

'So it was about Ellen being more likely to give in to you because of the way she looks, was it?'

'Ellen bein' ready for a man wasn't because of the way she looks, but 'cos of the way she feels, and that was down to you.'

Connor stared fixedly at Niall. 'Just what are you saying?' he asked, his voice iron-hard.

'Oh, come on, Conn,' Niall drawled. 'If I can sense it, so can you. You're close to her in a way that I'm not. She's a woman and she wants what a woman wants, and she's clearly not getting that from you. I'm guessin' that you go to bed, do what you have to do to get that son of yours and roll over.

240

Well, let me tell you, a woman wants more than that.'

'The women in the roadhouse may expect to be used differently, but Ellen's not like that.'

'Listen to yourself, Conn! Women are women. It don't matter where they live.' He paused and sat back. 'Nothing happened tonight, brother. I'm not sayin' it wouldn't've done if you hadn't come back when you did, with her wanting it as she did, and me bein' only human, but you did come back, and as you saw for yourself, you turned up before a single button had been undone.'

Connor's eyes narrowed. 'So you're saying that she wanted you to bed her? I don't believe that. She doesn't strike me as the sort of a woman who'd suggest something like that, especially not if that man was her husband's brother.' He shook his head. 'No,' he said slowly, 'she'd not do that, not Ellen.'

Niall gestured with his hands. 'Look at Ellen, I ask you. Is she the sort of woman I'd ever go after? Think about it, Conn. You know I go for women who are easy on the eye. I'll give it to you, Ellen's a pleasant gal . . . but that face. I grant you one raccoon's pretty much like another in the dark, but really. . . . When it was clear what she wanted, though . . .' He shrugged his shoulders. 'And think about this, too.' He leaned forward. 'How likely am I to suggest doing something with her that would make you refuse to give me my money if you found out?' He laughed dismissively. 'You

241

know me better than that. I may like a wager or two, but takin' a chance of losin' ma yearly due from the farm, that would be too big a gamble, even for me.'

'But you wouldn't expect to get found out, would you? No one who does wrong ever thinks they'll be caught. And as for it being too big a gamble, you always did love having an element of a risk in what you did. The greater the risk, the greater the sense of excitement. And that's what you crave from life, isn't it? Thrills and excitement.'

Niall leaned forward in his chair. 'You say she wouldn't do something like that.' Niall cut in. 'But just how well do you know her, Conn? You been married for just over two months, or thereabouts, and during that time you've been in the fields for most of the day and she's been in the house. You haven't had time to get to know her yet. Most you can say is that she doesn't seem that sort of person. But lookin' as she does . . .' He shook his head. 'I reckon she'd be very careful about the sort of person she seemed to be. Face it. You know nothin' about her.'

'I know she's been badly treated by her brother and his wife. Her brother treated her like a servant, and he and his wife made her hide away whenever they had visitors. And her father was as bad.'

'And you know that for a fact, do you?' Niall's voice was tinged with incredulity.

Connor stared at him, his forehead furrowed. 'I guess I don't,' he said slowly. 'That's what she told me.'

'After we both saw what she was willing to do this evening, thinkin' you wouldn't be back till mornin', you don't think there's a chance that she might've been lying to you? Maybe she hasn't even got a brother. Maybe she was working for a man, tried to fool around with him, and his wife found out. Couldn't that be the truth?'

'I suppose it could,' he said slowly. 'It's just that it doesn't seem like her.'

'You don't want it to seem like her, and I don't blame you. She comes across as real nice, and she's in your house, lookin' after your daughter. Of course you want to think only the best of her. And 'cos of what happened in the past, and 'cos I haven't wanted to help out on the farm since I got back, you want to think the worst of me.'

'I guess there's some truth in that,' Connor said slowly. 'You're my brother, and I sure would like to believe what you say.'

Niall stood up. 'It's late. It's been a long night and I'm turnin' in. I'm guessin' you won't want me anywhere near here when you talk to Ellen, whether you have that talk tonight or in the morning, so I'll take my bedding and bunk down in East Barn.' He paused. 'Don't worry about Ellen. She'll not step out of line again – this will have been too much of a shock for her. She won't want to risk losing her home.' He paused. 'I sure hope you can forgive her this. Given your part in what happened, I reckon she deserves a second chance.'

He started to go across to the pile of bedding in the corner of the room, and stopped suddenly.

He turned to Connor. 'It plumb went out of my mind that you've been hunting the animal killers. Did you find anything?'

'We sure did – a number of bloodied carcasses.'

'No trace of the varmint who did it?'

'Not a thing. I reckon they're gonna be mighty hard to catch. I'll go into town tomorrow and see if the others had more luck, but I think it's unlikely.'

'I might just go along with you,' Niall said, tucking his bedding under his arm. He went to the front door, opened it and stepped out into the raw night air. 'See you in the morning,' he called to Connor.

For a moment, Connor stared at the front door, then he moved his gaze to the table by the window, and then to the door of their bedroom.

He sat back in his chair. How could he have been so wrong? Ellen had seemed a genuinely pleasant woman, easy to talk to and undemanding. After his initial shock at her appearance, he'd got used to having her about the place and had come to enjoy sitting with her at the end of the day. And Bridget, too, although still sharp with her at times, had clearly started to accept her. Altogether, there was now a warmth in the house that had been missing since Alice had passed away.

So could he really believe that it had all been an act, that she'd lied about her background and the type of person she was at heart? No, he didn't think he could.

But looking back at what Niall had said about her loneliness, at what Niall had made him see, that had a ring of truth to it that made his pain worse.

The night before, something had stirred between him and Ellen, something that hadn't been there before. She'd felt it, too, and had moved towards him, as if wanting him in the same way as he had wanted her.

But he'd pulled back from her.

It hadn't been his fault that he'd had to go to Bridget, but later . . . alone in the bedroom . . . He put his head to his hands. If only he hadn't told himself that her response was no more than wifely duty; if only he hadn't gone to bed and acted as if nothing had changed between them, as if it was an ordinary night, just like all the other nights he'd shared with her . . .

As he'd lain there afterwards, aware that sleep would not come to her either, he'd known in his heart that he'd left them both unsatisfied.

No wonder she had been tempted by Niall, a good-looking man who had the ability to turn on the charm when it suited him. He could see now that in a moment of weakness, his failure could have led her to act in a way that was out of character.

If it had been any man but Niall who had put the blame on Ellen, he might not have believed him. But he knew enough about Niall to know that he would be repelled by the way Ellen looked. And he had no need for Ellen. It was well known in town that he regularly visited the women who lived in the rooms behind the roadhouse. No, Niall would have been telling the truth about this being Ellen's idea. But being a man who was morally weak, he'd have gone along with her for the hell of it if she'd made it clear that that was what she wanted.

Connor put his head in his hands. His brother and his wife – no wonder he was so distressed. More than distressed, in fact. He'd felt something stronger than that when he'd opened the door and seen her standing so close to Niall, her hair loose about her shoulders. A surge of misery and disappointment had stabbed him like a sharp knife. She'd been ready to betray him, and with Niall.

Any man would have felt as he had at that moment.

So where did that leave him and Ellen?

He stood up and reached for the lamp. Niall would have to move out the next day, and he wouldn't be wanting to take Ellen with him, so it would be just the two of them again and Bridget. If he was prepared to let Ellen stay. He stared at the place where he'd seen her with Niall. He'd never be able to forget what she had been willing to do with his brother. He'd be reminded of it every night. So did he still want her to be his wife and the mother of his child?

He glanced across to the bedroom door, and turned away. It wasn't a question he was able to answer.

'Where did you sleep last night?' Ellen asked, going into the living room and seeing Connor at the table, nursing a mug of coffee.

'In here.'

'And Niall?'

'In East Barn.'

She sat down opposite him. 'Why didn't you come in to me?' she asked quietly.

He glanced at her and raised his eyebrows. 'I reckon I don't need to answer that.'

'I think you do. It's obvious that you mistook what you saw when you opened the door last night, and you should have given me the chance to tell you what happened. Or what didn't happen, as nothing happened.'

'Niall explained it all.'

'I picked up snatches of what you and he said to each other, but not clearly enough to follow your conversation. I doubt very much that he told you he suggested that we lie together, but I refused. That's what happened, though. It was an offer he made, if you like. There was no force on his part. It was just a suggestion, I refused and he accepted my refusal.'

'Nope, that isn't quite what he said. You were

willing to go with him, as I understand it. And it was your idea.'

Her stomach gave a sudden lurch. She raised her eyebrows. 'And you believe him without hearing me speak?'

'I reckon I do. Lord knows, I don't want to, but I saw you standing there, not moving, not protesting, Niall with his fingers in your hair. What he said fits in with what I saw.'

She felt numb. She stood up. 'I thought you knew me by now, but obviously I was wrong. Just as I was wrong in thinking you a fair man.' She moved away from the table. 'I won't be staying here. I'll get about my chores now and then go for Bridget. I'll also pack the last of the turnips and put them in the cellar. I ask only that you take me to Baggs tomorrow so that I can get the first stagecoach back to Rawlins.' She turned towards the kitchen. 'I'm disappointed in you, Mr Maguire,' she said over her shoulder. 'I thought you were a better man than you've proved to be.'

He thumped his fist on the table. 'He's my brother. Of course I believe him.'

She stopped, turned back and looked at him in surprise. 'So you really think that Niall has earned the right to be believed without question merely because he was born to the same folks as you? You believe that he'll always do right by you just because he's your brother? Well I've got a brother who didn't do right by me, even though he was born to the same parents as I was.'

248

'If he *is* your brother.'

She stared at him in amazement. 'If?' she said. 'If?' she repeated with growing anger. She took a few steps towards him. 'So he's been making you doubt what I told you about my family, has he? And because he's always been the perfect brother, full of family feeling, ready to put his interests aside to support you at the time when your folks died and you were desperate to keep the farm going, you believe him now without question. And despite his losing everything, you're confident that he'd never be jealous of you or do anything to threaten your comfort in your home. That's a good description of Niall, is it?'

'You know it isn't.'

'Well, it sounds as if you think it is.' She paused. Forcing herself to calm down, she went and sat opposite him again. 'I know he's your brother, Connor, but I also know that you've seen him for what he is and that for some reason which I don't understand, you're now choosing to shut your eyes to his casual morality. You once told me that you believed in honourable behaviour. How honourable do you think it is to accept without question what one person has said without asking the only other person present for their account of what happened?'

'You can tell me your side, then,' he said, crossing his arms.

She shrugged her shoulders, dismissively. 'There's no point, is there? You've already judged me and nothing I can say will alter that. As I said, I'll leave tomorrow.'

He stared at her, his face drawn and strained.

'I know I should want that, but I know that I don't,' he said quietly, letting his arms fall to his sides in helplessness. 'I think maybe I could have done things differently in the last couple of days, and I feel that I must take some of the blame for what happened. If you agree, we can try to put this behind us.'

'You think I had – maybe even still have – feelings for your brother, yet you're prepared to let me stay on?' Her voice rose in surprise.

'I can see now that what happened the night before, when I came upon you by the bath tub as I did, may have unsettled you. And then, coming back to an empty house with Niall, an attractive man. You had your needs and you acted without thinking. In my heart I know that this will have been out of character, so yes, you can stay on if you want.'

Staring at him, her eyes cold, she rose from her chair.

'Forgive me if, despite a scarred face which should make me prepared to accept any crumbs thrown from the table, I'm choosing not to stay with a man who believes that I would approach his brother for sexual favours in his absence.'

Connor stood up and faced her. 'I hope you'll think some more and change your mind. I'm gonna tell Niall that he must move out today. He's down by the fence, staring at the creek. You'll not see him before you set off for Bridget, and he'll be gone before you're back. I must go into town today and I'll ride in with him.' He took a step towards her. 'I would like you to stay, Ellen. Let's try to put this behind us.'

She hesitated.

'When I lay alone last night,' he said quietly, 'I looked back over the months you'd been here, and I felt I'd chosen well. You've been a good wife to me, and you're kind to Bridget. And I think you are a fair woman. Will you ask yourself if wanting to believe in my brother is so wrong that you must end this marriage?'

She looked up into his eyes, and saw the wretchedness in them. She nodded slowly. 'I'll think about what you've said. But now I must collect the eggs and then go to Peggy's.'

She turned around, picked up a basket and walked out of the kitchen into the cold dawn, her vision misting.

# CHAPTER 21

'**I**'d like a word,' Connor said, walking across the yard to Niall, who was sitting on the fence, staring beyond the creek to the blue-hazed mountains.

Niall glanced down at Connor. He gave an exaggerated sigh. 'I thought you might. And I'm guessing it's still about last night.'

'Well, you thought right.' He climbed up on to the fence and sat down next to Niall. 'Ellen's taken the buggy and gone to Peggy's for Bridget.'

'You climbed up here to tell me that? Why, whatever next? But you needn't have bothered. I worked out that she'd be the one to go for Bridget as you were gonna go into town, and I came out real early, to be out of the way before she got up. I didn't know if you were gonna talk to her today, or if you'd chewed the cud last night, but either way I figured she wouldn't want to see me.'

'You figured right.'

Niall threw Connor a quick glance, then turned back to the view. 'So what's this word you'd like to have? I already said all I'm gonna say about last night. Either you believe me or you don't.'

'I'm choosing to believe you. You're my brother, and I wouldn't want to think you'd try to do something that would come between me and my wife. I think she acted out of character in a moment of weakness.'

'So what else is there to say?'

'Just that I reckon it's time you left. In fact, I'll put it stronger than that – I want you gone before Ellen gets back. You were gonna leave anyway. What happened last night just means that you're gonna leave that little bit sooner. I said I'd give you money to help with your lodgings, and I will, and you can move into town today.'

'And if I can't find any lodgings?'

Conn gave him a wry smile. 'I know you well enough, Niall, to know you've already found somewhere to stay. What's more, I reckon you've been staying there on the nights you've not returned here. I'm guessing that you've made more money gambling and doing odd jobs than you'll have needed for your whisky and whores, and that some of that money will have gone on lodgings.'

Niall grinned. 'Yup, you sure do know me, brother.' He jumped down and brushed the dust from his trousers. 'I'll go get my things ready, and I'll leave today. But I ain't leavin' without seeing Bridget first.'

'You're not—'

'I'm real fond of Bridget,' Niall cut in, 'and I'm not goin' anywhere till I've said goodbye to her.'

'You'll see her in town.'

'But it won't be the same as livin' with her. When I've got my things together, I'll go sit by the creek and see if I can catch me some fish. If I do, I'll leave them for your dinner tonight. You can send Bridget down to me when she gets back. That way, I won't be meeting your wife again. Leastways not so soon after last night.'

'OK, I'll go along with that.'

'Just as well you get your living room back. You may wanna bed down there in the future again.' Niall laughed. 'I'm guessing that's where you spent last night.'

'Maybe it was. But like I say, you'd have to go at some point. We'll need the space when we have another child.'

'And I hope you get one soon, I really do. You deserve it after what you're havin' to do to get it.' He looked around him. His eyes returned to Connor, and he smiled. 'I reckon I was about ready to move on, anyway. To be honest, brother, I'm kinda bored here.'

He gave Connor a slight wave, and strolled off towards the house.

'So that's brought you up to date,' Connor said, walking with Aaron past East Barn towards the house. 'It's kinda late now, so I'll have to leave going into town till tomorrow morning, but there's a chance I might go over to William and Peggy's later today. I'd like to hear if one of the other groups got closer to the hunters than we did.'

'If they didn't, in a few days' time, after we've finished in the fields, I'd like to ride out with the townsfolk on occasions. I know we don't wanna leave the farm unprotected, but there might be a time when you'd prefer to stay back and I could go in your place.'

Connor nodded. 'I'm sure there will be. By the way, I saw you'd done the last of the ploughing so all the fields are now ready for seeding in the spring. That's real good, but I thought we were gonna leave the last patch till tomorrow and do it together?'

'I changed my mind,' Aaron said. He hesitated. 'I picked up that things were tense between you and your wife and I decided that today would be a real good day to get out in the fields and finish the ploughing.'

Connor glanced at him quickly, then looked away.

'You decided right. It was a misunderstanding between us.'

'I thought it was something like that. And seeing as she's bin gone for most of the morning, I reckon I'll take my lunch into the bunkhouse, and let you two and Bridget eat alone.' He hesitated. 'You haven't long been wed. I know I normally eat with you when the hired hands have left, but I don't mind carrying on eating my meals in the bunkhouse. I don't have to join you. You could use more time alone, I'm thinking.'

'Thanks, Aaron,' he said. 'But you're a part of

this family and you'll eat with us as always over winter. This once, though, I'm grateful for your offer and I'll take you up on it for a couple of days. There are things Ellen and I need to sort out. We can go back to normal after that.'

'If you want, you can send Bridget out to me when she's had her food. She can help with the new calves.'

They reached the kitchen door. As Connor put his hand on the handle, they heard the sound of the buggy coming down the track.

'I'll take something from the pantry and go,' Aaron said quickly.

Connor nodded. 'And I'd better check where Niall is.'

He went hastily through the house to the front door, opened it and went out. The rattling of the buggy was louder. He started to run towards the fence, then stopped when he saw Niall down by the creek, staring towards the water, his back to the house. He would have heard the buggy, but he showed no sign of moving.

With a sigh of relief, Connor turned away and walked slowly towards the gate. He reached it, raised the iron bar and was swinging the gate open as Ellen came into sight. Her eyes straight ahead, she slowed the horses, steered them through the gateway and into the yard, and brought them to a stop in front of the house.

'Pa!' Bridget screamed, clambering down at speed.

Connor pulled the gate shut, lowered the iron bar and turned around to walk back. He stopped in surprise at the sight of Bridget running towards him, arms outstretched. Smiling, he bent down to her and she flung her arms around his neck.

He hugged her tightly, then held her away from him and looked into her face. His smile faded and he looked worried. 'What is it, honey? Is something wrong?'

'What's the matter with Ellen?' she asked, her voice a loud whisper. 'She didn't speak to me all the way home. I'm not complaining, but it was funny.'

He straightened up. 'Maybe she's got a headache. If so, it'd be a kindness to leave her be. I know she was planning to pack away the last of the turnips today and put them in the cellar. Maybe you could do that for her.'

She frowned up at him. 'If she'd got a headache, she'd have said so. She wouldn't have just sat there like that, looking unhappy.'

He glanced towards the buggy. Ellen had tethered the horses and they were drinking water, but she was nowhere to be seen. He looked back down at Bridget. 'Then all the more reason to do something to make her happy.'

'I don't like it when she's like that. I will do the turnips, I promise, but can I do them tomorrow, when I get back from school? I've got something planned for this afternoon. It's to do with Peggy. Look!' She grabbed his hand, and pulled him after her towards the buggy. Releasing his hand when she got to the buggy, she reached across to her seat and pulled out a fishing net.

Beaming at him, she held it up and waved it in the air. 'It's William's old net. He won't be using it any more so Peggy said I can have it. She said William won't mind. He came back home very late last night and he went into town real early this morning. He came back just before Ellen collected me, but Peggy had already said it was fine for me to have it. I was gonna go to the river and catch some fish now. We can have them for supper. I won't be able to go fishin' when the water freezes over.'

He looked at her in mock surprise. 'I didn't realise you were so keen on fishing.'

She nodded. 'I sure am.'

'And it's nothing to do with not wanting to pack the turnips for winter?'

She vigorously shook her head.

He laughed. 'I'm not fooled. But I guess the turnips can wait. Also, Uncle Niall's down there, and I know he wants to speak to you. Remember, though – you must throw any littl'uns back.'

'I will,' she said. 'I'll get a bucket for the fish.' And she ran into the house.

He started to follow her in, but Ellen appeared in the doorway and he stopped.

'I thought Niall was going to be gone before I returned,' she said, her voice cold.

'I'm sorry. He insisted on speaking to Bridget before he left. He's packed his things and put them in East Barn. He won't be coming back into the house.'

She turned away from him. 'As long as I don't have to see him.'

'You won't. I promise.'

'Don't make promises you may not be able to keep,' she said sharply. He followed her into the living room. 'Before you go, I've got a message for you from William.'

He stopped and looked at her, his eyes hopeful. 'Is it news of the hunters?'

'Yes. One of Elijah Carey's men told them all that it was more than just the killing of animals that folks had to watch out for. There's also been some cattle-stealing in the area. William thought you'd want to keep a closer eye than usual on the grazing cattle.'

'So not good news, then. I'll let Aaron know, and we'll pass the word around to the folks south of Liberty. The rustlers must be in cahoots with the hunters. It's unlikely that two different bands would hit the area at the same time.'

'Whoever it is, I hope they've gone.' She glanced beyond him to the open doorway. 'Bridget will have left her overnight things in the buggy. I'll get them. Then maybe you'd put the buggy away and deal with the horses.'

She started to walk past him.

'Ellen,' he said, lightly putting his hand on her shoulder. She stopped and looked up at him. 'Are you gonna stay?'

'I guess I am,' she said quietly, and she continued walking.

Relief coursing through him, he followed her to the buggy and reached up for Bridget's bag at the same moment that she stretched out her hand to take it.

Their hands touched. She glanced up at him, and their eyes met. Neither of them moved.

'I'm sorry,' he said.

She withdrew her hand from the bag. 'What exactly are you sorry for?'

'I don't rightly know, but I know that I feel sorry. I feel as if I lost something sometime between last night and today, but I can't say what.'

'I think we both lost something,' she said, her voice low, 'and I don't know if we can find it again.'

He nodded slowly. 'I feel I want to try.' He paused. 'Do you?'

'I think I do,' she said. 'More than that, I know I do.'

She moved back as he lifted the bag down, turned and went into the house. Connor's eyes didn't move from her back as he walked behind her, Bridget's bag in his hand.

'Uncle Niall!' Bridget called, clutching her fishing net and a bucket as she ran through the small side gate in the fence. 'Uncle Niall!' she shouted again, and sped towards the fallen log at the edge of the river where Niall was sitting, his jacket slung on the log next to him.

Reaching Niall, she slowed down, went past him and sat down on the log as close to the creek as she could get. Then she straightened her skirt, held out her net and lowered it into the water.

She glanced back at him, and he grinned at her. 'I see you know how to fish,' he said.

'William taught me. Pa doesn't like fishing.'

'He never did. Fishin's too much like playin'. Your pa's a man who doesn't like to play.

'Playin's fun. I'm gonna catch a lot today. This is William's lucky net.'

'Then I'm sure you will. I was gonna fish today, too, but I'm real glad that I changed my mind about that. I'm sure you'll catch more fish than I would've done, and you'd have made me look a very poor fisherman.'

She giggled.

'Next time I come to dinner, I expect to be given a plate of the fish that you caught in that very net.'

'You're gonna have my fish tonight,' she said. 'Pa said we can have everything I catch for dinner.' She beamed at him.

'I'm afeared I won't be here tonight, honey. That's what I waited back to tell you. I'm movin' on.'

She pulled the net from the water and stared at him in sudden panic.

'What d'you mean, you're moving on?' The net slipped from her hands to the ground. 'I don't want you to go.'

'I reckon I've been here long enough. Your pa and Ellen need to have their living room back, and

261

I need to be in town if I'm ever gonna find me some work.'

'But I don't want you to go.'

'I was never going to stay forever, honey. I'm not sayin' I wanna go quite so soon – I would have liked to be here a while longer, get to know my niece better – but it's not my house, it's your pa's, and he and Ellen want me gone.'

'Why?'

'I guess they're hoping to have an extra person in the house in the comin' months, and having me around will be one person too many.'

'What d'you mean, an extra person?'

'Your pa's always wanted a boy, hasn't he? Even when he was real young, he used to talk about running the homestead alongside his son. They're hoping you'll have a brother, and if you do, I'll be in the way.'

Her stomach turned over. 'Has she got a baby in her belly? Is that why you've gotta go now? Is it?'

He put up his hands in front of his face. 'Whoa! Not that I know of. Not yet, that is. But I reckon it'll happen. That's why your pa took a wife. So's he can get a son.'

'Does *she* want a son?'

'Sure she does. She'll want a baby of her own. Women always do. And Conn took her in, lookin' like she does, so she'll want to please him and give him what he wants.'

She glanced towards the house, then back at

Niall, tears welling up. 'You could say you wanted to stay, couldn't you? It's your house, too. You're Pa's brother, aren't you? If you worked the farm with Pa and Aaron, he wouldn't need a son.' She looked at him with sudden hope. 'He wouldn't, would he?' she said in excitement, and she wiped her eyes with the back of her hands.

'It ain't just need, honey. It's about wantin' something. Your pa wants a boy. Your ma tried hard enough to give him one, Lord rest her soul, and he's gonna keep on trying with his new wife till he gets one. If I insisted on staying put, they'd build another room, but they'd come to hate me for being at the table with them every day. I'd be in the way of them bein' alone with the baby. It's different, you being here – you belong here. But I'm not wanted here, and that's the truth.'

'Can't you stay just till the baby comes? I like it when you're here.'

He slid closer to her and put his arm around her. 'I know you do, honey. And if it wasn't for you, I'd have left long ago. But I can't live where I know folks don't want me, and I'm not wanted here. I'll find me somewhere in town, and that's where I'll see you. Your Miss Quinn's a real good friend of mine, and she'll bring you to visit. And I can pick you up from school and walk part of the way home with you.'

She brushed her arm across her face, wiping away the fresh tears. 'Promise me you'll come and see me.'

'I promise. You won't be able to keep me away. For a start, the fish in town won't be near as good as the fish you're gonna do for me,' he said with a smile. 'Nope, I reckon I'll be seeing you so often that pretty soon, you're gonna be fair sick of the sight of me.'

She put her arm around him. 'No, I won't. I love you, Uncle Niall.'

He kissed the top of her head. 'I know you do, honey, and I love you, too. I reckon you're the only thing I do love around the place. Well, you and my horse. But maybe not in that order.'

She laughed.

He jumped down from the log, picked up the net and handed it to her.

'Bye, Bridget.' He gave her a big smile, touched his hat to her, turned and started to make his way back to the house.

She stared after him as he walked across the grassy slope to the fence, went through the side gate into the yard and started to go towards East Barn. Then she scrambled on to the log, stood as tall as she could and strained her neck to see him until he'd rounded the corner of the house and was hidden from sight.

Sitting back down on the log again, she stared at the water as tears ran down her cheeks and fell unheeded to the ground.

# CHAPTER 22

Ellen stopped in the middle of shaping scraps and odd pieces of pork into sausages. She wiped her forehead with her apron and looked around her.

It had been a long, tiring Monday, and she felt the strain of it. The pain of the weekend was still raw inside her. That Connor had believed what Niall had said without question ate into her. Since then, she'd been desperately trying to put her hurt behind her, but it wasn't easy. Hopefully, the tasks ahead of her for the next few days would help her put it to the back of her mind.

At the start of the day, Aaron had butchered two hogs that would see them through winter, and she'd begun her work on them as soon as Bridget had left for school. She'd worked steadily since then, but she knew that she was going to have to go even faster in the following days if she wanted to avoid having to throw away meat that could have served them well in the winter months.

She wiped her hands on a cloth, and then rubbed her shoulders. It wasn't surprising that she was tired, she thought wearily. Apart from the amount of work she'd already done that day, she hadn't slept properly on either of the previous two nights.

All night long on Saturday, she'd stared in bleak despair at the place that lay empty beside her, waiting for the grey light of dawn to lift the night's oppression so that she could rise and seek out Connor and explain to him what had happened. She'd been so confident of her voice being heard, she thought wistfully.

And then last night, the tension in the house after Bridget's emotional farewell to Niall had rested heavily upon her and had driven away any hope of sleep.

Bridget hadn't openly blamed her for Niall's going – she'd have had no reason to connect her with his sudden departure. Nevertheless, when Bridget had gone back into the house after Niall had ridden off, and she'd tried to comfort her, Bridget had drawn sharply back from her. More than that, she'd looked at her accusingly. For the rest of the evening, Bridget had sat without speaking, and she'd been just as withdrawn this morning. She'd eaten her breakfast as fast as she could and had promptly left for school.

And Connor had said little more to her than had his daughter. Words may not have been spoken, but what had happened with Niall hung in the air between them, and felt to her a silent reproach.

She pulled herself together. The past was the past, and dwelling on it wouldn't change anything.

She must look to the future. If there was to be any sort of future for them as a family, she must return their home life to normality as soon as possible.

She stared down at the pieces of pork spread out on boards at the side of the kitchen. It was good to have something to do, something that might take her mind off the atmosphere in the house.

She'd cook the ribs at once. They could have some of them for dinner that evening, along with kernels of corn and potatoes. The rest she'd pack away and store in the woodshed attic where they'd freeze throughout winter until they were needed. The hams she'd leave for the next day, but she'd make the brown pork-pickle for curing them while the ribs were cooking. She could then put the hams and shoulders into the pickle the following morning.

She went into the pantry, took the salt, maple sugar and saltpetre from their shelves, and returned with them to the kitchen. Then she reached up to the shelf for a bowl. Next year, she'd make the pickle a week or so before she needed to use it. That way it'd have time to stand a while.

She stopped abruptly mid-action, her arm stretching up to the bowl. Maybe she shouldn't think so far ahead. What had happened with Connor had shaken her. If he could doubt her word as easily as he'd done, something else might come up between them, and when next year came, she might no longer be living in Liberty. She might be alone once more, with Connor no longer a part of her life.

A gulf of emptiness opened up in front of her.

She pulled the bowl to her chest and took a deep breath. She mustn't let herself think like that. She and Connor had both said that they would try to capture what had been lost, and that must be her focus. She had the cooking and preserving to do, and then Hannah Carey's wedding at the end of the week. Nothing else must be allowed to dwell in her mind.

She looked back at the meat. She was close to having done enough for one day. When she'd done the hams the next morning, she'd pack the fat pork in salt and put it in the barrels in the cellar. Her last chore for the next day would be to grind the remaining leftover meat and shape it into balls. They'd have some of the meatballs for dinner in the evening, and the rest would join the ribs in the woodshed attic, along with the backbones, heart, liver, tongue.

The day after that, she'd make lard by boiling the fat from the hogs' insides and straining it through a cloth into one of the stone jars in the pantry, and then she should be finished with the hogs for that year.

By the time she'd finished dealing with the hogs, she should be feeling a little better.

She picked up the water jug, saw it was almost empty and stood it in the sink under the spout of the pump. What had been lost was the sense of companionship that had developed between them: nothing more. Anything more than that had been in her imagination. She pulled the pump arm up and down with ferocious determination. If Connor was ever to feel a husband's affection for a woman who wasn't Alice, that woman wouldn't be someone who looked like her. The past few days had clearly shown her that.

As soon as she'd finished the day's tasks, she'd go back to her room and set her mirror in a place where it would be the last thing she saw every night, and the first thing every morning. Her reflection would be a constant reminder of what Conn saw every time that he looked at her.

'You've been so busy with the hogs today that I've not yet asked you about the sewing bee,' Connor said as they started eating their ribs and corn. 'How was it?'

'It was as I thought it'd be – everyone busily sewing and me acting as if I was enjoying it, too. It's a long time since I went to such a gathering of women. I rarely went before my accident; as for after . . . I didn't miss going to them, though. It's not something I've ever liked doing.'

'Were the women friendly?'

She smiled at him across the table. 'You're asking if they stared at me. The answer is, not much. They seem to have got used to my appearance by now. In fact, everyone was very kind, especially Oonagh. She helped me a lot with my dress and she ended up sewing my lace collar on for me. I hadn't been able to get it to lie properly.'

'She's real good at needlework,' he said. 'She used to make her clothes from very small. Her ma taught her.'

'What about you, Bridget?' Ellen asked, turning to her. 'It occurs to me that I've never seen you pick up a needle. Is that because, like me, you don't like sewing, or because you don't know how to sew?'

'I'm not like you in any way,' she said sharply, and she furiously stirred her food around the plate.

Connor glanced at Ellen, then at Bridget. 'What's the matter, Bridget? You've hardly spoken since you got back from school. For that matter, you've hardly spoken since your uncle left. It can't be that you miss him being at the table with us as he was hardly ever here in the evenings. Or in the day, for that matter. He spent most of his time in town. You'll find that even though he's moved out, not much is gonna change.'

She glared at him. 'It nothing to do with Uncle Niall.'

'So what's it to do with?'

'Nothing.'

'Well, it's clearly not nothing, is it? If something's bothering you, you must tell me. Or is it something you'd rather talk to Ellen about? When I've finished my meal, I'm going to have a word with Aaron and then check the corrals. If it is, you and Ellen could talk while I'm outside.'

'I don't wanna talk to her. I don't wanna talk to you. I wanna go to bed.'

She threw down her knife and fork, jumped down from her chair and ran to her room.

Connor stared after her, bewilderment on his face. He looked at Ellen. 'I know she's still upset about Niall, but I don't think this is about Niall. It doesn't feel like it. Did she say anything to you about what's bothering her?'

'Not a word. She dumped her pail and bag when she got back, grabbed a basket and went out to collect the eggs. Then she did the milking. She didn't say anything to me, not before she went out nor when she came in. Looking back, I think she deliberately stayed out till it was time to eat. I can't think what it can be other than Niall going.'

'Maybe,' he said. 'But I'm wondering if this is to do with what's happened between us in the last couple of days. I've done my best to be as I always am, but she could she have picked up that something was wrong, and that could have unsettled her?'

'I wouldn't think that's very likely.'

'She was worried about you yesterday morning,' he said. 'She told me you weren't like you usually were on the journey home, and she wondered why. Of course, I didn't tell her,' he added quickly. 'I said you probably had a headache, and she seemed OK after that. And she was cheerful enough when she went off to the creek to see Niall.'

'Then it must be about Niall.'

'I sure hope you're right. If you are, it'll pass. She'll see him in town often enough. But somehow I think it's more than that, though I surely don't know what it could be.'

# CHAPTER 23

'**D**o you know where Connor is, Aaron?' Ellen asked, stopping on her way to the outside pump. She put the two empty pails she was carrying on to the ground. 'I haven't seen him since lunch and I wanted a word with him.'

'He's bin in West Barn all afternoon. With the freeze gettin' that bit closer, he's bin banking the walls with straw and tightening the nailboards. I reckon he'll do the same in the main house next week, ready for when the snow flies.'

She glanced towards West Barn. 'It's just that I wondered if he wanted me to get his clothes out for the wedding. We've an early start tomorrow. If I hadn't been dealing with the last of the hogmeat all day, I'd have asked him sooner. I hung up my dress this morning, and I've set out the hat and boots I'll be wearing. I could get his things out, too, if he wanted. I know what he's planning to wear. Bridget will want to do her own things when she gets back from school.'

'I'm goin' over to the barn now and I'll ask him.' He started to move away. 'Bridget's already home, by the way,' he added, 'or she was. She came back while I was fixin' the top strut of the gate. She went into the house and came out again mighty quick. She was headin' for the river.'

'How strange. Or maybe not. She's not been herself all week. She's hardly said a word since Niall left.' She picked up the pails. 'Now I'm out here, I'll fill these with water and take them back to the kitchen and then I'll go down to the river and talk to her. I'd like to try and get things back to where they were before Niall left. With the wedding tomorrow, it'd be a sight easier if she was in a good humour.'

'Conn'll be just about finished by now. I'll ask him to come across to you about his clothes. I'd hold off goin' to Bridget till you've spoken with Conn.'

She laughed. 'Thank you, Aaron. I can take a hint. You're right in what you're thinking – Connor would be the best person to talk to her.'

With a grin, Aaron raised his hat, thrust his hands in his jeans and turned in the direction of West Barn.

Still smiling, Ellen went across to the pump, put the pails down on the ground and started to lever the pump arm up and down. When she'd filled both of the buckets, she made her way slowly back to the kitchen, the heavy pails awkward to carry, and put them down on to the floor by the sink. Wiping her damp hands on her apron, she went to her bedroom, pushed open the door, stepped into the room, and gasped aloud.

Her bright green dress lay on the floor in tatters.

She took a step further into the room and stared down in horror at the dress.

The skirt had been cut into several pieces. The bodice had been ripped apart and looked as if it had been trampled upon with dirty feet. Each of the sleeves had been slit from the wrist to the shoulder seams, and the lace collar that Oonagh had sewn on had been torn from the dress and thrown to the opposite side of the room.

She cupped her hands in front of her mouth, and breathed deeply into them.

'Well I'll be darned! What's happened?' Connor's voice came from behind her.

She turned and looked up into his face, her hands still in front of her mouth. He stared beyond her to the floor, then he looked down at her, his face questioning, disbelieving.

'Not Bridget.' He shook his head. 'Bridget couldn't do a thing like this.'

He looked again at the tangle of vivid green on the floor, and then back at Ellen.

'You've gone white, Ellen,' he said, and he quickly took her by the arm. 'Let me help you sit.' He half-carried her to the edge of the bed, sat down next to her and put his arm around her shoulders. 'Your dress,' he said quietly, shaking his head.

'It must be her,' she said, her voice a whisper. 'She must really hate me.'

He stood up. 'If you feel strong enough for me

to leave you, I'll go and get her. Aaron saw her go to the river.'

Connor sat at one end of the living room table and Ellen at the other. Bridget sat between them, a sullen expression on her face.

Connor sat back in his chair and stared at her. 'We're not going anywhere. I'm not going outside. You're not going to your room. We're not leaving this table until we know why you acted in such a way. You're not a mean girl, Bridget, but that was a real mean thing you did, and I wanna know why you'd do a thing like that.'

Bridget stared at the table in silence.

'You've not been yourself all week,' he went on. 'Something happened last weekend that turned you against Ellen. And not just Ellen – I've felt you hostile to me. I wanna know what it was.'

'Nothing happened.'

'Yes, it did. Whatever it was, it upset you deeply. So deeply that several days later you're still hurting so badly that you destroyed the only dress that Ellen had for the wedding. Now what was it?'

She threw a bitter glance at Ellen, tightened her lips and turned away. Folding her arms, she stared straight ahead of her.

Ellen stood up. 'I'll leave you to talk while I have a stroll around the corrals. I might as well do that as anything else – the dress is beyond repair.' She walked across the room to the kitchen door.

'The light's going,' he called after her. 'Remember

276

there's been rustling in the area and stay close to the house, won't you?' He heard the door click shut behind her, and he turned to Bridget. 'Now, young lady, what's this all about?'

She stared down at the table.

'Come on, Bridget. There's nothing you can't tell me. I think this is about more than your uncle leaving. Am I right?' She kicked her foot against the leg of the table, her eyes still on the table. 'Have you done something you shouldn't, and you're feeling guilty? Apart from Ellen's dress, I mean. If you have, I can help you sort it out.' He paused, but she said nothing. 'Are you upset because someone's hurt you? Has Ellen done something to upset you, and has that made you act unkindly towards her? Does your hostility to me mean that I'm being blamed all over again for bringing her here?'

Silence.

'Say something, Bridget.'

'I haven't done anything wrong, and no one's been nasty to me. There, I've said something.'

He stared at her thoughtfully.

'Is this about Ellen's appearance?' he asked at last. 'Are you worried about the folks coming to the wedding who haven't seen Ellen before, fearing that they might stare at us? Was destroying her dress a way of trying to stop her from going?'

She glared at him. 'Of course not. I don't care what people say about her. It'd be her they'd be staring at, not me. It's nothing to me.'

'I'm not so sure that it's nothing to you, but I'll accept that it's not what's upset you this week. So what is it, Bridget? We're gonna stay here till I know, however long it takes. This is not just about your Uncle Niall, is it?'

'I'm sorry he's gone,' she muttered. 'I like him.'

'That'll have made you unhappy at the weekend. It doesn't explain you destroying Ellen's dress a week later. And anyway, I was the one who told Niall to go, not Ellen.'

'It's what Miss Quinn said today,' she blurted out.

'Oonagh!' he exclaimed. He stared at her in amazement. 'What did she say?'

'Nothin'.'

'I'll forget you said that. Now tell me what she said that's got you mad?'

'It's about what Ellen told her at the sewing bee.' She stopped, and bit her lip.

'And?' he prompted.

She looked up at him, her eyes accusing. 'Ellen told her that you and her . . . that you didn't love Ma any more.'

He stared at her in surprise. 'But you know that's not true, don't you? I'll always love your ma. I've loved her since the moment I first saw her, and I'll never stop loving her just because I can't see her.' He paused. 'You know that, don't you?'

Her eyes on his face, she nodded slowly.

He leaned forward. 'And I think we've both known Ellen long enough to know that she'd never tell anyone that I'd stopped loving your ma. She knows I haven't, like I know she still has feelings for her dead husband. You don't truly think she'd have said a thing like that, do you?'

'Miss Quinn wouldn't have made it up.'

'I'm not saying that she would, but she might have misunderstood what she was being told.' He stared at her for a moment or two, his brow furrowed. 'I'm curious,' he said finally. 'Why did Oonagh bring up the subject of Ellen and me?'

'She kept me back at the end of school today and said she was worried about me. She said I seemed sad and she asked if I was unhappy. I said I was.'

'That'll be about Uncle Niall moving out, won't it?'

She glanced up at him, then quickly looked away. 'A little.'

'Only a little? What else were you unhappy about?'

She sat still. He could see that she was nibbling the inside of her mouth.

He leaned closer to her. 'Come on, honey. Tell me,' he said gently.

'It wasn't just what Miss Quinn said – it was what Uncle Niall said, too. Down by the creek, he said you wanted a son. He said you'd always wanted a son, and so had Ma, and that's why she died. And he said that Ellen wants a child who's hers. I'm yours, not hers. And he said he had to move out because he'd be in the way once you've got a new baby.'

He drummed his fingers on the table, then stopped. 'You're only eight, Bridget, and I don't know real well what to say to you. Part of what they've told you is true, and I won't tell you that it isn't. But only a part of it, and the way they've put it together has made it come out all wrong. I'm sure they didn't mean to tell you something that wasn't right, but that's what's happened.'

'I thought Miss Quinn was wrong about you and Ellen,' she said triumphantly. 'And Uncle Niall was wrong, too, about you wantin' a son?'

'That part's true.'

She slumped in her chair. 'So he *did* have to leave 'cos you want to be alone with the baby and he'd be in the way.'

'It's not exactly that, it's more . . .'

'And what about me? Will I be in the way, too?' she said sharply, sitting upright. 'It'll be you, that woman and the baby. I won't be wanted any longer.' She stared at him, hurt in her eyes.

He got up, went around the table to her and hugged her. 'There'll never be a moment in my life when you're not wanted. I'll always love your mother and I'll always love you. Nothing will ever alter that.' He kissed the top of her head, pulled his chair around to the side of the table and sat down next to her.

'But when you get a son . . .'

'You will still be every bit as important to me as you are today, as you've been since the moment you were born. Nothing's gonna change that. But

280

most farmers want a son. There's men's work on a ranch and a woman's work. You know that. Every homesteader needs a son to take over the man's work so that the farm can pass from generation to generation. I'm no different.'

'I can farm. You said how good I was.'

'And that was true, and it still is. But take a look at yourself, honey.' He smiled at her. 'You're already beautiful, and you're going to be even more beautiful when you grow up, just like your ma was. Someone is going to come along, marry you and take you away. That someone will live close by, I hope,' he added with a grin. 'I'd like to think you'll never be far from me. But with you gone . . .' He gestured helplessness with his hands.

'Then he could do the man's work for you and be your son.'

'But we don't know that, do we? He might have his own farm to run.'

'Suppose you don't get a boy? Martha's not got a brother.'

'Then I hope one of you will live here with your husband. Or all of you. We'd build another house.'

'Why didn't you build a house for Uncle Niall?'

'The truth is, he'd hate living on the homestead. He's always known that, and that's why he walked out all those years ago. He came back because he hit hard times, and that's the only reason. And he was only ever going to be here till he got himself sorted out. Whatever he let you think, that's the truth. I may have given him a little push, but he was always gonna go. He found lodgings in town a while ago, and was staying there when he wasn't here. He's like Oonagh. They both belong in a town – it's where they're happiest.'

'Is that why you didn't wed Miss Quinn?'

He hesitated. 'Nothing's that straightforward,' he said. 'And that brings me back to the subject of Ellen's dress. Why did you do such a nasty thing, Bridget? You can't truly blame Ellen for me wanting a son or for Niall leaving. So why?'

'I know Ellen's ugly, but I've got used to her face and you will have, too. And when Miss Quinn said that about you and her . . . and then I got back from school and I saw the dress hanging there . . . She thinks it makes her look as good as she can look . . . I didn't want her to look good.'

'Your ma was beautiful inside, and I think Ellen's a good woman, too. People like that always look good, whatever they're wearing. I'm disappointed in you, Bridget. If you'd come and talked to me as soon as you got back from school, this might have been avoided.' He paused a moment. 'You like Ellen, don't you? You say you've got used to her face. I thought you seemed to be getting used to her as a person, too.'

She shrugged her shoulders. 'She's all right, but not as all right as Miss Quinn would have been. I would've preferred Miss Quinn to be your wife.'

'As you made very clear at the time,' he said dryly.

She gave him a wan smile.

'You've got a lot to make up for, young lady. Ellen has the right to be real angry with you, and so have I. After all, she'll be walking in at my side tomorrow.'

She looked up at him in alarm. 'I forgot that.'

'I figured you did. Everyone will be in their best clothes, but not her. The day was going to be hard enough for her as it was, meeting so many people who hadn't seen her before. You've made it that much harder. You go and apologise to her. When we've had time to think about it, we can decide on a fitting punishment. You'll find her outside. She won't have gone far from the house.'

She turned and hugged him tightly. 'I'm sorry, Pa,' she said, her voice muffled by his shirt, then she slipped down from her chair and ran off to the kitchen. He heard her open the door and run outside.

'She's in bed,' Ellen said, coming from Bridget's bedroom into the living room. 'And she's apologised again. I think I've now had three apologies. She hasn't told me why she did it, though.' She went into the kitchen, picked up the water jug from beside the sink and filled the deep pan on the top of the stove with water. 'I'll do the dishes when the water's boiled. Then I'll go to bed, too.'

She went across to the window table and sat down. Connor got up from the dinner table and took the seat opposite her.

'Did she tell you why she did it?' she asked.

'I reckon we got it sorted out. Little bits of truth had been put together in such a way that they came out all wrong. Between them, Niall and Oonagh managed to give Bridget the wrong impression about why Niall left.' He shifted to a different position. 'And about what I feel for you.'

'What do you mean, what you feel for me?'

'It's something you said to Oonagh. She repeated it to Bridget, but in a way that made it sound different from what I'm guessing you said.'

'I told her I thought we were closer than we used to be.'

'She made more of it to Bridget than it was. I'm sure she didn't mean to do that, but it's easy for things to be taken wrongly.'

'I won't speak to Oonagh in such a way again,' she said quietly.

He nodded. 'There's something else, too, and it got me thinking. I told Bridget that you were a good woman and that she could trust you to be honest in what you said, and she accepted that.'

Her eyes met his across the table. 'Is this about last weekend?'

He nodded. 'I reckon I may have got things wrong. When I said that to Bridget, I knew at that moment how much I believed it myself. I tried to talk myself into going along with what Niall said, but I don't think I ever truly thought that you would have gone into the bedroom with him if I hadn't come back when I did.'

'Thank you. It means a lot to me to hear you say that.'

'Are we friends again?' he asked with a wry smile.

'Cautious friends,' she said, and she got up. 'The water's ready. I must wash the dishes.'

She went across to the kitchen. Connor got up and followed her. Leaning against the wall, she felt his eyes on her as she organised the dirty dishes.

'Have you something in mind to wear tomorrow?' he asked after a few minutes.

She glanced at him over her shoulder. 'I'll find something, but I've got a limited choice.'

'I'm real sorry about what Bridget did.'

She stopped what she was doing and looked at him. 'I know you are, Conn. And I believe Bridget is, too. Maybe it's for the best, though. The other dress was very bright. It would have drawn attention to me and I wouldn't have liked that. No, I truly think it might be for the best.' She turned back to the sink.

'It's mighty kind of you to take it like that. A lot of women wouldn't have. And now I'd better go and check on the animals,' he said.

She nodded to him, and he went across to the kitchen door, started to open it, stopped and turned back to her. 'I've been wondering all week,' he said.

Hearing the awkwardness in his voice, she looked at him questioningly.

'When you stood close to Niall on Saturday night, real close, did you feel anything for him? You know what I mean. He's a good-lookin' man, easy with women, easier than I am. Please tell me truthfully.'

His blue eyes were clouded with anxiety.

She shook her head. 'No, Connor. Nothing like you mean. I felt nothing for Niall. You wed me despite the way I looked, and I'll not forget that. You can trust me to be true to you in every way – in what I think and what I do. You're a good man, and I'm lucky to be your wife.'

'This sounds like dutiful Ellen speaking,' he said, with a sudden grin. 'Not the spirited Ellen I started to see before Niall came into our lives.'

'Dutiful or not, it's the truth.' She smiled slowly. 'The other Ellen's still there. She's just been a little overwhelmed by what's happened in the last week or two.'

'She'll come back, won't she? I was starting to like her.'

'Of course she will. After all, wasn't spirited Irishness a part of the bargain?'

He shook his head. 'Back to that bargain again, are we?' He stared at her long and hard. 'I think I mean something else, Ellen, but I don't rightly know what I mean.' He took his hat from the peg by the door and put it on. 'I won't be long.' He opened the door wider, took a step outside and turned back to her.

'You're wrong, you know,' he said. 'It's not for the best that Bridget damaged your dress. You would have looked well in it.'

And he pulled the door shut behind him.

# CHAPTER 24

'Are you ready?' Connor shouted towards the bedrooms as he pulled the front door open. 'If we're gonna see the Reverend do his part, it's time we left.'

He picked up two of the baskets that had been placed by the door, went through the open doorway and turned towards the side of the house. Seeing Aaron coming towards him, pulling the horses and a ribbon-garlanded wagon, he stopped and waited for him.

'Feels mighty strange to be wearing my Sunday suit on a Saturday,' Aaron said, grinning at Connor. 'But I expect it's nothin' to the fuss that Bridget and Miss Ellen will be makin'.' He ran his fingers between his neck and shirt collar.

'I reckon Ellen hasn't got a lot to make a fuss with,' Connor said, lifting the baskets into the back of the wagon. 'But I'm sure she'll look well enough. Bridget's planning to wear the blue dress her ma made for her. It was too big for her when Alice made it, but it should look real good on her now.'

'Ah, here's Bridget!' Aaron exclaimed.' Oh . . .' He broke off and looked at Connor in surprise.

Connor took a step forward and stared at Bridget in amazement.

She stopped walking and stared back at him.

'Why are you wearing your school dress?' he asked. 'You were gonna wear the dress your ma made.'

'I think I'll wear this. I can wear Ma's dress another time.'

'But why? This is a wedding. Women always get dressed up for a wedding. Girls, too. Everyone else will be wearing pretty dresses.'

'Ellen won't,' she said bluntly.

'Who wants me?' Ellen asked, coming out of the house. 'I heard my name.' She stopped short. 'Bridget, what are you wearing?'

Bridget glanced at her over her shoulder, then looked back at the ground in front of her. 'My school dress.'

'I can see that. But why?'

Bridget kicked a clump of grass with the toe of her boot. Connor looked over Bridget's head at Ellen. He shrugged his shoulders and gestured helplessly.

Ellen came forward and placed herself in front of Bridget. She put her finger under Bridget's chin and raised her face. 'Is this about my dress?' she asked gently. 'I can't wear my pretty dress because of what you did, so you won't wear yours either?'

Bridget nodded slowly.

Ellen put her arms around her and hugged her tightly. 'You've said sorry several times since yesterday, and I've accepted your apology each time. I already believed that you regretted what you did. But by putting your school dress on today, it tells me that you truly did mean everything you said. I'm so grateful for that, Bridget. So very grateful.'

Bridget looked up at her. 'Why are you crying?'

She released Bridget and wiped her cheeks with her hand. 'I didn't realise I was,' she said with a laugh. 'It's just that you've made me feel as if I matter to you. I can't describe to you what that means to me.'

Connor moved to Ellen's side. 'You've done the right thing today, Bridget, and I'm real proud of you.'

'Can I ask you now to do one thing for me, Bridget, before we set off?' Ellen asked.

Bridget nodded.

'Can I ask you to go in and put on the dress your ma made for you?'

Bridget stepped back and opened her mouth as if to protest.

Ellen caught her hand. 'It would please me very much if you did that. I'm extremely comfortable in what I'm wearing.' She looked down at her check-patterned brown poplin dress, and looked back at Bridget and smiled. 'I'll feel quite at ease today. I've not liked dressing up for some time now. But it would please me very much to see you in the pretty dress your ma made for you.'

Bridget looked from Ellen's face to her father's.

He smiled reassuringly. 'Go and get changed now, but be quick about it.' Ellen released her hand. Bridget hesitated. 'Off you go now,' he said.

She turned and ran back to the house.

'That was a very kind thing you did, Ellen.'

'I think she's been punished enough, knowing how disappointed in her you were.'

'I hope so.' He ran his eyes over her dress. 'You may not be wearing what you wanted to wear, but you still look mighty nice.'

He saw Ellen go red at his words and pull her overskirt down as if trying to make it lie smoothly over her stomach.

'I don't look any different from usual, but thank you for saying it,' she said.

He nodded. 'While Bridget's changing, we'll finish loading the wagon. There are a couple more baskets by the door, I think.'

'That's right. One's got the plates and white table-cloths in it, and the other a bowl of peas, some sponge cakes and marmalade. Those are my contributions to the wedding dinner.'

'I'll get the baskets, and I'll hurry Bridget along. Aaron will help you into the wagon.'

As Ellen turned towards the wagon, he started to walk towards the house.

Bridget came running out of the house at speed. 'Ellen!' she shouted.

'That was very quick,' Connor called after her as she sped past him.

'I said I wouldn't be long,' Bridget said, panting

as she ran up to Ellen. 'Look!' she cried. With a rustle of petticoats, she turned full circle, showing off her blue lawn dress with a polonaise.

Ellen smiled warmly at her. 'Your mother was a talented needlewoman. It's a lovely dress, Bridget, and you look very pretty in it.'

Bridget giggled.

'Ellen's right. You look mighty nice, Bridget,' Connor said. 'Now I'd better get those baskets.'

'That you do, girl,' Aaron called, and he unhooked the reins from the post.

'So why did you tell Bridget what Ellen told you about her and me, and in such a way as to suggest that there was more between us than there was?' Connor asked Oonagh as they lingered on at the long table, empty of everyone but themselves. 'I was going to ask you earlier, but I couldn't since there were others around. Now that we're by ourselves, I'd like an answer.'

'I don't know what you mean,' she said lightly. 'It's true I passed on something that Ellen said, and looking back I shouldn't have, but I did no more than repeat her words.'

'You've talked to Ellen so you know she's a good woman, but one without many friends. And you know Bridget, and the difficulty she's had in accepting Ellen, hurtin' as she still is after her ma, and fearing that I'll forget her ma now that I've gotten me a new wife.'

'I do know that,' she said quietly.

'You were a good friend to Bridget and me in the months after Alice passed on. I'd hoped you would be a good friend to Ellen, too. By saying what you did in the way that you did, you were not being a friend to any of us.'

Oonagh's violet eyes filled with regret. She rested her hand on his arm. 'I'm so sorry, Conn. I didn't mean my words to come out as they did, and until you spoke just now, I didn't know that they had. Ellen didn't say any more to me than would have been proper, and I didn't intend Bridget to think that there was anything more than a warm friendship between you.'

'Between what you said, and what Niall had told her earlier about having to leave so that he wasn't in the way when a baby came, Bridget's a mighty unhappy little girl.'

'Would it help if I spoke to Bridget, do you think? I could tell her she misunderstood me.'

'I think not. She'll feel that you're saying what I've asked you to say and she won't believe you. In fact, it could make her all the more certain that it was true. Both bits of it.'

Her shoulders slumped. 'If you think of any way in which I can undo the damage that Niall and I seem to have done, you must tell me and I'll gladly do it.'

He nodded. 'I'll remember that.' He glanced at her, and raised an eyebrow. 'So is there a Niall and you? The whole town reckons there is. They've seen you out together and they're rootin' for it.'

'Not my pa,' she said with a laugh. 'Not at all. He lectures me nightly on not being taken in by surface charm and a good-looking face. He thinks Niall is the unreliable wild type, happiest with a card in his hand, a glass of whisky at his side and a woman he can leave the next day.'

'And you?'

She shrugged her shoulders. 'I'm still heart free, if that's what you're asking. You know me – I like the idea of a little excitement, and Niall sure is that. But having a bank manager for a pa means that I'm used to being able to buy what I want, and I'm thinking about what would happen if Niall hit a losing streak.'

Connor frowned. 'Is he gambling a lot?'

'I suspect he is. But one game is one too many in Pa's eyes. Niall loses a few, but overall he wins his hands. He must do. He's always got money to spend.'

'He must also be finding work, then. I'm glad. Do you see much of him?'

'Being a schoolteacher, I couldn't go into the saloon, but I see him at other times in town and we go for buggy rides together. He comes to the school on occasions, and he's also visited my house.' She twisted her features into a pained expression. 'Just once. My folks sat with us and Pa's face was something to see.'

They both laughed.

'But why are we sitting here talking about Niall!' she exclaimed. 'I hear the fiddle and the mouth harp. Let's dance, Conn. You know how much I love to dance. Come on.'

'I should dance first with Ellen.'

'She's serving food. You can dance with her later.' She got up, caught hold of his hand and pulled him up after her.

'You always were a high lifer, Oonagh,' he said as she led him by the hand to the dancing area at the back of the hall. 'I still wonder at times that you chose to teach school. And that you do it as well as you do. I hear what Bridget says, and I know that you're a fine teacher, Miss Quinn.'

Ellen stood in the hall, her back to the long, half-empty food tables, staring at the people dancing.

It seemed an age since Hannah Carey, steadying the coronet wreath on her head with her hand, said 'I will', and then beamed up at the man next to her as he repeated the same words.

And even longer since Connor first stepped on to the dancing area with Oonagh. The afternoon light had been strong at the time, but the mellowness of dusk had now crept into the room, and still he was dancing with her.

But of course, he would be, she thought, angry at herself for the despair and distress that she felt.

He would want to be with Oonagh, would relish the time he spent with her and would cling on to every minute of it. All of his former feelings for her must have flooded back the moment that she'd come over to the long wooden table at which they'd sat with their wedding meal. She'd looked radiant in a dress of a blue that was the colour of cornflowers. She could never have looked lovelier than she looked that day, and not surprisingly, everyone around them had stared at her.

She'd placed herself on the other side of Connor from Ellen, put her plate of food on the table and sat down. Then she'd leaned in front of him, smiled at Ellen and commented upon how lovely Hannah had looked.

Her arm had brushed Connor's but she'd seemed not to notice it. He'd moved slightly back and she'd looked up into his face, and Ellen had seen the sparkle in her violet eyes.

'That's a lovely dress, Oonagh,' she'd said.

'I'm glad you like it,' Oonagh had replied, turning away from Connor. 'I got it from the shop that's just opened in town. It's larger than O'Shaughnessy's, and the dresses much prettier. I may not be making so many of my clothes in the future. And they've men's clothes, too, Conn,' she added, glancing back up at him.

'Is that so,' he'd said.

She'd laughed and looked back at Ellen. 'You should get a dress there, Ellen. They . . .' Her eyes had flickered to Ellen's plain brown dress, and she'd stopped abruptly. 'Why aren't you wearing the green dress we trimmed? I thought you were going to wear it today.'

'I spilled something on it.'

'What a shame that you'd no other dress to put

on. Not that it matters, of course – you already have a husband, and he's the best-looking man in Liberty.' She'd thrown Connor a glance of amusement, turned to her food, picked up her knife and fork and had begun to eat.

Connor had looked as if he were about to say something, but then he, too, had stared down at his plate and started to eat.

Ellen had turned to Peggy and asked if William was missing his fishing net.

'Do you know that we haven't danced together in years, Connor?' she'd heard Oonagh remark a short while later. 'I'll expect you to dance with me at least once today.'

'Maybe,' she'd heard him say. 'But first I'll dance with my wife.'

It hadn't worked out that way, though.

Knowing there'd be a large number of people at the wedding whom she'd never before seen, she'd intended to stay as close to Connor as she could. But just as they'd finished their meal, one of the women at the sewing bee had approached her and asked if she would take a turn at serving behind the food tables, and she'd been obliged to relieve the woman at the table laden with meat, pickles and sauces.

That had left Oonagh alone with Connor, and they'd been together ever since.

The last trace of the happiness she'd felt earlier in the day when Connor had said she looked fine, and when Bridget had shown how sincere in her apologies she'd been, had disintegrated. And now, as she watched Oonagh smile up into Connor's face every time that they faced each other during the square dance, she felt close to crying.

Oonagh may not have wanted to marry Connor, but she was clearly more than willing to dance with him or she would have left his side long ago, no matter what he wanted. That must mean that she now regretted not marrying him, despite what she'd said about not wanting to exchange one kind of jail for another.

She shook herself. She must lift herself out of the mood into which she was sinking. Connor was a good husband, and the fact that he was enjoying being with Oonagh didn't alter that. From what she knew of him, she knew that he'd have done his best to put his feelings for Oonagh behind him from the day that they'd wed. But some feelings can be too strong to be cast aside at will.

None of this was his fault.

And seeing him so happy at being with Oonagh was a timely reminder of something she'd do well not to forget. Their marriage was one of convenience and mutual respect, and no more than that.

Misery welled up within her. It hurt her to think that way, though she didn't know why it should: it was only the truth.

A ranch hand came to her side, offering her ice cream and coffee. She indicated her refusal, and took a step closer to the dancing area.

Niall sprang to her mind and the fact that she

hadn't seen him since the start of the wedding. Dragging her eyes from Connor and Oonagh, she looked around the hall. He, too, could be wondering about Oonagh and Connor if he'd been watching them all afternoon, just as she had.

Not for the first time in recent days, she wondered about the situation between Oonagh and Niall. If he was thinking about a future with Oonagh, it would explain why he'd moved into Liberty rather than go further away in search of work with cattle. Conn had repeated to her Niall's dismissive comment about cattle ranching having become another sort of farming, but Niall could have said that because he knew of the hopelessness of finding such work around Liberty, and yet he intended to stay there.

From what she'd heard, he had money to spend – more than the sum given him by Connor could account for – so he'd obviously found some work and was probably also making a bit of money from gambling. Gambling was an unreliable form of income, which he would know, but he might be hoping that one of the casual jobs he took on would lead to something more permanent in the future.

On Oonagh's side, she hadn't wanted to live on a homestead, and Niall wasn't a homesteader, and never would be. He might have fairly wild ways at the moment, but many men like him had given up such ways when they'd taken a wife. Oonagh would know that, and she might well be thinking that a future with him would give her more freedom than her present life which she was increasingly finding too constricting.

And what about *her*? Did she want Oonagh and Niall to marry and probably settle in Liberty?

A part of her did. If Oonagh married Niall, she wouldn't be as interested in spending time with Connor. But on the other hand, she'd always be anxious that Niall living so close to them could be unsettling for both Bridget and Connor. On the whole, the further away they both were, the better.

'What are you doin', standing here by yourself, Ellen?' Niall's voice came from next to her.

She turned sharply, and took a step back.

'You made me jump, Niall,' she said. 'Bridget's with Martha and her school friends. I don't expect to see her till it's time to leave.'

'But you should be dancin' with your husband. Why aren't you?' he asked. In feigned annoyance with himself, he tapped the side of his head. 'Oh, of course. You can't. He's too busy dancing with Oonagh. I've been watching them. Just like you have.' He looked across at Connor and Oonagh, and gave a loud sigh.

'Can I help you with anything?' she asked stiffly.

'Nope, nothing at all. I'm just thinking how lovely Oonagh looks today. I swear I've never seen her lookin' better. Her skin is smooth and creamy like buttermilk. It's no wonder my brother can't take his eyes from her face. What a face that gal's got!'

300

Glancing at Ellen, he shook his head in wonderment and grinned at her.

'Why shouldn't Connor dance with Oonagh? They've been friends for years,' she said sharply.

'So they have,' he drawled. His eyes crinkled at the corner in the way that Connor's eyes crinkled, she noticed. 'No hard feelings about the other night, I hope.'

'You mean about you leading my husband to believe that I'd been about to lie in bed with you? And that I'd suggested it? Why should I have hard feelings about a little thing like that?' she asked with exaggerated brightness.

He nodded slowly. 'I guess you *are* mad. But think of it from where I'm standing, from my point of view.'

'You mean there's another way of looking at it? I can't wait to hear it.'

'Well, if I'd told Conn that you'd turned me down, my pride would have been lower than a snake in the grass, and a man needs his pride.'

'I assume that your pride would have suffered because you'd've had to admit that someone who was homely enough to scare away the crows had turned you down.'

He laughed. 'I guess I'm making it worse. Can we start again?'

She gave him a slight smile. 'You *are* making it worse, and no, you can't start again. I think we'll let the subject lie.'

'I agree. But not in bed.'

In spite of herself, she laughed.

She turned her head to look at Connor and Oonagh. At the same moment, Connor glanced at her across the hall. Their eyes met. She saw him miss his step, stop mid dance and stare first at her and then at Niall. Then she saw Oonagh catch his arm and pull him into the dance again.

'You'll excuse me if I have a cigarette,' Niall said, and he pulled out a packet of cigarettes from his jacket pocket. 'Ah, here's Conn. And he doesn't look too happy. I reckon I'll make myself scarce.'

'I'm ready to leave, Ellen,' Connor said curtly as he reached her side. 'I'll get Bridget. We've been here long enough. Goodnight, Niall.' He took Ellen by the elbow and led her away, his face grim.

# CHAPTER 25

'How's Bridget?' Connor asked as Ellen came back into the living room.

'Asleep. I've left her in her dress. I'd have to wash it tomorrow, anyway, and I didn't want to wake her. She's exhausted. And she's not the only one. I've left the baskets with the dishes I took to the wedding in the kitchen, and I'm leaving them as they are till tomorrow. I thought I'd go outside for a few minutes, and then go to bed.'

'Won't you sit a while?' He went and sat at the table by the window, and indicated the chair opposite him.

She remained standing.

He glanced up at her. 'You were very quiet at the wedding and you said nothing on the way home.'

'I'm surprised that you noticed anything at all at the wedding, you were so occupied with Oonagh,' she said. She picked up her shawl, wrapped it around her shoulders, took a lamp from the wall and went out.

★　★　★

303

Her tone had been sharp, which was unusual, he thought, as he stared at the table in front of him. No, not sharp. She'd sounded upset. And of course she was right to be upset. More than upset, in fact; she had a right to be angry with him. He'd neglected her on the very day he should have stood beside her.

Surrounded by so many people she didn't know, with a face so badly scarred, and wearing clothes that were dull compared with the finery of the other women, she would have naturally looked to him for support, and he hadn't been there to provide it. He'd badly let her down, and not for the first time.

And he'd let himself down.

A wave of fury at himself for the way he'd behaved that day swept through him. He got up, grabbed his coat and went out after her.

'I didn't have much say in the matter,' he said, catching her up. He could hear that his tone of voice was defensive, and it shouldn't be. His behaviour was completely indefensible. He should be trying to show her how deeply he regretted the events of the day, how truly sorry he felt. 'She was there every time I turned around, and every time one dance ended, she pulled me into the next. I couldn't get away. I'd wanted to dance with you. I'm sorry I didn't.'

She stopped walking, her face turned away from him, the lamp held out to the side. 'You don't have to say that. There's no reason why you shouldn't dance with Oonagh. You've been friends for years.'

He stared hard at the side of her face. The ridges on her left cheek stood out, pinched and stark, reddish purple in the cold night air, and he was pretty sure that she was close to crying.

'I'm sorry,' he said again. He reached out to touch her arm, but she pulled her arm away from him. 'I wish I could wear my school dress tomorrow to prove the depth of my regret,' he said, and he risked a half smile. 'But I can't – it no longer fits.'

She glanced at him and smiled. But with her mouth only, he noticed; not with her eyes. 'Did you want anything else?' she said quietly. 'If not, I'd rather be alone. If you're already in bed when I come in, I'll try not to disturb you.'

She turned from him and continued walking towards the fence. He watched her go, a haze of amber light encircling her, then he went back into the house.

He pushed the door closed behind him, leaned back against it and stared ahead of him, frowning. Had he just been totally truthful with Ellen, or was there something about himself that he'd rather not see, rather not admit to her?

It was true that Oonagh had been at his side throughout the day. But he'd lied when he'd said that he couldn't get away from her. Of course he could've, but he'd chosen not to.

If he was brutally honest with himself, after the pity he'd seen in the eyes of the folks who'd looked first at Ellen and then at him, it had felt darned good to know that he was the envy of every man there because he was the one who was dancing with the beautiful Oonagh.

That was the truth of the matter. Bridget had started the day with a generosity of spirit, and then so had Ellen. But he had filled the rest of the day with the opposite.

He moved away from the door and sat down by the window, staring with unseeing eyes around the room.

And Ellen, too, would realise that he'd chosen not to walk away from Oonagh. She'd have seen from the moment that Oonagh sat down at their table, that she'd gone out of her way to monopolise his attention, and he had let her.

He put his head in his hands, and groaned. How he must have hurt Ellen. If only they could return to the start of the day, he'd do things so very differently.

But they couldn't. He had let Ellen down that day and so, too, had Oonagh. She must have known how much Ellen would need him by her side.

When Oonagh had been talking to Ellen after the sewing bee, she must have given her the impression that she genuinely liked her. If she hadn't, Ellen would never have been so relaxed that she'd told Oonagh that they'd grown closer.

Ellen had wanted a friend, and Oonagh had led her to believe that she was going to be that friend, but her actions had betrayed her. That day, her friendship for Ellen had been shown to be a shallow thing, something to be picked up, played with and dropped at will.

It would not be easy for Ellen to take steps towards a friendship with anyone else of a similar age to hers again.

And what about Niall? What must he have thought of Oonagh's behaviour?

He sat back in his chair. Thinking about it, why *had* Oonagh behaved towards him as she had?

He was a married man, and the only interest he'd shown in her was as a friend, not as a woman. If she'd wanted attention of a different kind, he'd have expected her to look to Niall. But Oonagh had decided to celebrate the Carey wedding with him, and had left Niall by himself.

But not by himself for the whole of the day.

He remembered the sharp stab of pain he'd felt when he'd looked across the hall and seen Niall standing next to Ellen, both of them laughing. He'd instantly stopped dancing and made a move to go over to them, wanting to come between them. Oonagh had tried to draw him back into the rhythm of the dance, but the mood had been broken. For the first time that day, he'd shrugged off her hand and had continued to walk across the hall to his wife.

That Ellen had been alone with Niall at the wedding hadn't been her fault; it had been his. It was going to be hard to make up for the hurt he'd caused her that day, but he was determined to do it.

He peered through the window pane, wondering if she was about to come in, but the dark shades of night threw back the pale contours of his face, and he couldn't see beyond the anguish in his reflected eyes.

He stood up. He couldn't go to bed and leave things as they were.

The kerosene lamp stood on a log behind her, a golden globe of light.

She leaned against the fence and stared ahead of her at the moon, which hovered low over the distant mountains, outlining the shadowy peaks with a pale, translucent light. All around her, the dark-purple hue of night deepened.

She sighed and drew her shawl more tightly around her shoulders.

'I've been sitting inside, waiting for you to come back in.' Connor's voice came from behind her.

Startled, she turned to look at him. He was standing amid the pool of lamplight, and she could see the misery in his eyes.

'I thought you'd have gone to bed by now,' she said.

'Well, as you see, I haven't.'

She turned back to the horizon. 'You need not wait up for me. The scent of pine is strong tonight and I'm enjoying the night air.'

'So I see.' He came up to the fence and stood

beside her, his arm resting against hers. 'I kind of reckoned you were planning to enjoy the night air till you could see that I'd gone to bed, so I thought I'd come out to you.' He paused. She sensed that he expected her to say something, but she stood there, silent. 'What are you thinking about?' he asked.

'Need I think about anything? Can't I just enjoy the beauty of the night?'

She moved her arm away from his, and continued to stare ahead in silence.

'Talk to me, Ellen,' he said quietly, after a few minutes. 'I can't make this right if you won't speak to me.'

'Maybe you can't make it right, whether I speak to you or not.'

'That's as may be, but you must let me try. I've done wrong. I know that. And I know it's not for the first time. And I regret it. Won't you tell me how I can make things better again between us?'

She started to say that nothing could do that, but she stopped. She suddenly knew that something could.

She turned to him. Moonlight traced the rugged planes of his face, the laughter lines around his eyes, his firm jaw, the cleft in his chin, his broad shoulders. Her eyes lingered on him, then she looked away. It would be easier not to be looking at him when she asked him what she had to ask.

If she was ever going to be able to put the day's events behind her, there was one thing she desperately needed to know. Until that moment, she hadn't known how much she needed an answer to the question that she hadn't dared put to him in all the time she'd been there, but now she knew.

'I need to ask you something, Connor,' she said quietly, staring ahead of her. 'And I need you to tell me the truth. I wasn't ever going to ask you, but I think maybe I have to. Please don't tell me what you think I want to hear. I want the truth, no matter what it is. If you truly want to make things better between us, you must promise me that, and you must be true to your promise.'

'I promise.' She heard puzzlement in his voice. 'You've gotten me real curious now,' he said. 'What is it you want to know?'

'I know it isn't my business and I shouldn't ask . . .'

'Whatever it is, it's bothering you, and that makes it my business.' He turned to her and rested his elbow on the bar of the fence. She felt his eyes on her profile, and she flinched involuntarily. 'What is it, Ellen?' he asked, his voice gentle.

'Why did Oonagh turn you down? And do you still care for her? After today . . .' She stopped abruptly and bit her lip.

'Turned me down?' His voice echoed hers. 'You're thinking that I'm pining after Oonagh? Who told you that she turned me down?'

She turned to face him. 'It's obvious. I can see that you care for her. Of course, you would – she's beautiful. And Bridget clearly wanted her to be your wife. That you didn't wed her means that she must have turned you down. And Niall as good as told me that. Oonagh, too. And I saw you with her today. I think you still care for her, and I wonder if you regret marrying me. I can live with the truth more easily than I can not knowing it. I thought I didn't need to know, but I do.'

He gave her a wry smile. 'Of course, there could be another reason why I didn't wed Oonagh?'

'Another reason?'

'A pretty obvious one, I would have thought.'

'What reason?'

'That I didn't ask her.'

Her heart jumped. 'You must've. She's beautiful.'

'I didn't ask her, Ellen.'

'You didn't?' She felt a bolt of surprise shoot through her. Her mouth fell slightly open. She put her fingers in front of her lips and stared at him.

'Nope,' he said slowly, shaking his head.

'But why not? She's lovely.'

'She's lovely outside, I'll admit. But not inside.'

'I don't understand.'

'I fell in love with Alice when I was eight. I've always loved her and she's always loved me. Everyone knew we'd wed as soon as we could, including Alice's best friend, Oonagh. One day, when we were about fifteen or sixteen, the three of us were out together and Alice became ill. We took her home, and then Oonagh and I set off in the direction of Liberty. We hadn't gone far when she suddenly stopped and said we were near one of Niall and Jeb's hideaways and she'd take me there, if I wanted. And she started talking and acting towards me in the way that a woman shouldn't.'

He paused. His eyes studied her face.

'I reckon I don't need to go into details. It's enough to say that I was pretty sure it wasn't the sagebrush blooming around the hideaway that she wanted to show me.'

'But she knew you loved her best friend! That's a terrible thing to do.'

'That's what I thought. But that wasn't the thing that really showed me what Oonagh was like as a person. After all, everyone has days when they do something they shouldn't, something they later regret,' he said, giving her a rueful glance, 'something they hope they can be forgiven for. Nope, it was after that, when Alice was better. The three of us would go out together as usual, and Oonagh was just as friendly towards Alice as she'd ever been. More so, in fact, even though she'd done her best to come between us.'

'But that's sly!'

He nodded. 'It showed me there were two sides to her. I could never wed someone I knew to be dishonourable like that, and I would never let such a person help me raise my daughter. Oonagh was very kind after Alice passed on. She helped Bridget and me through a terrible time, and I'm real grateful to her for that. But I'll never forget what she tried to do behind Alice's back, nor her false friendship for Alice, and I never for one moment considered asking her to be my wife.'

'But at the wedding . . .'

'At the wedding, I behaved badly, but it was not to do with any feelings I might have for Oonagh.' He ran his hand through his hair. She sensed his discomfort. 'I'm gonna tell you why, but you've gotta know first that I'm ashamed of myself.' He paused.

'Well?' she prompted.

'It was that I was enjoying knowing that all the men in the hall were looking at me with envy, me being with Oonagh. I said I'd be honest with you, Ellen, and I have been. I'm not proud of myself, and it won't ever happen again, I promise you.'

'I'm glad you told me, Conn. In a strange way, it makes me feel better about things.'

He stared at her, surprise in his eyes.

'I don't understand,' he said, his voice questioning. 'I thought you'd be real hurt and angry.'

'Of course I'm hurt, but maybe not as much as you feared. It's hard to explain, but I know what I look like, and I prefer it that you're honest about my appearance, and don't try to pretend that it doesn't matter, because it does.'

He opened his mouth to speak, but she reached out and pressed her fingers to his lips, and stopped him.

'I don't blame you for feeling as any man would feel when approached by Oonagh. Whatever you might know about her as a person, she's a beautiful woman, and other people will see only that beauty. They don't know her as you do, so of course they'll envy you. And they'll pity you when they look at me with my damaged face. I don't criticise you for wanting to be near her at times, just to enjoy looking at her.'

He took her hand from his lips and held it. 'Because the accident damaged your face, Ellen, you think always of the way you look, and you put much importance on the way other women look. Too much importance, to my mind. I reckon there are different kinds of beauty,' he said slowly. 'I've been thinking for a while now that you're one of the most beautiful women in Liberty.'

She felt a lump come to her throat. She shook her head and looked away. 'Please don't talk like that. It makes me feel uncomfortable.'

'I'm saying only what I feel,' he said quietly. 'And I'm also feeling that it's late now, and that it's time that I went to bed with the woman I'm glad is my wife.'

His gaze was warm on the side of her cold face, and she turned back to him.

'Before we go to bed, I have something else to ask you, Conn,' she said. Her voice was shaking, she realised.

She took a deep breath to steady herself. 'Am I right in thinking that I go to the doctor in Liberty if I believe I'm with child?'

'Stop, Pa. It's Martha! She's with her folks,' Bridget cried from up on the wagon between Ellen and Connor. 'Let me get down. I wanna go in with Martha.'

'Careful, Bridget,' Connor said as she started to stand up. He drew the wagon to a halt. 'You girls will be able to learn even better today as neither of you has had to walk to school.' He glanced across at the Carey wagon. 'I wonder what Abigail and Elijah are doing in town on a Monday.'

'They left things from the wedding at the school 'cos they couldn't take everything home with them. I 'spect they're gonna collect them today,' Bridget said impatiently. 'Martha told me. Now can I get down?'

'I reckon you've forgotten something, young lady.'

'Please.'

'That's better. Mind you don't kick Ellen as you get down.'

Bridget glanced curiously at Ellen, then looked back at her father. 'Why's Ellen come into town with you?'

'I'll tell you now if you want, but it's a long story and Martha will have gone into school way before I've finished.'

Bridget looked across at Martha, who'd gotten down from the wagon and was hopping up and down, waiting for Bridget to join her. 'You can tell me tonight, can't you?' she said, and she waved at Martha. Then she clambered past Ellen and jumped to the ground.

Ellen leaned across the seat and handed down her school bag and lunch pail.

'If you're going to Massie's, Pa,' Bridget called up, 'will you get me a new slate pencil, please? My old one's almost worn out.' Then she ran off to join Martha.

'Bridget! Come here, would you, honey,' they heard Abigail Carey call, and they saw Bridget go over to the Carey wagon. Abigail called something down to her.

Connor shook the reins and started to walk the horses forward.

'Wait, Pa!' Bridget shouted, and she ran back to the wagon. 'Martha's ma and pa are gonna pick us up tonight. They're gonna be in town all day.'

'You lucky gals,' he said, smiling down at her. 'We'll see you a little earlier this evening, then.'

'Come on, Bridget. We'll be late and Miss Quinn will tell us off,' Martha said impatiently, and she turned and ran towards the school. Bridget waved up at the wagon and ran off after Martha.

Abigail Carey smiled across at Connor and Ellen.

Elijah touched the brim of his felt hat, turned the horses around and headed their wagon into town.

Connor turned to Ellen and smiled broadly at her. 'And now for the doctor,' he said, his voice filled with excitement, and he urged the horses forward.

Hand in hand, they walked out of the doctor's office, each of them beaming, and found themselves face to face with Abigail Carey. She glanced towards the office door behind them, then her eyes went from one face to another and she broke out into a wide smile.

'Is it what I'm thinking it is?' she asked, clutching Ellen's hand. 'I'd be so happy. We all would.'

Ellen glanced at Conn. He smiled back at her. She nodded at Abigail and Abigail threw her arms around her in a hug.

'I'm real happy for you,' she said, and Ellen saw that her eyes were glistening.

'We can't take it in yet,' Connor said. 'Ellen told me her suspicions on the night of the wedding. What a moment that was! I can't tell you how it made me feel. And now to know for sure . . .' His voice caught.

'It was a lovely wedding,' Ellen said quickly. 'Hannah looked beautiful. Her dress was clearly made by a skilled needlewoman. Was that you?'

'No,' Abigail said, shaking her head. 'It was made by Hannah herself. She's very good with the needle. Always has been. That's what I'm in town

317

for, among other things. Hannah's gonna make the curtains for her ranch and she couldn't decide on the material. She's now made up her mind, and I told her I'd pick the material up when I collected the dishes left over from the wedding. So you thought it went well, did you?'

'I sure did. And Connor, too. There can't have been anyone who didn't have a good time.'

Connor glanced quickly at her, and squeezed her hand.

'Well, I reckon I oughta get on now. Lots to do, and I won't get it done if I stand here talking, pleasant though it is. And I'll be seeing you soon, anyway, at that Thanksgiving Dinner you've planned.'

'I'm looking forward to it,' Ellen said.

'Good day to you both,' Abigail said. She started to move away, then paused. 'Remember, we're giving Bridget a lift for part of the way home tonight,' she added, and she moved off briskly in the direction of the livery stable.

Connor stared after her, then turned back to Ellen, his eyes suddenly anxious.

'Maybe we shouldn't have said anything yet. It's not yet three months. Just in case . . .' He stopped abruptly.

'In case things go wrong, like with Alice. You can say the words, Conn. We both know it can happen.'

'And so will Bridget. She watched her mother suffer several times. Sure she was very young, but she'll remember it, and we don't want her to fear for you sooner than necessary. It'll be your early Thanksgiving Dinner in two weeks. I think we shouldn't tell her till after that.' He paused. 'But maybe having the neighbours over will be too much for you now. You need to rest as much as possible.'

'It won't be too much,' she said hastily. 'I've already started preparing the food. They've all made me real welcome, and I want us to celebrate my first Thanksgiving here with them. They obviously can't leave their homes in November, with the risk that snow or a sudden blizzard could keep them from getting back to their animals, so making Thanksgiving in October is a good idea, and they think so, too.'

'Well, if you're sure it won't be too much.' He sounded uncertain.

'Bridget will help me,' she added. 'I promise I won't overdo things, Conn.' She put her hand on her stomach and gave him a reassuring smile.

He looked down at her hand, then back at her face, and he, too, smiled.

'You must let Bridget do the evening milking from now on,' Connor said, coming into the barn and seeing Ellen on the low milking stool, her shoulders pressed against the cow at whose udders she was tugging. 'The cows will soon get used to being done a little later than you've been doing them. I'll tell Bridget tonight.'

319

She finished milking the cow, pushed back her stool and looked around at Connor.

'The milking was one of the chores you insisted that Bridget give up when she started school. I know she helps out at times, but if you make it a regular thing from now on, she'll wonder why. She's smart and she'll soon work it out. Wait until after our Thanksgiving, Conn.' She bent down for the pail of milk beneath the cow.

He put his hand on her shoulder and stopped her. 'I don't want you doing too much,' he said, reaching down for the pail and lifting it up.

She stood up and put her hand gently on his arm. 'I want this baby as much as you do. After the accident, I thought I'd never have a child of my own, that no one would look at me again, but they did, and this is the result.' She ran her hand lightly across her stomach. 'I know Alice lost several babies, and I know she worked very hard. But that may not be why she lost them. Sometimes women lose babies for no good reason. I promise I'll stop if I feel I'm doing myself a harm, but I want to do my chores for as long as I can. Bridget shouldn't be given too much to do at the end of her school day. She has lessons to learn.'

He nodded. 'I guess you're right.' He turned to leave with the milk. 'I'll take this to the kitchen, and then go across to the bunkhouse to see if Aaron's finished banking dirt around the foundations. I'll come back with him and do the animals' feed this evening.'

'And what I said about having a child of my own, Conn,' she said quickly. He paused. 'I've grown to love Bridget and nothing will change that. It's not something I can say to her – and she wouldn't believe me if I did – but I'll make sure that she always knows inside her that I love her as if she was mine.'

He gave her a broad smile. 'I'm sure she will. Just as having a son won't make her mean any less to me.'

'Or a daughter. We don't yet know which it'll be.' Her face clouded with sudden anxiety, and she took a step towards him. 'I know you love Bridget. And I know you now want a son very much. But if you have another daughter, you will love her, too, won't you? You won't be too disappointed?'

'I *will* be disappointed, just as I was when I first saw Bridget. But that feeling will pass as quickly as it did with Bridget, and I'll love her just as much as I would have a son. And I'll hope that she looks like you.'

She threw back her head and laughed. 'I'm not about to put her – if it *is* a her – in the way of a horse, so she will never look very like me.'

He gave her a slow, lazy smile. 'Yup,' he said. 'I chose well for the mother of my future children.' And he turned and went out of West Barn.

She stood still and stared after him. Then she raised her hands to her face and found that her cheeks were wet.

★   ★   ★

'Ellen's been feelin' a bit tired these last few days. I'm gonna take some of her chores from her, if I can. Maybe get Bridget to do a little more,' Connor said as he and Aaron walked past the corrals towards West Barn. 'Here, if you give me one of those sacks, I'll start on the stalls on the left. You do the right.'

They went into the barn. Aaron handed one of the two sacks he'd been carrying to Connor, went to the far end of the barn and started tipping pieces of carrot and potato into the cows' feed box. Then he suddenly stopped and looked up.

'I think we've got a visitor, Conn,' he shouted. He dropped the sack, ran to the back entrance to the barn, stood still and listened.

'Someone's comin', boss,' he shouted into the barn to Connor. 'It's a horse not a wagon, so it won't be anyone bringin' Bridget. They sure are movin' fast.' He ran out of the barn, across to the fence and stared up the track. 'It's only one horse,' he called over his shoulder to Connor, who was running up behind him.

Conn stopped in his tracks. 'Only one that we can see. There could be more behind him. I'll get my gun. It's not the time of day for visitors.'

He turned and started to run back through the barn.

'I'll wait in the barn to catch sight of the rider,' Aaron called after him.

Connor waved his hand in agreement and continued running. He ran past Ellen, who was

322

approaching the kitchen with a pile of firewood in her arms, threw the kitchen door open, ran in and grabbed his gun.

'It's only Elijah Carey,' he heard Aaron call. 'I'll open the gate.'

Ellen followed Connor quickly into the kitchen and dropped the wood in the basket by the stove, anxiety on her face.

'No need to worry. I expect you heard Aaron – it's just Elijah,' Connor told her, putting down the gun. 'I'll go and see what he wants.'

He went through the house and out the front door just as Aaron was pulling the gate open. His head still down, Elijah rode straight through. Aaron swung the gate shut and followed Elijah across the yard.

Elijah pulled hard on his horse's reins, brought it to a stop and climbed down from the saddle.

Connor went forward to take the reins from him, his face anxious. 'There's nothing wrong is there, Elijah?' he asked as he led the horse to a pail of water. He ran his hand along the horse's back as it dipped its head to drink. 'We don't often see you ride like that. There's sweat dripping from your horse's belly. Why aren't you with Abigail?'

Ellen hurried out of the house. 'Why, Elijah. What a surprise,' she said with a welcoming smile.

Panting heavily, he touched the brim of his hat to her.

'I got bad news, Conn,' he said, drawing his

breath with difficulty. 'Real bad news. Bridget's been bitten by a rattler. She's at the doc's.'

'A rattler!' Aaron exclaimed. 'Is she bad?'

'How come?' Conn asked. 'No, don't tell me now. Tell me later. Saddle up for me, Aaron.'

'I'll ride with you,' Ellen said quickly. She started to undo her apron.

'No, you must stay here.'

'But I want to go with you.'

'You're not to ride.'

'Then I'll follow on the wagon. I'll bring some of Bridget's things in case she has to stay the night at the doctor's. And if she doesn't, we'll need the wagon to bring her home.'

He stared at her for a moment, then nodded. 'OK, but I don't like it. You must go carefully. I'll hurry Aaron along.'

He turned and started to walk quickly along the front of his house just as Aaron rounded the corner with his horse. He took the reins from him. 'Ellen's gonna take the wagon,' he said. He checked the cinch, then he swung himself up into the saddle. 'Harness the horses for her, will you? I must get off. And you'd better check that there's nothing's cooking.'

'Sure thing, Conn.'

He trotted his horse across to Ellen and looked down at her. 'I wish I could send Aaron with you, but I can't. He's the only man here today and I need him to watch the place. There's nothing you can do for Bridget – Doc will do what has to be done – so you be sure to drive slowly.'

'I will.'

'I'll ride beside you, Conn,' Elijah said. He pushed the pail away from his horse and climbed back into the saddle. 'Abigail and Martha are at the doc's with Bridget, and I've left the wagon there. I wanna see how the gal's doing, anyway.'

Ellen took a step forward and looked up at Elijah, concern written across her face. 'Martha wasn't bitten, too, was she?'

'No, ma'am. Just Bridget.'

'Let's go then,' Connor said.

Spurring their horses into a canter, they rode through the open gate, turned on to the dusty track and broke into a gallop.

# Chapter 27

Ellen leaned forward on the wooden bench in the doctor's front room, her eyes on the closed door opposite her, straining to listen to what was going on inside the office. She heard the sound of movement and conversation, and occasionally she heard Conn's voice above that of the doctor, but it was indistinct and she couldn't make out what anyone was saying.

She turned her head slightly and glanced down at Martha, who was sitting between her parents. Martha's cheeks were wet with tears and her eyes red and swollen.

'How did it happen, Martha? Do you feel able to tell me?' she asked gently.

Martha looked up at her, her eyes full of fear and misery. She sniffed, and wiped her nose with the back of her hand. 'It wasn't my fault.'

'No one's blaming you, Martha,' Abigail said gently. 'Are they, Mrs Maguire?'

'Of course they're not.' She smiled reassuringly at Martha.

'Just tell Mrs Maguire what happened. She'll want to know, like I would if you'd been hurt.'

Martha wiped her cheeks with the cuff of her sleeve. 'I was sitting on the wagon with Ma and Pa, waitin' for Bridget to come out of school. Suddenly she ran out. Real angry she looked, and like she was crying. She knew Pa was going to collect us both, but she didn't come over to us. We kept calling her. We *did* try.'

'Don't distress yourself, Martha,' Ellen said hastily. 'Whatever happened, I'm sure you're not in any way to blame for this. So where did Bridget go, if not to you?'

'Straight around the back of the school, and out into the long grass. She knows we're not allowed to go there 'cos there might be snakes there. I called for her to come back, but she just ran into the grass without stoppin'. Pa and I got down as fast as we could and we ran after her, but she was going real fast. Miss Quinn ran after her, too, and she kept shouting for her to stop.'

'Miss Quinn was there, too?'

'She came out of the school just after Bridget,' Abigail told Ellen. 'But I don't know why Bridget would stay after everyone else had gone. Do you know what held her up, honey?'

Martha nodded. 'Miss Quinn came over to us at afternoon recess and asked her to stay behind after school. Bridget thought she might've done something naughty, but she couldn't think what. But I guess Miss Quinn must've been real angry with her about something to make her run off like that. I wish she hadn't.' Her eyes filled again with tears.

Elijah put his arm around his daughter. 'It's like Martha said, Miss Quinn came running out of the schoolhouse right after Bridget. But Bridget just kept running. She'd picked up a stick from somewhere and she was hittin' out from side to side, like she was real mad. I guess she frightened the rattler, maybe even stood on it. She suddenly stood still and screamed that she'd been bitten, then she turned and started to run towards us. They know not to run if they get bitten, but I guess she forgot. I yelled at Martha to get back, and to Bridget to stand still, and I ran up to her, picked her up and carried her back to the schoolroom.'

'Where was she bitten?'

'Her leg, thankfully. I could keep the place she was bitten lower than her heart.'

'Are you sure it was a rattler?'

'It must have been a prairie rattler. You don't get faded rattlers in these parts – that one's a real dangerous rattler.'

'How dangerous is the prairie rattler?'

'Nothin' for an adult to worry too much about, but with a child, you never know. Depends on whether Bridget actually stepped on it, or hit it with her stick, or just frightened it. Unless you're really pestering the snake, it's only going to slap at you. I'm hoping it was more of a quick warning bite. Those only come with a small amount of venom. A snake would rather save its juice for something it can eat.'

'There were snakes on the farm owned by

Robert's parents, but not many poisonous ones, and no one was bitten while I was there. In fact, I never saw more than a couple in the year I was there. Did you try to suck the poison out?'

'We sure didn't. It don't do any good, and there's a mighty strong risk of the poison getting into the person who does the suckin'. No, ma'am, the leg was swelling fast and changing colour so we just wound my bandanna around her leg above the bite, and got her to the doctor as quick as we could. In case you ever need to know, you must be real careful not to stop the blood from flowing. It would do more damage than the poison.' He held up three fingers. 'You gotta be able to fit two or three fingers under any bandage. Best thing is to get to the doctor, though.'

'How lucky you were there. Miss Quinn would never have been able to get her to the doctor as quickly on her own.'

'Yup, I guess it was.'

The voices in the back room sounded loud behind the door. All four turned instantly towards the door. It opened, and Connor and the doctor came into the front room.

She saw that Connor's face was strained and drawn, and she stood up and took a couple of steps towards him.

'How is she?'

'She'll be fine, Mrs Maguire,' the doctor said. 'She's a strong girl, and a lucky one. I don't reckon there was much venom in the bite, and she should get over its effects quite quickly. I reckon I've cut enough away to get out all the poison. The skin around the bite had dried up and was already flaking off, which helped us get the right place. I've given her some Echinacea, and that'll help with any venom left in her, but the wound will need to be kept real clean or she could still lose the leg. She's in some pain, but that should soon pass.'

'Can we take her home now?' she asked.

'I guess there'd be no harm in that. There's nothin' else I can do for her. It's just a matter of letting time and Echinacea take their course.'

'What made her so angry?' Martha asked.

Elijah put his hand on her shoulder. 'That's not for you to ask,' he said. 'No doubt Bridget will tell you when she wants to. And since it looks like she's gonna be fine, I reckon we'll get off home now. Abigail will come around in the morning and see how things are with Bridget, won't you, Abigail?'

'Of course I will.'

Martha looked up at her father. 'Can I go and see Bridget with Ma tomorrow?'

'You've got school tomorrow,' Abigail cut in.

Elijah shook his head. 'Like your ma said, it's a school day, and you'll go to school like you always do. And Bridget will need to rest a while. Maybe you can see her at the end of the week, if her pa thinks she's well enough.'

Connor smiled down at her. 'She'll be ready to see you by then, I'm sure.'

'We'll be off now, Conn,' Elijah said. 'She's a strong gal, so don't you worry.'

'I'm mighty obliged to you for coming as fast as you did, Elijah, and for gettin' Bridget to the doctor so quickly.' He looked down at Martha. 'And I'm real grateful to you for all you did, Martha. You were a good friend to Bridget, rushing out into the grass like that to try and stop her. I'll be going into the school to see Miss Quinn tomorrow, and I'll tell you then how Bridget's getting on.'

'Night then, Conn. Doc. Miss Ellen.' He inclined his head to them, and he and Abigail took Martha by the hand, and they went out.

Ellen glanced towards the back room. 'Is Oonagh still in there with Bridget?'

The doctor shook his head. 'She left just after they set Bridget down. I'm guessin' that she and Bridget didn't see eye to eye about something. Whatever it was, it made Bridget mighty upset when she saw Oonagh by the bed. She got herself riled up all over again, and had trouble breathing. We didn't have to ask Oonagh to leave. She could see the harm she was doing by bein' there, and she'd gone before Conn got here. Isn't that right, Conn?'

He nodded, his face grim. 'It sure is. I'll be speaking to Oonagh in the morning. I wanna find out what went on. But it's time I took Bridget home.' He glanced down at Ellen. 'Ellen, too,' he added. 'She looks quite pale.'

The doctor glanced at Ellen. 'Didn't expect to see you twice in one day,' he said with a smile. 'Conn's right. You *do* look pale. You need to go carefully.'

'I feel a little tired. That's all. The wagon's outside and there are some blankets in it, Conn,' she added.

Connor moved towards the door. 'I'll get them. We'll keep Bridget real warm on the journey back.'

'You can leave her here tonight, if you want. You said you're coming in tomorrow, so you could collect her then.'

'Thanks, Doc, but no. Home is where she'll wanna be when she wakes up in the morning.'

'I expect you're right. I'll give you some Echinacea to take back with you. When you've seen Oonagh tomorrow, would you stop by and have a word with me? There's something I want to talk to you about.'

Connor turned sharply and stared at the doctor. Ellen saw alarm spring to his eyes.

'It's nothin' to do with Bridget. She'll be fine. Or Mrs Maguire.' The doctor smiled at Ellen. 'She's fine, too. No, it's something else, something I've been meanin' to talk to you about. Should've done so sooner.'

Connor frowned slightly. 'Now you've gotten me wonderin'. OK, I'll come over as soon as I've spoken to Oonagh. I can leave off seeing Niall till later. He'll want to know what's happened, maybe come down to the ranch to see her, and I want him to know he can do so. We'll be off now. If you give Ellen the medicine for Bridget, I'll get the covers.'

The next morning, Ellen went quietly into Bridget's room, carrying a tray with a plate of biscuits and eggs and a mug of sweet milk. She saw that Bridget's eyes were closed, and hesitated. Standing for a moment at the side of the bed, holding the tray, she stared down at her. Then she placed the tray on the low table next to the bed, and went and sat on the chair in the corner of the room.

Bridget opened her eyes. 'I heard you come in.'

'I rather thought you did.' Ellen smiled and moved to sit on the edge of the bed. 'How are you feeling this morning?'

Bridget pulled the quilt up to her chin and stared at the ceiling.

'I've brought you your breakfast. You didn't have dinner last night, so you must be hungry by now.'

Silence.

Ellen waited for a few minutes. 'Does your leg hurt?'

No answer.

'You spoke to me a moment ago so I know you're able to speak. Are you in pain? Are you angry about something I've done? Is that it? If so, you must tell me what it is. I can't help you if I don't know what I've done to upset you.'

Bridget turned on to her side, her back to Ellen.

Ellen moved closer to her and leaned over her.

333

'Please, Bridget,' she said gently. 'Tell me what's made you so unhappy that you ignored everything you've been told about safety. I'd like to help you if I can.'

Bridget pulled the quilt over her head, and Ellen heard muffled sobs coming from beneath it.

'I wish I knew what to say that would help.' She waited quietly for a few minutes, listening to Bridget cry, then she stood up. 'I'll leave you to eat your breakfast. I'll stay in the house all morning so you can call for me if you need anything or if you want to talk.' She stepped away from the bed, then impulsively turned back, pulled the quilt away from the top of Bridget's face, kissed her lightly on the side of her forehead, and replaced the quilt. 'We love you, Bridget, and we want to help you. I hope you'll let us.' She straightened up and started to move away.

'Where's Pa?' Ellen heard her ask from beneath the quilt.

'He's gone into town. He went on the horse.'

Bridget pulled the quilt down from her face, turned and stared up at Ellen. 'You don't love me. You'll love the baby and you won't want me. I want to live with Uncle Niall.'

'Oh, Bridget, honey. Of course we'll always love you.' She bent down and tried to take Bridget's hand, but Bridget pulled it away.

'You've got a baby in your belly, haven't you?' she snapped, her voice accusing. 'I know you have – Miss Quinn told me. She kept on telling me you'd still want me, even if the baby was a boy, but I could tell she was sorry for me. She kept saying I wouldn't be in the way, but I know I will. That's why you didn't tell me.'

'I only told your pa a couple of days ago. We didn't even know for certain till I saw the doctor yesterday. It's why we went into town. I don't know how Miss Quinn found out. I'm sure your pa didn't tell her. He couldn't have, in fact, as we were together all of the time. We were going to tell you in two or three weeks, when the difficult time had passed. We didn't want to worry you. I don't know how she can have found out. I'm real sorry you had to hear it from someone else.'

'Then you shouldn't have told anyone.'

'But we didn't. We decided . . .' She stopped short and put her hand to her mouth. 'Yes, we did, but we didn't mean to. We met Martha's ma as we were leaving the doctor's office, and she guessed why we'd been there. But she was going to be in town all day, so I don't see how Miss Quinn would have learned of it before school got out.'

'I saw Mrs Carey talkin' to Miss Quinn when she brought Martha's lunch pail into school. Martha left it in the wagon by mistake.'

'So that's what happened! Well, we didn't think to ask Mrs Carey not to tell anyone as we got into talking about the wedding.'

Ellen sat down on the side of the bed, close to Bridget.

'The baby's not going to change anything. Your pa loves you, Bridget, and he always will. The fact that he'd like a son doesn't alter the way he feels about you, and it never will. He can love more than one person. He loved both your ma and you, didn't he?'

Bridget twisted the corner of the quilt. 'I guess. But now that you're gonna have a baby . . .'

'You and your ma will still be important to him. Your pa will never love anyone else like he loved your ma. I know that, Bridget. But I'd like to think he feels comfortable with me. He works hard, and he needs a home where he can relax when his day's work is done. I don't ask for more from him than that he's content to sit at the table with me at night.'

Bridget stared up at her. She bit her lip.

'Ma died because of the babies. You might die, too.'

Ellen smiled at her. 'I'll try not to,' she said lightly, and she stood up. 'Now eat your breakfast. I fear that the eggs are already cold. Here, let me help you to sit up.' She slid her hands under Bridget's arms and raised her into a sitting position. Releasing her, she moved back.

Bridget reached out and caught her arm. She stared up at Ellen. 'I don't want you to die.'

Her vision blurring, she gazed down at Bridget. 'And I don't want me to die either. I'm very happy living with you and your pa.'

'You must try very hard not to die. Pa likes sitting with you. I can tell he does.'

Ellen bent down and kissed her on the top of the head. 'Enough talking,' she said, her voice shaking slightly. 'You must eat your breakfast.' She smiled down at her and ran her finger down Bridget's cheek.

Bridget smiled back.

She turned and walked to the door.

'Ellen,' she heard Bridget call after her.

She looked back at Bridget. Bridget had turned her head and was staring at her. Ellen took a step towards her. 'What is it? Do you need something?'

'It's funny, but when I look at you now, I never notice that mark on your face.'

# CHAPTER 28

Connor went straight to the schoolroom when he reached town, getting there before any of the children, as he'd known he would.

Oonagh was in the corner of the room, lighting the wood in the potbelly stove. She glanced up at him, then carried on with what she was doing.

He sat down on one of the tables and stared at her. 'You're obviously not the least bit surprised to see me.'

She raised an eyebrow in his direction. 'Of course I'm not. I know you, Conn. I knew you'd be here as soon as you could get here after sunup.' She slid the iron lid back on to the stove, went across to her desk and sat down. 'How's Bridget?'

'She's doing fine. What I want to know is why any of it happened.'

'She ran into the long grass, which she's been told not to do. That's what happened.'

'And what made her so mad that she'd do a dangerous thing like that? What did you say to her, Oonagh?'

'I mentioned the baby. I assumed you'd have already told her.'

338

'How did you know about the baby? I didn't tell you. You're the last person I would've told after what you said to Bridget the day before the Carey wedding, and the way you said it.'

'Abigail told me. Martha forgot her lunch pail and Abigail brought it into school. She'd met you outside the doctor's office, she said, and she was still very excited about your good news. As everyone will be. We all know how much you want another child.' She paused. 'I wasn't to know that you hadn't already told Bridget. How could I know that?'

'By the fact that Bridget didn't mention it, didn't in any way seem different from the way she usually seemed. If Bridget had been told, you'd have known. And I reckon you know that. And a moment's thought would have made you realise that we wouldn't want Bridget to be worried sooner than necessary. You saw the way she was when Alice kept on losing her babies. How did you think she'd feel when she learnt that Ellen was carrying a child? This is the second time you've deliberately hurt Bridget. Why?'

Oonagh leaned forward and stared at Connor, her violet eyes full of remorse. 'I didn't think, Connor. That's the truth. None of this was deliberate. I completely forgot that Bridget might fear for Ellen, even though she doesn't like her. It's just that my pleasure at your news blacked out all other thoughts, and I told her on the spur of the moment how thrilled I was.'

'Hardly the spur of the moment,' he said acidly. 'Abigail told you before the end of the lunch recess. You told Bridget at the end of the day. You planned the time and the way in which you'd tell her, and I'm guessing that you managed to make her think we'd stop loving her as soon as the baby arrived.'

She started to stand up. 'It was a thoughtless error on my part . . .'

'Don't waste your breath.' He stood up. 'Between you and Niall, you seem to be making Bridget one unhappy little girl. Both of you say that you're fond of her, but giving pain is a strange way of showing affection. I'm not surprised about Niall. Bridget's no more than a temporary distraction for him – something new, something different. In truth, he hardly knows her and he's never really thought about anyone but himself. But you, Oonagh. You're a woman. You're meant to have a woman's feelings. Where were those feelings when you decided to hurt my daughter?'

'Connor, I'm so sorry.'

'I don't wanna hear it. The rattler's not the only one that's full of venom. I've said my say, and now I'm gonna see the doc, and then I'm going home to my family. But just to bring you completely up-to-date with my family situation, I reckon you're wrong about Bridget not liking Ellen. Very wrong.'

He turned and walked out.

★　　★　　★

'That's the heifers and calves taken care of. I'm sorry I was gone so much of the day that we didn't get this done sooner.' Connor shut the gate of the far corral.

'Well, they're done now,' Aaron said. He nodded towards the cows. 'It's good to see that so many of the mother cows are already carrying next year's calves. It's gonna be a good year next year. Babies all around, I reckon.' He gave Connor a knowing smile.

Connor grinned at him. 'I figured you'd work it out. Yup, you're right about next year. But as far as this year goes, I'm about to ride out to the ploughed fields and check that we've manured them all. I reckon we'll have snow within the month and we need to be ready to dig the first of it into the soil. Don't know what it is about the snow, but it sure helps the crops to grow.'

'Right, boss. While you do that, I'll fill in the outhouse pit and move the outhouse to a new spot. If there's time after that, I'll top up the wood in the bunkhouse.' He started to walk away, then turned around. 'I plumb forgot to ask. Did you find out what you wanted to know from Miss Oonagh and the doc when you went into town this morning? You said that the doc wanted to see you.'

'Yup. I'll tell you and Ellen later on at dinner. I wanna catch the last of the light.'

With a slight wave of his hand, Aaron turned and went towards the bunkhouse. Connor dropped the iron ring over the corral gate, went across to his horse and untethered it. He swung himself into the saddle and headed past the vegetable garden and out towards the fields.

His head bowed in thought as he rode, he ran over what he'd been told that morning. That Oonagh, whom he'd felt sure was genuinely fond of Bridget, could repeatedly hurt her, was something he still found hard to believe, despite what he'd known for years about Oonagh's character. She must have been so angry that he'd married Ellen, a woman with a damaged face, and not her, that she'd pretended friendship with them all while doing everything she could to keep Bridget from accepting Ellen.

He slowed his horse as he turned on to the fields, his eyes scanning the newly turned earth for any large patches that they might have missed when spreading out the manure.

It had been real bad luck, Abigail coming upon them as they'd been leaving the doctor's office. She wouldn't have known about Oonagh's mean streak and that it was important that Oonagh shouldn't be told. She would assume, as anyone would, that Oonagh would realise that he hadn't yet told Bridget, and that it was something that Bridget should hear from her father.

He rode to the end of the furthest field, his eyes on the ground, but the light was going and he realised that he'd have to leave checking the rest of the fields until the following day. He'd make an early start in the morning, and he'd come out with Aaron. They'd get through it more quickly that way. He turned the horse around and started slowly down a track that ran between two fields.

What Oonagh had done had been malicious and spiteful. But Bridget would recover, and with Ellen looking after her, she'd have nothing worse than a slight depression in her leg around the bite. No, Bridget's situation was no longer as worrying as what he'd heard from the doctor.

He hadn't known what to expect when he'd gone into the room behind the office and had sat down at the table with the doctor. He'd known only that it must be important. The doctor was a busy man, who wasn't given to wasting time in the daylight hours, and he wouldn't have asked to see Connor if it hadn't been something serious.

'I'm sorry to have to tell you this, Conn,' he'd begun.

'From the look on your face, I'm guessing this is about Niall,' Conn said.

The doctor nodded. 'There've been some more animals killed in the foothills leading up towards Sage Creek.'

Connor stopped midway in the act of lifting a glass to his lips. 'And that's to do with Niall?' He put the glass back on the table.

'I'm afeared, we're thinking it might be. For the last couple of months, there've been a few mean-lookin' strangers hanging around the saloon in the evening. If you'd been in Liberty at night, you would've seen them. Just a day or two at a time and then they're gone. A week or so later, they're back again. They keep themselves to themselves, sitting around a couple of tables, drinking, playing a few hands of poker, not causing any trouble, not mixin' with anyone except Niall. We're thinking they might be the hunters.'

'Is there any evidence against them, or is it just that they don't look so good and come and go?'

'Not as yet. I guess it's more of a hunch. A hunch that a few of us have gotten.'

'You think Niall knew them from before?'

'We asked him, and he said he did. He said he knew them from way back, but had been surprised to see them when they turned up in Liberty.'

'And you don't believe him, I take it?'

'Whether he already knew them or not isn't important. It's what he's doing with them now that matters. He often comes into town with them, and goes out with them. Niall's got lodgings in town, but we reckon the men are probably holed up in one of the discarded claims north west of Liberty. We think they're using that as a base for their criminal activities. It's hard to see why else they'd be hangin' around Liberty.'

Connor shrugged his shoulders. 'So Niall's not choosy about the company he keeps. It doesn't mean that he's out slaughtering animals for their hides. And nor that his friends are, no matter what they look like.'

'I agree. But it's a possibility that it *is* them, and

344

that Niall's involved.' He paused. 'One or two of the townsfolk have been wondering how Niall's got so much money to spend. There's work to be had, but he doesn't seem to be asking for any of it, yet he keeps spending.'

Connor stared at him, frowning. 'He does odd bits of work around the place, doesn't he? He's done stuff for Jack Massie, and in the livery stable, and I know he's done some bits of carpentry in the new buildings, and he mentioned something about hauling lumber.'

The doctor shook his head. 'The sheriff's been asking around. It's quite a time since he did any work for anyone in town. There's no way he's getting his money from any of the folk around here.'

Connor's shoulders slumped. He sat back in the chair and looked around the room. 'Well, I can't rightly say I haven't asked myself how he could be spending so much,' he said at last. 'Like I said, he told me he was working, but I didn't see any sign of it, and no one ever came up and mentioned that he was working for them, like folk often do.'

'You gave him some money, or so he said, didn't you?'

'Yup. It was probably enough to pay for his lodgings for a while, but not for all of the things he was spending money on.'

The doctor gave a slight shrug of his shoulders. 'Anyway, we thought you oughta know the way we were thinking.'

Conn stood up. 'I must get back and see how

Bridget's doing. I was gonna go and tell Niall about what happened to Bridget after I'd spoken to you, but I reckon I'll go straight back home. Oonagh will have told him anyway, or someone else in town will have. When you see him, maybe you'd tell him he's welcome to visit Bridget whenever it suits.'

'Of course I will.'

'Thanks for telling me about Niall. I appreciate it. I admit that there are things that don't seem to add up, but I'd need to hear some solid evidence before I believed that of my brother. I can't see him killin' animals. Nope, not Niall.'

And that's what he told himself all the way back to the homestead.

# CHAPTER 29

Still breathing heavily after the strenuous brushing down he'd given his horse, he dropped the bar across the doors of East Barn and leaned back against the door. His bare arms steamed in the chill evening air, and he rubbed them with his hands as he stared up at the darkening sky.

After years of studying the sky, trying to work out how late he dare leave the wheat and the corn before harvesting it, knowing that if he misjudged it, a single downpour of rain would be sufficient to ruin the whole crop, he'd gotten pretty good at being able to forecast what was coming and when, and he knew that Ellen's early Thanksgiving would be the last time that the neighbours would come to them that year. Well before the end of November, the land would be buried beneath a mantle of snow and they'd surely have had the first of the winter blizzards. No one would be able to visit again until the snow had melted, which might not be before the end of April, or even later.

He started to walk towards the house. By the time that spring came, Ellen would move with

347

difficulty, he thought. She'd have to be careful not to slip over. He must make sure that the paths around the house were free of ice at all times.

He glanced towards the kitchen and saw her pass in front of the window. He wasn't looking forward to telling her the town's suspicions about Niall, and nor Aaron, but he couldn't put it off any longer. Apart from one question from Aaron after he'd got back, they'd kept from asking anything, and had waited for him to feel like talking about it. However, it was unfair to keep them waiting much longer.

Thrusting his hands into his jeans pockets, he sped up his steps. As he reached the kitchen door, it opened. Ellen stood in the doorway.

'There you are,' she said with an anxious smile. 'I was coming to tell you that dinner was ready.'

'Let me wash my hands and I'll be there.' He put a bowl in the sink and started pumping water into it. Ellen brought a jug of hot water across to the sink and poured some into the cold water in the bowl. 'Thanks,' he said. He leaned over the bowl and immersed his arms to his elbows. 'How's Bridget doing?'

'Much better now, I'm happy to say.' She unhooked the drying cloth and stood next to him while he washed his hands and arms. 'The pain's not as bad.'

'That's good. Doc did real well. Elijah, too. There, I'm done.' He turned to her and reached out to take the cloth from her with his wet hand. With a laugh, she moved the cloth out of his reach, took hold of his outstretched hand and began to run the cloth along his bare skin, backwards and forwards, wiping away the droplets of water that shone silver in the hairs on the back of his forearm.

He gazed down at her hand. 'Ellen,' he said quietly.

He looked up into her face. Their eyes met, and locked. Then she smiled, released his first arm, leaned across in front of him and lifted his other arm. Slowly she slid the cloth the length of his arm and brought it back again.

'Ellen,' he repeated, his voice low.

She glanced up at him and laughed. 'I think you've already said that.'

'I guess I have,' he said, grinning at her. 'And you know what, I'm mighty tempted to say it again.'

'Then we'd better go back to the subject of Bridget,' she said, running the cloth between his fingers, first one finger, then the next, and the next. 'She was feeling so much better that she even suggested getting up for dinner, but I told her she had to stay in bed. She wasn't too pleased, and said so several times, but when I looked in on her a little while after that, she was fast asleep, and she was still asleep when I checked her a few moments ago. It'll do her good. There, your arms are dry now.'

He gave her a lazy grin. 'I'm mighty tempted to plunge them into the water again.'

Laughing she turned away, hung the drying towel

back on its hook, and went across to the stove. Glancing over her shoulder, she saw that he was still standing there, watching her. She half-smiled at him. The clear-blue eyes that gazed back at her were warm on her face.

'Aaron's already at the table,' she said.

'I guess I can take a hint.' He moved away from the sink and took a few steps towards the living room. As he passed close to her, he hesitated a moment, then went on through to the living room.

'I've roasted a sage chicken,' she said, following Connor into the living room shortly afterwards, a plate of food in her hands for each of the men. 'With mashed potato, peas and string beans.' She went back for her plate, returned with it and sat down opposite Connor. 'I've put a plate aside for Bridget. She'll be hungry when she wakes.'

Connor bit into the chicken. 'This is real good. I didn't realise how hungry I was.'

Aaron picked up his knife and fork, then put them down again. He stared at Connor. 'We can talk about the food if you want, Conn, or we can talk about what's really in our minds. Did you find out about Bridget, and what did Doc want?'

'So now you know everything I know,' Connor finished.

'Nothing can surprise me about Miss Oonagh,' Aaron said. 'I never did like that one. But I reckon they're wrong about Niall. I can believe a lot of not-so-good things about him, but he was real

350

good with cows, and I sure find it hard to believe that he'd stoop to killin' animals for a few lousy bucks.'

'That's the way I see it, too,' Connor said, nodding. 'Making a bad choice of friends is one thing, but slaughtering animals is another.'

'So what are they gonna do?' Aaron asked. 'Did Doc say?'

'He didn't volunteer anything and I didn't ask. I guess they'll keep an eye on him. There's nothing more they can really do. I told Doc to tell Niall that he was welcome to visit Bridget. If he comes, we might pick up something from him, but it's a long shot.'

Ellen got up, collected the empty plates and carried them out into the kitchen.

'I've made an apricot pie,' she said, returning to the living room a moment later, a dish in her hand.

Aaron stood up. 'I reckon I'll go back to the bunkhouse now.'

'Won't you have some pie before you go?' she asked, putting the dish on the table.

'I won't, thanks. There's still some cracks around the window frames, and I need to stuff more cloth into them. I've a good chance of finding the cracks tonight as there's a slight wind getting up. I'll soon feel where the cold air's comin' in.'

''Night, Aaron,' Conn said.

'Night, boss. Night, Ellen.' A moment later, the kitchen door clicked shut.

'I'll see if Bridget's awake,' Ellen said. She wiped

her hands on her apron and started towards the door to Bridget's room.

'Wait,' Connor called. 'Come and sit down. Bridget will make herself heard if she wants food. It's her leg the snake got, not her tongue.'

Ellen hesitated, then returned to the table and sat down again.

'You haven't said anything yet about what Doc said. Aaron spoke readily enough, but not you. What are your thoughts?'

'He's your brother. I obviously hope that everyone's suspicions are wrong.'

'Obviously,' Connor said dryly. 'And now that you've made the comment a dutiful wife should make, in your heart what do you think?'

She hesitated.

'Tell me, Ellen. I want to know. Be honest. I'd like to hear what you think.'

'I don't really know what I think. On the one hand, Niall says he cares about animals and that he cares about Bridget. And if his feelings are genuine, I think he'd be unlikely to join in with killing animals.'

'And on the other hand?'

'If something he shouldn't do presents itself, and he can make money from it, then I'm not so sure that Niall wouldn't do it. He's lazy and has loose morals. I'm remembering his suggestion to me that night you were out with William, and I'm remembering that, despite him saying several times how fond he was of Bridget, he deliberately put ideas into her mind that he knew would hurt her. And much as he was supposed to be keen on cows, he wasn't keen enough to make an effort to get another ranch. In fact, he's done very little with animals since he got back.'

'All that's true.'

'Also, his friends are the sort of men who play cards for money, who drink a lot, visit a type of woman. Such activities cost money, and the men who do them aren't always bothered about keeping to the right side of the law when they go after the money they need.' She paused. 'I'm sorry, Conn,' she said quietly, 'while I don't believe that he would have gone out of the way to look for something illegal, I *can* believe that if it landed in his path, he might get involved with it.'

He nodded slowly. 'That's fair enough. I'll just have to hope that you're wrong.'

'We'll both hope I'm wrong. I very much want him to be innocent in all of this.'

'I appreciate that. And now we should think about something more pleasant. Let's talk about our early Thanksgiving dinner. Are you still sure you wanna go ahead with this? They'd understand if you didn't. You'll be feeling more tired than usual. Alice always was. With every baby, she was sick at the start of the day.'

'I haven't felt sick at all, and I'm looking forward to having a Thanksgiving with visitors. When I was growing up in Omaha, the weather wasn't a problem in the same way as here, since people didn't have animals they had to get back to, and we always had a large gathering at home. I loved it. I'd like to do the same here.'

'We could ask them to bring food? They'd be happy to and it'd give you less work.'

'No,' she said smiling. 'It's my way of thanking them for welcoming me as they did. I'd like to do it by myself. If Bridget's better, though, she might be willing to help me.'

'Fair enough.' He looked curiously at her. 'You never talk about yourself, do you? You never say you have a headache, or you're tired, or you've hurt your hand or anything. You must say if you don't feel well, even if it's nothing to do with the baby.'

'I'll remember that. Thank you. The only difference is that maybe I'm a little more tired than I was.'

'You must stop and rest whenever you feel you need to. We've looked after ourselves for a year. With help, maybe, but it's been only Bridget and me, and Aaron, of course. We can do that again, with you helping us whenever you can. But only when you feel strong enough.'

'I won't take any chances. Thank you.'

'You mustn't thank me. You're having my child. I don't need thanks for wanting to take care of you like I should. Besides,' he added with a grin, 'I seem to recall saying that I never wanted to hear those words from you again.'

She laughed. 'So you did.'

He stared at her for a moment, then got up, moved to the chair closest to her and sat down. 'In the years after Alice gave me Bridget,' he said quietly, 'I watched her suffer as first one baby, then the next, died in her belly. And then, finally, I held her in my arms as she died, our baby lying dead beside her.' He took her hand. 'I want to help you, Ellen. You must let me.'

She nodded.

'I'm not thinking now about our baby. I'm thinking about you. Sure I want a baby, but you being all right when your time comes is more important to me than the baby.'

Surprise in her eyes, and disbelief, she looked up at him.

He pushed a strand of hair behind her ears, and his hand lingered there. His forehead slowly creased in amazement. 'And that's the truth,' he said, his voice full of wonder. 'But I guess I didn't know it till now.'

# CHAPTER 30

Ellen opened the kitchen door to go for the eggs. The morning air stung her face. Shivering, she glanced up at the sky. Leaden dawn had only just begun to fragment into merging bands of milky white.

She pulled her buffalo skin coat more tightly around her, and quietly shut the kitchen door behind her. Bridget hadn't yet appeared for breakfast and she didn't want to disturb her. She began to make her way quickly to the hen house, the crisp layer of frost that covered the ground crunching beneath her feet.

They'd need extra water with the Thomases and Careys coming for their Thanksgiving dinner, she thought as she passed the pump. She'd fill up some pails from the outside pump for that. The pump arm was sure to have thawed by the time she was ready for the water, or at least she hoped it would've. She had memories of chipping away at the ice-bound pump when she and Robert had lived on his parents' ranch. It had been one of the few tasks that she'd hated doing.

She reached the hen house and put her hand on the latch to open the door.

'Ellen!' she heard Bridget call, her voice coming from the direction of West Barn.

She stepped back in surprise and glanced across the empty corrals to the barn. Bridget was half-running towards her, carrying a large pail with both of her hands. Her movements were jerky as she tried not to slip on the frosty ground, and milk was spilling with her every step.

'Be careful now, Bridget,' she called, and she started to go quickly towards her.

Panting, Bridget came to a stop in front of Ellen. She bent down to put the pail on the ground, and remained bent over, breathing heavily.

'Mind you don't fall and find yourself back in bed so soon after leaving it. Martha's looking forward to seeing you today. It'd be a pity to be stuck in bed when she gets here.'

'I won't be.'

'I thought you were asleep. You must have been up very early to have done the milking already. It's kind of you to want to help like that, but you mustn't do too much too soon. You're still quite weak. And the mornings are cold now. You must stay inside the house and leave the milking for me. Just till you're stronger.'

'It's Daisy,' Bridget said, straightening up, fear on her face. 'Where's Aaron?'

Ellen glanced towards West Barn, then back at Bridget. 'What's wrong with her?'

'I don't know, but she's ill. She's not walking properly and I can tell she doesn't feel well. One of the reasons I did the cows this morning was to see her. I was worried about her since she didn't look right yesterday.'

Ellen put her arm around Bridget's shoulders. 'Poor Daisy. She's never been very strong. Motherless runt calves often aren't. She's done well to have lived this long. Lots of dogies don't.'

Bridget shrugged off her arm. 'Aaron will make her better. He always does,' she insisted. 'Where is he?'

'Behind East Barn with your pa. We're not the only ones who are up early. They've already started roasting our Thanksgiving pig. None of the neighbours will want to get back home late.'

'Uncle Niall would know what to do. I wish he was coming to lunch. He hasn't yet been to see me since I was bitten.'

'Your pa told him he was welcome to visit you any time. He'll have been busy, honey, or he would have come.'

Bridget nodded. 'The last time he came to the school to see me, he said he had lots of things to do.' She picked up the pail and clutched it to her chest. 'It doesn't matter anyway. Aaron will know what to do,' she said, and she stepped sideways to go around Ellen to East Barn.

'No, you don't,' Ellen said, stopping her. 'Go and put the milk – or what's left of it – in the kitchen. And then you'd better have a glass of buttermilk and some biscuits. You haven't had breakfast and you need something to keep you going. It won't help Daisy if you get ill all over again.'

'But Aaron must—'

'I'll go and get Aaron,' Ellen interrupted. 'When you've had something to eat, you can go very carefully back to Daisy. And I mean carefully. You don't want another accident, do you?'

'What's the matter with her, Aaron?' Bridget asked, staring anxiously at him as he walked the calf in a circle, then knelt down and ran his hands up and down her hind legs.

Ellen stood at the edge of the stall and watched him.

'She's certainly lame, and she's got a lot of small swellings on her hocks,' he said at last. 'I'll wager she's got 'em from lying on the hard floor, or possibly from fallin' down. She slips quite easily, I seen. You say Daisy's bin feedin' all right?'

'I'm sure she has or I'd have noticed.'

He ran his hand across the calf's stomach.

'She's not gaunt and her stomach doesn't bounce when she walks in the way that a sick cow's stomach bounces. Her head and ears aren't drooping, and she seems to be feedin' all right, so I reckon the swellings aren't a sign of illness.'

'That's good, isn't it?'

Standing up, he shook his head, and eyed the calf thoughtfully. 'I don't know. There's something about the way she looks that ain't right.'

'What're you gonna do?'

'Stop the swellings from getting larger. We don't want them to burst and become infected. I'm gonna wrap some rags around her legs to keep them dry and clean, and stop them from gettin' scratched.'

'And what should *I* do?' Bridget asked anxiously.

'You can clean her stall while I take care of her legs. When the stall's completely dry, we'll fill it up with a mass of fresh, dry straw. We must clean the floor of the barn, too, and make sure it's not slippery, just in case the swellings are because of her slippin' over. When the snow comes, we must make doubly sure that we wipe as much of it off our boots as we can before walking through the barn. We don't want any more cows with problems like this.'

'Will Daisy be OK? She will, won't she?' Bridget gazed up at Aaron with trust in her eyes.

He smiled down at her reassuringly. 'We'll both do our best to see that she is. We'll watch her closely, and hope she'll be back to normal in a few days' time.' He paused. 'She's done well to get this far, honey. Dogies don't usually last as long as she has. I can't promise you she'll get better, but we'll do our darndest.'

Bridget stared at him in alarm, then she put her arms around the calf's neck and hugged her. 'She's gonna get better. You are, Daisy. Yes, you are. I promise you.'

'You can start on the stall now, Bridget. Pile the

old straw into a heap. When you've done that, I'll take it outta here and give Daisy some fresh new straw.'

'How's she looking?' Connor asked, coming up to them.

Ellen stood aside and let Connor pass in front of her to the calf's stall.

'Aaron thinks she might have slipped over. She's gonna be all right, though,' Bridget said. She knelt down beside Daisy and scratched the small horns that were starting to harden in the soft hair around her ears.

Connor looked questioningly at Aaron.

'She got some swellings on her hind legs,' he said. 'It's nothin' we can't try to fix. But I wouldn't like to say that she's gonna be all right. You know what it's like with runts.'

Connor nodded. He looked down at Bridget. 'I know you want to stay with Daisy, but we don't want you catching a cold. You'll not be as strong as you were before the snake got you. I want you to go back to the house and stay in the warmth. Just for a few days.'

'But, Pa . . .'

'There's no "but, Pa" about it. That's what's gonna happen. Anyway, you've gotta get ready for when everyone gets here, and I reckon that Ellen could probably use some help with the meal.'

Tears started to roll down Bridget's cheeks. 'I've gotta clean her stall.'

Connor bent down to her. 'I'm sorry, honey, but

we must see that you're all right. That's the most important thing.'

She gave a loud sob. 'Daisy's important, too.'

'I've a suggestion, boss,' Aaron cut in. 'I reckon we could move Daisy to East Barn, just for a while. It could give her a better chance of pullin' through. It's drier there – has to be with all the food and grain we've got stored – and it's closer to the house so it'd be easier for Bridget to slip out for little bits of time to see how Daisy is. I could make a stall for Daisy just inside the entrance.'

Bridget's face lit up. 'Can we do that, Pa?'

'I don't see why not. I'll walk with you and Ellen back to the house, and then I'll clear a spot for Daisy. Thanks for that, Aaron. It was a mighty good thought.' He turned back to Bridget. 'When I've done the stall, Aaron will move Daisy, and then you can go out and see her for a few minutes.'

'Can't I stay and help Aaron, Pa? Daisy could be scared, bein' moved like that, but she wouldn't be scared if I was with her. You don't need me, do you, Ellen?'

'I guess I could manage without your help. But it's down to your pa what you do.'

'Please, Pa? Ellen doesn't need me. You heard her.'

'OK, I guess so. But as soon as we've got her into East Barn, you're to go back to the house and have a rest.'

She clapped her hands in glee and turned back to Aaron. 'Now what should I do?'

Connor turned to Ellen. 'Like I said, I'll walk back with you. We don't want you slipping over like Daisy did.'

She laughed. 'Are you likening me to a cow?'

He grinned at her, and held out his hand.

# CHAPTER 31

'I know it's not really Thanksgiving, and it's a Sunday, not a Thursday, but it's a better Thanksgiving than last year,' Bridget remarked, pushing back her empty plate. 'I like Martha being here. And everyone else, too,' she added quickly. 'Can I take Martha to see Daisy, Pa? We've both finished. I can't eat another thing. And you can't either, can you, Martha?'

Martha shook her head. 'I'd like to see Daisy,' she said. 'Can I, Pa?'

'I'm not surprised you're both full up, my dears,' Peggy said cheerfully. 'I don't think I've ever seen two girls eat as much as you before.' They giggled. She turned to Ellen, beaming. 'That sure was a fine meal, Ellen. I don't know as I've ever had a tastier chicken pie.'

Ellen burst out laughing. 'Thanks for trying to make me feel better. It needed more juice in it, I thought.'

'Peggy's right, it was a real fine pie, Ellen,' William said. 'With all you've had to do recently, I'm surprised you didn't just put the whole chicken on the table, still squawkin', and let us get on with it. And Conn's never done a better roasted pig.'

'That was Aaron's work, too,' Connor said.

'And difficult work it was, too, putting the pig on a spit across the fire, and turnin' it once in a while,' Aaron said with a grin.

Ellen pushed a dish of vegetables towards Peggy. 'There are some mashed potatoes and parsnips left, and a few candied carrots, if you've room for more. Or anyone else who wants some. Aaron, do you want some more?'

He shook his head. 'I reckon I've eaten my fill.'

'What about you, Elijah?' Ellen asked.

Elijah leaned back in his chair and patted his stomach. 'I'm thinkin' I'd better save some space for your pumpkin pie. Bridget told me she helped you with it.'

'That she did. She was a great help.' She smiled at Bridget.

'Is it all right if I take Martha to see Daisy now?' Bridget asked plaintively. 'Daisy's ill,' she added, looking around the table. 'We've put her in East Barn and Aaron's gonna make her better.'

'Aaron's gonna try,' Aaron said with a laugh. 'I can't promise I'll be able to do it.' Bridget's face fell. 'But I'm gonna do my best. When we've had our pie, I'm gonna go out and check her. Does that make you feel better?'

'Not as better as I'd feel if I went to see Daisy with Martha now. I can tell her you're coming. Can I, Pa? Please?'

Connor looked around the table. 'If no one objects? OK. Off you go.'

Bridget jumped down from her chair, with Martha following her. They ran into the bedroom where the coats were piled up, and a few minutes later, bundled up in their thick coats, they ran through the kitchen and out of the back door.

'It's good to see her looking so well now,' Abigail said, staring after her. 'She's a lucky girl that it wasn't worse.'

'And she's a lucky girl that you and Elijah were close by,' Conn said. 'We'll not forget that in a hurry. I doubt she'd have been going back to school tomorrow if Elijah hadn't acted as fast as he did.'

'And you're looking mighty fine, too, Ellen,' Abigail said with a smile. 'And after doing all this in your condition.'

Ellen flushed.

Peggy leaned over the table and squeezed her hand. 'Conn told us as soon as we got here, but I didn't like to say anything in case you wanted to keep it quiet till you were further along the way. He also told us that Bridget knew, but I felt it better not to mention it while she was around. I know I don't have to tell you, William and I couldn't be happier about the news.'

Connor smiled at Ellen, then his face became more serious. 'Now that the girls are out of the way, is there any news about the hunters? With Bridget being ill, and with a lot of catching up to do on the farm, I've not been into town since I spoke to the doctor. You'll know, of course, their suspicions about Niall?'

William and Elijah nodded.

'We found some more carcasses earlier in the week on the low slopes of the mountains, and there's been more stealin' of cattle,' Elijah said. 'It's a reason not to stay out late today. I don't have many cows, and I want to keep the ones I've got. I've left a man there, and there's no reason for anyone to think we'll be away from the ranch today, but all the same . . .'

'I guess it's lucky I never had more than a couple of cows,' William said. 'But there's other things folks can take, if they're so minded.'

'With snow most likely in a couple of weeks, I reckon there'll be little more killin' and stealin' before the spring,' Aaron said. 'There's a slight risk that they might strike once or twice while the snow's still thin on the ground, fallin' regularly enough to cover their tracks, but they'll soon have to hole up for the winter.'

'I reckon you're right,' William said, nodding. 'What about you, Conn? Are you and Aaron gonna be enough here if there's trouble?'

'We'll manage. We shedded the cattle a week ago. It means we'll have to feed them for longer than we might've, but it'll be a sight easier to keep an eye on them now that they're housed.'

'Talking of food,' Ellen said, looking around the table. 'If we're all ready, I'll clear the table and bring in the pies. I've also made a layer cake.' She stood up and started to move around the table, collecting the plates.

'You must let me . . .' Peggy said, rising from her seat. She stopped sharply at the sound of horses coming down the track.

'Hello the House!' they heard a voice call from the other side of the gate.

'I'd know that voice anywhere,' William said. 'It's the doc.'

Connor went to the window and glanced through it. 'Well heard, William,' he said 'It *is* the doc. He's in the buggy. Strange – it's kinda late in the day for him to visit.' He unhooked his jacket from next to the front door, put it on and went out.

There was a sudden clatter from the back of the house as the girls flung open the kitchen door and rushed through the kitchen into the living room. A column of cold air gusted into the room after them. Then the door clicked shut.

'There's someone coming,' Martha panted.

'We couldn't see who it was,' Bridget added. 'They were in a buggy. Maybe it's Miss Quinn.'

'It's the doctor,' Ellen said. 'Your pa's opening the gate. I'm sure they'll be coming in here in a minute. Take off your coats, both of you. He might have come to see how you're getting on, Bridget, though it's a bit late for such a visit.'

The buggy sounded outside the front door, and they heard the distant clang of the gate as Connor shut and barred it. Then they heard his footsteps as he returned to the house.

With Peggy and Abigail's help, Ellen hastily started clearing the table, piling the plates by the sink. The two girls returned from putting their coats in the bedroom and helped them remove the last of the dishes.

'What brings you out today, Doc?' they heard Connor say from in front of the house. 'Come in and have something to eat while you tell us.'

The front door opened and the doctor came into the room, rubbing his gloved hands together.

He nodded towards the table, and looked back at Connor. 'I saw the buggies outside and figured you'd got company. I'm mighty sorry to be interrupting you all, but I've got some news that Conn should have.' He took off his gloves, unwound his scarf and blew into his hands. 'It sure is cold today.'

'Let me get you something to eat,' Ellen said quickly.

'That's real kind of you, Mrs Maguire, but I mustn't stay long. I need to get back before the light goes. I'd take a mug of coffee, though.'

'Bridget, go and get the doctor a chair,' Ellen called as she went swiftly across to the kitchen. A moment later, she returned with a pot of coffee and a slice of apricot pie, which she put on the table in front of the doctor.

'Thank you, Mrs Maguire,' he said, smiling up at her. He turned to Bridget, who was hovering behind him. 'Lookin' at you, I'd say you've completely gotten over your snakebite, young lady. You're lookin' real pretty today in that green dress.'

'She sure is,' Peggy said, beaming at Bridget. 'It fair sets your hair off a treat, my dear.'

Blushing deeply, Bridget sat back down on her chair. 'Aaron's gonna look at Daisy in a minute,' she told the doctor. 'She's ill. Martha and I are gonna go with him. Will you come with us and see if you can make her better?' she asked, her voice hopeful.

'Daisy?' The doctor looked questioningly at Connor.

'A runt calf,' he said.

The doctor turned back to Bridget. 'Poor Daisy,' he said gravely. 'But I'm afeared I only know how to make people well.'

Bridget's face dropped.

'I'm sure she'll be fine, bein' looked after by you and Aaron,' the doctor added.

He picked up his mug, caught Connor's eye, glanced at Bridget, then put the mug to his lips.

'I've an idea, Bridget,' Connor said. 'You're obviously still worried about Daisy. Why don't the two of you put your coats back on and go with Aaron to look at her now? You can have your pie when you come back in. You might have some room for it by then.'

Bridget and Martha exchanged pleased looks, and jumped up. 'Thanks, Pa,' Bridget said.

They ran to the bedroom, and were back a moment later, once again wrapped up in their coats, each with a woollen scarf wound around their head and neck.

'Let's go, then,' Aaron said. He glanced at Connor and looked back at the girls. 'Maybe I'll check out the other cows, too, while we're outside. Do you think you girls could help me?'

They nodded vigorously, their eyes shining. He moved towards the kitchen, and they started to follow him.

'One moment, Martha,' Elijah called quickly, getting up. He threw a quick half-smile to Connor.

Martha stopped, turned around and stared anxiously up at him. 'I'm just going to see Daisy again. And the cows, too. I can, can't I?'

'I'm thinking we oughta be going home now, honey. We've got the cattle to think about. We've left them for long enough.'

Martha and Bridget looked at each other, disappointment written across their faces.

Elijah turned back to Connor and the doctor. 'I reckon it's time for us to thank you and Ellen for a darned good Thanksgiving, and then make a move. I'll be in town tomorrow, so if you need men for anything, Doc . . .'

William stood up. 'You know, I'm thinking we'll be off, too, Conn. Like Elijah said, best not to leave the place for too long. Up you get, Peggy. We're leavin' now. I'll be heading for town tomorrow morning, too, Doc.'

The doctor nodded. 'I reckon we'd be pleased to have your help.'

'Why don't you say goodbye to everyone and then come out with me, Bridget?' Aaron suggested.

'OK,' she said, throwing Martha a rueful look.

She went around the table, hugging the Careys and Thomases, and then followed Aaron out through the kitchen.

'You'll help everyone with their coats, will you, Conn?' Ellen asked, and she hurried into the kitchen.

She came out, a basket in each hand, just as they were opening the front door.

'It's only right that you have some of the pumpkin pie,' she said. 'I've put some pieces of the pies into a basket for each of you. Here.'

'That sure was kind of you, Ellen,' Peggy said. She hugged her and took one of the baskets. 'It's bin a real treat today, comin' here and bein' entertained by you like this. I'm mighty grateful to you. And William is, too.'

'Thank you, my dear,' Abigail said, taking her basket. 'You've done us real proud. Conn's a lucky man.'

'We've enjoyed your visit,' Connor said, his breath misting in a silver column in front of him as they crossed the yard to the buggies. 'I'm sorry it had to end so suddenly.'

'Doc won't be here without a reason. I sure hope it ain't a bad reason,' Elijah said. He shook Conn's hand and gave his arm to Abigail to help her into the buggy.

When both couples were sitting in their buggies, a rug wrapped over their knees, Connor moved over to the gate and stood waiting to close it. Ellen waved to them as they set off, and then went back into the house. She'd just filled the doctor's mug again when Connor returned.

'Before I do any more today,' she said as soon as Connor had sat down and she'd given him some coffee, 'I think I'll have a short rest. I hope you'll both excuse me.'

As she closed the bedroom door behind her, she heard Conn say, 'So, Doc. What's this all about?'

# CHAPTER 32

'Let me guess, it's about Niall again,' Connor said.

'It is, I'm sorry to say. This time, it's the evidence you wanted. Well, maybe not wanted, but you know what I mean.'

Connor sat back in his chair, the blood draining from his face. 'Reliable evidence?'

The doctor nodded slowly. 'I'm afeared so. It's from eye-witnesses.'

'So tell me.'

'Jeb Barnes was out Saratoga way a few days ago with some of his ranch hands. They'd been talking to a rancher out there about buyin' some wood before winter set in. On their way back to Liberty yesterday morning, they came across several animal carcasses.'

'Not again!' Conn exclaimed.

'Yup, again. Despite the chill in the air, the carcasses were still warm so they knew that the hunters were around and they kept a watchful eye. They were just about to go over one of the hills when they heard a load of hollerin'. They stopped where they were, got off their horses and went real carefully up the hill. Keepin' their heads low so's not to be seen, they peered over the top and saw the strangers I mentioned. They were in the saddle, huddled in a group, talking to each other and pointing in various directions.'

'How close were Jeb and his men to them? Could they see their faces or were they just guessing who they were?'

'They were some way off, but not so far that they didn't recognise some of them as men they'd seen in town. And they were close enough see the hides slung over the horses' backs. But the strangers outnumbered them, and they had guns. Jeb wasn't gonna let anyone take any chances and they stayed put till the hunters had gone. All but one of the hunters went towards the deserted claims north west of Liberty. It's where we'd thought they might be staying. The one who didn't go with the others headed for town.'

'You're gonna say you think it was Niall, aren't you?'

'I sure hate having to tell you this, Conn, but it *was* Niall. Niall all but grew up on the Barnes's Ranch. He and Jeb have been friends since they were young lads. It hurt Jeb to have to tell us this about someone who'd been a close friend. You can be sure he wouldn't have said it unless he was plumb certain.'

'But the man would have had his back to them as he rode. And he'd have been a long way off.'

'Think about it, Conn. Jeb knows the way Niall

holds himself in the saddle, the way he uses his right arm when he rides. And Jeb knew the horse. Niall hung around him a bit in the early days after he got back. Jeb would know Niall's horse anywhere.'

'What about the cattle stealing? Do you think it was the same gang, with Niall involved in that, too?'

'More likely than not, I'd say. I reckon they've not been fussy how they got their money. Animals they could sell on, they stole. Animals they couldn't sell, but with hides they could sell, they skinned. They're intent on taking everything they can, no matter what they have to do to get it. When a gang like that finishes with an area, they move on somewhere else.'

'I'm not excusing Niall, but he lost everything he had in the last winter. I reckon that set him on this road.'

'A lot of other people also lost their life's work. But this is a growing country and there's work to be had for those who are prepared to start building their lives again, no matter how hard it is. But that's not the way of Niall and his friends. They've been goin' for a fast, easy buck.'

'Do what you've gotta do, Doc. Like I say, I'm not excusing Niall. What he's doing is wrong and he's gotta be stopped. They all have. I'll ride out after the hunters with you.'

'I appreciate you wanting to support us, Conn. This can't be easy for you. Like I said, Jeb spotted them a few days ago. We had enough men and we couldn't have got to you in time. What's more, we couldn't risk making them suspicious. We had a chance of catching the gang and stopping the carnage, and we had to take it.'

Connor sat straighter and stared hard at the doctor. 'What are you sayin'?'

'As soon as Jeb filled us in, the sheriff sent a couple of men to watch Niall. If he'd left town again, they'd have done their best to follow him and see where he went. But he didn't. He went from the saloon to his lodgings and stayed there all night. First thing this morning, the sheriff went over and charged him. He couldn't risk Niall seein' groups of men gathering in town, guns in their belts. He had no choice. You know that, don't you, Conn?'

Connor nodded.

'But it's the people doin' the organisin' that we really wanted, and the sheriff told Niall that whatever happened, he'd be charged and go before the district court next week. But he said they'd go easier on him if he gave us the names of the gang and told us where they could be found.' He paused. 'I'm sorry, Conn. He's your brother and I know this must hurt.'

'You had to do the right thing. I appreciate you telling me this, and also giving Niall the chance to make things better for himself. So what did he choose to do?'

'He gave us their names. The sheriff left Zack

377

Carter with him in his lodgings so he couldn't warn the hunters, and a posse rode out with the sheriff, took the varmints by surprise and got them all. We figured that because it was Saturday, with more folk moving around before the snows came, going into town and the like, the hunters had felt there was a greater risk of being seen, and they'd stayed put. One of the hunters was hurt, but he'll live. They've been thrown into jail and they'll be transferred to Laramie tomorrow.'

'And Niall? Am I gonna be able to see him?'

'We've left Zack with him.' The doctor gave him a wry smile. 'We figured it wouldn't be a good idea to throw him into jail with his former friends. You can see him tomorrow morning. I told him I'd come by and tell you what happened and I promised we wouldn't move him until you'd had a chance to see him. We thought you'd wanna say goodbye, whatever he'd done.'

'You thought right.' He linked his fingers behind his head and looked up at the ceiling.

'Out of respect to your family, Conn, the towns-folk will be careful what they say about Niall, especially in front of their children.'

'I appreciate that, Doc.' He looked back at the doctor. 'I know you told me Niall said he knew the men from way back and was surprised when they turned up here. Do you reckon that's what happened, that he was here, bored, and they turned up in the saloon, recognised each other, started drinking together and later they sensed he could be one of them and encouraged him to hitch up with him? Or do you think he came back, knowing they would be coming here and that he'd be helping them? That when he went to the ranches around, like the Barnes's ranch, saying he wanted work, he was really just checking out what there was to steal?'

'I guess we'll never know, but I'm inclined to think that he wouldn't have spent time with you and your family if he'd come here intendin' to slaughter animals. And he wouldn't have taken lodgings. He would have stayed out at the claim with the men. Nope, if I had to say one way or the other, I'd say he met them here, was at a loose end and was attracted by their offer of easy money. Knowing Niall, he'd have found a certain excitement in the whole thing.'

Connor nodded. 'I'd like to think it was like that, too.' He paused. 'You don't think Oonagh knew what Niall had gotten into, do you?'

Their eyes met. The doctor dropped his eyes first.

'We did wonder,' he said. 'They were often seen talkin' to each other. But they've been friends for years so that doesn't mean a thing. He didn't say a word about her so we'll never know.' He glanced in the direction of the kitchen, and then looked back at Connor. 'I reckon you did well when you took that lady to be your wife. Yup, I reckon you did at that.'

*    *    *

379

The sound of the doctor's buggy was receding into the distance when Connor walked out into the backyard, stood still, his hands deep in his jacket pockets, and looked to his left. The corrals were empty now that the cows had been shut away for the winter and all the horses had been put in the shed behind East Barn. It was depressing not to be able to see animals around the place. The farm was as much the animals as the crops to him, and he missed seeing them whenever he stepped out of the house.

And the thought that he was unlikely to see Niall again after the following morning made it all seem more depressing than ever.

He started to walk slowly towards East Barn. Niall hadn't been part of his life for years, and when he *had* returned, he'd spent as much time in the town as he had at the homestead – more so, in fact – so there was no obvious reason why he should feel any regret that he wouldn't be seeing him again, but regret it he did. Maybe it was the thought of his folks, and how unhappy this would have made them, that made him feel so wretched.

And there was Bridget, who would have to know the truth within a day or two at the most. The children would soon hear it from their folks and were sure to taunt her about her uncle's part in the killings. He didn't look forward to telling her the truth. In the short amount of time she'd known Niall, she'd come to love him. And she loved animals. What he'd done would be a tremendous shock to her, and the whole thing was bound to upset her greatly.

He reached East Barn and stood for a few moments at the entrance, watching Bridget. Her head was bent low over the calf as she stroked its back. Aaron was standing above her, looking down at her.

'You just keep lovin' her, honey,' he heard Aaron say. From Aaron's tone of voice, he didn't need to go closer to know that Daisy hadn't yet responded to the treatment. 'She's a tough little thing. Don't you give up hope.'

Bridget looked up at Aaron, and Connor saw that her face was streaked with tears. 'She's no better, Aaron. Can't you do anything?'

He went up to them. 'Not much change in her, then?'

Aaron glanced around at him. 'Not yet. There's time, though. She doesn't look that lively, but she could rally. I guess we'll know tomorrow.'

Connor stared down at Bridget's grief-stricken face. He'd vaguely wondered whether he should tell her about Niall that evening, but seeing her already in such distress, he knew that he couldn't. And there was no need to.

From what the doctor had said, it was unlikely that news about Niall's part in the killing would have reached her school friends by the following morning. They'd hear it from their parents in the evening, and he could leave telling Bridget till then. By then, Daisy might have rallied a little. If so, Bridget would be feeling more cheerful in herself, and that would help.

'It's school tomorrow, Bridget. I want you to say good night to Daisy and come in with me.'

'You go in and I'll follow you. I promise.'

'I think not. We'll go back together. When you've gone, Aaron will top up her stall with clean straw, won't you, Aaron?'

'I sure will. She'll be the warmest and most comfortable calf there ever was.'

She leaned forward and kissed the calf on its neck. 'Night, Daisy,' she whispered into its ear. 'I'm gonna come and see you in the morning before I even have breakfast. You've gotta be better by then.'

She stood up. Connor picked up the scarf she'd dropped on the ground and wrapped it around her neck. 'I have to take the wagon into town tomorrow so I'll drive you to school.'

He saw the misery in her green eyes, and he took her hand. 'Let's go in and see Ellen,' he said gently.

Ellen smoothed the blue lining of Bridget's brown wool hood into position with her fingers and picked up her needle. Feeling Connor's eyes on her, she looked up. His face was etched with sadness, and her heart ached for him. She paused. 'I wish I knew what I could say to help you, Connor.'

'There's nothing to be said. It's knowing what

Niall did that's weighing on me, and knowing I'll be seeing him for the last time tomorrow.'

'Of course it would,' she said quietly. 'He's your family.'

He nodded. 'Yup, he is. I shouldn't feel anything for him after he left Alice and me like he did, and after the things he's done since he returned, but I do, and it's hurting.'

'The pain will be less tomorrow night. Once you've said goodbye to him, and have spoken to Bridget, you'll be able to start putting it all behind you. You'll still feel sad when you think of him, but it won't be as sharp in your side.'

She reached for her reel of cotton.

'You're right. It's what's in the future that's important, not the past, and we've a future we can look forward to.'

'Yes, we have.' She smiled at him, then moved Bridget's hood closer to the lamp and bent over it.

'You hate sewing, don't you?' he said after a few minutes.

'I guess it's obvious from the way I'm doing this,' she said with a rueful smile. 'I noticed the lining was torn when Bridget took her coat off, and I don't want it to get any worse. The idea of having to make a whole new lining is quite terrifying.' She laughed and turned back to her work.

'You mustn't do anything more than mending in the future; not if it doesn't please you.'

She gave an exaggerated sigh. 'Alas, this is too

cold an area in which to send a baby out without clothes.'

He grinned at her. 'I agree.'

'And as I fear that Bridget is no keener on plying the needle than I am, and since making clothes is a woman's work, I must do it.'

She smiled across the table at him, checked that the lining was still in the correct position, and began to thread her needle.

'But it's a man's work to provide for a woman, so you've got to let me provide for this in the future.' He pointed to the hood on the table.

'You do provide,' she said in some surprise. She indicated around her. 'You've provided me with a home that I'm very happy in.'

'And I'll also provide you with the clothes that we wear. And that our baby wears, too,' he added. 'In the spring, you can go to the new store that's opened up in town, and buy our clothes there.'

She shook her head. 'No, much as I dislike sewing, I'll make our clothes as my mother did before me, and as I'm sure Alice did, too. Clothes made by other people are not something you should spend your money on. What kind of wife would I be if I let you waste your money?'

He leaned forward. 'When my pa was a lad, his pa worked on a farm back east and they had to take on a lot of men to help with the harvest. They cut the wheat with a reaper. If they were lucky, they could cut as much as half an acre a day. Then men would then pitch the wheat on to a wagon, take it to the threshing area and using a flail, separate the grain from the stalks and husks. Now we use a thresher. It's all done by a machine and a couple of horses. We get through everything quicker and more easily, and with fewer men. It means we save on wages and have more time for other tasks, and the horses and cows have more grazing time. That's progress.'

'I know that,' Ellen said with a smile. 'But why are you telling me?'

'Because just as new ways of doing things are making farming easier for men, new ways are making it easier for women, too. If they let them. When I was a young lad, Ma used to make our soap and candles. Maybe in towns like Omaha, folks were already buying them back then, but not out here in Liberty. But by the time Ma had passed on, Massie's was selling them, and she could buy them. It gave her more time for other things, and that's good.'

She smiled. 'I understand. Thank you. I'll buy the baby's clothes.'

'All of our clothes, Ellen. You can buy them all.'

She stared at him in anxiety. 'Do you have such money to spend?'

'Aaron's been checking the bales of hay. We've more than we need for animal feed so we'll be selling the extra. We'll also be selling a couple of colts. As Niall realised, they'll bring in more than two hundred bucks apiece. Even with the money I've given Niall, by the time we've sold everything we don't need, and bought coffee, rice, salt and anything else we can't produce ourselves, plus any new tools we need, we'll have money over. Buy the clothes, Ellen.'

'I will. Thank you.'

'If you say thank you again, I'll take back the offer,' he said with a laugh.

'All right, I won't. But you know that I feel it inside me.'

'I do,' he said quietly.

'That's done,' she said a few moments later, cutting off the cotton. She straightened up, gathered her sewing things, put them in the basket, picked up the basket and stood up. 'You're looking very thoughtful,' she said, staring down at him with concern. 'Are you thinking about Niall again?'

He shook his head. 'Nope. I'm still thinking about the future. Our future. You, me, Bridget and the baby.' He looked up into her eyes. 'I'm mighty glad that you're part of my future, Ellen Maguire.'

She clutched her basket tightly to her.

'Me, too,' she said, feeling warmth rise to her face.

He stood up, took her basket from her hands, put it on the table and looked down at her.

'And it isn't just because of this,' he said, and he ran his hand slowly across the front of her skirt, outlining the slight swell beneath the material. He dropped his hand. 'It's because of you and how you are.'

A deep silence filled the room, broken only by the sound of their breathing.

He moved closer to her and put his hands lightly on her shoulders. Looking down into her face, he began to lower his lips towards hers.

Panic welled up inside her. She stepped quickly back from him. 'Don't, Conn. There's no need for you to do that for me to believe that you enjoy my company. No need at all. My face is ugly, and your lips might touch the edge of my scar. It wouldn't be pleasant for you. I've never expected you to do this, and I never will.'

'But I want to.'

'I don't want you to. If you want to please me, you won't go further. It'd embarrass me.'

'As I do want to please you, I'll listen to you.' He took her hand. 'But I can't always promise that I'll obey you in the future. As you said yourself, men have a streak of stubbornness in them.'

He raised her hand to his lips and kissed it.

'I guess I'll have to make do with that,' he said with a wry smile, dropping her hand and stepping back from her.

'Thank you,' she said. Holding her basket with both hands, she turned away.

# CHAPTER 33

Connor jumped down from the wagon and pulled the horses to the hitching post next to the trough of water. He tethered them, checked that the water in the trough hadn't frozen and then walked across the rutted track to the sidewalk. Turning down by the side of the new clothes' shop, he made his way towards Liberty Town Hall.

The doctor was coming out of the town hall just as he reached the door.

'Ah, Conn!' he exclaimed, stopping in front of him. 'The sheriff knows you're seeing Niall this morning. He said that if I saw you before he did, I was to tell you that you could go straight over to Niall's lodgings. We told Mrs Palmer to leave her house till Niall had left, just in case there was shooting. You'll find Zack Carter there. He took over the watch again this morning. Reckon he's pretty fed up with seeing Niall by now.'

'Right, I'll do that. I'm keen to get this over with. It's been preying on my mind since I learnt what happened.'

'It would. I'll let the sheriff know you're with Niall. When he's finished what he's doing, he's gonna check that he's got enough men going to Laramie. That'll take a bit of time, so you'll be able to sit with Niall for a while.'

'I appreciate that.'

'Leave Niall's door open. Zack's armed, and he'll stand just outside.' He paused. 'I'm sorry, Conn, but you know how it is. I'm on my way to the livery stable to let them know how many wagons to hitch up. Niall will sit up front on one. We'll have one of our guns in the back of each wagon, watching the men there, but our thinkin' is that he'd be a mite safer up front.'

Connor nodded. 'I reckon you're right about that. OK, I'll get over to him now. And while you're at the stable, ask them to saddle up a horse for me. I'll leave my wagon there if it's not needed. I'm gonna ride with the sheriff so you can tell him to count me in. Ellen knows I won't be back tonight, and she knows not to let Bridget go to school tomorrow, not till I've spoken to her.'

'I dunno. I reckon the sheriff will have enough men without you. And without Jeb, too. We've told him to go back to his ranch. He's pretty shaken about what a man he'd liked so much has done, and I reckon he was glad to be out of the way this morning. No, I'd go home, if I were you. This is going to be hard enough as it is, saying goodbye to Niall, knowing what he's done. Don't make it harder on yourself. When the sheriff comes for him, walk away, get on your wagon and go home to your wife and daughter.'

He nodded slowly. 'Maybe I'll do that. But if you find you need an extra man, my offer's still there. Seeing those killers get justice, including Niall, is more important than anything else.'

'I think we're all agreed on that. See you later, Conn.' The doctor went back into the town hall. Connor turned around and made his way back to Main Street.

As he reached Main Street, he saw a number of men on the sidewalk, walking towards him from different sides of the town. They'll be making for the sheriff's office, he thought. Doc was right – he wouldn't be needed.

His head down, he turned right and headed for the wooden house where Niall lodged. Yes, he'd go back to Ellen as soon as he'd seen Niall. And he'd look in on Daisy to see how she was doing. Both he and Aaron had thought that there were signs of improvement that morning, and Bridget had been beaming as she'd run out to the wagon, waving her school bag and pail.

He lifted his head and looked around him. He'd say goodbye to Niall and then he'd start living a life that a year ago he'd thought he'd never have again. His steps speeded up.

Reaching Mrs Palmer's house, he lifted the latch and walked in. He glanced quickly at the door leading to Mrs Palmer's rooms, saw that it was shut, and walked straight through to the back of the house where Niall had a room.

Niall's door was closed. He knocked on it. 'It's Conn Maguire, Zack,' he called, and he stepped back and waited for Zack to open the door.

There was silence.

He knocked again. 'Niall. Zack. It's Connor.'

Still no reply.

Frowning, he leaned close to the door and listened. A faint, intermittent sound came from inside the room. But hard as he tried, he couldn't make out what it was.

'Zack,' he called again, and he rapped on the door.

He pressed his ear to the door and strained to hear. The muffled noise coming from inside the room sounded louder, more urgent.

He moved back slightly and tried the door handle. It turned, and he cautiously opened the door. Frantic thudding came from inside the cupboard on the far wall of Niall's room. So that's where Zack is, he thought. By the sound of it, he was gagged and in the cramped space of the cupboard, was trying to kick at the inside of the door.

He pushed the door to the room wider open so that its back touched the wall. There was no one behind the door, and there was no one inside the room. Apart from Zack, he thought dryly as he walked into the room and looked around.

His eyes settled on the flimsy cotton curtain that

was fluttering in the breeze that blew in through the open window. Well, Niall would hardly have gone out through the front door and run the risk of being seen.

The movement inside the cupboard took on a new desperation. Ignoring it, he hurried out of the room, and peered inside Mrs Palmer's rooms. They were empty, too, as he'd thought they would be. Niall wouldn't have hung around the house. Assuming he could take a horse without being seen, he'd have got far away from Liberty as quickly as he could.

Or would he?

He paused and leaned back against the wall.

Niall would know that it wouldn't be long before they found he'd escaped. And he'd know that neither the sheriff nor any man in town would let him get away without giving chase. Their anger against him was such that they were sure to go after him, and there were enough of them to split up and cover the most likely routes of escape. They'd be fresher than he was, and with horses that had been newly fed and grained, and they'd outride him. Niall would know that.

No, he wouldn't do anything as hopeless as attempting to outrun them. That wasn't Niall's way. He'd find somewhere to hide, somewhere in the hills where his horse wouldn't be seen, and he'd stay there until he was sure that they'd given up, no matter how long he had to wait. Only then would he make his escape.

So where would he go to hide?

He thought back to the things they'd done together as children. The trouble was, he'd rarely played with Jeb and Niall when they were young. And on the few occasions he'd done so, he'd never been allowed to visit the secret places they used as hideaways, so he had no idea where they were. The only person who'd been permitted to visit their haunts had been Oonagh.

He straightened up. Oonagh! Of course!

Oonagh would remember where they used to play. Niall could even have reminisced with her about them in the last few weeks. When people came back after a long absence, they often talked about things they'd done in the past, and about the places they used to go to. He might even have taken her to some of those hideaways since he got back.

The townsfolk must have seen them together often enough to think that they were likely to wed. Oonagh's folks would never have allowed a man in her room, no matter how innocent the purpose, and it may well be that on occasions she and Niall had taken the buggy and gone for a drive together. One of Niall's hideaways would have been a likely place for them to head for.

He went quickly to the front door, and stopped. If he went out that way, someone would be sure to see him and might send word that he'd left. If so, they might come for Niall earlier than they'd planned, and he wouldn't have time to try and

393

stop things from being worse for his brother than they already were. If he could get Niall to give himself up, they might still go easier on him.

But that meant that he'd have to find him first.

He glanced back towards Niall's room. Overcoming Zack Carter and locking him in the cupboard will have been a spur of the moment action on Niall's part, and from the noise Zack was making, he hadn't been hurt. It couldn't matter if he stayed in the cupboard a mite longer.

If he was quick, he had time to get to Oonagh and ask for her help. She'd know, as he did, that at heart Niall would never wish to become a man with his face on a wanted poster, at risk of arrest if he ever again entered the territory in which he'd been born.

He ran back to Niall's room and climbed out through the window, deliberately deaf to the sounds of Zack Carter.

Keeping close to the back of the houses and shops, he made his way towards the schoolhouse. Oonagh would be inside with the class and he'd have to attract her attention from the outside. He'd make for the window that looked towards her desk, and he'd have to hope that she'd see him standing there and come out to him at once.

If she did, he'd beg for her help. She'd know of Niall's guilt by now, and if she had any feeling at all left for him, she wouldn't want him to become an outlaw on the run, any more than Niall himself would, when he had time to stop and think.

★　★　★

He reached the schoolhouse without seeing anyone, and without being seen, he hoped. He edged around the wooden building, and paused when he reached the window that would give Oonagh a clear view of him, should she look in his direction.

Carefully inching forward, he looked through the window into the room, but it was one of the older pupils who was standing in front of the class, watching the pupils do their work. There was no sign of Oonagh. He jumped quickly back against the wall, his heart racing. What to do now, he wondered.

She must be somewhere else in the schoolroom, he decided, and he edged towards the window again. To his great relief, the older pupil was bending down, talking to one of the children in the front row. She was pointing to something on the child's slate, and had her back to him.

Taking advantage of the moment, he crouched low and crossed swiftly to the other side of the window. Cautiously raising himself up, he glanced at the back of the room. Then he slid down from the window again, his heart pounding in his chest, hoping he hadn't been seen. She wasn't with one of the pupils at the back, nor was she heating a lunch on the potbelly stove, which Bridget had said that she sometimes did. She definitely wasn't in the schoolroom.

So where was she?

And then he heard the faint hum of voices coming from beyond the building. He moved away from the window, stood up and ran along the side of the wall towards the noise. Peering around the end of the building, he saw Oonagh standing with Niall a little way off at the edge of the long grass. Niall had his back to him, and Oonagh was half turned away.

He couldn't hear what they were saying from where he was standing, but from their tone of voices, and from the way in which they were using their hands and arms, Niall seemed to be trying to persuade her of something, but she wasn't of a mind to listen.

He left the cover of the building and walked over to them.

'Conn!' Oonagh exclaimed.

Niall spun around and stared at him. 'Ain't that the darndest! I might've known.'

'I haven't told anyone you've escaped, and I've left Zack in the cupboard. But they'll find out soon enough that you've gone. Hand yourself in before they do, Niall. If you do . . .'

'Save it. I know the arguments, brother, and I'm not convinced. I'm choosing freedom, and I'm off. Unless of course, you're planning to arrest me.' He gave him a dry smile. 'If you are, you should know that I won't go quietly. Brother will take up arms against brother.' He pursed his lips, drew in his breath and shook his head. 'I reckon Ma and Pa wouldn't like that. No, sir, they wouldn't.'

'I don't wanna take you in. I want you to give yourself up.'

Niall laughed in his face. 'That's never gonna happen.' He turned to Oonagh. 'So are you coming with me or not?'

She gestured helplessly. 'Like I said, I've got a job, Niall. I've got a home. I live my life in comfort. What can you offer me? Nothing.'

'You call what you've got a life! Sewing bees and Sunday School. Rules and regulations. The moral folk of Liberty, upright, deadly dull, around you night and day. Oh no, not at night. Your folks would never allow that, would they?' He threw back his head and laughed.

His laughter died away. He took a step closer to her.

'It's your choice, Oonagh,' he said, his voice caressing her. He trailed his fingers slowly down her cheek. 'A lifetime of knowing that you're dying inside before you've even had a chance to live, or a lifetime of what I can give you. Excitement, fun, places you've never been to before, people you've never met before. I'm offering you the freedom to be you, Oonagh – to have the next best thing to what you really want.'

'How do you know what I really want?'

'You want my brother, honey. You have for years, from when we were very young. I seen the way you moved when he was near, the way your skirts were always slipping up, your bodice always that bit undone. I wished you luck, thinkin' it might loosen him up a bit, but my good brother turned his back on the sins of the flesh you offered. He—'

'Don't listen to him, Oonagh,' Connor cut in. 'You're worth more than life on the run with an outlaw, 'cos that's what Niall will be if he runs from this.'

Niall's eyes didn't leave Oonagh's face. 'You couldn't get him then, and you ain't gonna have him now, not ever, but you can have me, and that'll be a helluva lot more fun, I can promise.'

She stared up at him. 'I don't know what to do. For once I really don't.'

He smiled at her. 'I do. You and me, we're alike. We both want to live life to the full, and if we want a thing and have to do something we shouldn't in order to get it . . .' He shrugged his shoulders. 'If you dare to start living, you'll get your bag, get on your horse and ride out next to me. It's decision time now, Oonagh. Either way, I'm off.'

'Don't go with him, Oonagh. He won't get far,' Connor said. 'I'm going for the sheriff.' He made a move as if to run.

'No, Pa!' Bridget's cry came from behind them. He turned sharply.

Bridget was standing there, fear on her face.

'What's happening, Pa?' she gasped. 'I saw you through the window. Why are you and Uncle Niall arguing?'

'You've no coat on, Bridget. Go back to the schoolroom. I'll explain later.'

She stood firm on the ground, her face white. Her gaze went to Niall. 'Why are you leaving? I don't want you to go.'

He stepped forward, his face softening. 'I'm sorry, Bridget. I've let you down. I've done something wrong and I've gotta leave town.'

She stared up at Niall's face. 'But I thought you loved me.'

'I do, honey. You're the best thing about this place. But I'm in trouble and they'll come after me if I stay here. Your pa's gonna try and stop me from going.'

She looked at Oonagh, then back at Niall. 'Is Miss Quinn going with you?'

Niall turned to Oonagh. 'Is she?' he asked.

She looked from him to Connor, then back at Niall. She nodded. 'Yes, she is.'

Niall grinned broadly. 'And she's gonna get me a horse?'

She nodded. 'You can have Pa's.'

'Get a few things from home and go for the horses. I'll see you behind the horses' shed. Be quick.'

Oonagh nodded. She looked down at Bridget.

'I'm sorry, Bridget,' she said. 'But I've got to do this.' And she picked up her skirts and started running in the direction of her house.

'Get back to the schoolroom, Bridget,' Connor said. 'I'm off to the sheriff.'

Niall lunged towards him, but Bridget moved faster.

'You can't,' she shouted, lurching forward and grabbing Connor's leg. 'I love Uncle Niall. Please don't tell the sheriff, Pa. Please don't. I love him,' she cried, tears streaming down her face as she clung to his leg.

'Bridget, honey,' Niall said. 'I'm so sorry.' His voice caught in his throat.

Connor glanced at him. He was staring down at Bridget, his face full of wonder as he gazed at her, and of regret. And he looked down at Bridget, hugging his leg tightly, stopping him from moving.

He felt a tightening in his chest. 'I think we'll go straight home now, Bridget,' he said quietly. 'The wagon is across the street.'

Her body relaxed and her arms fell to her sides.

'And we're not gonna tell the sheriff, are we?' she asked, looking up at him.

'No, honey, we're not gonna tell the sheriff.'

Turning his back on Niall, he held out his hand to Bridget, who took it, and together they started to walk towards Main Street.

'Bridget's with Daisy,' Ellen said, coming into the living room as Connor was bringing in an armful of wood for the stove. 'Daisy's definitely on the mend, but Aaron thinks we'll be going through something like this with her again before too long.' She went across to the front door and closed it behind him.

'I'm sure he's right,' he said, dropping the wood into the basket. 'So sure that I think we'll leave her stall in East Barn. Bridget can fuss over her when she gets back from school in the evenings.

It'll be good for her to have something to take her mind off what happened today. I'm just glad that she doesn't have to say goodbye to Daisy as well, right now.'

'And it's been a difficult few days for you, too. Why don't you sit down for a while and have a coffee? Lunch will be ready before too long.'

'That sounds real good,' he said, and he went across to the dinner table.

'Bridget left her lunch pail at school. She said she'll bring it back tomorrow night,' she told him, coming back into the room with a mug of coffee. 'She insists on going into school tomorrow, although there may not be any school, not if there isn't a teacher.' She put the mug in front of him and sat down opposite him.

'I'll take her in with me. I'll obviously have to go into town.'

'Will you get into trouble?' she asked, her eyes anxious. 'For leaving Zack where he was, as well as for letting Niall go?'

'I doubt it. Maybe folks will be less than friendly for a while, I don't know. But I doubt there's any man in town who could've turned his brother in, and they'll know that. They're fair people and they'll not hold it against me for long.'

'Do you think they'll catch him?'

He gave her a wry smile. 'I'm guessing they won't. I reckon he'll hole up somewhere till he's fairly sure that they'll have given up, and then he'll move. But he'll still be watchful. He's been

401

hunting since he was a lad. He'll know the way that hunters think, and he'll be able to work out what to do for as long as there's the slightest risk of someone out there looking for him.'

'Being with Oonagh will slow him down.'

'That's true, but he'll plan for that. I reckon he'll get out of Wyoming Territory as fast as he can and go somewhere where it'll be hard for them to follow him. With the cold spell coming, and few warm clothes and provisions, they'll probably head for the south west, putting mountains and bad weather between us and them.'

They heard the kitchen door close, and Bridget came into the room.

Ellen smiled at her. 'I'm getting lunch, Bridget, but it's not quite ready. Would you like a glass of milk?'

'No, thanks. I sure am glad we came back when we did. I'm tired.'

'That's not to be wondered at,' Ellen said. She stood up and helped Bridget with her coat. 'This was your first day back at school after being ill. If you want, you can go to bed now. Take your Mother Goose book with you. If you'd like, I'll bring your lunch into your bedroom.' She smiled at her. 'Would that be a good idea?'

Bridget nodded, her eyes on Ellen's face.

'Can I get you anything first?' Ellen asked, taking the coat, hanging it on the hook and coming back to Bridget.

Bridget shook her head.

'Off you go to bed, then,' she said. 'I'll bring you in a biscuit to keep you going until lunch is ready.'

Still Bridget didn't move.

'What is it, Bridget?' she asked quietly, bending down towards her.

Bridget lifted up a hand, put it on Ellen's shoulder and pulled her nearer to her. Half-smiling into her face, Ellen looked at her curiously.

Raising herself on to her toes, Bridget angled her head to look closely at Ellen's left cheek. Then she gently touched the scarred skin. Her breath warm against Ellen's face, she ran her fingertips along the ridges and lightly pressed the livid skin, moving her fingers backwards and forwards across its roughness.

Then she sank back down to her heels, wrapped her arms around Ellen's waist and hugged her hard. Her arms fell to her sides and she stepped back, her face serious.

'I'm real glad Pa wed you, Ellen,' she said, and she ran off to her room. She reached the door and turned back. 'Real glad,' she repeated. Her face broke into a wide smile, and she flung the door open and ran into her room. 'You can read to me if you like,' she called.

Connor stared after Bridget, and then he looked up at Ellen's face.

He got up, went over to her, picked up the corner of her apron and wiped first one eye with it and then the other.

'Bridget's come to love you, Ellen,' he said quietly. 'And so have I. I'm glad you didn't tell me about your scar in your letter. You were right. It would have stopped me from choosing you, and I would've lost the chance of having you as my wife. I couldn't have found myself a better wife, nor one I'm happier to look at.'

'Oh, Conn,' she whispered.

He smiled down at her. 'I reckon Bridget had the right idea. She wanted to do something, and she did it. There's something I've been wanting to do for quite some time now, but I listened to you and I held off.' He took her face between his hands. 'But I'm not gonna hold off any longer. What I want to do is kiss my wife, the woman I love.'

Her eyes opened wide as he lowered his lips to her left cheek, and kissed the mottled centre of the damaged skin.

She drew in a long, deep breath.

'And now the other side,' he said, 'or it'll feel left out.' He leaned down and kissed her on the right cheek.

Raising his hands to the sides of her face, he ran his fingers down each of her cheeks, his eyes burning into her with deep blue intensity.

'I love you, Conn,' she said, gazing up at him, her voice shaking.

His face broke into a slow smile. 'Then I insist on you joining in with this, wife,' he said, and he lowered his lips to her mouth.

She started to reach out to him, hesitated a moment, then she slid her arms around his back, sank against his chest and met his lips with the same passion as his met hers.

# EPILOGUE

*Laramie Sentinel*
Saturday, June 30, 1888

**M**AGUIRE – In the town of Liberty on the 4th instant, to the wife of C.D. Maguire, a son.

Crowning almost a year of marital felicity, the arrival of Daniel Connor Maguire, named after his paternal grandfather and his father, brought great happiness to Connor, his wife and his daughter, securing as it did for posterity their homestead, name and lineage.